FOREIGN AND DOMESTIC

CAMPAIGN II:
BATTLE
FOR THE
MIDDLE STATES

FOREIGN AND DOMESTIC

Campaign II:
Battle for the
Middle States

Michael Mannske

Radius7 Pressworks
Plymouth, Minnesota

FOREIGN AND DOMESTIC
Campaign II: Battle for the Middle States

Copyright © 2007 by Michael Mannske.

All rights reserved. No part of this publication may be reproduced, stored in a retrieval system or transmitted in any form or by any means, electronic, mechanical, photocopying, recording or otherwise without the prior written permission of the copyright holder, except brief quotations used in a review.

Banner Graphic by Pixel Candy
Illustrations by FMTrauts
Middle States Flag by Brandon Wind

ISBN: 978-0-9796759-0-4

Published by Radius7 Pressworks
3500 Vicksburg Lane #320
Plymouth, MN 55447
www.radius7.com

PRINTED IN THE UNITED STATES OF AMERICA

10 9 8 7 6 5 4 3 2   07 08 09 10 11 12 13

Dedicated to the Air Force flight surgeon whose
"Oh, what the hell"
changed my life forever.

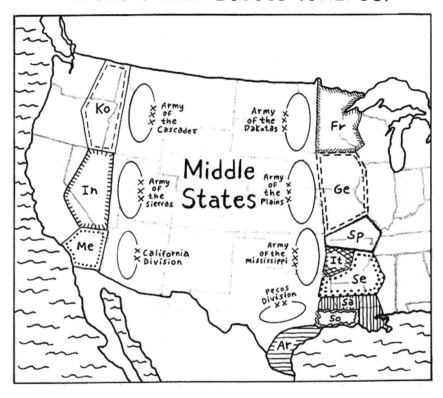

PREFACE TO WAR

Civilization's greatest conflicts begin with the smallest of things. A pretty face incited the Trojan War. A scrawny Bosnian teenager sparked World War I. So it was with the US–UN War. It was started by a six-year-old Cuban boy named Elián Gonzáles.

The Elián affair set many chilling precedents for America, the gravest being the boy's handover to the Cuban Army at Andrews Air Force Base. For the first time, sovereignty of an American military base had been surrendered to a foreign power. Billionaire insuranceman, Harold 'H. B.' Budd, determined it would be the last.

With the U.S. no longer able to rely on the president to protect it from foreign invaders, Budd recruited a force that would; a select group of veterans he dubbed the Ex-Nihilos. Ex-Nihilos were patriots. They swore their allegiance not to a piece of land and not to any person. They gave their oath instead to an idea, the Constitution of the United States. This distinction would prove critical when it came time to fight their president, Milton Cummings Earle.

Earle should never have become president. Like disco, he was something everyone loved to hate and only won election because of a last-minute campaign gimmick. To win re-election and reverse his drop in the polls, he tried another trick; he signed the UN's *Declaration of Dependence.*

Liberals hailed this OneWorld endorsement as courageous and progressive while conservatives screamed *treason.* Sixty thousand moderates thought it a curious enough novelty that they voted to re-elect him; Earle, the man who changed the face of the nation forever.

But dependency came with a price and it was put to the test in New Mexico when two Americans were jailed for the murder of a Mexican citizen. When UN Peacebuilders arrived to forcefully extradite the two for trial in The Hague, the locals took up arms. As more detachments were brought in, it soon became evident the blue-helmets no longer intended to go home. Budd's premonition had come true and he sounded the klaxon: Invasion.

The administration pledged to support the Secretary-General and when Earle sent troops to reinforce the invaders, the Ex-Nihilos had a second enemy. The patriot's key weapon in fighting this new foe? The mothballed fighter jets in the desert boneyards of the American Southwest. Fully-restored and battle-ready, these forgotten warships represented the largest air force in the world and gave the Ex-Nihilos the power necessary to persuade U.S. forces to repurpose their loyalties. Initially, their plan succeeded, but due to their small numbers, the veterans could not hold on for long. On the East and West Coasts, their efforts collapsed as Special Operations Forces loyal to the president counter-attacked. Only in the country's interior where the populace was vigorous and sympathetic were the patriots able to consolidate and repel the commandos. The Ex-Nihilos named these occupied territories the Middle States and the civilians and militia who joined their cause became known as the Sovereign Forces.

The U.S. military, trained only to deter outside aggressors, were not prepared for an attack from within. After decades of defense cuts and three thousand nuclear warheads now in Sovereign hands, it was clear President Earle was going to need help putting down the traitors. He called the United Nations.

After only a few years of taxing authority, the UN Secretariat had become a military superpower in its own right. Flush with trillions of dollars from global income and Internet taxes, it created UNIFUS, the United Nations Interim Force in the United States. This coaxial coalition of like-minded nations sent armies from around the globe which quickly overwhelmed the SF. As reward for pushing the independents back, Coax members were allowed to control whatever territory they reclaimed. These territories ringed the Sovereigns and were grouped into eleven zones called protectorates. In the states where these international entities operated, not even their governors were allowed to intercede.

Surrounded on all sides, the MS stood alone in the world. With no trade, no travel, no fiber cable, phone lines or power grid, its fledgling economy faltered until an intricate network of agrarian communities sprang up to form an innovative breed of decentralized industries. The Sovereigns recovered and, despite their ragtag status and lack of high-tech weaponry, still managed to sport a nearly twenty-to-one kill ratio over their foes.

Secretary-General Burin Zzgn began awarding mandates to break the stalemate. UN mandates gave a protectorate the full rights and privileges of a new country. It allowed the parent nation to set up its own borders, install its own government and gain its own seat in the General Assembly.

The promise of owning a slice of the most prosperous country on earth proved a powerful incentive for the Coax members. They now poured even more troops and weapons into the fight and, eager to settle old scores, fought with untold savagery and barbarity. The media didn't report on these atrocities, instead portraying the UN as protectors, a picture most comfortable Americans were all too happy to accept.

The U.S. president maintained control of the East- and West-Coast economies. Commonly referred to as the XUS, the Americans here fell into two camps: the symps and the bluebirds. Bluebirds were loyal to the president. These transnationals felt death was not enough for the flatlanders of the Middle States and believed their creeds of freedom, nationalism and independence had to be extinguished before infecting others. If the bluebirds weren't actively fighting for the UN in frontline units, then they were busy back in the XUS spying on friends and policing their families.

Symps did not support Global Oneness. While not all agreed with the Sovereign's provocations to war, they certainly sympathized with their motives. From harmless TV weathermen who denied global cooling to militant Freemartins—the underground resistance force who fought the occupiers in their own cities—these disparate groups risked losing jobs, homes and worse in a country that was no longer theirs.

Two years have passed since the rise of the Ex-Nihilos. With their backs against the missile fields of the Dakotas and their flagging forces ready to unravel, the Sovereigns are desperate to reverse their fortunes and defeat their enemies—both foreign and domestic—before the families they left behind pay the ultimate sacrifice.

This is their story: the Battle for the Middle States.

ACT I

INTRODUCTION

Sheriff Arroyo surveyed the ranch from the bottom of the dusty drive. He had visited this troublesome place many times since his bogus election, but had never committed it to memory. Now he wished he had.

"Oh, Holy Mother. He's bloating already."

Arroyo wheeled around and slapped the binoculars from his officer. "Put those down, baboso. Get your shit together or you'll wind up like Martinez yourself."

The blonde-haired marshal turned back and glassed the expansive mansion before him. The estate was nestled in the middle of 240 acres of pecans, a lush green bowtie in the middle of the dry desert scrub. It had bubbling fountains and colorful gardens and fresh-cut lawns. The staff had their own pools and the owners enjoyed purple-mountain vistas through dozens of airy, arched porticoes. It was through one of those windows his deputy had been ambushed and now lay lifeless across his blood-drenched squad car above.

Oscar, where do I get idiots like you? Arroyo said to himself. He ran a tongue over his newly-installed braces and queried his watch; he was going to be late to the dentist's again.

The marshal sent a six-man team east behind the stables with their Land Rover G4 then sent the rest west to occupy the pump house. That left him his *enforcers*: two teenage gangbangers slipped across the border compliments of the Mexican Army. Wearing baggy jeans, wrinkled blue uniforms and the latest Oakley wraparounds, they had driven up dirty from Chihuahua in a new two-toned leather-upholstered Escalade pickup complete with armor plating and a military-issue .50-caliber machine gun.

This was not his daddy's Cadillac.

He glared as the two reclutas fought over the stereo. Stoners. Why does the colonel keep sending me these slackers in their crackmobiles? He wanted them gone but needed their firepower. He banged on the hood and motioned the men to follow as he walked up the drive, gun drawn.

The grade was steep as Arroyo strained up the slope. Too much desk time, he thought. Cresting the rise, he crawled behind a large boulder to catch his breath as the two conscripts drove lazily by into the kill-zone. "Vato loco! Are you crazy? Back up! Get down!"

The punk behind the gun gave Arroyo a vulgar salute before the truck stopped and did as ordered. Arroyo waited for the teams to call in before adjusting his radio to broadcast over the squad's loudspeakers. "Hermosa, why do you have to make this so hard?" he announced, refusing to use English. "Why couldn't you chicanos leave peacefully like your gringo neighbors?"

No response. He crept the rest of the way to the black-and-white and freshly-red squad car before flattening himself against its fender. His sergeant's hand dangled before him, the blood dripping off his fingers in sticky crimson icicles. Arroyo slapped it out of the way and reached inside the door, turning off the car's camera. "Jorge, I really have to admit, I never thought you had the cajones for this," Arroyo baited. "Impressive, truly."

Still nothing. Arroyo relaxed. His two teams had the compound surrounded and with the family trapped inside, he could take his time. He enjoyed this part of the hunt, the part where he got to torment his prey. "Not coming out? That's OK. Don't bother. We won't be taking prisoners today." He slapped his deputy's cheeks absently, the head lolling on the hood. "All these months I so looked forward to you serving as my jailhouse chaparros. That won't be necessary now. Today, we will be killing you all."

Dirt crunched a few feet away. Arroyo and his rent-a-thugs chambered their weapons and readied for an ambush. "There," pointed the gunner. "In the bushes."

Arroyo jumped up and aimed into a thick tangle of yellow roses, one of many lining the drive. "Old man! What are you doing? Get up! Now!"

An elderly gentleman stood in a bent perma-stoop and gazed serenely at the gun. "Oh, it's you Miguel," smiled Jorge Hermosa. "What took you so long?" Hermosa was the ranch's owner and a first-generation chicano. Born in Oaxaca, Mexico, he immigrated to the U.S. in 1945 where he worked the fields as a boy. Later, he married, taught himself English, became a citizen and worked his way up in the pecan business until, now, he owned the biggest grove in the state. Once considered an inspiration to other poor immigrants seeking the American Dream, Hermosa and his family were now decried as sell-outs—*pochos*—by the illegals who were hell-bent on kicking them and the anglos out of Aztlan-America.

"Who did this to Oscar?" asked the sheriff. "You, old man?" Arroyo eyed the mansion's darkened windows with suspicion as a deep drone rose from the back. He smelled a trap and rounded the car to close with the leathery rancher.

Hermosa ran a hand through the dead sergeant's hair. "This boy here? He said he was here to collect our guns."

"He was doing as I ordered."

"You didn't tell him, did you, Miguel?" the old man asked softly. "That there would be trouble if he tried to disarm us. But that's why you sent him here alone, isn't it? So you would have an excuse to come kill us."

The manicured marshal flushed. Partially from shame. Partially from the fact his radio was broadcasting every word to the rest of his men. He grabbed the codger's sweat-soaked shirt and pulled him closer.

"Get your hands off me," Hermosa spat. He lashed out with a garden spade. The sheriff pulled back a set of bleeding knuckles.

Arroyo suddenly felt like a child; like he was back in Mexico being scolded by his father for stealing eggs. He snarled then knocked the farmer to the ground and kicked him in the head. "Angel. Rene. Move in." He turned to the soldiers in the pickup behind him. "You, cover them. Shoot out all the windows, second-floor first." The machine-gunner gaped into the wind. "Hey, toad-licker, I said NOW!"

The sheriff squinted. Something approached in the soldier's glasses. Something big and dark that blotted out the sun. Arroyo turned. It was an Apache. He recognized the attack helicopter from SWAT training. There, at Ft. Bliss, he had seen them from a distance; morning, noon and night they flew. Far away, they looked like gnats. Now—up close—*he* was the insect. His lunch dropped a foot inside him as the gunship floated toward him.

"Well, if it isn't our favorite import, Sheriff Arroyo," came a voice from his radio. Arroyo fumbled with his walkie-talkie, wondering how they had got on his frequency. "We've been listening in on the excitement. Hope you don't mind," said the pilots.

The misshapen warship was hideous and bulged with threatening appendages and armaments—missiles and rockets and antennas and sensors. The chopper bounced gently in the air as it cleared the compound's roofline before coming to a hover over the front yard. Arroyo made out two helmeted men inside.

"That's my son-in-law and his boy. Both ex-Army," the old man boasted from the dirt. "Pretty impressive wouldn't you say? Built from parts on the Internet, I understand. Military surplus. You arrived just in time for their maiden flight."

Arroyo's men stood rooted in the open, the air rending about them as the superheated downdraft cooked their faces. "What do we do, sir?"

"How the hell should I know? Shoot! Shoot it down!"

Arroyo pivoted and dove for cover as Alpha and Bravo teams opened fire on the chopper's flanks. Bullets littered the ground like spitballs as the deputies fired on the armor-plated cockpit. Arroyo looked behind to yell instructions to his Caddie-crew. The truck was empty. *Putos.* Obviously, bravery and courage were still purely theoretical concepts in the Mexican military.

In a few seconds, the deputies' guns were silent. As they scampered to reload, the Apache's chin turret traversed right then left before locking onto the Escalade in front. The chopper's gatling gun spun and in a long thunderous burp, sent a shimmering column of shells into the vehicle's thick metal plating. The rounds toyed with the hood, blew off its doors and crumpled the roof like Reynolds Wrap. Arroyo choked, the barrage engulfing him in a micro-climate of dust and debris. Hot metal peppered his back as he dove for the dirt, praying to the Blessed Virgin for protection. In slow motion, the pickup folded in on itself and slouched to the ground. When all that remained was a small fire, the cannon quieted.

"Grandpa, get out of there," crackled the pilots over the squad's intercom speaker. "You've made your point."

Hermosa stood and waved his grandson off. "Not until this corrupt Reconquista gets off my property and out of my country."

Arroyo rose and patted himself slowly. He hurt. Hurt bad. The old man shuffled up and planted a bony finger in his chest. "Your terrorizing is over. You are *not* going to run us out. You've disarmed all the ranchers and run them out, but not us."

"*I'm* Otero Sheriff," Arroyo spit back. "I am the law here!"

Hermosa moved closer. The rancher had known his share of Arroyos before; the ungrateful young men who felt the world owed them, the overcompensating bullies who thought themselves better than everyone else. The patriarch had never backed down from them before and wasn't about to now. "You are not sheriff. You are illegal. You were voted in only after you flooded this county with cholos and other Z-card aliens. If we leave, then Otero County is next, then New Mexico after that. This stops now. We are not leaving. *You* are."

Arroyo couldn't think. Nobody had ever rebuked him like this. This man twice his age and half his size had him stammering and he smoldered inside. "You disgust me, old man. You turncoat. You and your family. You turn your back on your own people and sell your soul to be like them, to be gringo. You're a fossil, a petrified chicano relic."

"Miguel, you bleach your hair and date white women. Who is *gringo* here?"

Arroyo's jaw locked. He yanked the rancher off his feet and turned him to face the Apache. "Nobody calls me that and lives, bolillo," he hissed, hitting Hermosa hard in the kidney.

The old man blinked but steadied, surprised by what little pain he felt. "This is America," Hermosa said. "We are done handing it over to you." Arroyo hit him a second time. "Is that all you've got? I'm still not licking your boots." A third time. Hermosa's eyes fluttered. Arroyo released him and the old man laid down in the grass, three bright red spots staining his linen shirt.

"GRANDPA!" cried a voice cried through the speakers.

"Arroyo, you son-of-a-bitch!" came another.

The sheriff glowered at the gunship and closed his bloody blade as Team Bravo re-emerged from the pump house, firing grenades. All went wide of the chopper except one which glanced off the windshield, spiderwebbing it harmlessly. Before the men could retreat, the helicopter banked sharply on its side and swept down on them, its blades chopping them off cleanly at their belts. Team Alpha watched in horror from across the yard as six pairs of legs ran helter-skelter for the trees, colliding with one another on the way.

The Apache continued its turn and circled north, disappearing behind the house. The deputies froze, heads swiveling, until the bird reappeared from the foothills behind them. Climbing incredibly a half-mile over their heads, the warship stalled then swapped ends before swooping to their rear and ventilating their Rover in a single burst. The six ran for the horse barn but only three made it inside, the pilots nailing the stragglers to the stable doors with thousands of metal flechettes from their rockets.

Arroyo was running. He was almost to the highway and could see his black-and-gold Navigator glistening invitingly in the sun. I'm going to make it, he thought, as the stable exploded behind him. He gave a burst of speed and was fifty yards away when a blast-furnace of heat peeled away his face and threw him backward into the gravel. In an instant, his SUV was a pyre, a roiling fireball lifting high into the air above it. Out of the flames, the Apache reappeared. "I'm in hell," he whispered to himself.

"Not quite yet, Miguel," burst the radio as the chopper descended and slowly approached.

"*What do you want?*" the lawman cried, looking down the barrels of its cannons.

"We want our country back," replied the pilots. Arroyo threw a handful of gravel at the gun, rolled right and ran for the groves. The turret followed and cut down a swath of trees twenty-feet wide in front of him. "We want our neighbors back." Arroyo changed direction, running for cover to the other side. Those trees exploded, too, showering him with supersonic splinters. "We want our padrone back, *illegal*."

Arroyo had nowhere left to go. He slumped, angry for being defeated. Angry for having come so far. His blood spattered the dirt as the last drips of adrenaline left his body. Was it true? Was the Hermosa's defiance the backlash the Americans had been threatening for so long? Was this the start of the great revolt the Aztlan leaders blustered would never occur? If it was, Arroyo knew he would never see the result.

The Mexican shouted against the din, spitting all the vindictives he had heard growing up: the devil has white skin and blue eyes, he is exterminating us like Hitler, we are not illegal in our own homeland. Between his mad rants, he fired his gun, the shots ricocheting off the silent bobbing Apache. Finally, he said his last. "FOR THE RACE, EVERYTHING. FOR ALL OTHERS, NOTHING!" He swayed in the buffeting rotorwash as his words trailed off into the gale.

"Time to go to the Mother, Miguel."

Arroyo snapped his automatic to his head as the gatling gun spun. He fired. The shot entered his temple, but—like his vendetta on the Hermosas and his coup against their country—it had come a second too late; the Apache had already turned him into a pink cloud of sizzling flesh and bone.

So began the tale of the US-UN War.

CHAPTER 1
HVA

Memos, binders and folders lay forgotten in the dusty corners of the corridor, as if evidence of a hurried move. With no electricity, the hallway was dark. From the far end, a lone ninja star spun through the air, bounced off an up-turned cafeteria table and skittered to a stop on the cracked linoleum floor.

More rotation, thought Aboud Tanner. The lab-coated scientist jotted new calculations into his folio, wound up and heaved another projectile. It hit the make-shift target sideways and dribbled into the corner, waking the spiders. "I inhale."

Despite the bad aerodynamics, Tanner liked this building. It was the last on his rounds, cooler than the others, quiet. And his stash was here: a decades-old vending machine full of well-preserved Camels, Kools and Chesterfields. Some janitor had hoarded it away in the basement pre-Kyoto. When Aboud found it, he had wrestled the machine into the elevator and stuffed it in the ladies' room with the other Coke, Little Debbies and Kotex machines. He dropped in his daily quarter and yanked back the knob as a thirty-year-old pack of Benson & Hedges 100s clattered down the chute. "God is good," he said, lighting one.

Aboud puffed a few times, raised his leg high in the musty air and let loose with another disk. He slipped as the orb sailed over the table and buried itself firmly in the metal door at the other end of the hall.

Bang! Aboud was up in a shot and sprinted down the corridor. He peeked outside. Goobers. A surveillance camera was staring straight at him from atop its pole looking for the source of the noise. He hugged the wall and looked at his watch. It wasn't time for his rounds to finish but if he didn't do something within thirty-eight seconds, the camera would throw an exception and alert StanEval. He stubbed out his cigarette, adjusted his lab coat and entered the cool summer day. Behind him, the door slammed shut, revealing a powder-blue warning sign:

3M FRINGE SCIENCES LAB.
BLDG 115.
KYOTO POSTED. OFF-LIMITS.

The camera looked down on the scientist, whirring as it pulled back. The device was waiting for something. Removing the folio from his coat, Aboud flipped its polymer pages to his security checklist and tapped away as the servo zoomed in to watch. *I hate Great Brother,* he wrote in digital ink, sauntering to the next building so as not to trigger the camera's behavior recognition routines. By the time Aboud had crossed the terrace, the camera grew uninterested and broke lock. As the eye meandered off on its normal sweep of the campus, Aboud shot it a quick Iranian obscenity. The camera whipped back just as he made it to the door and dove awkwardly inside. Aboud stood, dusted himself off and repeated his gesture to the sentinel. "Idiot," he said. "You cannot be the fox of me. I designed you!"

Aboud was in darkness again. He ran his hand along the wall and stopped at the fifth door down. *SURPLUS,* it read. Aboud fumbled for his keys and cursed as a pocketful of hollow-point .45s went clattering to the floor. He chased them blindly as they rolled away before returning to the door to unlock it. Inside, a great cave of hardware gaped, dripping with stalactites of cables and harnesses and power strips while underneath, stalagmites of ancient desktops, modems and dot-matrix printers were piled high. It was a gallery of computer museum-pieces going on endlessly in both time and space. Paradise, he thought.

Tanner waded through myriad floppies and loose connectors as he made his way to a small work area in the back. Unnoticable from the door, the retreat contained all the necessary furnishings of an office: desk, workbench, coffee maker, microwave, mini-fridge. Even a dread-locked mannequin.

"It's just me again, Marley, you ugly snoot," he said, surprising the plastic sentry with a clumsy tae-kwon-do ab-crotch-face combination. Aboud fired up his monitors and waited for their green ectoplasm to light the sanctuary before connecting the motherboards and network cards of his home-brew computer. On the wall, a Strawberry Shortcake clock told him he had just under thirty minutes. Enough time, he judged, to begin his first act of espionage for the day.

Aboud was no stranger to sedition. Revolutionary fervor had surrounded him growing up in his native Iran, where friends and family had been killed for their crazy dreams of freedom. The ayatollahs and mullahs there were ruthless and had held his country with an iron fist. Tanner had not wanted to die for what he considered a hopeless cause, so he escaped to America where he buried himself in his studies and graduated with a triple-Ph.D. in just four years. As it turned out, resistance hadn't been crazy; Iran was now free and democratic thanks to those same heroes who had given their lives for it. This shamed him.

The United Nations arrived shortly after Tanner started working and oppression began oozing up here, in America of all places, the Land of the Free. Subtle new regulations and restrictions were introduced; homeschool closures, criminalization of UN flag desecration. His American friends loved these policies but Aboud knew where they were leading and vowed never to run from tyranny's shadow again. That was why he had taken up the Sovereign Cause. That was why he was now sending them his former employer's secrets.

3M provided the perfect medium for his sedition: black fiber. Dozens of Worldcoms and Global Crossings had failed over the years; hundreds of world networking projects had come to a halt. Many were incomplete and most undocumented. Some of those undocumented network cables hung in this room now. These pirate networks were what had enabled Aboud to work undetected for months.

The scientist connected a router to his computer and waited for the LEDs to settle before jumping on the Tarantella sideweb. Sidewebs had popped up after the U.S. government took over control of Google for antitrust violations and granted the UN regulatory power over cyberspace. The NextWeb Act had two goals: one, track activity by assigning users unique GPS-based IP addresses and, two, generate revenue by taxing those who resisted. Surfers refused both options and the Web fragmented into hundreds of cobbled-together networks that only specially designed page-hopping browsers could access. Tarantella was one of those networks, one of the Big Five, and a nasty one at that. Noted for its crushing flood of porn, bestiality and snuff, its backbone groaned under the load. That's why he used it; he was a needle in a haystack here. Only this wasn't a haystack. It was a cesspool.

MANBLA was his first stop.

"Hmm, Marley. What do our friends at Man-Boy have for us tonight? I know you want to know."

MANBLA.TV, the first company to pioneer direct net-to-satellite broadcasting, proved that anybody with pedestrian technical know-how and a couple of cheap servers could sling whatever filth they wanted farther and wider than all the major networks combined. Aboud read that night's schedule. "We have *Uncle Earnie at the Petting Zoo* at seven o'clock, then *Confessions of an Altar Boy* at nine and at eleven we have *So You Want to be a High School Teacher*. I guess that's a reality show. What do you think?"

He opened *Uncle Earnie* first and shuttled through at X8 speed. No good; it was filmed outdoors, had too much saturation and too much contrast. On to *Altar Boy*. Filmed indoors, it had a flat luminosity and carried a uniform golden cast: the perfect carrier. "Oh, *goop*, here we go."

Aboud took off his glasses and planted his nose flat against the monitor glass. He had learned this method of previewing after sending hundreds of classified files. This perspective allowed him to analyze a porn clip's hue variations and frame transitions while avoiding its nastiness. Turning the volume down and the video rate up, Aboud began tagging his key-frames. Five minutes later, the hard part was done.

With a loud yell, Tanner hopped in the air and delivered an inept crescent kick to his friend's jaw. He missed, landing awkwardly on his knee. Chastened, he crawled back to his computer and pulled out his mobe.

Mobes were portable pamnetic memory device that remembered enough of a person's programs, documents, favorite movies and last year's shoe purchases to practically be considered a brain prosthetic. Depending on lifestyles, some carried their mobes in an iPod or cellphone, others in a folio or beneath their skin. Tanner had surreptitiously imbedded his in the Zippo his father had given him just before he had been murdered by Iranian Guards. The lighter's heavy metal case shielded his signal just enough to prevent notice by near-field detectors. He waved the mobe in front of his monitor as a one-hundred-page research document leaped onto the screen.

ULTRANANO DIAMOND COATINGS:
FABRICATION AND PROPERTIES.

Aboud scanned a few chapters of the paper before dragging a test page onto one of *Altar Boy*'s key-frames—a smoky still-life of a candlelit church altar. In seconds, text began disappearing, letter by letter, revealing the picture beneath as small dots flashed with each encryption. First slowly, then faster, in no particular order, green spots, red spots, yellow spots sprinkled across the frame turning the scene into a fireworks of pixels. When the routine ended, the image of a goblet, bread and table remained, seemingly unaltered. Pleased, Tanner dragged the remaining pages of the bootlegged document onto the rest of the *Altar Boy* video and set his PIXMERGE program to batch-encrypt.

His watch chimed. His next caretaker round started in ten minutes. Not enough time to post the file to a staging server. He eyed Marley warily and felt in the thigh pocket of the fatigues underneath his coat for his new nunchucks. He decided he would skip the safety of the staging procedure and upload the file directly to MANBLA's public server.

Just this once.

<p style="text-align:center">~~~~~~~~~~~~~~~~~~~~~</p>

Paul Phillips had had it with Ahrmenta. Since he had taken over as the National Security Agency's new SUBDIR of Signals Search, he was growing more and more concerned over her handling of EPAULETTE. Her propensity for taking shortcuts had alarmed him when he apprenticed under her; now that he was her boss, he aimed to address it more concretely.

"No, Paul. Your ideas are fine for most protocols, but not this. And not now. We have a new breed out there now. They—"

"We've had hackers before, A."

"Yes, but those guys numbered in the thousands. Now we have millions. NextWeb disaffected most everybody and sent them underground and now they're innovative as hell."

"Well, I still can't justify the funds. How can I look Broderick in the face and tell him we're using pattern-recognition hardware to detect *non*-patterns?"

EPAULETTE was a *listener* in spydom terms. Where ECHELON had eavesdropped on the world of audio and spoken-word, this next-generation enhancement cataloged all graphics and videos in the known universe. Its goal: identify a picture's content and decipher any clandestine messages concealed inside. Its priority: the war plans of the Sovereign Forces.

"So what you're telling me is we've been wasting our money investing in pattern-recognition. That it?"

"These people are not stupid, Paul. They read books and watch *24* reruns. They know how the NSA works and they cover their tracks pretty damn well."

"Easy, A. Pull it back a notch. I don't work for you anymore, remember?"

"Is that what this is about?" she accused. "You get promoted so you can get back at me? You were in over your head before and you're in way over your head now."

Phillips could see he was getting nowhere. "Well, I guess we're done here." He got up from his chair, gathered his papers and looked at Ahrmenta two tiers up. She had disappeared behind her monitor; he could hear her typing. How could she still make me feel so worthless? he thought. He strode for the door and opened it. "This won't go away, doctor. We'll be seeing each other again."

"Wait, Paul. Don't go. ULTRAMARINE found something. An MPEX file on Tarantella."

"So?"

"So. It got caught in one of my filters. A file that's modified but hasn't changed."

"One of *your* filters? I could've guessed. You're already implementing algorithms, aren't you?"

"Someone had to," Ahrmenta retorted.

"Put it on overhead." The doughy director bounded up the stairs to get a better view. "What am I looking at?"

Ahrmenta leaned back and pointed to the wall diffuser where two multi-colored cubes rotated side-by-side in tandem. "The file on the right is brand new. It was changed just a few minutes ago."

"And?"

"The file on the left is the original."

"I can't see the difference."

"That's because there is none."

"Even the size and timestamps?"

"Yep, but look here." Ahrmenta typed a command, stopping the spinning cubes and splitting them apart like cheese slices. She twirled and picked at them with a laser manipulator. "Compare the hues. Purple here but deep purple there. Not a lot. But enough."

"Enough for what?"

"Hiding something."

"But wouldn't a new color change the file's checksum?"

"Not necessarily," she said. "And that's the beauty of it. If the encryption software was programmed just so, you could theoretically keep those sums intact. A *one* here means a *zero* has to go there."

"What are we talking about?"

Ahrmenta typed some more. "On this frame alone, we have over forty thousand altered pixels. That means half contain data and the other half are just compensators. How elegant."

"Save your admiration for later. Do we have the source?"

"Standby." Ahrmenta ran a HEADTRACE to find the file routing. "Yes, got it." She stood, brushed passed Phillips and bolted for the door.

"Where are you going?"

"To the NCI Room. We've got to get a ping on this."

"No you're not!" We're going to run this through EPAULETTE and figure out exactly what we have first." Phillips sat down and began tapping on her station.

Ahrmenta pulled up and turned back to her boss. "Paul, DON'T!" Up on the projection screen, the cubes turned red, vibrated violently, then broke apart in a bright flash.

"What the hell was that?" asked Phillips, sheepishly.

"A trigger. He attached a trigger, you ass."

"He. He who?"

"Whoever posted the file. Now he knows."

"Knows what?"

"Knows that someone is on to him," railed Ahrmenta. "Tell me how you got promoted again?" The boyish Phillips reddened. "Come on," she said. "We need that ping now more than ever."

~~~~~~~~~~~~~~~~~~~~

Stripped to his fatigues and straining to keep an arm lock around the six-foot-two Rastafarian, Aboud plunged a twelve-inch KA-BAR into Marley's kidneys just as a tone sounded. He ran to his computer.

WARNING. FILE DELETED, MODIFIED OR COPIED.

His trigger. It couldn't be. It had to be something else. A server crash. A traffic spike. A new webbot. He called up the MANBLA server. The file was gone, self-immolated as designed. *No!* He opened his trojan and scanned the header, his eyes hovering on the scariest fricking thing he had ever seen:

ARMY.FTMEADE.NSA.GOV

Aboud put his hands to his head. "UNSAT! UNSAT! UNSAT!" Slapping off the computer, he pulled out all the cords and cables he could think of and then held his breath.

~~~~~~~~~~~~~~~~~~~~

Ahrmenta ran down the hall and barged into Network Attack. She loved this room. Big as an arena with fourteen levels of wall consoles, its rotunda encircled a huge four-sided LCD array hanging from the rafters like an NBA scoreboard. The only thing missing were the hoops. She flashed her ID at the napping duty officer then raced up to the NCI station. Elbowing the tech aside, the computer picked up her mobe signal and launched an exact copy of her desktop. The tech flew backward onto the floor. "Can I help you?"

"I'm Doctor. Brown with EPAULETTE. I need you to clear your pipeline. We have an emergency ping request."

"No we don't." It was Phillips, puffing up behind her. The room hushed as he grabbed her and wheeled her around. "What are you doing, A?" he said, forcing a smile.

The duty officer followed next. He opened his mouth but Ahrmenta showed him her hand. "We finally have what we've been looking for, Paul. A file packaged perfectly; precisely designed to slip through our filters. If we don't find out now who sent it, it won't matter *what* he's sending."

Phillips wasn't buying it. Non-Cooperative Interrogation was reserved for big stuff and required the whole net be brought down; all work brought to a stop. As a new SUBDIR, he relished his name being up in lights, but not that way.

Grabbing his lapel, she pulled him down to her. "Look, this guy put a trigger on that file. Not many people know how to do that. Why would someone do that for a porn flick, for Pete's sake? Something's hinky, Paul. I'm thinking it's war-related. I'm thinking we may have found the comm-link between the SF and the Freemartins."

Phillips fingered his tie, trying to avoid Ahrmenta's gaze. He didn't know what to do. He had never shutdown NETOPS before. Looking around the room, he found little inspiration. Shit.

"*Now*, Paul!"

Phillips nodded at the tech. "Do it."

The duty officer stepped back as Ahrmenta took control of the monitor again, dragging the address header from her desktop onto the NCI queue.

> WARNING: NCI REQUESTED. NEEDS D OR SUB-D SIGNATURE APPROVAL.

Phillips waved his hand at the screen and the dialog disappeared. All attention went to the node map on the scoreboard. In two seconds, NSA servers around the globe trapped and cached all the Web's net-request packets. With Web pages no longer being requested, it only took another three seconds for the entire Internet to trickle to a stop. When the network had stilled, the NCI ping went out, lighting up cyberspace bright red.

~ ~ ~ ~ ~ ~ ~ ~ ~ ~ ~ ~ ~ ~ ~ ~ ~ ~ ~ ~

Aboud could hear his eyes flitting in their sockets. They sounded like bat's wings and were the only thing moving in the still dark cavern.

He had shut down everything in time, he was sure of it. Sure, they had found his file, but they hadn't found him. He sucked in a great gulp of air, wiped his brow and began holstering his weapons.

"Dear *Marley*, that was close!"

~~~~~~~~~~~~~~~~~~

The packet circled the globe several times, interrogating every router, switch and computer on the way until it found the right device. Then it hit it hard. Like a shot from a bullet, the ping unleashed a devastating waveform, shaking its electronics to the core. The chip fought off the blow but in doing so, sent an atomic reflection back down the Web, a waveform uniquely shaped by the impurities designed into its chemistry. Electronic companies had been tattooing their chips for the government for decades and storing their IDs at NSA headquarters in Maryland. Now, ULTRAMARINE, the NSA mainframe, waited as the silicon fingerprint echoed back down the Internet's deserted superhighways.

"We have it!" cried Ahrmenta. "Doing a MAC lookup now."

At center court, the World-Wide-Web morphed into a map of the United States. In the top center, a star appeared. St. Paul. "It matches a router owned by 3M. Their Fringe Sciences Lab."

"Great. That tells us a lot," Phillips said. "They must have thousands of employees. Which one?" Phillips sat down and took over the station, waiting for his desktop to pop up. Ahrmenta watched over his shoulder. "No Paul, 3M was Kyotoed over a year ago, remember? No one's there anymore."

Phillips didn't remember. He called up the agency's corporate casebook and typed in *3M Fringe Sciences* "You're right. It's posted. Everyone's gone. But it still has a skeleton crew."

"How many?"

"One. A Doctor Aboud Tanner. Iranian ex-pat. He directed Fringe Sciences. And he's HVA!" Phillips picked up a phone and dialed the duty desk at Minneapolis Center. "Minneapolis? Sub-Director Phillips at Meade. We have a high-value-asset needing an extraction, stat. Use your tactical people. Tell your ops officer I'm sending his docket now."

"Oh, and tell him I prefer the target ambulatory."

~~~~~~~~~~~~~~~~~~

Time for his last rounds. Aboud lit a candle and in the soft glow, gave his surroundings one last go-over. He crouched to retrieve an errant ninja star lodged under his desk. In the corner his router blinked knowingly at him. Scabbard! How could I have forgotten to unplug it? He reached back and yanked whatever he could grab, threw the box against the wall then paced the room. I should leave. Should I leave? I have two hours left. What about the cameras?

Bam! Bam! Bam! The exit doors at the end of the corridor bashed against the walls as they exploded off their hinges.

The scientist froze. I am not ready for this, he thought, struggling to remember the escape plans he had so painstakingly rehearsed for the last year. He grabbed a backpack hanging on a hook, pulled out an incendiary grenade, set the timer and pulled the pin. He ran for the hall forgetting his helmet. He dashed back to Marley to snatch it from his head. "Am I scared?" he replied to his friend. "That is a true statement."

The NSA agents poured into the hallway entrance as Aboud bounded out the storage room door and flattened himself against the opposite wall. He couldn't tell how many there were, the sunlight was too bright. Their target lasers came on and he counted three beams dancing on the floor. I can take them, he thought.

He flung out his right arm as a jet-black .45-caliber Beretta slid down his sleeve and stopped in his hand with a sharp metallic *click*! He thumbed its safety and fingered the trigger as he pulled a glass reticle down over his eye. Circuits in his helmet whirred to life as heat signatures from the three officers were projected on his retina along with a red crosshair that floated on their center-of-mass. The agents walked forward and Aboud felt time compress. He lost his hearing and tunnel-vision hit. He fought it off. God is giving me a glorious chance to redeem myself. I am not taking the coward's way. Not this time. I will not flinch in the face of death again.

Bam! Bam! Bam! pounded the doors behind him. Another team. More radio chatter. More sun. He whipped his head around and flicked out his left arm, another Beretta clicking into place. Guns were going both north and south, impact points computed both fore and aft. He looked ahead to the first team, then back to the others. Take the closest first, he said to himself. No, take the new ones first. His arms trembled but he couldn't pull the triggers. I can't die now; what about the mission? What about the SF? Ten seconds later, he ran like a scared schoolgirl as the incendiary grenade lit up the hallway in magnesium-white.

The tactics team fell back as the corridor filled with bits of plastic, glass and doors. They rushed the burning computer room where Aboud stood waiting for them in the flames. They dove for the floor firing, dismembering him in a hail of bullets. A helmet rolled towards them from the blaze. When the heat had subsided, a sergeant went in to recover Aboud's body. When he returned, he was carrying Marley's half-melted head by its dreadlocks.

CHAPTER 2
HOTPIT

Along a straight pine-guarded section of I-94 in the Dakotas border region of Minnesota, a handful of airmen smoked and laughed in the hidden glade, waiting for their pilots to return. Spider landed first, pranging his A-10 roughly onto the northbound lanes of the interstate with little polish or skill. He turned off the makeshift strip halfway down and barreled into the refueling pit at top speed. Behind him, Shank, Om and Hoop followed in close pursuit. The wide-eyed crew chiefs stood fast as the four jets careened to a tangled stop, spraying them with gravel.

"What the hell's the hurry?" hollered Beak Brucato, head crew-chief, gesticulating angrily at the pilot. "Monster Trucks in town?"

Spider's canopy snapped open as he waved the pissed-off airmen away. "INCOMING!"

The chiefs dove for cover as a formation of delta-winged Mirage III jet fighters screamed by overhead. Their camo netting fluttered in the attacker's wake as anti-aircraft fire arced skyward after them. A tracer shell exploded its target and somersaulted it into the evergreens a half-mile away. The rest of the enemy formation swerved to miss their fallen comrade and continued westward without him.

"YEEHAW! Splash one Frog," cheered Hoop over the radio. "Think they saw us land?"

"How couldn't they?" answered Shank, opening his canopy. "They flew right over."

"Then why aren't they circling back? They blind?"

"They're worse than blind," Spider said. "They're French." John 'Spiderman' Trent was the leader of Hogsbreath Flight, a four-ship of A-10 Warthog attack jets fighting for the Sovereign Forces. He also commanded Dispersed Operating Location Yankee, the hidden mobile mini-base where they ate, slept and had been flying out of for the past several months.

Brucato and his men peeked up from behind their sandbags, helmets askew. He stood up and plugged into Spider's aircraft. "Friends of yours?"

"I invited them for a beer," replied Spider. "Guess they had something better to do than shoot the shit with four raggedy-ass Hogs."

"You could have warned us," Brucato scowled.

"I didn't spot them until I turned final," replied the major. "Sorry about the furball. Any damage?"

Beak surveyed the bunched-up jets. "You're in the grass. Nothing bad. You won't be getting any bombs or bullets though until we pull you out."

"That was a real cluster-fuck, John," radioed Om, Spider's number three wingman. "A few more feet and we'd be in each other's laps." Noah 'Om' McCardell was new to the A-10, having just transferred in from the Sovereign's last functioning F-16 squadron. McCardell was a lieutenant colonel, but despite outranking everyone in the flight, he was not its commander; partly, because of inexperience, mostly, because the others would have fragged him long ago.

"Up yours, you wiener," railed Bill 'Hoop' Hooper, an Irish-Italian brawler from New Jersey who piloted aircraft number four and who didn't give a damn about much, least of all anal frat-boy lieutenant colonels. "Why didn't *you* see them coming? I thought you were the F-16 god."

"They had Exocets," explained McCardell. "They weren't after us."

"You didn't know that until they just flew by."

"We would have died just the same, piling into here like this."

"Spider, that was a shit-hot Judy," remarked Green 'Shank' Williams, the number two wingman, wanting the colonel to know where his affections lay. "I never saw them coming."

Hooper agreed. "You got us down in the nick of time. You saved our asses, sir."

Spider touched hand to helmet, saluting. "Nothing but the best for my hogs." McCardell shook his head.

Brucato's only tug was sitting on blocks in the weeds again, awaiting parts. He hitched up Thelma and Louise, the camp's two aging jennies, and pulled the jets out of the grass as if they were Conestoga wagons. His chiefs hooked up fuel lines and duck-taped bullet holes while the pilots looked down from their cockpits, engines running. Hotpit refueling may have maximized aircraft turn times but the ritual disheartened the grimy weary pilots who desperately needed twenty minutes alone with a cot before being sent off into the next battle. Beak marched lunch and a drink up to the hungry pilots before they nodded off. "I put your next mission in here, too," he told Spider.

Spider squinted at the form, pulling it close and rotating it in the sun. Damn. What the hell did it say?

"You got the frag?" asked Shank over the flight's VHF radio.

"Yep, standby." Spider slid a pair of bifocals on under his visor as the rest of the flight tore into their Jimmy Johns and Pudding Cups.

"Hey, Hoop, look," needled Shank. "The old man's got cheaters."

"No way. Mr. Hawkeye himself?"

Beak and his crew laughed. "So *that's* why he almost ran us over."

For the last two years, Trent's men had mocked his creaky back and pantomimed his over-g'd hemorrhoids; now they knew about his failing eyes. Trent dug around his cockpit for a used piddle pack and tossed it at Shank, the round bag bursting against the lieutenant's fuselage, splattering on his sandwich. "I've got more where that came from if you delinquents keep it up." Spider went back heads-down to his mission planning.

From the pad, Brucato grinned up at the grumpy flight-lead. "Happy Jorge Hermosa Day, sir."

"Yeah, what's so happy about it?"

The maintenance specialist pulled a cart-load of five-hundred-pound bombs out onto the gravel. "Look what the powder fairy brought us."

Trent looked down at the bombs, non-plused.

"They're live, sir."

"Live? You mean they go *boom*?"

"You got it. Compliments of squadron."

"And bullets? We've got real bullets this time?"

"Armor-piercing. High-explosive. Incendiary. Full combat mix. For everybody."

"The last time we had live anything was over a year ago," remembered Shank. "Is depot finally back on its feet?"

"Don't count on it," answered the sergeant. "Tomorrow, you'll probably be back dropping concrete bombs and shooting slugs, so enjoy."

Hoop started unstrapping. "I'm coming down to kiss you full on the mouth, Beak."

"Save it, Brokeback." Spider flipped his map over and started jotting new targets. "We're going to Ripley. Start planning."

"But the frag has us going to Wadena," McCardell complained, scribbling turn points and timing hashes onto his map with a pocketful multicolored pens.

"Wadena's not there anymore," answered Spider.

"What?"

"The Haitians overran the town last night."

"That's not what intel briefed this morning."

"Intel's full of shit," Spider responded. "I went into Fergus last night. I've got my own sources."

"Smoking cigars with a bunch of Fergus Falls townies is not intel."

"They weren't locals. They were escapees from Wadena. What they told me wasn't pretty."

"What'd they say?" asked Shank.

"That the town was encircled before everyone could be evacuated. Not many got out. Why?"

"My sister's in Wadena."

The chatter grew quiet. "Sorry, Green."

"And *so*?" queried McCardell.

"So we're going to Camp Ripley instead," Spider replied. "The Foreign Legion wheeled back there from Wadena this morning. The Haitians will be with them."

"Whoa, whoa, whoa. That's a FUN tank garrison now. It's way too risky."

"Risky for who?" asked Hoop.

McCardell changed direction, ignoring Hoop's insinuation. "It's not our mission."

"What *is* our mission?" Spider probed.

"Preserving assets."

"You mean preserving *your* ass," hissed Hooper.

"Enough, Hoop." Spider swiveled in his seat looking down the line of attack jets to his second-in-command. "Safety may be your goal, Noah, but my mission is to grab Kermit by the throat and stab him in the heart so I can go back home and bounce my little grandson on my knee. Treat me for shock if you think I'm wasting all this high-explosive on a ghost-town."

McCardell held up his orders. "But the ATO."

Spider held up his orders, crumpled them and tossed the paper over his shoulder and into his engines. They fluttered out the other end as confetti. "What ATO?"

Two more poofs of confetti followed as Shank and Hoop tossed their air tasking orders into their intakes. "Yeah, what ATO?"

The lieutenant colonel threw up his hands. "I'm shutting down. I'm not going to be a party to insubordination."

Spider wearied. "Don't go tits-up on us, Om."

"Let him shutdown, sir. I'll take his jet." It was Brucato. Spider looked down at him. "You sure, Beak? You ready?"

"What do you mean, *ready*?" stammered Om.

"Beak is one of our auxies," replied Shank. "He's a private pilot and is going to A-10 school."

"Yep, ol' Sergeant Beak here has enough trainer time to replace any one of us," added Hoop. "Even you, colonel."

Beak put a foot up on Om's ladder but not before McCardell hit the retract switch, sucking it up into the fuselage. "That ain't happening, gas jockey. They don't make oxygen masks big enough for your dago schnozz."

"You playin' or stayin', Om?" asked Spider.

"Think careful," said Hooper. "You don't want your backbone getting sucked down your engines."

McCardell shot Hoop a radioactive glare. "I'm in. But this goes against every fiber in my body."

"Flexibility," declared Spider, returning to his map. "Key to Airpower."

Spider raised his landing gear and banked north into the clear bluebird sky as Shank, Om and Hoop climbed after him. He eyeballed their jets as they formed up, their bulbous noses, fat green wings and yawning top-mounted engines looking as attractive as pregnant toads. When they had all stabilized and were in position, Trent plugged Slayer into his headphones, cranked the volume and pushed over for the ground.

Spider didn't use a map for navigation. He read the countryside, preferring to follow its wavy wrinkles, folds and creases instead. He stuck close to the water—rivers, creeks, lakes—any topographic low-road he could hug against to hide his approach to the target. Over the months, his wingmen had caught on, too. They were down there with him now, comfortable as the fields and pastures blurred by below, able to judge their height by just inches. All except one.

"Three is way too high," called Hooper. "He's highlighting our position."

"Three, you taking a whizz up there?" asked Spider.

"No," insisted McCardell.

"Then get down here. You're going to get us shot down." The F-16 pilot complied but only by a few feet. "Noah, we're not in the Rockies," coaxed Spider. "This state is as flat as a fourth grader. You're still too high." McCardell dropped a few additional feet but could stomach no more. Spider cursed and gave up.

Hogsbreath was behind enemy lines now, behind the line-of-contact where 120,000 blue-helmeted French regulars and Foreign Legion lay gunning for them in the forests and farmlands below. The French had come as part of the United Nations Interim Forces in the United States. They had been the first Coax nation to volunteer to help President Earle quash the Sovereign independents and had brought with them their colonial forces, too. Not only did the French-UN soldiers hope to kill a cowboy American or two and bring back glory to France, they were also in it for the money; the UN paid fifty thousand dollars for every A-10 shot down.

"Hogsbreath, we're five minutes from target. Ready for brief?"

"Two."

"Three."

"Four."

Trent started the checklist. "Targets are tanks and armored-personnel-carriers inside grid UNIFORM-MIKE-NINER-ZERO."

"Two."

"Three."

"Four."

"Threats are SAMs, small arms, helos."

"Two."

"Three."

"Four."

"Three, you'll be first-shooter. Loft your bombs into the basket from the north. Two and Four, follow me and stay tight. We'll use the bombs for cover. They'll never see us coming. Copy?"

"Two."

"Four."

"Three, you copy?"

"What am I supposed to do while you three are having all the fun?" nittered McCardell. "Touch myself?"

"You orbit at the release point," said Spider. "You're our air cover for today."

"How the hell am I supposed to dogfight Mirages and Rafales in a piece-of-shit A-10?" he asked.

"You're the air-to-air puke," replied Spider. "You tell me."

"If I were flying a real jet, I would."

"Your F-16s are all hangar queens, colonel."

Hoop snorted. "Not to mention your bombs are always landing in somebody else's zipcode."

"Why are you doing this, Spider?"

"You saw those Mirages this morning," he replied. "We're losing air superiority. We have to provide our own fighter cover."

"Why are you doing this, Spider?" McCardell repeated.

"And you piss me off."

"Two."

"Four."

~ ~ ~ ~ ~ ~ ~ ~ ~ ~ ~ ~ ~ ~ ~ ~ ~ ~ ~ ~

The air was still as Captain Louis LeCounte checked his vehicles and readjusted his camouflage projectors before bunking down. Around his garrison, the Haitian Machetes lay about their APCs in drug-induced stupor from the previous night's raid. The drugs were military-issue and that angered him for it was his commander that was supplying them. But, so far, he was right, the pills *were* cheaper than feeding the voodun plus, it kept them from killing each other between battles.

The Machetes were descendents of the Tonton Macoutes, the infamous voodoo death-squads organized by former Haitian dictator 'Papa Doc' Duvalier to suppress dissidents. It was not soon after General Faisson assigned them to his unit that LeCounte began considering resigning. And it was not soon after LeCounte was ordered to set them loose in Wadena that he had wished he were dead. That night—last night—amid the horrid screams and chilling music, he had witnessed the maddest images of hacking and flaying and raping a human being could take. And the plunder. It took an entire fleet of commandeered FedEx vans just to carry away all the electronics and appliances and jewelry they had stolen. He stared horrified at one such piece now, a gold engagement ring hanging from the neck of a slumbering voodun, a woman's finger still attached. Yes, he thought. He would tender his resignation tomorrow.

~ ~ ~ ~ ~ ~ ~ ~ ~ ~ ~ ~ ~ ~ ~ ~ ~ ~ ~

"Hogsbreath. Arm 'em up. Fight's on."

McCardell heard the signal and plunged for the ground. When he could go no lower, he rocketed for the sky, lofting his payload like a slingshot into the enemy bivouac five miles away. He peeled away as Spider and the others continued into the camp, their heat-signatures masked by the cold metal casings of the Mk82s as they whistled mindlessly through the air ahead.

Spider scoured the horizon for French armor. He saw nothing but flat, featureless scrub. And shadows. That was a recurring problem the FUN had with their new domed projection systems; the shelters hid vehicles and troops well by replicating the surrounding vegetation, but on a sunny day, they couldn't hide from their own shadows.

Beneath the A-10s, McCardell's bombs reached the end of their broadcast day and hit, sending tangerine fireballs mushrooming high overhead. "We've got secondary boomers! Must be the fuel depot," yelled Shank.

Spider searched the terrain again. Where were the French? No petrol tanks. No fuel trucks. He dug for his glasses.

The Legionnaires of the 13th Demi Brigade awoke, dazed by the explosions and panic-stricken by the roar of the jets. They roused from their pads, fired up their vehicles and abandoned their camouflage.

"Holy shit, Lead. We've got Leclercs and AMXs all over."

Hoop rolled upside-down to take in the scene for himself. "Lead, they're uncloaking. They've got cloaking devices. We're fighting fucking Klingons!"

Up ahead, white smoke trails laced the skyline. "HOGSBREATH, THREE SAMS. ELEVEN, TWELVE, ONE O'CLOCK!"

Shank and Hoop broke out of formation and headed for the weeds as Spider jinked and juked. The missiles sailed by his canopy, uninterested, homing instead on the diesel fireballs to his rear. Spider followed his wingmen in a wide arc away from the SAMs, while, in the center of the camp, a cloud of dust arose and headed east.

"Pierre's getting out of Dodge, guys," Spider transmitted. "Two, drop your stick in front of their column. Four, drop yours to the rear. Bottle them up. I'll take care of the chewy center."

"Two."

"Four."

Shank and Hoop split off on their bomb runs while Spider took out a cellphone. He watched the undisciplined Haitians stampede for the exit as he checked his display. Three bars! He dialed his wife's work number and waited for the operator.

"Women's Chemistry Department. How may I direct your call?"

John almost dropped the phone. He had never gotten through to his wife before. "Hello? This is John Trent. Can you hear me?"

"Hello," came the reply. "You've reached the University of Minnesota. Is anyone there?"

"Yes, this is John Trent. I'd like to speak with my wife, Laura," he said, yelling above the wind and the racket of the cockpit.

"Say again. I can barely hear you," replied the mousy-voiced attendant.

"*IS LAURA THERE?* I've got to talk to her now while I'm in range."

Ahead, two black dots appeared above the hills.

"Two's in hot," radioed Shank.

"Four's in hot," repeated Hooper.

Spider cleared them in with his best Gladiator. "Unleash hell."

"Laura? I'll go get her. It'll just be a minute." Trent couldn't believe his ears. She was there. It had been two years since he heard her voice.

What would he say? What would she do when she realized it was him? Would she cry? Would she hang up? The cellphone played a few bars of Barry Manilow, then went dead.

In the distance, Shank's bombs hit their targets as a geyser of sparks lanced the sky like a Las Vegas fountain show. "TAKE THAT YOU BERET-HEADED SURRENDER-MONKEYS!" he cussed. Hooper's stick struck in the rear of the column, blocking the retreating mechanized forces. In the middle of the confusion, the surviving French officers regained control of their vehicles and dispersed into the trees. It was Spider's turn now.

"One's up."

Spider yanked hard on the control stick, pointed his nose to the sun and flipped upside-down to scan the bedlam below. He watched through the top of his canopy as a mass of armor made for the treeline. He pulled and rolled towards them.

"One's in hot."

~ ~ ~ ~ ~ ~ ~ ~ ~ ~ ~ ~ ~ ~ ~ ~ ~ ~ ~

LeCounte wiped the blood from his goggles and mounted his turret. He had managed to reverse course and race north for a tall stand of tamarack after shooting two of his mutinying Machetes down below. Now he scanned the sky for more of the American tank-busters, recalling the terrifying stories he had heard from tankers in other units about how the A-10's engines whistled harmlessly above while a single round from their guns could slice a tank in two. He heard the whistle and raised his machine-gun to the sun. Too late. One of his tanks dissolved behind him as the jet flew by and disappeared behind the hills. Two, three, four, five more bombs he counted, as the fireballs walked closer in quick succession. LeCounte didn't make it to number six.

~ ~ ~ ~ ~ ~ ~ ~ ~ ~ ~ ~ ~ ~ ~ ~ ~ ~ ~

"My God!" whispered Spider through his teeth. Each of his marks found a tank and either blew off a turret, shredded its chassis or left it spinning high in the air. He didn't want to imagine what the insides were like.

Spider turned west just as the far side of the camp came alive with helicopters. "Lead, I've got choppers on the flight line. They're spooling up. Where are they coming from?" Shank and Hoop turned back for them as the birds leapt into the air and headed for safety to the east.

"Two's in hot."

Spider called him off. "Two, ABORT, ABORT, ABORT! They're Cobras. They're U.S. They're pitching out of the fight."

"They're still Coax with the UN. I can take them out now."

"No. We don't fire on Americans."

"Well, they're firing on you," cried Hoop. "Two Sidewinders, your six."

Spider twisted in his seat and scanned his tail. "No joy." He swivelled back the other way and saw two rocket plumes helix towards him. "Tally-ho the 'winders." With no time to think, Spider pulled his nose vertical and waited as his airspeed bled off to zero. Not now. Not yet. *Now.* Spider kicked full right rudder, flipping the jet end-for-end just as the American missiles sailed past. They'd been tricked. Deprived of their heat-source and unable to turn back, the warheads exploded harmlessly behind him.

"Lead. SAM. Left nine o'clock. Low."

Not again. Spider sat back in his seat as a missile sprang out of the trees and got big in his canopy. There was nothing he could do. All his maneuvering had slowed him down. He was out of airspeed and ideas. He closed his eyes and prayed. Prayed that some lazy Gaul at the Mistral plant had forgotten to connect the fuze.

F-L-A-S-H! B-O-O-M!

His cockpit lit up like an arc welder as a great quake passed through the jet. The wind got loud as the A-10 headed for the ground. Spider opened his eyes. I'm still here? he thought, jettisoning his bomb racks and relighting his engines just in time to miss a smouldering tank-hulk by inches.

Shank and Hoop couldn't bear to watch. "LEAD, EJECT, EJECT, EJECT."

"Not tonight boys. I heard the snail here is awful." Spider fought to keep his wobbling Hog airborne as staccato puffs of dirt scampered along beside him. He looked back. The Cobra was firing and gaining on him.

F-L-A-S-H! B-O-O-M!

His cockpit lit up again but this time the chopper was the one hit.

He watched it in his mirrors as the gunship smoked, flew sideways then disintegrated into splinters behind him.

"FOX-FOUR THE ROTORHEAD!" whooped McCardell.

"You didn't have to shoot them down, Om! They were U.S."

McCardell, rocking his wings in victory, zoomed overhead. "Now they're *ex*-U.S."

Spider's dry tongue stuck to the roof of his mouth as his arms shook with fatigue. He fumbled for the glasses that had slid down his nose all the while trying to milk altitude out of his faltering turbines. Warning tones buzzed in his helmet as his fighter flew on the edge of a stall. A grove of trees loomed for him ahead and he yanked his control stick, just barely clearing a grove of firs. Hoop joined up on him from behind and gave him a report.

"Lead, engine number one is smoking and you're peppered with shrapnel underneath. You're losing fluids. Hydraulics. Maybe oil."

"That it?"

"And you're trailing a pine bough."

"Don't worry, John. We'll get you home," assured McCardell.

"No," countermanded Spider. "Two can take me the rest of the way. You and Four to go back and complete the mission."

"Say *again*?"

"I said finish the mission. Ripley is too target-rich to call it quits. I want those bastards to pay for Wadena."

"They just spanked our four-ship. How long do you think *two* of us would last?"

Spider didn't push it. He was twenty miles behind enemy lines and barely flying. He might as well have had *KICK ME* painted on his tail. "Fine. Set up escort and point me home."

Spider's knuckles whitened as oil spewed out behind him and his hydraulics decayed. He squinted out his windshield to find a safe place to ditch when his phone rang. He fumbled for it and slipped it into his helmet. "Laura, it's me, John. I love you, babe. I've missed you so much."

"Umm, sir, this is Audrey."

A big bang sounded from behind Spider's seat as warnings flashed across his dash.

"Lead, you OK?" asked Shank. "Your number one just spit out a shitload of fan blades."

Trent cut off the engine and activated its fire extinguisher. "Audrey, of course, sorry," Spider apologized. "Is Laura there?"

"Laura's right here."

"Hello, this is Laura."

It was her. Laura. His wife. She sounded gorgeous, her sweet, silky alto swirling in his ears. It uncurled his toes and blotted out all else. "Hi, hon. It's me, John. You aren't going to believe where I am right now so I'm not even going to tell you."

"*Hello*? This is Laura. Can I help you?"

Trent pulled the phone away. One bar. He was close to friendly territory: too close. The technically-challenged Middle States didn't have cellphones as their towers had been bombed out of existence by the Coax. He had but a few seconds of signal before he would lose it all together. He continued to sink earthward as his engine got hotter.

"Honey, I don't have much time. I wanted to let you know—"

"Look," interrupted his wife. "I don't know who you are but I'm in a meeting. I'm going to count to three. After that, I'm hanging up."

Spider's shoulders slumped. She's not hearing me. "I can't stand being without you, Laura," he said into the blind. "I can't stand thinking of you alone, without me there."

"One."

"I know you're probably still bitter," he said softly, the trees getting bigger outside. "Still mad at why I left. The way I left."

"Two."

"I just want you to know I'm sorry. I *had* to leave. You'll see someday why." He heard his wingmen calling, saw them turn back for him and circle overhead.

"Three."

"Anyway, I wanted to let you know I'm OK." More lights flashed at him. More bad news from his engine. "That I'm still alive. That I love you more than ever. And I want you. I want you to join me."

"Sorry, whoever you are. I've got to go. Try again when you can afford a better phone!"

The phone went dead in his ear. *Shit*! Did she hear any of it? he wondered. Had he endangered his life for nothing? The trees reached for him now, scratching at the bottom of his jet. For the moment, he didn't care because for the first time in two years, he had finally gotten to hear his sweet wife's voice. And it sounded great.

CHAPTER 3
SHOPPING

How much can one man eat? Laura did a quick scan of the cart. Ten cartons of jumbo eggs, a drawerful of English Muffin bread, two cafeteria-sized vats of baked beans, a five-gallon pail of New England Clam Chowder and a crate of Florida oranges. And that was just the bottom rack. Laura shook her head as she tried to find a safe place for her grapes. This was the first time she had shopped with Abby. It would also be the last she would share a cart.

"What are you staring at? Why is everyone looking at me?"

Laura turned back to the apples.

"You don't think I'm hoarding, do you?" Abby asked. "You don't think we're not going to eat this, do you? This is what Wade eats every week. Honest. You don't think there's going to be a problem, do you?"

"No one's looking at you," Laura said. "Why should you have to put it back?"

"The shelves are pretty sparse," Abby offered. "It seems there are less and less brands to pick from. The rest are pretty mangy."

"Uh huh."

"Just look at these. You call these bananas? All they give us is these little deformed things from South America somewhere. I think they look like someone stubbed their toe."

"Well, they certainly made up for it with these," said Laura, palming a giant yellow fruit as if it were a basketball.

"That's not a grapefruit," replied Abby. "That's a pomelo and it's half rind and half air." She threw the orb back into the bin. "Where are all these things coming from anyway? The circus?"

Laura smiled.

"Anyway, I should probably put some of this back, huh?"

The Fredricks were her husband John's friends, but she enjoyed Abby. Her honesty, her quirkiness. She was entertaining and a welcome escape from another moldy day at the university. "Are you always this hyper about fruit?"

"It's just not like him to not write, Laura. I don't know what it could be. I'm worried sick."

"Is that what you wanted to get together for? August?"

"I told him not to go. But his father said he was old enough to make up his own mind. I could've kicked him right then and there."

Laura leaned into the cart, willing it to the meat section.

"Everything seems to have gotten worse since all this mandate talk started." Abby checked over her shoulder. "Since the *French* arrived, I mean, with their soldiers and teachers and policemen."

"How so?"

"I mean the border, the phones, the Internet. Ever since France began claiming us as their own, our contact with the MS seems to have clamped down."

"A mandate is perfectly justified," said Laura absently. "It's like an Indian reservation. The UN puts it aside for countries that are here to help contain the Middle States."

"Laura, what if he's dead? What if Auggie's been killed? How would I find out? How would I know?" Abby rubbed at her eyes. "There's no mail, no news. I want my boy. I want to know he's OK."

"It's OK. He's fine."

"Are you sure?"

"I'm sure," Laura repeated, looking for the steaks.

The farmer's wife exploded into smile. "Thank you, Laura! I'm so glad I can talk to you. Wade was right, I needed to get out of the house. You were the only one I could talk to. You are a true friend."

"You're a true friend, too."

Abby put a hand over her mouth. "Hon, I'm so sorry. I forgot all about John. Have you heard from him? It's been almost a year, hasn't it? How have you been making out?"

"Two years," Laura corrected.

"*Two* years! And here I'm going on like I'm the only one in the world hurting."

"I'm not hurting. It happens. Professors take leaves and sabbaticals like this all the time. Sometimes they're gone overseas four or five years. Researching rainforests. Studying in the Antarctic."

"But they're not fighting, Laura. They're not in combat."

"Neither is John. Hostilities are over."

"How do you know?"

"Know what?"

"That an all-out war isn't raging across the border? This very minute?"

Laura raised her hands, taking in the store. "Because everything's fine. We'd be watching it on the news if it wasn't."

"So, you're OK then?"

Laura returned to the beef, nodding.

"Then why are we in the meat section?"

Laura blinked at the package in her hands. "For you."

"We don't buy meat. We have five thousand cows!"

"I like meat!"

"You're a pasta person. And Cody's a vegan."

"I've been known to have a T-bone or two."

"Laura, these are *dog* bones not *T*-bones."

Laura looked lost in her raven black curls. Abby took the package and returned it. "It's OK. I did the same thing with Auggie. I kept buying him his God-awful Maple Pop-Tarts even after he left. I still have a cabinetful. Honey, you going to be all right?"

Laura retrieved the package of bones, slapped them in the cart then piled on five more. "You know, I really wish you'd quit your *honey*-ing. It's really starting to get annoying."

Abby gave her a stunned look then grabbed the cart and wheeled away, Oreos and Velveeta trailing behind as she went. Laura followed her to a deserted aisle where she found her friend bent over a broken bottle of Ragu, crying. "You dropped these."

"I know. They're mine. I just wanted to go. I'll run my stuff through and pay for it quick. Then you can take me home."

Laura knelt beside her, moving the sauce around with a couple of paper towels. "Sorry about that back there. It's not you. It's me. I'm just a little frayed today."

"No, it's me," said Abby "Wade said it, too. I'm getting clingy." Sobbing. "I miss him so!"

A man rounded the far end of the aisle. Laura waved him over. "You can clean this up now. *We're* obviously not having much luck with it." Abby laughed and wiped her sniffles.

"I do not clean!" boomed the reply.

The pair looked up. A tall solid Negro towered over them. He wore tan pants and a tan shirt with an Ivory Coast crest on its sleeve. In one hand he carried a half-full shopping basket. In the other, a powder-blue beret. "Who's tings are these?" he asked, poking through their cart.

Abby stood first. "They're mine. Or, I guess, both of ours. But mine mostly. Not *mine*, obviously. It's for my husband and—"

The black man thumped Abby's cantaloupe then dropped it into his basket. Laura's jaw fell. "Excuse me. Can we help you?"

The African held up a white palm as big as Laura's face and kept rummaging. "You cannot leave with all tis. You will put it back."

Laura dug in her handbag. "There must be some mistake. I haven't heard about there being any problems."

"There is a rationing. You have too many such tings," he gestured, wrinkling his nose at a jar of lutefisk.

The man's name tag said *BEETLESMANN*. "There is no such thing, Mr. Beetlesmann." Laura flipped open her cellphone. "It would've been on the news. But I just happen to know Governor Johnson. I work with his son at the U. We'll see what he has to say about this."

"TIS I SAYS!"

The officer's voice carried through the store sending Laura and Abby into animal crouches. "It's OK," Abby whispered to Laura. "I've got this." She flashed her card then handed it to the UNsman.

"What'tis?"

"It's my clearance card. We run Fredrick Dairy. We supply milk to your base. These are the provisions our farm needs for the week."

The giant studied the badge, then threw it on the ground. "T'means not'in. You get by like t'rest."

Abby bent down to pick up the card. She reappeared, holding the back side to his face. "Then I will have to tell Commander Faisson that his signature is no longer being honored by his officers."

The African gawked at the autograph then straightened and gave her a quick half-bow. "I completely sorry, Miss," he said, returning the cantaloupe and other commandeered items. "Tese are UN, for UN use, of course. You may go. Many blessings." He turned and disappeared into the gathering crowd.

Abby yelled after him. "Here's a discount card! Five gallons, get one free." She turned back to her cart. "The nerve. What right do they have telling me what I can and can't buy?"

"I'm sure he was just following orders," Laura said, turning her back to the stares. "It has to be pretty tough on them. Being in a strange land, so far from home, trying to keep our half of America at peace with the middle half. Don't you think?"

Abby nodded. "Let's get out of here before the midday rush starts." She leaned her tiny body into the cart and huffed it to the checkout.

"Sorry, ma'am." The girl at the register held up an egg. "This is a restricted purchase. Only one allowed per month."

Abby spun around. "Say what?"

"Easy, easy. It was just a joke."

Abby gave the woman a second look. "Barbara?" It was Barb Hanson, fellow soccer/hockey/football/wrestling mom. "Barbara, I haven't seen you since Roy's graduation. You scared me there for a minute. Wow, girl. You look good."

"Thanks. It's this Fredrick Dairy Euphoria Juice," she replied, pulling a bottle of milk from behind her register. "I can't get enough of it. What's in it?"

"Wade could tell you more than me. He feeds the cows peppermint for digestion, wild dagga for stress, catnip for alertness and blue lotus for that certain happy feeling in bed. It even has some aspirin in it."

"Aspirin? That explains why I've been able to get along with the boss lately," tilting her head to Bret Robillard, their bagger.

Robillard avoided Abby's eyes. "It's our best seller," he noted. "That and the Key Lime."

"Limes were my idea," Abby beamed. "We grind rinds in our rations so the city folks can't complain to the UN about our manure. The lime flavor was an unexpected side-effect."

"Too bad," Barb said. "I love the smell of manure. Screw the blueberries."

Robillard eyed the growing checkout line. "Barb?"

Hanson took another pull of milk and continued ringing up the groceries. "How is Auggie? Everything still a go for the big wedding?" Abby dropped Wade's Leinenkugels on the jelly donuts, flattening them. "I mean, Cheryl hasn't backed out, has she? He is so lucky to have her."

Abby dug through her purse and threw a handful of hundreds on the counter before cantering out of the store. Robillard scowled as Hanson watched her go. "What? What'd I say?"

"I'm sorry," Laura said. "It's nothing you said. She's had a bad day. I'll pay whatever's left."

"It must be the war," said Hanson. "Poor thing. It's got everybody strung higher than hummingbirds on meth."

Laura closed her wallet and padded away. "There's no war. I wish people would stop saying that."

Abby wandered the parking lot looking like a lost five-year-old in her flowered sundress and flip-flops. Laura turned to her Pathfinder and opened the doors with her remote.

Bwip! Bwip!

"Over here, Ab!" Abby jumped in and, after filling the back with bags, Laura joined her. "Auggie will be fine. He'll find a way to get something to you."

Abby shook her head. "I just have this awful feeling. Every time something reminds me of him, my heart starts chugging. Like it's pumping cookie dough."

"If something's happened, it was from an accident. Not fighting."

"But that's why he snuck into the MS in the first place, Laura. *To* fight. He and his friends didn't risk getting thrown in prison just to sit on the border and play cribbage. They went because they heard things were tough. That they were needed."

A knock sounded against the window. "Mrs. Fredrick?"

Abby rolled down her side. It was Robillard, the store owner/bagger, holding a box of Special K cereal.

"You left this at the checkout."

"Not me. I didn't buy that."

"It's on your receipt."

"I think you've got the wrong person," Abby said. "If it doesn't have chocolate or sugar in it, Wade won't eat it."

"Still, I'm quite sure you bought it. I even put your receipt inside."

"No, *I* wouldn't even eat that."

"Still—"

She rolled up her window. Robillard stuck in his hand and held the glass fast. "I insist," he said, lowering his voice. "Compliments of Cottage Grove Byerlys."

"OK-OK," Abby relented. "But someone's going to be back in a minute looking for this and then you'll be sorry." She took the box and threw it in back. She startled as Robillard's puffy face came in her window.

"Remember, the receipt's in the box," he recited.

She leaned away and rolled the window shut.

Quiet returned to the car as Abby took a tissue and continued talking into it. "You're really sure, Laura? That's all it is? No battles. No fighting. And Auggie is all right?"

"Yes," she replied. "Now are we ready to get back to our normal boring everyday lives?" She shoved the key into the ignition and started her engine..

"What was *that*?" Abby pointed out the windshield as four triangular shapes shooshed by overhead. They were gray with French-UN red-and-blue roundels under their wings. They sliced through the air with the faintest of whispers and, in a blink, were gone, disappearing into the humid Minnesota haze, their tailpipes aglow. "Wow, they were low!" Abby said. "How come they didn't make any noise?"

Laura grabbed Abby by the head and shoved her into the footwell. As an Air Force wife and married fifteen years to a fighter pilot, she knew what was coming next. "*GET DOWN!*" she shouted as a sonic boom rolled across the mall like a giant wave of water, knocking panes from their casements and turning cars into clouds of bright glitter.

From all across the lot, Laura heard muffled shrieks and cries and low moans as the shock subsided. Abby was screaming beside her, her sundress torn and splotched, her head and arms bleeding. Laura had the windshield in her lap. All she could hear was a thick gurgling in her ears. She touched her own cheek and felt glass grind underneath the skin. "NO, NO, NO!" Laura hollered as she hammered her horn in unison with the others. "I will not permit you to do this! I will not allow you to touch me!"

Helicopters streamed by above and armored personnel carriers raced by below them as Laura's carefully coiffed world shattered and rained down on her with the rest of the glass. In the pandemonium, she saw John. He stood in the doorway of their farmhouse and was leaving, backlit in the setting sun. "It'll happen slow," he had said, picking up his flightbag after giving up on begging her to join him. "You'll do what they ask at first because they'll seem reasonable. But then, when they've got enough soldiers on the ground, they'll tire of sugar-coating everything. Then things will move fast," he told her.

"Then it'll be too late. Don't wait until it's too late."

CHAPTER 4
STOWAWAY

Grease slicks came free of charge at the Come-On-Inn Cafe. "It keeps the silverware from rustin'," his dad loved to repeat. Wade was looking at one now, floating in his coffee. He stabbed at the stain with his spoon and swirled it absently as he read the letter for the hundredth time.

"You going to eat those, Chewie?" asked his waitress. "They look cold."

Wade folded the note roughly and shoved it into his pocket. "Not today, Peg. I had breakfast at home." He pushed her his congealed eggs. "I don't know why I ordered it." He pushed her his steak, hash browns and sticky bun, too.

"Hi, Wade. How the ladies doin'?" asked Pete Fredrick.

"Cows are doing good, Pete. Hanging in there." Pete was Wade's down-and-out uncle. He had been a dairyman at one time but lost his farm in the eighties. Now he just hung around downtown in the coffee shops, pretending to be one.

"Et's good," Pete continued, waiting for an invitation to sit. "Corn's looking good. Ain't usin' genetics again, are you? Stuff's bad shit, Wade. Rot your herd like gangrene."

A rusty Olds Ciera puttered up the street, stopping several times and holding up traffic. "I'm meeting with someone, Uncle Pete. I'll catch you later." Wade watched the car swing into an open stall and its slight gray-skinned driver get out.

"What's this? Nother 'grint you bringing in?"

"A student from River Falls. He's going to be helping out our herdsman this summer."

"*Moo-U*, huh?"

"Sorry, Unc. Gotta go." Wade brushed past the frail figure and made for the door. "Say hi to Aunt Jill for me." Outside, he regarded the driver and his movie-star glasses, off-kilter beard and Indiana Jones fedora. He extended his hand. "I'm Wade. You George?"

Aboud turned, startled. "Yes. George. That is a true statement. I am George."

"Glad to meet you, George. Let's go inside."

The man leaned in to Wade. "Just because Stone says it, doesn't make it so."

The farmer grinned. "Sure." A block away, a powder blue golf cart appeared and drove erratically down the sidewalk towards them. Wade furrowed his brow and hurried his guest inside.

"I understand you specialize in butterfat production," Wade announced loudly, seating him at his booth. "Ours is a little low. If you could help us get our premiums up, you'll be worth your weight in gold." Peggy brought a pot of coffee as the other farmers went back to their visiting. Fredrick had hired foreign kids before; South Africans, Pakistanis, Thais. With Mexican help priced so high, overseas laborers were as common in Hastings as silos. Even rednecks like Wade needed global outsourcing.

"Just because Stone says it, doesn't make it so," Aboud repeated.

"What? Talk sense," Wade whispered back.

"I cannot talk to you until you give me the right password."

"Password? Are you 007 or something?"

"I have to be sure who you are being. You could be anybody. CIA. TSA. StanEval. Any number of them would like to eat my head."

Wade stuck out an arm and shoved it under the Iranian's nose. "Take a whiff, Austin Powers. Take a deep whiff. Know many feds that smell like cow crap?"

Tanner turned his head away. "No, but they can be *very* smart."

Out his window, Fredrick watched as the two teenagers in the golfcart stopped beside the Olds. They flattened their noses against Aboud's windows and tried opening his doors. Across the street, a pretty blonde fifteen-year-old appeared. She had just left the Ben Franklin with a bag of fabric swatches when the boys began yelling after her. She turned and walked away as they jumped into their caddy and putted in pursuit. Wade stood. "I'm going."

Aboud tugged at his shirt. "OK. OK. Sit down. Please. I believe you."

"No. I'm going. Now," Wade repeated, grabbing his John Deere hat and cup of Skoal juice. "If you want to come, then throw your stuff in the truck." Wade looked again to the street. "There's trouble."

"Get away, pervert!" cried Bettina Schoerman, kicking at the two boys to let her alone.

"We just want to talk, perky-tits, or are you too good for us?" Darren Taylor taunted. Darren and Dieter Taylor were Pax Cadets, a civilian body comprised of thirteen- to twenty-year-olds that provided watcher services to the local UNIFUS warrens. Darren, a rolley-polley sixteen-year-old, was well on his way to becoming a hoodlum. Dieter, his 21-year-old brother, freshly freed from jail to enlist, already was one.

"Please let me go. I haven't done anything wrong."

"I don't know about that," replied Darren, moving closer. "I don't recall you ever coming over to talk in school. You preferred preppies." Dieter snuck up behind and pulled the blouse out of her shorts. She screamed and wheeled around to slap him. Dieter caught her arm. "Hitting a Peacebuilder is a felony." He pulled her close to smell her. "We're going to have to call this in. You'll have to come with us."

Schoerman's fear grew as each of the early-morning shoppers around her sidestepped the confrontation to duck into the nearest store. Her assailants beamed confidence when Wade yelled from across the street. "Honey, it's time to go. Stop flirting with the cute cadets and hop in. We've got chores to do!"

The brothers turned just enough for Tina to wriggle free. She bolted for Wade's open door and scooted in beside Aboud. Wade hauled the door shut and waved to the two UN youth. "Thanks for looking after my girl. Keep up the good work." He watched them in the mirror as he pointed his Dodge Ram toward his farm. One jotted down his license, the other called on his radio. Damned Nazis.

Tina gave her door a gentle slam. "Thanks again, Mr. Fredrick," she said, framed by the fragrant hedgerow of her mother's lilacs. "I'm glad there are still people around like you."

"No charge," Wade replied. "Just don't go downtown without your brothers anymore."

The heat began toying with Aboud's beard. It drooped off his chin as Bettina stuck her head back inside the cab. "Nice meeting you, too, George," she said.

Tanner held his whiskers on with one hand and waved with the other. "Nice to meeting you, too."

Fredrick backed Black Beauty down the drive and continued home. He scavenged for his chew tin then offered the scientist a wad.

"No thanks," Tanner said. "That's illegal."

Wade shrugged, shoving a plug into his cheek. "So's smuggling spies."

Aboud stared out his window as the newly planted corn fields raced by and fidgeted. "You did not know her?" he finally asked.

"No, was I supposed to?"

"You endangered us for a stranger? The mission could have been compromised."

Fredrick rankled. "Look, Jose. I don't know how it works in your country, but here we help each other. No one is more important than anyone else."

Aboud turned back to his view. His legs bounced on the seat as he sat on his hands. "I thought at least you knew her."

Wade watched Aboud sulk. "Get a spine, my man. If you can't well up the guts to confront a couple of pimply-faced blue-baggers, then you have no business going to the MS."

The pump hummed happily as it filled the Fredrick Dairy truck with milk. When the transfer was complete, Wade turned it off, uncoupled the hose and stowed it back in the parlor. "You just about ready?" he called into the shadows.

"One more of a minute," replied Tanner.

Fredrick grabbed the man's sleeping bag and marched it to the top of the tanker. Aboud had designed it himself. He called it a cocoon. It was thick and white and warm and airtight. Tanner had brains, that's for sure, Wade thought. Why were the little guys always the smart ones? The farmer shoved the sack into the hatch as he racked his brain trying to recall a smart big guy.

Wade's farm rested on five hundred acres of prime Mississippi River bottomland. It had taken three generations of Fredricks to subdue the plot from a millennia of woodlands, rock and swamp. When his turn came to run things, he retired the dozen cows that had fed and supported their family for years and installed a new mega-tech rotating parlor that milked five thousand premium-bred heifers three times a day. Not bad for a high school dropout. From the top of his perch, he swept his eyes about him, wondering if this was the last time he would see the homeplace.

Aboud scampered out the barn and climbed the ladder, half-naked. "Don't look," he told Wade, as he ran for the cocoon and jumped in. "OH, HOCKEY!"

"I told you it'd be cold."

"It is. It is," Aboud chattered through his teeth. "It will just take a minute to warm up." Then: "Why does it have to be so cold again?"

"To keep it thick. It's been ultra-filtrated to remove the water."

"To maximize your load?"

"And for your ride," Wade added. "You'd be banged against the sides like road kill if it were liquid."

Aboud dipped in a finger and licked. "It is like jello."

"Like riding inside a marshmallow," Wade recited. His stowaway's lips were still blue. "You sure that thing's warm enough?"

"I will be all right," shook Aboud.

"Good, then you won't be needing this." Wade reached down inside Aboud's underpants and pulled out a Glock automatic.

"Give me back my gun."

"No doing," Wade said. "They've got radar at the checkpoints and this will make them hotter than a bull in a pepper patch."

"But the cocoon absorbs radar."

"Not taking that chance." Wade pocketed the sidearm then reached into the bag again to pull out a small gas cylinder. He tossed it down into the dumpster before attaching a small hose to the shroud. "*This* is your air supply. It's from the airbrakes. It won't smell great but at least you won't run out of air. It's going to take us at least three hours to get you to Montevideo."

Aboud looked as if Wade had just snatched a pickle from his Big Mac. No one had ever modified one of his designs before. Wade grabbed the hatch and banged it on his head to close it. "Before you go, I just want to say a thing." Aboud gathered his thoughts. "You were right to help that girl back there. It was admirable. Something I would like to do someday."

"Yeah, well."

"You have a low opinion of me, I know. Will it effect how you carry out this mission?"

"You have *nothing* to do with my motivation," Wade replied.

"Then why *are* you doing this? For freedom? For patriotism?"

Wade looked to the west where feathery mares-tails whipped high above the horizon. A storm was brewing. He blinked rapidly at the clouds before producing a worn, crumpled letter from his pocket. "Here. A Freemartin at the grocery store gave this to my wife last week."

> FROM: SF/QS/ADMIN (QUARTERSTAFF PERSONNEL)
> TO: MR/MRS WADE FREDRICK
>
> WE ARE SORRY TO INFORM YOU THAT YOUR SON CORPORAL AUGUST WADE FREDRICK WAS RECENTLY KILLED IN ACTION IN MINNESOTA. HE WAS ATTACHED TO 1211INF ARMY OF THE DAKOTAS WHERE HE WAS ENGAGED IN HEROIC EFFORTS TO EVACUATE CIVILIANS IN WADENA. IT WAS THERE HE RECEIVED A FATAL WOUND FROM A UN SNIPER. WE REGRET THAT UNAVOIDABLE CIRCUMSTANCES MADE NECESSARY THE UNUSUAL DELAY THIS NOTICE HAS TAKEN TO GET TO YOU. IT IS OUR HOPE THAT IN TIME THE KNOWLEDGE OF HIS HEROIC DEFENSE OF THE UNITED STATES OF AMERICA, EVEN ONTO DEATH, MAY BE A SUSTAINING COMFORT TO YOU. HIS PASSING REPRESENTS A DISTINCT LOSS TO THE SOVEREIGN FORCES.
>
> EDWARD F WITSELL, GENERAL OF RECORDS

"I am sorry, Wade."

Out on the highway, a small blue three-wheeled Whispa slowed and pulled into the drive. Wade pocketed the note. "Get down and zip up," he said. "We've got company." He screwed the hatch tight and descended the ladder.

"You smurfs here for some freebees?" Fredrick yelled as he inspected his rig and got it ready for the road. Alongside, the tiny canvas-sided runabout pulled up with a Pax Cadet and a neighbor boy inside.

"Milk's for kids," announced the cadet. He wore the blue dickey and tan pants of a Patrol Leader, a small step up from the motley jeans, sneakers and baseball cap the boys in town wore.

"That's good," replied Wade. "Because this load is going to the front. It's for *real* soldiers."

"Ha, ha," repeated the passenger, kicking his feet up on the dash. "*Real* soldiers."

The cadet elbowed his friend. "Shut up, asshole, or I'm not taking you on any more ride-alongs."

Wade ducked under his truck's axle. He came up a moment later, wiping grease from his hands. "I need to go, boys. I'm late for my delivery."

"I'm afraid I can't let you do that," said the cadet, getting out. He produced a clipboard of reports. On top, a wanted poster of Doctor Aboud Tanner-Geha flapped in the breeze. He showed it to the farmer.

"Never seen him."

"This man in Middle Eastern. We have information you hired an Indian or an Arab."

"Your information sucks."

"I'm not kidding," the cadet said. "This is official business. Anything you say will be used against you."

Wade snatched a glance to the milk tank. He didn't have but a minute to get the truck running and get Aboud some air. "If this were official, the Provost would've sent real police with real guns, not kids with Fluror spray."

The stringy teen inside the cart taunted his cadet friend a second time. "Dude, you're being so serious. Just kick his ass."

Wade marched over to the ultra-light and stuck his head inside. "Haven't I seen you before? Aren't you Nick Burlissen's kid? The kid that broke into my folk's house last Christmas? How did you get out of juvie so fast?"

Burlissen cowered and scampered to the back seat.

"Back away from the car!" wavered the patrol leader. He had a hand on his baton. Wade moved toward him, flexing hands as big as shovels. The cadet thought twice about pulling it, producing a can of incapacitant instead. "Stop or I will use this. It's Fluror and will freeze your mucus membranes in an instant."

Wade cursed. "You worthless bed-wetting turncoats. You don't do a lick of work on your own, but when the UN offers you a chance to spy on your neighbors and harass people you don't like, then all of a sudden you're model citizens."

"Stop! Stop right there!" The youth went for his radio. Fredrick went for something behind his back.

"He's got a gun!" yelled Burlissen.

The trainee retreated and stumbled backward into the calf lot. He fell into a fetid puddle of cow urine and manure as the big man pulled out a wallet. Fredrick snickered.

"Mom's going to love you when you get home." He opened his wallet, attached a manifest to the boy's clipboard and tossed it on top of the cursing cadet. The mullet-headed teen yelped as the metal pad hit him square in the chest. He opened his eyes to check for a wound.

"W-w-what does it say?" the plebe asked, cringing in fear as the baby animals sniffed his head.

"It's a requisition for fifty thousand pounds of cottage cheese." Wade threw him a pen. "Sign at the bottom, kid."

"But I though that was milk in there."

Wade slid a pair of Ray-Bans on his nose, climbed into his cab and fired up the engine. "It is, but if you keep me here one more minute, blueberry, *it will be* cottage cheese."

CHAPTER 5
MILKRUN

An American was loose somewhere in their lines. "Has it cleared the checkpoint yet?" asked Lieutenant Colonel Lucie Rèmé, 515 Bataillon du Trains' matronly night duty officer.

"Three hours ago," replied Michel DuGuay, her aide.

Three? Merde. How am I going to cover this up?

"Should I notify 1st Armored?"

"No," she replied.

"They can send out patrols." The corporal tapped his headset.

"Don't bother the combat units. We're supposed to be supporting them, not the other way around. Let's take the initiative and show them we can be self-sufficient for a change." She took the receiver and woke Captain Zizou, the unit's combat escort officer.

"Madame?" replied a raspy voice

"Capitaine? You awake?"

"Colonel, not you again. My men just got back from last night's *emergency* mission to Duluth. They are finally asleep."

"When the général misses his foie gras, that is an emergency. Minnesota's sole goose farm is twenty miles from here. So we take him geese!"

"They make Spam twenty-miles from here, too. Send *that* next time and see if he notices."

"Georges, we have a problem."

"It can wait till morning. I am not waking my men."

"An American dairy tanker passed through the border at nine last night. It was supposed to be at the cantonment at Sleepy Eye at midnight. It is not there. No one has seen the man. We think he is lost."

"You want us to scout for it?"

"No. Just you."

"Why me? The Lone Ranger will turn up on his own."

"I am afraid the truck might have made its way to the LOC."

"All the way to the front? How could it get there? Is this another one of your initiatives?" he asked.

"The farmer called saying he had surplus."

"And you said you would take it?"

"He was going to dump it. I thought our boys would enjoy real milk for a change instead of powder."

"Lucie, you are retiring in a month. You do not have to impress people anymore."

"If you do not help me find this tanker, I will be discharged, not retired."

Rèmé hung up and left the control shelter for the latrines. On her way back, she stopped to watch the stars and enjoy a Gitane. As she lit her third one, the dispirited night-duty officer sat down against a forklift and fell asleep. When she roused, Rèmé found a Jumbocruiser tour bus parked in front of her transport headquarters, engine idling.

"Who's the rock star?" she asked, fingering the custom pearl trim and peering through the smoked windows. The stoney guards gave her no notice. She marched past them. "Doesn't he ever sleep?"

"Well, good morning, Lucie," welcomed General Sean Faisson, five-star commander in charge of the UNIFUS French Protectorate in Minnesota. "How is Logistics doing tonight?" He was sitting in her chair. He didn't get up.

"I am sorry I was not here to greet you, général," she saluted. "I didn't know you were coming. I was powdering my nose."

He put his feet up and weighed her blocky figure. "Powdering your nose? How wonderful. You use makeup!"

Rèmé was plain, she knew. That was why she worked nights. She had given up competing with the younger officers years ago; the wasp-waisted waifs with long-legs and round-hips. But still, the commanding general was here now. He had stopped in to see her and that made her feel special.

"As you can see, it is a quiet night," she said, bending over him to type on her laptop. "No problems. Fuel is rotating to the front on schedule. No Freemartin attacks tonight."

"Then everything's accounted for?"

"Yes, sir," she replied. "As can reasonably be expected during war."

"Anything in the log mentioning missing deliveries?"

"No, sir. Nothing in the log about that." She wasn't lying. She had purposely left it out.

Behind them, a radio sputtered. "LIMA-XRAY-TWO-THREE? This is FOUR-FOUR." It was Zizou. "I think we've found your milk truck. It is just to the northeast of Redwood Falls at UNIFORM-KILO-THREE-EIGHT-FIVE-THREE-SIX-FIVE."

Faisson keyed the microphone. "Good work, FOUR-FOUR. Maintain contact but do not engage. Understand?"

Zizou didn't recognize the voice. "Authenticate, base."

"This is FOXTROT-CHARLIE-ZERO-ONE."

If the captain didn't recognize the voice, he certainly recognized the callsign. FC was short for French Command. ZERO-ONE told him General Faisson himself was talking. "Yes, sir! Affirmative ZERO-ONE!"

Rèmé yawned wide. "I will have to consult a map. I do not know where Redwood Falls is." The trim olive-skinned general regarded her as he tumbled two silver-metal spheres in his palm. "Where is the topo?" she asked DuGuay, rummaging about her.

"No need to play dumb, colonel," Faisson told her. "The caporal here told me everything while you were napping."

"Yes, ma'am," DuGuay piped in. "I told the général how you took the initiative. How you wanted to build Logistics Command into a self-sufficient force that we all could be proud of!" Rèmé's eyes bulged at him, but she said nothing.

"Why, pray-tell, do I have *Americans* roaming behind my lines?" Faisson hissed.

"It was my idea," she answered.

The general clicked his balls louder.

She continued. "We have no dairy tankers of our own. The Freemartins blew them up a few days ago. I thought this would be the best way to feed our soldiers."

"And you thought nothing odd of the fact that the Americans chose something as worthless as milk trucks to blow up?"

Rèmé's eyes fluttered as Faisson stuck his nose close.

"Help! Help!" sputtered the radio.

"FOUR-FOUR. Is that you? Report."

"ZERO-ONE. FOUR-FOUR here. We are under water. Repeat, we are under water. We were parked in a field of some sort and the irrigation gates opened up and ... swamped us and ..."

"I am not interested in your hearing a farm report, capitaine," interrupted Faisson. "Did the American see you? Over."

"I—I do not know, sir."

"Explain."

"I do not know because he is gone."

~ ~ ~ ~ ~ ~ ~ ~ ~ ~ ~ ~ ~ ~ ~ ~ ~ ~ ~

Aboud gasped as he sucked in a year's worth of breath. "I am not drinking milk ever again!"

"Sorry for the wait," said Wade "But I couldn't see keeping you down there another hour." Aboud fell onto his back and closed his eyes to the night sky, panting. "How did you make out with your cocoon?" the farmer asked.

"Never again! The zipper leaks, it is dark, I am stiff and numbing, it smells like diesel," Aboud recited.

"You shouldn't need to go back in." Wade surveyed the bean field above them. He had passed through the border check four hours ago, dodging military patrols as he made his way to the frontier. When he arrived at the Minnesota River, he stashed his tanker in this gully as he was told and waited for a signal flash from the treeline to his front. "Something's not right, doctor. They should've been here by now. What do you want to do?"

"Walk."

"Walk? Are you crazy. The UN's out there. If they don't pick you off, the Sovereigns will."

"I will prefer my chances." The scientist dipped his hand into the tank and flipped out a handful of slimy white goo. "Anything but this." In back of them, in a field along the river bed, Wade heard men swearing and saw lights flash. He froze.

Tanner turned and began signalling them with his laser. "Finally they are here!" Fredrick slapped the light out of his hands. "No, no, Aboud. *Crap.* Those are not the good guys."

"Who are they then?"

"I don't know but they're not swearing in English." Wade pulled a small yellow magnetic device out of his coat and pressed a button on its side. He waited for the transmission indicator to start blinking before slapping it onto the hatch.

"What is that? What are you doing?"

"We're making a run for the lines. The Middle States are just a mile on the other side of the river." Fredrick grabbed Aboud's ankles and dragged him back into the tank.

"But you said I could stay out. Don't make me go back in there!"

Wade pushed his head down and closed the hatch. "I changed my mind."

~ ~ ~ ~ ~ ~ ~ ~ ~ ~ ~ ~ ~ ~ ~ ~ ~ ~ ~ ~

Faisson called for his staff to begin hooking their battle management equipment into the command post's network. Before they started work, he addressed the room. "Everyone may be wondering why I have invaded your quiet little corner of the PBZ. I am here hunting a spy. He is an American scientist who the Freemartins are trying to smuggle into the MS. We believe he is in possession of many valuable military secrets and is inside the missing Fredrick Dairy truck.

"I am here because for some inexplicable reason, things only work when I am involved." He glanced at Rèmé. "I am sure you dislike having me as much as I dislike being here, so, please, drop everything you are doing and give full assistance to my staff. Your cooperation will dictate how much I will overlook your negligence in this matter."

A phone rang. "Général, it is a Mr. Murray from the Coax Office," said Corporal DuGuay. "He wishes to speak to you."

"Anyone receiving calls from our Coaxial allies—*especially* the Americans—tell them to go to hell," Faisson instructed. "We are busy."

"Sir, he said the NSA has picked up a beacon in the Redwood Falls quad. It may be the missing tanker."

The commander growled and snatched the phone away. "Faisson here."

"General, Tom Murray, OCC. Are you aware an emergency locator beacon is emanating from your Le Sueur peacebuilder zone?"

"Why, no, Mr. Murray. Why would that be a concern of mine? They go off all the time."

"This one's encrypted. It's on a non-standard frequency."

"Meaning?"

"Meaning it's either Sovereign Forces or Freemartin."

"I see," said Faisson. "Very well. Thank you for your help. We will have a look at it. Good night."

"General? We have an HVA missing," hurried Murray.

"Tell me more."

"I'm afraid I can't. It involves national security interests."

"That is a shame. What *can* you tell us, Mr. Murray? For instance, is he a physicist, is he Iranian, has he ever worked for 3M?"

"Son-of-a-bitch, who told you?"

"Come, come, Mr. Murray. You still think the U.S. owns the only monopoly on clandestine competency? We have our methods, too."

"I'd like to come down and help coordinate," replied the agent.

"Like you helped alert us before the spy broke through our border?"

"Look, I don't know what you're getting at, but we want to keep him out of Sovereign hands just as much as you do. We have to help and rely on each other."

Faisson snorted. "If we had to rely on the questionable loyalties of the U.S. during this war, we'd be eating Freedom Fries with our bouillabaisse."

Murray ignored the accusation. "I'll be there in five minutes, general. *Don't* do anything until I get there. This is still only a protectorate. This is still U.S. domain."

Faisson slammed the phone into its receiver.

"Do you wish us to detain him when he arrives?" asked his captain-of-the-guard.

"No, adjutant. Let him in. I derive much pleasure from tormenting these fat slave-owners. Caporal, get me the Blackwings."

The DAOS Blackwings were Commander Faisson's special ops helicopter unit. They flew the Tigre Eurocopter, the French equivalent to the American Apache, only slower, heavier and less capable. A voice on the other end answered, thick and groggy. "Special Forces Aviation. Colonel Airiee."

"Good morning, my good friend."

"Général Faisson?"

"Felix, I am in need of your immediate assistance. We have an American trying to make a run for the MS."

"One?" Airiee reasked. "We have hundreds every day."

"This one is special. This one is an HVA. He is broadcasting an ELT. We are triangulating now."

"I see," said the helicopter commander, rustling for his flightsuit. "I can have a section of Tigres ready to go in sixty minutes."

"Too long," said the general.

"How long do I have?"

"When you hang up the phone."

"My WSO and I can be airborne as soon as we lace our boots," replied Airiee.

"I knew I could count on you."

"But I will have no support. It will only be me. Are you sure that is what you want, Sean?"

"Absolutely. This spy has the Americans by the short hairs. If we can kill or capture him, it would win us much favor with the Secretary-General."

Airiee sighed. "If it is that important to you, then I would be honored to fly the mission."

Faisson congratulated him. "Excellent, my friend. You are the *only* one I would trust."

"You can join me, you know, Sean. I can stop by and pick you up."

The general demurred. "I would love nothing more than to fly again. Perhaps when I am made governor of the new French mandate, then I will have the time to take you up on it."

~~~~~~~~~~~~~~~~~~~~~

Zizou and his men righted their Sherpa and headed up the ravine after Wade. Fredrick caught sight of their headlights and muzzle-flashes as the ox-like tanker lugged up the hill. "Come on, Babe." He stomped the accelerator but the Sherpa's speed made him wonder if he was in reverse. He crested the ridge, cussing, as bullets penetrated the tank. He thought of Aboud. They must know he's in there. The soldiers were close now. They disappeared behind his rig as a dark shadow slid down the tank's side and crouched on its fender.

"ABOUD!" Wade hung out his window, pointing wildly. "The valves! The valves!" Tanner reached down to a bank of metal levers and opened them all, splattering the road with thick white chunks of ultra-filtrated milk. Fredrick watched his speed dwindle as his back wheels spun and fishtailed in the glop. In his mirror, the soldiers reappeared covered in white, tobogganing sideways through the slick. They slid off the road and into a ditch filled with barbed wire. Wade pumped his fist. "That's my boy! We'll make a farmer of you yet!" Straight ahead and fifty feet above him, a helicopter approached, filling his cab with its tungsten blue searchlight.

"FOXTROT-CHARLIE-ZERO-ONE, THIS IS TIGRE-ZERO-ONE. Have the target in sight and awaiting orders. Over."

Wade covered his eyes as he whipped the truck to the left. Too fast. The tanker did a ten-wheel drift through the intersection as Airiee blew by overhead.

Fredrick wrestled the groaning semi back to the ground and picked up speed to the west where he prayed a squad of Sovereign Green Berets were waiting to back him up. Above, Airiee sliced his gunship upward and cut a loose arc through the lightening sky to give his weapons officer enough room for a rocket attack.

Fredrick adjusted his side-mirror just as the road in front of him lit up like a disco dance floor. The blasts were so close he couldn't hear them. The explosions lifted great domes of tar from the pavement as his rig went airborne over the still-glowing craters. When he landed, he crashed back into his seat as Airiee drew up alongside him.

~ ~ ~ ~ ~ ~ ~ ~ ~ ~ ~ ~ ~ ~ ~ ~ ~ ~ ~ ~

"General, you can stop this by shooting out his tires or taking out the engine." Agent Murray chomped urgently on his Bazooka bubble gum as he watched the images arrive from Airiee's gun camera.

Faisson feigned helplessness. "That sort of accuracy is quite impossible at these speeds and distances, I'm afraid, Mr. Murray."

"But the HVA must be taken alive. It is of *vital* importance."

"Importance to whom?" asked the five-star. "Why don't you tell me what our Doctor Tanner has done and maybe I will see what I can do."

Murray ran a hand through his hair. "I can't tell you that. He's a spy is all I can say and the U.S. needs him alive for interrogation."

Faisson's eyes crinkled as he continued to play with the American. His troops needed to see the impotence of these cowboys. It didn't matter if they were Sovereign *or* U.S. They all were mutant-sized apes with baboon-sized brains.

"This is TIGRE-ZERO-ONE," coughed the radio. "Target will be in Sovereign territory in one mile. Request permission to terminate."

Murray banged the table and stomped his foot. "General, I represent the president in this matter and I *forbid* it.

"Ah, so sorry *Americunt*," Faisson replied in French to the howling approval of his troops. "I represent *the world*!"

Murray looked around the clapping CP. "What did you say?"

Faisson picked up the mike and smiled. "I said, TIGRE-ZERO-ONE, Terminate."

~~~~~~~~~~~~~~~~~~~

Wade pulled Aboud's .45 out of his belt and emptied the clip at the hovering warship. He was surprised when it pulled up and disappeared behind him.

Airiee strained to see into the cockpit ahead of him. He could not raise his weapons officer on the intercom. He fumbled for the override and switched his armament panel to missiles. Five miles downrange, he fired on the tanker himself, trying to follow the weapon's flight over the slumped body and blood-splattered windshield of his WSO's cockpit.

The hundred-pound fire-and-forget TV-guided Tigrat hit the milk tank dead center, shredding its thin aluminum skin and turning its cargo into a quarter-mile-diameter ball of sticky white fog. Wade fought to drive through it. He turned on his wipers to clear away the spray when Aboud's severed arm thudded across his windshield, smearing blood as it went.

Wade was sick. It was over. He had failed Aboud and he wasn't going to see his farm again. He took his foot off the gas, put his forehead on the wheel and listened as the wiper swatted against the limb.

Something dangled out his side window. It was Aboud's head. "Do not be slowing down, Wade. The helicopter is coming back!"

Fredrick jumped off his seat. "Oh, Jesus, God!" He put a hand up and looked away. "I'm not talking to you. I'm not talking to a decapitated head!"

"I am alive, Wade. This is a true statement. The warhead didn't fuze. It went straight through the tank without going off."

Wade gave the little man a quick once-over then jerked him into the cab. "Stick your head out your window and keep me on the road," he yelled, wiping dry curd from his windshield. "And don't scare me like that any more." Up ahead, he strained to make out the road, tugging his wheel right then left. "There's the bridge. We're almost home!"

The Frenchman's last missile accelerated through the air. This time, the Tigrat's crosshairs were on Wade's cab. The dart corkscrewed right, then left, following Fredrick's turns and accelerations. Just as Wade turned onto the straightaway to Beaver Creek Bridge, his tattered semi disappeared into a thick glade of hardwoods, causing the missile to go stupid, lock its fins and bury itself into the trunk of a 150-year-old elm tree.

Wade and Aboud's world went cock-eyed as the explosion lifted the rig onto its left tires. Tanner hung from his seatbelt as Wade kept them on the road. "Don't let go," barked Wade. "I can drive this way all the way to Las Vegas if I have to."

Aboud pawed for a hand-hold. He was half-in and half-out his window when he slipped off his perch and landed in Wade's lap. Wade lost control, his tanker slamming into the bridge's side-railing where it launched into the air like a Hotwheels toy. After a graceful pirouette, they landed in the shallow creek below, upside down and facing backwards.

Nothing in the vehicle moved as Airiee's gunship circled and landed in a clearing. As its chin-gun hunted for survivors, something in the sky ahead caught his eye. He scanned the thickening overcast for a moment before making out four Vietnam-era UH-1 Hueys heading for him from the west in tight formation.

Airiee laughed at the ancient warbirds. You can't be serious, he thought. This is the cavalry? His multi-mission Eurocopter had Mistral air-to-air heat-seekers. He flipped his weapons selector to A-A, waited for two of them to lock then sent the missiles skyward to their targets. The Hueys stood their ground as the Mistrals wound toward them. Right before they hit, the pilots peeled out of formation and dove for the trees exposing two ugly, squat A-10s coming up fast behind to take their place.

"*Merde.*" The Blackwing commander was in enemy territory, alone, with a dead co-pilot and two American A-10 Warthogs coming for him. He pulled out of his hover, turned and raced for the safety of French lines.

In seconds, Spider was on him. He yanked hard on his control stick and popped-up over the hapless chopper. Trent had never dive-bombed a moving helicopter before. He didn't even know if it was possible but had always thought it would be cool. He rolled out, pulled his piper ahead of the fleeing Frenchman and puked off two Mk82 concrete bombs. The bombs went wide and sunk into the pasture below but not before smashing through the Tiger's rotor disk. The chopper's fiber blades splintered and sailed in every direction, leaving the aircraft to twirl and roll in the air before furrowing itself into twenty acres of soybeans.

"I don't believe it," radioed Shank.

"You're cleared in hot, Two. Finish them up. I want you to plant them deep enough in the soil so the farmer can still harvest in the fall."

Shank circled around from the east. When he rolled out and put his reticle on the crinkled hulk, a man climbed out and waved something white. Shank remembered the massacre at Wadena and thought of his nephews and nieces. He remained unmoved. "This is for you, sis." He pulled the trigger and held it firm as the chopper and its European occupants disappeared under six feet of rich black Minnesota loam.

~ ~ ~ ~ ~ ~ ~ ~ ~ ~ ~ ~ ~ ~ ~ ~ ~ ~ ~ ~

Faisson glared in silence as his screen filled with gray black static.

"That was masterful. A brilliant tour-de-force by the master tactician himself." Murray roamed the room, raising his hands in rhythm with his words. "Are you a stark, raving lunatic?" he said, marching up to the taciturn general. "Why did you do that?" Faisson smiled, fingering his ballistrae under the desk. "Not only did you lose a fifteen-million-dollar aircraft, but you managed to get your DAOS commander killed and may have just handed the Sovereigns their biggest weapon."

Faisson twirled his finger over his head. "Adjutant, remove Mr. Murray from this room, please. Our period of *coaxial cooperation* seems to have run its course."

Two hulkish Commando Hubert guards approached and placed their hands on the agent's arms. Murray shrugged them off. "I'm going, general, but I'm reporting this to the NSC. That means the president and after that, you'd better hope the Secretary-General doesn't get wind of it." Murray grabbed his folders then walked out the door.

Faisson waited until the American had left the compound before pulling out his FAMAS automatic and shooting Rèmè's laptop across the table and onto the floor. The HQ clerks all pushed away from the table and fled the flying keys and bits of circuit board until all that could be heard in the command post were his empty trigger clicks. He left the shelter in silence, boarded his motor coach and ordered his driver to take him back to Duluth.

"You save one of those bullets for me?" asked Lieutenant Colonel Rèmè, handcuffed to the front seat.

Faisson ignored her. He walked to the rear of the coach, turned on the shower and waited for it to warm. "No, Lucie. For tonight's debacle, I have something better in store. You will get to retire but as a combat soldier, not an officer. A common foot-soldier. A soldier with the Haitians." He turned and stripped before entering the water.

"And I pray you represent your gender proudly. You will be their only female."

CHAPTER 6
REUNION

Spider jumped around underneath his fuselage like a cricket cornered by an eight-year old. He was trying everything he could to salvage his mission but Brucato wasn't buying any of it. "Well, just slap on some more duct tape. I've gotta go," he pleaded. He looked up at Shank and Hoop, who were pointing and laughing from their cockpits across the hotpit pad.

"There's nothing to tape to," responded Beak. "You lost three more panels this trip and your rudders are delaminating."

"I'll keep it slow."

"Right. And what about the bullet hole in the hydraulics?"

"That's why there's two systems."

"I just don't know how long we can keep her flying."

"Keep her flying?" Spider repeated. "We just got her. She's brand new!"

"Sir, this bird is a hand-me-down from Pigseye Flight. It belly-landed, skidded off the runway and caught fire. Nobody wanted it but you."

"It flies sideways a little but other than that, it's fine."

"Sorry, sir. I'm red-lining her. Just too many squawks."

"Dammit. The doctors finally clear me to fly but my own crew chief won't? That's just *wrong*." Om waved to Spider as he taxied out of the clearing. Shank and Hoop followed, horsing their engines and blasting Spider with hot exhaust.

Beak picked up a speed-wrench and went back to work. "Why don't you just use the time to take a bath, sir?"

Spider felt a presence as two huge arms encircled him from behind. They felt like massive steel hoops as they squeezed, pressing the breath out of him. Beak backed away, not knowing how to help as Trent was lifted off his feet and thrown upside-down into a nearby sand pile. Spider groaned and rolled slow-motion into a crouch. He groped and fumbled his gun.

"Don't shoot, don't shoot," said Wade. "I give up!"

"Chewie? Is that you?"

"Farmer John? Is that you?"

Spider holstered his sidearm and grimaced as he straightened and popped his back. The crew chiefs all came over to help. "Sir, that couldn't've been good. Do you want us to get your backboard?"

"Backboard?" Wade asked. "I was told this was a fighter squadron, not a nursing home."

"Spider crashed a few weeks ago," replied a young airman. "His spine compressed when he punched out."

Spider reached in the air with both hands, rotated his hips, then did some calisthenics. "Yikes. I'm afraid to say this but I think you might have actually helped."

"We aim to please," winked Wade.

Spider had known Wade for going on twelve years. The pilot had befriended the dairyman after he had left the service and tried starting a farm of his own. Since then, Wade had been his constant companion because the pilot was a disaster as a farmer.

Spider introduced his friend to the unit then lead him to his hootch for a lunch of peanut butter crackers and musty Tang. "It's good to see you again, Chewie."

"Look at you!" Wade replied, yanking at Trent's flightsuit. "I never knew you were important. Do I call you John or Spider or major?"

"I go by Spider in this alternate world."

"And you can fly that?" Wade asked, pointing to the battle-worn jet resting in the shade.

Spider shrugged with feigned modesty.

"Then how come you never learned to plow a straight line?"

"It's been two years since I sat in a tractor, Chew. How *is* the farm?"

"I'm up to five thousand head now," Wade crowed.

"Not your farm. How's mine?"

"I've been cutting your hay for you but your back forty is getting pretty scary. It has more weeds than a prairie restoration project."

Spider wasn't surprised. He knew Laura wasn't interested in the farm. Neither were the boys. That had been his passion. His dream. He couldn't give them the desire if he had hypnotized them, although he had tried. "You've been feeding your cows my alfalfa? Sounds like you owe me some money."

"I'll send you a check when I get back."

Trent stood and started walking. "Follow me. I've got something to show you." He led Wade out of the median, across the abandoned interstate and down an embankment where a newly-hoed plot of veggies lay basking in neat green rows.

"What's a fighter pilot doing growing a garden?" Fredrick asked. He pointed to a struggling sapling with yellowing leaves.

"It's a lemon."

Wade yucked then caught himself.

"It'll recover. Just needs a little more rain."

"What happened to all his buddies?"

"That was a tangerine. That was a lime. That was a grapefruit."

"There's a reason they don't call Minnesota 'The Citrus State,' you know."

"I'll figure out a way to do it. Then they'll name a fruit after me." Spider showed him his berry patch next.

"Strawberries?" Wade asked, cocking his head.

"What's wrong?"

"Where are the berries? Everyone back home has been picking for a week now."

Trent looked perplexed. "But look at the leaves and blossoms. They're huge."

Fredrick bent down and ran his hands through the bushes. "Yeah, they are, but something's missing. You spray them with anything?"

"2-4,D for thistles and Malthion for the cutter bugs."

Wade picked up a dead insect from the ground. "Well, you killed the bees, too. No berries for this year."

"Well treat me for shock," mumbled Spider. "People are going to be pissy now."

"You must really like farming to be doing all this in the middle of a war."

"I love growing it and my guys love eating it," replied Spider. "Farming's the second best job in the world."

Wade craned his neck skyward as a pair of Marine Cobra's appeared for a moment, their rotors beating the air as they raced for battle somewhere to the west. "John, we lost Auggie."

"Lost Auggie? How? When?"

"He left for the MS six months ago. He wanted to fight. His friends had gone and ever since then, he wanted to go, too." Wade took off his John Deere hat and stared at the logo. "He was killed last month."

"I'm sorry. I didn't know." Then: "I'm proud of him, Wade. There's not many people back on the economy that think their country's worth fighting for anymore."

"Abby found out first. She's hysterical. I can't even talk to her. I think she blames me."

"Is that why you joined the Freemartins?"

"They've been hounding me for months. Last week, I finally did it. To honor him."

"Let's go back to camp. I'll make you some coffee."

"No, John. Thanks. I'd love to talk, but I've got to get going. I've got to be heading back."

"Back where?" asked Spider.

"Back home. I've gotta get back before someone notices something's up."

"You don't think they'll know something's up when they see your tank blown to shreds and catfish floating in your cab?"

"I won't bring it back," Wade responded wearily. "I'll just say it was totalled in an accident."

"OK, I'll just call Northwest Airlines then," cracked Spider. "They can pick you up at Fergus Muni and fly you back to Minneapolis in a DC-9."

"They will?"

"Like hell," said Trent.

"Then why are you being a jerk about this?" railed Fredrick.

"Because you can't go home."

"*Like hell.*"

"I don't know how to break this to you, Wade, but you're in the Middle States now. We're at war with everybody. We aren't part of the U.S. We aren't part of the world. We're cut off and alone. No information. No commerce. No travel."

"That wasn't supposed to be part of the deal," said Wade. "I was supposed to go to town, meet some little guy, stick him in my tank, drop him off in Redwood Falls then be back in time for morning milking."

"I don't know anything about your deal," Spider said. "But you and me both saw what the French will do. They know who you are. You won't be safe at home anymore."

"That was you up there? With the Hueys?"

Spider nodded. "You can't go back until we get our country back. And somehow big guy, I think you knew that going in."

Wade plucked a green bean and crunched on it. Maybe he knew what he was getting into and maybe he didn't. Maybe he smuggled Aboud out of revenge. Maybe it was guilt for his noncommittal fence-sitting or disgust for profiting from the conflict when others were dying. He didn't know. What he did know was his previously well-managed life was gone and he kicked himself for his recklessness. "How am I going to get Abby?"

"The Freemartins will bring her. Don't worry about that end. Hundreds cross over every day. They've got pipelines in place for that."

"And what about the farm? I'll lose the cows. What is there for me to do here?"

"You can start by fixing this," Trent said, sweeping his hand across the garden.

"I'm serious," said Wade.

"How about crew chief? You're good with machinery. You can be my new crew chief. Beak can train you in."

"Don't I need to go to school? Don't I need training? I'm too dumb to learn anything new."

"Wade. We're in a war. We're loosing our arses. We aren't picky. We can use anybody and everybody. Even Abby."

Wade hooked a finger of Copenhagen from his cheek and threw it on the ground. "Thanks for your offer, John, but I'm going back on my own. I'll get across fine. I'll be all right."

Spider relinquished. "OK, but you'll need help. Let's go back where you can lie down and take a nap while I see what I can do. You can have my cot. Then we'll talk. All right?"

"You can do that? You're not too busy?"

"If you didn't already notice, my jet's on the DL list." Spider patted Wade's broad Cinemascope back and ushered him up the rise. When they arrived at his hootch, Wade rolled onto the cot without argument.

"How long has it been since you heard about August?"

"Four days," replied Wade.

"How long has it been since you've slept?"

"Four days."

"I'm sorry for your loss, Wade. He was a great kid."

"Wake me in an hour, all right?"

"Won't have to. My Hogs'll be back by then. They'll wake you." Spider waited for Wade's breathing to become a deep ploughing before turning to leave.

"John? I didn't see what happened to that French chopper. Did you waste 'em?"

Spider grinned, happy to give some good news. "Yeah, big guy. We wasted 'em."

CHAPTER 7
SILO CITY

"One more day and I'm kicking someone out of their jet," Spider told Beak as he watched Om, Shank and Hoop take off without him again. Beak and the others returned to their commander's grounded warbird, patching and stiffening and riveting its skin. Flying was hard. Not flying was harder.

WHOP! WHOP! WHOP!

Chopper blades. This better be my airframe specialist, Trent thought as a tar black UH-60 appeared through the leafy canopy above. It came in fast as if being followed and flared for a landing on top of them. "Not here, you idiots! Out there. On the road!"

The Blackhawk pelted the men with grit and sent their camo netting billowing into the trees. Spider picked up his M-16 and fired it into the air. Suddenly, three more choppers appeared. They hovered in a circle over him, soldiers and guns bristling from their sides. Spider threw down his weapon and held up his hands. The choppers landed and a pilot got out.

"Major Trent?"

"What the hell are you doing, captain? You just trashed Camp Snoopy!"

"We're delivering a package. We've been told to hand over custody to you. Follow me."

The man stuffed papers into Spider's hand then ushered him to a side door where a pair of burly UNCONs pushed a little gray foreigner at him. Spider stared at the man's baggy fatigues and bandages as the commandoes hopped back in their choppers and took off back into the overcast. "You're not my sheet-metal guy are you?"

"Aboud Tanner, reporting for duty!" The scientist saluted, nearly poking himself in the eye.

"You must be the doctor Wade smuggled in. You don't need to salute me."

"What? Why do you look at me like that?"

"I'm wondering who let you out of the hospital? You look pretty beat up."

"Do not worry about these," Aboud said, flapping the slings on his arms. "These are just precautions. I am being fine." Trent reached for the man's shoulder. Aboud pulled away. "It is just slightly dislocated only."

"And the cast?"

"It is a hairline. Of my tibia. It is very minor. I am ready to go on patrol."

"Aboud!"

Tanner turned and smiled. "Wade! You are here, too?"

Fredrick rubbed the sleep from his eyes as he hurried over from the hootches to make the introductions. "Aboud, this is John, I mean Major Trent. He was one of the A-10 pilots that rescued us."

Spider extended his hand. Aboud saluted. "Stop that."

"Man, they fixed you up fast," observed Wade. "How long were you at the hospital?"

"The medimacs had me for a day."

Wade turned and snarled at Spider. "A *day*?"

"It's been twenty-four hours, Wade. You slept straight through."

"I thought you said you'd get me up."

"So you could go get yourself killed? Sorry. Character flaw." Spider took a look at the orders still in his hand. "Looks like we're going to see Woody. General Patterson is the commander of the Sovereign Air Arm, our version of the Air Force. And he's sending his own personal Eclipse to ferry us in." Spider looked again at the skinny boy-man. "You really must be special."

"Unsat! Unsat! I am to be meeting a general?" Aboud picked up a hammer from one of Brucato's nearby tool bins and began bashing his cast.

"Hey, hey hey!" Spider yelled, holding him back. "What the hell are you doing?"

"If a general sees me like this, he will never let me fight."

The major backed away and shook his head at Wade and Aboud as plaster chips flecked his face. "I'm babysitting a pair of nutjobs."

The tiny twin-engine Eclipse jet picked its way through the rolling hills of North Dakota before it found the lush flat valley of the Mouse River. The air taxi followed the estuary north, its light wings flexing disturbingly in the afternoon thermals. Out the window, Minot approached, a small prairie city that lay burnt and empty, abandoned after years of FUN shelling and U.S. cruise missile attacks. Wade regarded the blackened rubble out his side window, brooding. "What's that?"

"Peacebuilding," replied Spider.

Across the isle, Aboud tinkered. He had dismembered an emergency strobe light and re-engineered it into an orthopedic stimulator. Spider could only see the whites of his eyes as the device sent high-voltage pulses through a wire wrapped around the scientist's swollen shin.

"UHHH. UHHH. UHHH."

"You promised," Wade said. "I could've been home by now."

"No, if you'd gone home you'd be like MacGyver here, only with wires hooked to your scrotum."

"UHHH. UHHH. UHHH."

"You promised," he repeated.

"So hate me. At least you're alive to do it."

The very-light-jet flew through the basin another twenty miles before popping up over the bright bustling town center of Minot Silo City. Silo cities were austere but close-knit communities. They thrived under the protective nuclear umbrellas of the thousand Minuteman III facilities that dotted the Middle States. Minot not only had its own silo, it also served as the headquarters for the entire Sovereign Forces.

The jet popped out of the river valley and made a quick arcing visual approach to the Minot airstrip. It lurched to a stop as Spider opened the hatch and let down the stairs. On the ramp, a HMMWV sat nearby, Middle States flags waving proudly from its fenders. Beside it, a pruney stumped-over seventy-year-old in a green flightsuit stood, puffing madly on a heater.

"Hey, Woody. Good to see you." Trent gave the general an informal half-wave–half-salute typical of the SF. Patterson returned it then shook his hand.

"I'm not happy to see you," the four-star whispered.

"What'd I do now, Wood?"

"Dammit, John, A-10s don't grow on trees, you know." Spider pulled his hand away but Patterson kept pumping. "That was a pretty stupid stunt."

"What was?"

"Going into Ripley like that. All by yourselves without orders."

Spider breathed a sigh of relief, glad Peterson hadn't found out about his cellphone escapades. "That's why we went. They weren't expecting it."

"You were playing fast and loose."

"No I wasn't. I had my reasons."

"And they're always hotheaded."

"Maybe, but I always seem to rack up kills, don't I?"

"Next time, you're going to rack up your own guys."

"I measure risk with reward. You taught me that."

"A four-ship against a brigade? *That math*, you learned on your own."

Spider burned from the rebuke. He had received many admonitions from Woody over the years: flying too low over Lake Placid Ski Resort as a new second lieutenant, mock-strafing the families on the lift chairs, sending the mayor's horse through a fence. Even as a fifty-year-old, Trent could still feel its sting. "What do you want from me?"

"Obedience, Trent! Just for once, a little obedience."

"You knew what you were getting when you asked me to fly for you."

"You're lucky Swenson didn't take your wings."

Trent bit at his lip.

"I would have."

"Yes, sir."

Patterson gave Spider back his hand and looked over to the Eclipse. "Major! You going to introduce me to your friends or do I have to guess who's who?"

Spider jumped aside. "General, I'd like you to meet Wade Fredrick.

Wade is the Freemartin who penetrated the French lines to bring us our scientist."

"Glad to meet you, Wade. You can call me Woody."

"General Patterson is one of the Quarterstaff. He's our Air Arm commander," added Spider.

Fredrick shook his hand.

"That was a brave and daring thing you did risking your life like that," said the general. "I want to thank you for the entire Middle States. You may just have saved the Sovereign Cause with the heroism you displayed."

Wade looked at Spider. "I did?"

"You did." The general grabbed a velvet purple case and a small walnut plaque from his vehicle. "I want to present this to you for rising to a calling greater than yourself." Woody opened the case and pinned a gold medal on Fredrick's round scrum-sized chest. Wade looked down at the medal. It had a silver-embossed Constitution at its center and hung from a navy blue ribbon with white chevrons and stars. "On behalf of the Quarterstaff of the Sovereign Forces, I present you with the Lay Medallion, the highest honor we can give a civilian."

Woody stepped back and saluted. Wade flushed. He had not wanted to come. He had not wanted to waste time with people he did not know talking about things he did not care about. He wanted to go home. But seeing this weathered soldier with silver hair and four-stars honoring him like this made him feel the trip hadn't been trivial. He returned the salute.

"Here is a plaque of our appreciation. This comes with an automatic commission to Chief Warrant Officer 2nd Class, if you'll have it." Wade hawed for words, swallowing his chew. Patterson pulled close. "There is nothing to be humble about, Wade. You just saved thousands of lives."

"I-I don't see how."

"You will," said Woody. "Just stick around awhile."

"I don't know if that's going to be possible. Can I get back to you on the warrant officer thing?"

"You've got family back home, don't you?"

"My wife."

"Don't worry about her. We'll get her out."

"The same way *I* got out?" worried Fredrick.

"No. I'll put UNCON on it," Woody assured. "Unconventional Ops are our Green Berets. They're our most elite fighters."

"Thanks." Wade stepped back, reading his award. "Sir."

"And this is Doctor Tanner," announced Spider. "The scientist Wade managed to smuggle over."

"Pleased to meet you, General Woody!"

"Aboud, it's General Patterson *or* Woody. Not both."

"Doctor, I'm your biggest fan," proclaimed Patterson.

"You are the man I have been sending my files to?"

Patterson nodded. "The entire Quarterstaff's been waiting to meet you." He shook Tanner's hand and got a shock. "Ouch! What the hell was that?" he said, flapping his hand in the air.

In the excitement, Aboud had forgotten all about his stimulator. He turned it off and ripped at his wires. "UNSAT! UNSAT! SORRY! SORRY!"

"No need to be sorry," Patterson said, rubbing his molars. "My fillings are still tingling. If that's a new weapon, we should start you working on it right away."

Aboud stopped untangling his wires and stood stiff and erect. "General, I did not come to work in a lab," announced Tanner.

"Oh?"

"I want to fight. I want to be a runt."

"I think he means *grunt*, sir," Spider whispered.

Woody regarded the timorous scientist. "You sure?"

"I do want not to be behind the lines. I do want not to be safe. I wish to fight and die for a cause greater than me. Like Wade."

"Tell me I didn't come all this way just so you could play GI Joe," protested Fredrick.

Spider agreed. "Doctor, with all the resources the SF has invested in you, I don't think the general is going to—"

Woody raised his hands and turned to his Hummer. "That's damned admirable, Aboud. We need men of your caliber."

"You do?"

"Yes." He motioned Aboud over. "Can you go to the front now?"

Tanner hesitated. "But I need to fill out some paperwork first, yes? I need training first I think."

"Nonsense." Patterson motioned to his driver. "Captain?" Frank Corriston, the general's driver, opened the back of the vehicle and dumped a pile of gear at Tanner's feet. "Here's an M-16. Start loading the clip."

Aboud groped for the shells with his bandaged hands before dropping them on the tarmac. "My fingers. They are a little burnt."

"Guess we'll have to practice at that," said Woody.

Corriston produced an armored vest and threw it across Tanner's shoulders. Aboud shrieked as his joints rebelled.

"Problems?" asked Patterson.

Aboud shook his head no.

"Good, we just about have it then."

"There's more?"

A seventy-pound rucksack went on next. Aboud's leg buckled and he fell over backward even before Corriston had removed his hands. Patterson bent over and put his hands on his knees. "Should we try that again tomorrow?"

"That is a true statement!" Aboud agreed. "Maybe in a few days."

"Good," said Patterson. "In the mean time, I've got something for that leg of yours." The general waited for Aboud to unravel himself from his gear before walking the trio across the ramp and into the carnival. Every silo city had a carnival, the merchant center of the settlement where everyone would go to shop, eat and be distracted. It was always in the center, the safest zone, and in Minot, carnival was on the airbase proper.

"We got the shit kicked out of us when we took over the MS," explained Woody, referring to the opening days of the US-UN conflict. "Cruise missiles, air strikes, artillery. Every town and berg in the Middle States took it in the shorts, but not here. Not at any of the other missile sites either. For some reason, the Coax left these alone."

"President Earle said if the SF is insane enough to attack the president, you're insane enough to use nukes," said Wade.

"Well let him think we're crazy then, because our entire economy is rebuilding itself under the shade of these ICBMs." Woody scanned the market looking for a craftsman for Aboud.

"There's been no news about battles," continued Wade as he veered away from an overly-pushy mime. "About towns being bombed. Except from a few banned blogs and video nets."

"President Earle's made his desires known; no coverage of the front, no mention of *war*. The media's only too happy to comply. He's their baby, after all," said Woody.

"And don't forget Blue Ops," added Trent. "News coverage of any UN battle is illegal."

Woody stopped at a bright yellow canvas booth where an Amish man stood staining some tables. He went in then came out with a shiny cherrywood walking stick and gave the cane to Aboud.

"Why … thank you, sir. How much do I owe you?"

"Thirty-four sovros."

"How much is that in dollars?"

"About ninty-eight thousand dollars. Things got a little expensive when the president cut off commerce. Where'd Wade go?"

"John is buying him something to eat, I think."

After a few minutes, Wade returned with a bucket of milk and a pail of chocolate-chip cookies.

"I see you found the dairy truck."

"I smelled it, actually."

"As you can see, farms are flourishing again, food is cheap."

"That's because the MS hasn't signed Kyoto," noted Wade. "You're cheating."

Aboud surveyed the base, the festive carnival merchants, the makeshift shipping-container homes. "Your silo city is protected like a medieval castle," he said.

"And they'll continue to be protected as long as Earle keeps thinking we're loonies with our finger on the button," answered Patterson.

"Would you use them?"

"There are no non-proliferation treaties here," answered the air arm commander. "We proliferate our missiles like rabbits. We've reclaimed all the mothballed Peacekeepers and Minutemans and re-MIRVed them with three refurbished warheads each." Woody pointed to a flat concrete slab a few blocks away. "That's Minot's missile there: *Headbanger*."

"But would you use them?"

"Doesn't do any good carrying a gun if you're just going to shoot someone in the kneecap." Woody lit a match and put it to another cigarette. "Yes, we'd use them. It's the only thing that's been keeping the president and these Bono-bastards at bay all these months."

The foursome continued to the SAGE building, a tall, gray windowless cube left over from the Cold War that now housed the Quarterstaff. Wade and Aboud trailed behind, taking in the puppet shows and veggie stands.

"Wood, I'm sorry for flying off to Ripley like that," Spider offered.

"No you're not."

"I put the lives of my men in jeopardy. For my own agenda."

"You're pounding sunshine up my ass. You want something."

"I let you down. It won't happen again."

"That's a shame. You do the best work I've seen."

"What?"

"Flying formation with Mk82s? Bombing helicopters? Someone's going to put that in a novel some day."

"Then why come down on my case every time?"

"Because I need that kind of thinking in a command, not a cockpit," answered the general.

"I didn't volunteer to fly some desk," said Spider.

"Look at you, John. Most pilots have a squadron by the time they're your age."

"So why don't you give me a squadron?"

"I can't. Not until you grow up."

"Looks like we're at a stalemate then."

Patterson turned away angrily and waved him off.

"I need a jet, sir."

"Sounds like a personal problem."

"We scavenged a broken down Pigseye bird but in the off-chance Beak can't fix her back up, is there a way you can expedite a replacement from the boneyard?"

"Not a chance," replied Woody.

"You're not even going to try?"

"Those techs down there are working through retirement just to mill spare parts. They custom-machine every gear and spindle by hand. Those junk-yard dogs put NASCAR to shame."

"Then what about a raid?"

"What about a raid? On who?"

"The Flying Tigers arrived from overseas last week. They're supposed to be Coaxial with a wing of FUN Rafales at Hinckley."

"You want to blow up a squadron of POTUS A-10s?"

"No. I want to get them to defect."

"I thought you promised not to embarrass me again," moaned Patterson.

"Thor Gunnar's their commander. I know Thor. He was raised in the Guard like us. He's people. He could care less about making colonel or general. He hates the UN, hates having the blueberries in his squadron giving him orders. And I know he's going to have major problems when Earle tells him to open fire on other Americans."

"How many would defect with him?"

"All of them," replied Spider. "Gunnar's awesome. If he augured in today, his men would follow him into the same smoking hole."

Woody pulled another pack of smokes from his flightsuit pocket. They were Novartis, laced with PKT and painkillers.

"Since when you smoke luckys?" Spider wanted to know.

"I smoke them when I get headaches."

"And I'm giving you a headache?"

"We can't have pilots running around on the ground like Rambo," Patterson recited.

"I wish we had those cloaking devices like we saw at Ripley," said Spider. "That would help."

"Shimmer fields," offered Aboud, limping up behind.

"That's what they're called?"

"That is what I call mine."

"You know about these?"

"I know the principle. The French use a projector-screen combination."

"And yours?"

Tanner rummaged through his Six Flags Over Tehran duffle Wade was carrying on his shoulder. "Mine is an interconnected matrix of camera-diodes. It is like a big plasma screen only you wear it. Each element has its own camera and is cross-axially addressed."

Wade helped Aboud untangle the device. It looked like a vest of clattering glass beads. The farmer draped it over the wincing doctor like a piece of chain-mail then turned on the battery pack.

Woody's cigarette dangled from his lower lip. "Will you look at that!"

Inside Tanner's stomach, a hole appeared as daylight streamed in from the plaza behind. Woody, Wade and Spider all bent down in unison to look at the street scene as if the scientist's torso weren't there.

"Can you make one for my A-10?" asked Spider.

"Too expensive. Not aerodynamic."

Spider walked around back and peered through Aboud's chest. "Hi Wade. Pass me a cookie?"

"What *can* it cover?" asked Patterson.

"A HMMWV maybe."

Wade stared transfixed at the sight. He nudged Tanner to the side and watched the image ripple. "When you move, it doesn't look quite right. It kind of—"

"Shimmers. That is a true statement. There is a small lag as the focal array tries to reconnect to the right LED. "That is why I call it a shimmer field. The image waves like a mirage until the processor catches up."

Spider looked at Patterson through the hole. "Woody?"

"No raid, major."

"But this could get us up to the ramp at Hinckley without being seen."

"And once you get inside? How are you going to hijack those jets without killing American boys?" Patterson challenged.

"Microwaves," Aboud interrupted.

"You've got one of those, too?"

"A small demo." He reaching into the duffel and pulled out what looked like a common everyday network router. It had a square black antenna with a small optical scope attached to aim it.

"It is called a POP gun; Pulsed Organoleptic Projectile. They have been around for awhile." He flipped the prototype on and the device began humming.

"You aiming that at me?"

"Do not be afraid, General Woody. Please hold out something harmless I can pop. A dollar bill?"

"A sovro?"

"A sovro bill. Yes. When aimed at a person, intersecting microwave beams can be focused on a point close to the skin resulting in a localized hotspot intense enough to explosively vaporize the air."

"What will that do to a soldier?"

"Depending on the power and tissue depth, anything from shock to unconsciousness." Aboud aimed his array at the bill and charged the circuits. Inside the plastic antenna, one hundred miniature microwave radiators rapidly began turning on and off. The out-of-phase sequencing caused ripples of energy to cancel and reinforce each other much like a handful of pebbles would produce when thrown into a pond. By using a microprocessor to control the phasing, a slender concentrated beam could be formed and steered. One such beam was being created now. It came to rest on the end of the cigarette dangling from Woody's lips and blew it up in front of his face. "Sorry! Sorry! Unsat! Unsat!"

"That's OK, doctor," said the general, pocketing the sovro and picking tobacco from his lashes. "I've been shot at before."

Aboud crammed everything back in the bag, averting his gaze.

"Is a bigger one possible?"

"In my bigger version, I can track multiple targets. It can knock down a platoon in half-a-second."

Trent pleaded to Woody with his eyebrows.

"Still no, major. The FUN would scramble their interceptors the minute the A-10s took off. They would be sitting ducks."

"Black Diamonds would work in that case," offered the Iranian.

"Downhill skiers?"

Tanner retrieved a vial of fine black powder from his bag. He poured some onto his hand, held it to the sun, then threw the dust onto the lawn. "I did not know what to call them so I called them Black Diamonds because they are black and shiny."

"What do I hear?" asked Spider, down on his hands and knees.

"They are nano-devices. They have tiny jaws. They are eating." One by one, unseen by the men, the tiny nano-robots marched around the ground in a programmed search pattern until their nitrogen receptors detected grass. When the feelers found a stem, they climbed up exactly one inch and began eating through the blade in straight cuts. When all the tips had fallen, a spot of newly-mown fescue appeared, cut out of the shaggy turf like a miniature crop circle. "3M programmed these for Sears to cut lawns."

Wade was enthralled with the trick. He took a vial for himself and tapped it into the lawn, spelling out his name.

"Add a diamond coating and tune their receptors for other compounds and these nano-technology devices can chew through anything. Metal. Glass."

"A runway?" wondered Spider.

"By targeting calcium carbonate, a *concrete* runway," answered Tanner.

"Still no," said Patterson.

"*Nano-technology* doesn't work for me," said Trent. "Too big. It needs a catchier name. How about NTs or nits or nanites?"

"*Nitnoys*," said the general.

"Huh?"

"*Nitnoys*. It's Vietnamese for *little things*."

"So you're on board, Wood?"

"Trent, you're getting up my nose. I'll think about it." Patterson picked up Tanner's bag from the ground and handed it to Corriston.

"That is mine!"

"There's no time to waste, doctor. This goes to our lab," ordered Woody. "In six months our guys can have everything reverse-engineered and combat-ready."

"You have a lab?" Aboud asked.

"Brand new. Hidden in the Badlands. Almost in South Dakota."

Aboud poked in the grass with his new cane. "But you need manufacturing capability. Why just the nitty-noids alone would require millions—"

"We have it," responded Patterson. "We have a garage economy, remember? Every household is an entrepreneurial center. Throughout the MS we have hundreds of backyard oil-shale refineries, pole-shed steel mills and mom-and-pop semiconductor foundries. We can do whatever needs to be done and do it faster than it would take at a huge industrial plant."

Aboud thought some more. "I can have these weapons ready in *three weeks*."

Patterson rested his hand on the scientist's shoulder. "No can do, son. We're sending you to the front, remember?"

"Oh, yes. I forgot." Aboud kicked at a pebble. "But maybe I can help with your lab temporarily, while I am healing."

"You sure? I don't want to interfere with your dream."

"I am being sure. Who is running your facility?"

"You are."

"*Me*? But I have never directed a weapons lab before. I was never able to get a clearance."

"Well, you've got one now," Patterson announced, dangling an ID badge with Tanner's picture on it. He jerked it away as Aboud reached for it. "You've got a lot of people counting on you, doctor. Chemists, semiconductor engineers, metallurgists, nuclear, a coalition of crack professionals who have left their jobs to work in the MS. I know it's pretty feeble compared to what you're used to, but everyone here is devoted one hundred percent to this. Are you?"

"On the condition I will still have a combat slot open for me. That once I have healed and completed my projects, I will be permitted to fight like a regular soldier."

"We have a deal," said Woody. "Until then, you will be in charge of our new R+D Command."

"Where is this place," asked Spider. "I've never heard of it before."

"I'm not telling. Full security. No one's allowed in. Not even the Quarterstaff can know, it's so remote."

"It sounds lonely," said Aboud. "Like a leper colony back home."

"So you don't feel homesick, that's what we'll call it then," declared Patterson. "The Leper Colony."

"And so you'll have a sense of inclusion, that's what we'll call you, too," added Spider.

"What is that, John?"

"As of now, your official callsign is *Leper*."

CHAPTER 8
ABBY CAPTURE

Laura bounced to the beat of Madonna's *Hung Up* while waiting for Cottage Grove's last stoplight to let her by. Evening storms had wrung the air free of summer's dingy haze, at least for a day or two. Ahead, glass and steel sparkled in the morning sun as the city skyline loomed ahead on the horizon.

It was Thursday. Her staff would be gone to their cabins for the weekend and she was looking forward to finishing her department's budget in peace. She cranked the volume and warbled along with the tune.

Traffic was thick. She veered left then took the shortcut, a long but bucolic route that corkscrewed through the last remaining holdouts of rural life left in the county.

Madonna gave way to news. Laura didn't like news. She stabbed at the buttons for a different station but not before it told her the state of Iowa and the northern-half of Missouri had been awarded to Germany as a mandate, that Congress had just capped her weekly credit and debit card purchases to $100 for gas and $100 for food, and that a fisherman from the Philippines named Alfonse had just won that week's two-billion-dollar Worldball jackpot.

Sirens droned up from behind as TSA squad cars and French-UN PVPs raced by. She turned off her FM and tuned in KOME, San Jose's Rock of the Bay, on the new Internet radio Cody had installed for her.

Just when she had figured out the controls, another traffic jam appeared up ahead. It was the Fredrick farm. She jammed on her brakes and lowered her window. "What's going on, officer?" she called out to a disinterested sergeant.

"None of my business, ma'am. Just keep moving."

The line crawled as gawkers peered through the flashing strobes of the police cruisers. Laura came abeam the farm, the backyard thick with gendarmes. In the middle of the fray stood Abby in bathrobe and slippers, waving a shotgun.

"HOLY—" Laura turned her head and kept driving straight ahead. What had Abby done? Where was Wade? As soon as she was past the roadblock, the traffic thinned and she floored the accelerator. I've got to get to work, she said to herself. I'm already late. She turned up Fleetwood Mac as loud as it would go as two rifle blasts boomed behind her.

Laura hauled her Wrangler onto the shoulder and reversed course for the farm, spitting gravel as she went. She shot a gap in the traffic, drove through a ditch and came to a stop beside the Fredrick Dairy signboard.

"Mam'zelle, stop," commanded a petite mall-tanned Frenchman in gendarme garb. You cannot come here. Go back immediately."

"I'm a friend. What has she done? What's going on here?"

"She has done nothing. Now you must leave."

Abby screamed as Laura watched the farmer's wife wheel her gun at the men encircling her. Across the cornfield, a blue-flagged armored personnel carrier plowed a path for them. It disgorged a black-clad RAID squad and pointed a menacing cannon. Laura ran around the policeman. She yelped as he grabbed her arm.

"What's the problem here, Constable?" asked a thick-shouldered brown-shirted Minnesota trooper.

"*You* are," said the European. "This is a UN matter. Go away."

"I'm Highway Patrol. *We're* responsible for crowd control. Not you."

"So do your job!" He shoved her at him, then left.

"Hi, I'm Timothy Bowe. Are you a friend of Abby's?"

"I'm Laura. Laura Trent and yes. Do you know the Fredricks?"

"Yes, but not well. From what I gather, the gendarmes are here to take Abby to a Reunification Center."

"A what?"

"An internment camp. The blueberries just opened them."

"For what purpose?"

"To reunite families with loved ones in the Middle States."

"You mean to take her to Auggie?"

"And Wade. Turns out he illegally emigrated last night."

"Look at her," said Laura. "She obviously doesn't want to go."

"It's for her own protection. So says the inspector anyway."

"Protection from who?"

"Neighbors. Cadets. You're considered a symp just for having family over there now."

"She's not a sympathizer. Why would anyone think that? Her family supplies the whole UN base for Pete's sake."

"I know."

"Well, can't you do anything?"

"Not while the French are here. They have jurisdiction." He looked her in the eye. "But you can."

"Me? What can I do?"

"You're her friend. You can talk to her."

Laura looked over to the scene for a moment. "The UN knows what they're doing."

"You really believe that?" replied Bowe.

"Look, I'm not political. I mind my own business. I run a department at the U. I can't be seen here." She watched the road as a Live@Five news van pulled into the yard.

"Mrs. Trent, as you can already see, this probably isn't going to end real well." The trooper motioned to the barn's roofline where a RAID marksman was perching himself for a shot.

Laura looked over his shoulder before covering her eyes. "This is straight out of a horror movie," she moaned. "Abby wouldn't hurt a fly."

The shotgun went off again, sending the pair for cover behind Bowe's squad.

"Will you help her?"

"I'll do what I can."

"Go ahead. Shoot me! Shoot me! I don't care," shrieked a hoarse and quivering Abby Fredrick. "I'm not going to go with you to your filthy, stinking camp!" One of the men had been counting shots. He held up four fingers as the circle of gendarmes got one step smaller. Abby crouched. "DON'T COME ANY CLOSER!"

Laura approached cautiously from the driveway. She pulled back her black greco curls and hooked them behind her ears. "Abby? Abby, honey. It's me, Laura." The ring of police parted and allowed Laura to walk through. "Put that thing down so I can come and talk to you."

"Laura, my God, you've come! Help me," she pleaded.

"That's what I'm here for."

"They want to take me prisoner. They said Wade's a traitor. That he's a Freemartin and helped smuggle a spy to the MS. They're going to arrest me and torture me as punishment."

Laura looked to the inspector. He stuck out his lip and shrugged his shoulders.

"They want you to go to a Reunification Center, not a camp."

"It *is* a camp!"

"No. Not like that. It's a place to process you."

"Like we process our cows? For slaughter?"

"You want to be with Wade don't you? Then you need to go," Laura reasoned.

"Lies!" Abby spit. "How can I trust you? You sound just like them."

"I'm your friend. Why would you ask such a silly question?"

Fredrick gathered her robe around her with a fierce pull. "Because you haven't returned any of my calls. I call and call and you don't answer. It's like you've forgotten about me."

Laura looked down at her Monolos. "Abby, I'm sorry. I've been busy."

"You're *always* busy."

"That's not true. We just went shopping, didn't we?"

"It took you two months to do that. And you only did it so you wouldn't have to see me for another two months."

"That's not fair."

"I'm just a hick to you, a farmer living out in the middle of nowhere with the manure and flies."

"I'm sorry."

"I used to trust you. You were the only person I could talk to. Now you just want to get rid of me."

Laura felt ashamed. Everyone eyed her. She *had* avoided Abby. She had been keeping her away. Partly for not wanting to hear more droning about August. Mostly for not wanting to be reminded of how much she missed John. Laura hung her head as a *click!* from the sniper's rifle-bolt reached her ears from the roof behind her.

"Up yours, *bitch!*" Laura's curse startled the men as she rushed across their circle, grabbed the barrel of Abby's shotgun and slapped the hysterical housewife solidly across the face.

"Owww!"

The gendarmes hooted and hollered in French as Laura pulled Abby close. "Snap out of this now!" she whispered. "You need to go with them, don't you understand? They aren't arresting you. They won't hurt you. They want to protect you."

"You're not just telling me that to get rid of me?"

"I wouldn't do that to you."

Abby dropped her gun and collapsed to the ground like a Muppet. "Oh, Laura. I called all night. I called and called. Where were you?"

"I'm sorry. I was—"

"THEY KILLED AUGGIE! AUGGIE'S DEAD! MY BABY'S GONE!" Abby howled into the dust and gravel of the drive.

"Oh, no honey."

"My son's gone. Laura, what am I going to do? I've got no one."

"I'm sorry. I'm sorry." Laura fell on top of Abby, bundling up her limbs to shield them from the rifleman's scope.

"Wade's gone some men came and said they had something for him to do and would he do it and Wade said yes he said yes because he was mad and angry at the UN the president everyone that Auggie was dead he never cried he just went and now he's gone too I don't know what to do what should I do Laura what should I do?"

The policemen surrounding them began to look serious again as Laura took her friend by the chin and shook it. "You need Wade, right?" Abby sniffed. "He's mourning, too. He's suffering. He needs you, right?"

"He would never say it but, yes, I know he does."

'Then you need to go with the police. They'll take care of you."

"Are you sure? Do you promise?"

Laura twisted around and searched for the moustached inspector. She found him talking to the sniper who was packing up to leave. "Yes, I promise," she said.

Abby raised her face to the sun. "Then I'll call Pete. He'll take care of the cows. He'll keep things running until we make it back."

"Cody and I can help, too."

"Thank you, Laura. I'm so lucky to have such a wonderful friend like you."

"I'm not that wonderful. I really *don't* like your flies."

Laura rubbed Abby's blood-shot eyes and helped her into the house. The inspector approached and offered his hand. Laura looked at it. "Let her alone. She's going to shower now. Just give her thirty minutes and she'll be packed and ready to go."

"And there will not be any more of such problems?"

"Not on her end."

"What do you mean?"

"I mean I told her she'd be safe with you."

"As safe as can reasonably be expected in a refugee camp."

"It's not a Reunification facility?"

"It is many things to many people."

"Tell me I did not just lie to my friend, *Clouseau*. Tell me that you are going to see to it there isn't one little scratch on her head."

The chief snickered, sticking out his hand a second time. "Thank you again, Ms. Trent. We will take it from here."

Laura's heart pounded with anger. She went white with rage at the man's condescending smirk and snatched his hand as John had taught her in Aikido class. She pivoted to the side and twisted his thumb with a vicious tug that flipped the man high into the air and onto his back. She followed him to the dirt and, kneeling beside him, pulled a sharpened credit card from her bag and drew its razor edge across his jugular. The Frenchman felt something warm trickle down his neck and, in shock, waved his men off.

"Oui, bien sur. Elle sera traite avec le plus grand respect. Cette une promesse," he replied, but in the wrong tongue.

"I'll take that as a yes," she said, leaving a mark.

Laura stood, trembling. From her fingers to her mud-crusted pumps, her body buzzed like she had just downed a steroid slushie. But she liked it. The excitement made her feel like she could crack-back a linebacker, like she could eat a car. The bony olive-skinned beauty sheathed her card and gave the gendarmes a New York once-over, daring them to say a word. They didn't and backed away as the trooper led Laura to her car and helped her in. She peeled down the driveway and headed for work. Once there, she locked herself in her darkened office where she replayed the events of the day, wondering what she had done.

CHAPTER 9
TERM LIMITS

The last of the flashbulbs died off as President Milton Earle's thoughts drifted to dinner. From across the White House lawn, the sharp tang of mustard-pulled pork hit his nostrils, inducing him to cut short his photo-op with his Middle Eastern guests.

"Mr. President? Any comment on your brothers?" asked one reporter. "From the early returns, it's looking like they are shoo-ins for the Republican nomination. As well as the presidency."

"Well, the election's still a few months away," replied Earle. "I'm not going to write off the Democrats just yet."

"Do you have any words of encouragement for them or is there still bitterness over the last time they ran against you?"

"Now Sal, can't you set a better trap than that? I love my bubbas. My word of caution to them: think twice before moving in here and tangling with the likes of you."

The gallery laughed as another reporter asked a question. "Mr. President, any thoughts as the twilight of your administration approaches? Some presidents have likened their retirement from office as an extinction or a bittersweet divorce. Any regrets?"

"Brady, the only regret I have right now is delaying BBQ Night one more second." He put a meaty arm around his guest for one last photo while whispering in his ear. "How 'bout some pickled okra, visor? Fresh-picked from my home state of South Carolina."

The vizier didn't seem to hear as he and his family marvelled at the Ford Pool, the Rose Garden and the huge columns holding up the White House's South Portico. Upon seeing the battalion-sized picnic tables under the ground's stout maples, their mouths gaped open.

"You don't think the visor's head's going to explode all over my slaw, do you, Peter?"

"That's *viz-zeah*, Mr. President," whispered Peter Laird, the president's stumpy ever-present chief-of-staff.

"Whatever. I'm hungry. Let's get some grub."

The dignitaries wore ghutra coverings and robes of red-and-white, the colors of their new dependency, the Badawl Republic of Tigris. The territory, freshly annexed by the UN from Al-Anbar, Iraq, was to be the new Middle Eastern homeland for all the worlds dispersed nomadic tribes. Earle addressed himself to the bedouin leader. "*Viz-zeah? Dinn-eah?*"

The president's chef explained the evening's exotic cuisine as the visitors sniffed at the Upcountry samplings of hush puppies, collard greens, sweet potato casserole, beer-butt chicken and peach cobbler.

The strapping comedic Earle hoisted his sandwich in honor of the emir and downed a bite. "If this doesn't give you a boner, Peter, I don't know what will."

"Is this pork?" the vizier's bearded nephew inquired, in proper Queen's English.

"Shipped in fresh from Maurice's Piggy Park," the president replied. "Life is good!"

The Arab and his family hastily replaced their sandwiches and exchanged them for the chicken instead as Laird picked through his corn bread, embarrassed.

The president and his guests all sat down and began eating as the emir launched into an animated exchange with his nephew. "President Earle, my uncle wishes to know about that long green building in the back, with the antennas. Is it a military command post or some sort of surveillance center?"

"You mean in the aide's parking lot there?" pointed Earle.

"Yes, what is it, my uncle is wondering?"

Laird coughed a mouthful of banana pudding into his napkin.

"Why that's where my ma and pa—"

"That's a museum," Laird finished.

"A museum! Can we see it?"

"I'm afraid not. After the president finishes eating, he really must go."

"Nonsense, Peter. Our guests are curious about our freedoms and opportunities. What makes America tick, heh, veesher?" Earle wiped pork grease from his mouth and stood. "What better way to celebrate the American Dream than introduce them to a sixties classic, the single-wide mobile home."

"But, sir."

"And Peter will be happy to show you," Earle announce.

"I would?" The aide gulped down his sweet tea and led the delegation to a sixty-foot-long lime green trailer resting on cinder-blocks in White House side lot. It had white trim, a CB antenna, a tattered canvas awning and an air conditioner dangling from a boarded-over bedroom window. On one of the satellite dishes, an orange Earnhardt Number 8 decal beamed proudly. Laird shuddered. "This is the childhood home of President Milton Earle." Earle gave an exaggerated bow. "He and his mother and father and brothers lived in this house in one of the poorest parts of America, the Piedmont of South Carolina. He has brought it with him to Washington to remind him of his humble beginnings."

"Ah, I see. So he doesn't get a big brain?" said the nephew.

Laird cocked his head.

"He means big *head*, Peter. Jeez, loosen up, grits-for-brains."

"Yes, big head," the boy corrected. "Ah, and what is that?"

"That is a trailer hitch, where the truck attaches."

"It moves?" The delegates and wives gestured excitedly.

"See Skeeter, they love it!"

"And what is that?" the nephew wondered, pointing to a blue plastic tank.

"Umm, that? That's a hygiene tank."

"And these?" he asked, looking up at a string of dangling multi-colored lights.

Laird rolled his eyes. "I believe those are called Chinese lanterns. A common decoration found in most upscale trailer parks and campsites throughout the South. Earle nodded his approval from the back, downing a fistful of boiled peanuts.

"And this?" The nephew pointed to a rusty cylinder laying underneath the home.

Laird put on his glasses and bent down for a closer look. "I don't know. If I had to guess, I'd say it was … HOLY—"

Two pink eyes glared at the chief-of-staff from the shadows below the trailer and jumped out at him. Laird rolled onto his back as a sinewy albino dingo sprang into the daylight and snapped at his face. Earle and his guests leaped away in unison giving Laird room to execute a lifesaving somersault. The mongrel barked its displeasure from the end of his overstretched chain as a voice boomed from inside the home.

"Hon, if you don't shut that tick condo up, I'm gone kick him so hard his pups'll be born dizzy."

Just then the door burst open as a flint-throated woman with big hair and a baggy rose-printed nightgown appeared, followed by her son. "Shithead, knock it off or I'll get the collar."

"Yeah. Bad dog. I kick you ass," repeated her son, sending the hound yelping with a string of BBs from his toy M-16.

The Middle Easterners stood rooted, quietly regarding the mother and her Huggie-clad two-year-old.

"Hon, you better come here," Tammy Stoddard yelled into the trailer. "We have guests."

Harvey Stoddard, Tammy's sweating and shirtless husband, ducked through the too-small door, a wet towel wrapped around his head. "Hi, ya'll!"

"Hi, Harv. Sorry to bother you," said the president

"Who the hell is he?" Laird groaned.

"Everyone, this is Harvey Stoddard, the first lady's brother. This is Tammy, his wife, and son Tyler."

"I kick you ass," Tyler threatened, jabbing his gun at them impotently.

The in-laws waved sheepishly as the delegation clapped.

"He's sorta between jobs right now, Peter. Don't let this get around."

Laird brushed off his Dolce & Gabbana fair trade trousers and stared as the foreigners fawned over the Stoddards. "They think they're bedouins."

"Must be the turban," Earle agreed.

The guests begged Harvey and Tammy to stay with them for the rest of the evening. Laird gave a reluctant yes, seeing the request as a reprieve from further mortification. After saying their good-byes, he grabbed his boss' elbow and walked him toward the White House.

"We have the Secretary-General waiting, sir."

"Hell, he's still here?"

"He's on your schedule, Milt. He's been waiting for over an hour."

"Why do you think I spent so much time with the camel-huggers? Because I like the smell of goat shit? I wanted the twit to leave."

"He's got your 7th Fleet, remember?"

"So? What else does he want?" asked the president.

"He doesn't want anything. *You* called him here."

Earle jerked his arm away and blazed down at his deputy. "No, Peter. *You* called him here."

"To tell him you want the 7th Fleet back."

"I don't give a happy horseshit about the 7th Fleet. If Zzgn wants to run the war, let him."

"I can't believe you're saying this."

"We can't be trusted to police ourselves, remember?"

"That's not fair, Milt."

"*You* said it."

"I said that when I was with Air America and Bush was in the White House. Things are different now."

"The only thing different is you're a policymaker now, not a sanctimonious talk show host. *You* advocated this Dependence and Alignment crap. You and your other World Village joy-germs. Imagine your horror when a presidential candidate actually took your plank and ran on it—*me*. This is your making so don't pee down my back. I'm the only honest one here."

"People can change."

"*I* changed. From Republican to Democrat, remember? Not you. You're *still* a wingnut."

Laird blinked.

Milton Earle reached down and scuffed the aide's hair. "You look like a frog caught in a rainstorm, Skeeter. Come on. Let's go see the Little General. I'm interested in how you're going to handle this."

The pair padded up the worn granite steps and into the golden glow of the White House's Entrance Hall. From there, they followed the red carpet of the cross hall to the West Wing where they met their guest waiting outside the Oval Office.

"Burin! It is so nice of you to come and meet me on such short notice. Welcome to the White House." The rangy Earle vaulted into the room like a steeplechase horse. In two steps, he had closed their distance so fast Zzgn had trouble scrambling for a smile.

"Mr. President, I am honored at the attention. It is always so humbling to visit you in your fine palace."

Laird waded into the ceremony with an outstretched hand. "He's the president, Mr. Secretary-General, not a *king*. We don't have royalty here. This is the people's house."

"Of course, Mr. Laird," bowed Zzgn. "Accept my apologies."

Earle ignored the two cackling hens and concerned himself with his own comfort. "Cigar, cognac, Mr. Secretary? Coffee enema, Peter?"

Zzgn fished a Macanudo from Earle's humidor as Laird regarded the South Lawn vista out the room's tall bay windows. When he spun back around, Earle had returned from the kitchen with a Schlitz and a sniffer of Louis XIII. "Now, Mr. Secretary-General, about the 7th—"

Someone knocked at the door. "Peter? Let them in, please."

Laird huffed over to the door, admitting a hive of groundskeepers who began personalizing the presidential suite by removing pictures, relocating furniture and moving the desk.

"Sorry," smiled Earle, planting his wide rear in a worn merlot-red lazyboy sitting near the fire. "I get the heebie-jeebies when my back's to the window."

"Let me get right to the point," continued Laird as he let the workers back out the way they had come in. "You have something of ours and we would like it back."

"Hmm, could you perhaps be more descriptive," teased the Sec-Gen.

"You have our Pacific Fleet, General and we are in need of it."

"You need it? For what?"

"We don't need to explain to you—"

The Secretary-General produced a pack of Saudi EMROs. He lit one of the skinny smokes and offered it to the president, who puffed it and hacked loudly.

"We are planning a new offensive against the SF in the Cascades," explained Laird. "We need our carrier groups to spearhead it."

"I see," replied the General. "You need them for your fight against the SF. Bit of an overkill, don't you think?" He looked to the president. Earle just shrugged his shoulders.

"The details of our request is not of concern to you," said Laird.

"I beg to differ."

"Your only interest should be to return command of our battle group to the president."

"Why would you need such superior firepower against such a small paramilitary force? You are warring with fifty-year-old men who employ weaponry just as aged."

"The war would be easier if we had our navy back. *And* more UN oil."

"That is up to the General Assembly to vote on. I cannot coerce them, only persuade."

Peter looked to his boss who had taken his shoes off and was running his toes through the astro-turf carpet.

Zzgn continued. "Whereas I have the entire Peoples Army of the Republic of China to battle in the event they should decide to advance on Taiwan or Japan. They have already tried to invade Korea during your American civil war."

"*That* is not of our concern, General Zzgn. We agreed to put the 7th under UN command only until the Chinese withdrew from the Korean peninsula. Now that that's done—"

"But Peter, the Secretary's correct," interrupted the president. "We are part of the world community. Isn't it our responsibility as an Alignee to help prevent bigger nations from bullying the small?" He smirked.

"A superb observation, Mr. President. The Korean Union would not exist if it weren't for the use of your ships." Zzgn took a pull from his maduro and blew smoke Laird's way. "And I needn't remind you of our StanEval officers standing beside your admirals every day ready to enforce the resolution."

"One word to our sailors from the president and your observers are overboard with bullets in their heads," warned the chief-of-staff.

"That is what I am fully confident *will never* happen," replied Zzgn, curtly

Earle took a sip of beer, dribbling on his exposed undershirt. He flicked it off with the back of his hand before replying. "I hate to rain on your parade, Burin, but Americans can be pushed only so far. They want our forces back."

"But your public supports peace," the SecGen answered.

"Not when it comes to kicking Sovereign ass. Then, even all my long-haired drug-addict bed-wetting pinko-commie friends love the military."

"You are concerned with what others think? Even when you are at the end of your last term?" wondered Zzgn. "A *hobbling duck,* so called."

"No disrespect for your goals, but that pig just won't fly here, Burin."

"I see. Public opinion is important to you."

"The president isn't interested in what it would mean for him personally," corrected Laird. "He is referring to what would happen to the country. What would happen to the progress we have made in the war should our party be swept out of power in the next election. Which it will if our forces are not brought back under U.S. command."

"But what if there were no election?"

Earle's rocking stopped. "What are you suggesting?"

"An automatic third term, Mr. President."

The room thundered with an accidental fart from Earle's seat cushion. "A what?"

"A third term of unlimited duration mandated by the Security Council under its Emergency Wartime Ordinance powers."

"Well butter my butt and call me a biscuit."

Laird launched to his feet. "Don't *even* go there, Zzgn. You can't meddle in our affairs. The UN can't manage our politics. Hell, *we* can't even manage our politics."

"No meddling. Just an insurance police to guarantee continuity of leadership."

"You wouldn't dare!"

"Just until the war is over. Temporary, of course."

Laird took of his glasses and stabbed them toward the Secretary. "Russia would never put up with this. I can call Ambassador Rubinov the minute you leave and I'd have his veto before you were in bed."

Zzgn swirled his cognac. "Anton will have no problem with it. And either will your Supreme Court. It's called a constitutional abeyance and precedents have already been set in the Sudan and Ukraine."

Earle leaned forward. "Burin, my friend, I'm afraid this won't work."

"Thank you, Mr. President." Laird gathered the hair that had flown over his shoulder and pasted it back over his scalp.

"At least not during peacetime," the president continued.

The stumpy aide put hands over his ears and paraded around the room. "Don't say what I think you're going to say!"

"But during war, a bloody civil one at that, the people *need* a coherent, focused strategy. Not the defeatist policy of appeasement a new administration would bring in."

"I can see your wisdom, Mr. President. Such leadership will bring victory and Alignment to fruition that much sooner."

Laird threw his folder to the ground. "You're buying this hook, line and sinker!"

"I admit it's a little far fetched, but—"

"But you're seriously considering it, aren't you?"

"I'd be a fool not to, Peter. The country expects its president to do all he can."

"This isn't about the American people. This is about *you*!"

"Get a hold of yourself, boy."

"This is about unlimited power. Unlimited rule."

"I'm warning you, you'd rather sandpaper a bobcat's bottom than take this course with me."

"You're right. Why don't I just go get your robe now, your Highness, or do you wish me to wait until your crown is poured?"

Earle pulled back a thick fist and mashed it into the side of his aide's face. Laird went cross-eyed and fell backwards on the turf. When he came to, the office was back in order and the Secretary, on his way out.

"Thanks for stopping by, Burin. I'll be in touch," waved Earle.

Laird sat up, rubbing his jaw. "This is blackmail, Zzgn."

The Ukrainian paused as he passed through the door. "That's a bit harsh, Peter. I consider it barter."

With his guest gone, Earle paced the room in silence, daydreaming about the possibilities the General had offered. No more campaigning, he thought. No more politics. No more cajoling the Southern Actors or containing the bluebirds. He could keep his servants. He could keep his bodyguards, his dalliances, his Air Force One. No boring memoirs, no peacock presidential library to raise funds for. Imagine, I could live out my life right here. He stopped at the portraits on his wall and regarded them. "Lookie me, pa! Looks like I'll be here another four years." Former Vice President Clifford Earle stared across the room plaintively, expressionless at the news. "And if they haven't carved your wrinkly carcass up for gator bait by then, I'll make sure I'm here another four years after that."

"Is that what this is about, Milt?" Laird wondered. "Spite? Validation? Revenge?" Earle addressed the two other paintings nearby, one of brother Congressman Cassius Earle and the other of eldest brother Senator Clive Earle. The commander-in-chief raised his snifter and spit a stream of brandy on the portraits. "You can't wait to tell them, can you?" guessed Laird.

"That their worthless no-talent brother has outfoxed them again?" he answered. "You bet your arse-crack I can't." Earle lumbered over to his friend and reached out a hand. Laird took it. "You know, Skeeter, you're about as useless as goose crap on a pump handle. Why couldn't you come up with any of this abeyance stuff?"

Laird shook his head. "Because I'm not a conniving, maniacal tyrant."

"I know," Earle agreed. "That's what I need. Think he'd ever consider becoming chief-of-staff?"

"No, sir. Why be a puppet when you can be the puppeteer?" Laird let his reply linger, then opened the door to leave.

"But I can have my resignation ready by morning. Just in case."

CHAPTER 10
TRIAGE

Hinckley Air Field occupied the far side of Grand Island Casino International. The base had just opened under a Memorandum of Understanding between the UN and a local Sioux tribe. Not that the Sioux wanted to pick sides in the war, but doing business with the UN did have its perks: it brought a lot of rich Third-World dictators to the tables and it came with its own seat in the General Assembly.

"We thank you for coming to Hinckley to see our wounded, Commander Faisson."

"No, it is I who wish to thank *them*," he replied.

"It does wonders for the men to see you."

"I was hoping it might be a morale builder."

"When morale is high, healing accelerates." Colonel Denice Villat ran 1RMED, France's field hospital regiment. The medical facility was, strangely enough, located in a converted corporate jet hanger on what used to be the general aviation side of the field. Villat wove the entourage through the beds as the general inspired and decorated the casualties.

"Merci," said Faisson, saluting a young para-marine with a head wound. He bent over and pinned a Barrer Pour Le Blessée, the French Purple Heart, on the man's frock. "From what battle did you come?"

"St. Cloud, sir. I was a tank gunner with the 6e-12e RC."

"Ah! A great victory, yes? The Sovereigns tried to gain our flanks with their overweight Abrahms, trying to trap us as we crossed the Mississippi, but we caught them in the open with our Leclercs and sent those colonial bastards running for their plantations, didn't we?"

The patients, caught off guard by their commander's colorful banter, responded loudly, filling the hospital with laughter.

"Better speed, better armor, better gunners. Proof that French tanks are superior." A smiling Faisson posed with the young enlisted as a hospital photographer took their picture.

"And what battle were you in, caporal?"

"Sir, I was wounded at the Stand of Minnetonka. We were ambushed by a squad of basketball players who booby trapped their property and shot at us from their mansions on the lake."

"Americans are cowards until it comes to giving up their extravagant frills. Then they fight like hysterical women." Faisson drew close. "But we made short order of the partisans, didn't we? We swept in house by house and asked questions later. That taught them to fear the French soldier. We've not had a problem with the Minnesotans since, have we?"

"No, sir!"

Faisson partook in more ceremony as Phillipe Laval, the general's aide, tapped his watch. "Sir, your intel briefing." At the end of the row, a doctor gently laid a sheet over the face of a dead soldier.

"Who is that, Phillipe?"

"That is nothing you want to see," replied Colonel Vallat.

"Nonsense. A man has given his life." The general pushed through his staff and turned down the aisle. When he reached the dead soldier, he pulled the sheet back to reveal a mutilated and burnt body with no eyes, ears, or nose and a freshly slit throat.

"This is not a man," Vallat confessed. "It is a woman."

"Mon dieu!" crossed Laval. "Where are her—"

"Her breasts? Eaten."

The doctor read her chart. "Her name was Rèmé. Lieutenant colonel. She was brought in late last night barely alive. She was beaten, raped and we believe made to drink gasoline before it was ignited."

"Who could do this?" sputtered the aide.

"The Machetes."

"The Haitians did this? To a French officer? Fragging is a serious charge. Do you have evidence?"

The doctor lifted the sheet further.

"What are those symbols? On her legs and back?"

"Voodun," replied the physician. "They are snake and phallus fetishes."

Laval turned to Faisson who was peering out a nearby window. "We have to report this to the inspector general, sir."

"We have already started the paper work," replied the doctor

"The Haitians didn't frag her," Faisson announced, watching the flightline activities outside. "It was the Americans."

"How? The SF were nowhere near her camp."

"The Freemartins are everywhere, doctor."

The surgeon adjusted his spectacles. "The Freemartins may be our enemy, but they aren't evil. *This* is evil." He grabbed the sheet and covered the body. "We have not seen this before. Not until the Machetes arrived."

"It could also be desperation," said Faisson. "The Sovereigns are finally realizing they are losing the war."

All eyes dwelled on the general.

"But would they do this to an officer? A woman?"

"She is not an officer," replied Faisson. "I demoted her to caporal last week."

"But her tags—"

A corporal lay drugged nearby, his leg in a cast. Faisson reached around the boy's neck, ripped off his dog tag and, with the heel of his hand, rammed it edgewise between Rèmé's two front teeth. Laval and the others turned their heads reflexively as Rèmé's palate split in two with a sickening *pop*! "She's a caporal now," said the five-star.

"General, please understand. My hands are tied. As a doctor under UN jurisdiction, I am required by the Geneva Convention to report all suspected cases of murder."

Faisson took a step toward the man, regarding him closely. "You aren't French, are you?"

"No, but I fail to see what that has to do with anything."

Faisson fingered his nametag. "Doctor Andresson?"

"Yes."

"American?"

"Yes. I'm a volunteer. I'm on humanitarian leave."

"Doctor Jon Andresson? Pediatric physician from Mayo?"

The doctor leaned back as Faisson pressed in. "Do I know you?"

Faisson slapped Andresson's clipboard to the floor, the doctor's mouth hanging open in stunned silence. Andresson bent down to pick up his charts. When he came back up, he was looking down the barrel of Faisson's black FAMAS semi-automatic.

"You don't even remember me, do you?"

"W-w-what is this about?" the doctor asked, raising his hands to half-staff.

The eyes of the infirmary were upon them, including many from the Red Cross. Laval had seen his commander's rages many times since becoming aide-de-camp. They had resulted in demotions, discharges and incarcerations. They were swift and merciless. Now, looking down at Rèmé, he knew they could also be murderous.

A squat tough-looking soldier, with heavy eyebrows and a thick handlebar mustache ran up. He wore three gold chevrons on his sleeve, a chief sergeant. "Sir, can I be of assistance?"

Laval didn't trust his general's intentions. He took control before Faisson could reply. "Sergent-chef, arrest this man immediately."

"On what charge?" laughed the doctor.

"Suspicion of sedition."

"Have you people gone completely mad?"

"And suspicion of murder in the death of Lieutenant Corporal ... I mean, Caporal Rèmé.

"For Christ's sake, I'm here to help you," cried the doctor. "*I'm on your side!*"

The guard lowered his rifle and stuck it in Andresson's ribs. When the surgeon realized the soldier meant business, he allowed himself to be goose-stepped out of the hanger. "BUT I'M AN AMERICAN CITIZEN. I'VE DONE NOTHING WRONG!"

"Tell that to my daughter," Laval heard Faisson say.

French-UN engineers scrambled to ready the military side of the airfield in time for the Death Storks, a squadron of Rafale omni-role fighters arriving soon from their home field in Dijon. Already, a unit of American A-10s, redeployed from their overseas base in Bentwaters, England, neared mission-ready status on their own ramp just to the west. All told, the small town of Hinckley, Minnesota would soon be hosting close to two hundred fighters and four thousand airmen in support of the UNIFUS mission. Until then, Brigade d'Intelligence had to carry out their functions amid the diesel engines outside and an overworked air conditioner inside.

"And that is the end of my briefing," concluded Sous Lieutenant Xavier Chack, that morning's intelligence briefer. "Are there any questions?"

Lieutenant Laval looked over to his general for a response but Faisson continued his occupation with the contents of his wallet. Laval continued to run the meeting for him. "Yes, Lieutenant Chack. I have a question on the increased battle damage we have been experiencing. How can we negate the Sovereign fighters use of live munitions?"

"We can not," Chack replied. "Their ammo dump has been restored but is located at the Red River Depot in Oklahoma, the German's area of responsibility."

"Can't we liaise with the Germans? Tell them our concerns?"

"The dirty Krauts aren't concerned with anyone but themselves. They do what they want."

"Then what is keeping us from taking out the depot ourselves if they will not? Are we afraid of the Sovereign F-22s and F-35s?"

"No."

"Why not?"

"Because we have not seen any lately."

"Because our pilots are all of a sudden becoming aces and have shot them all down?" Laval threw his pen onto the table. "*Come on*, lieutenant."

"I am sorry. I am nervous." Chack gave a quick glance to Faisson who seemed to be mumbling to the pictures in his lap. "We suspect their fighters have been grounded due to spares problems. They do not have the manufacturing or fabrication base to replace their damaged radar or fly-by-wire electronics."

"Can't they fly them without the computers?" asked the aide.

"No, when a black box fails, the whole aircraft is grounded. Even their boneyard F-15s and -16s."

"Xavier, do you have an updated Order of Battle?" asked a voice from the back row.

"I have a video." Laval nodded for him to proceed. "The Sovereign

Air Arm has been left to prosecute their air defense with mostly legacy airframes. Here is gun film from our most recent sorties." Chack hunched over the projector as it warmed up.

"What is that?"

"An A-7. Flown by the Sioux City Hooligans, I believe. Notice the lack of supersonic dash. They have no way of shooting our fighters down from behind. They have to take frontal shots. Very risky and ineffective."

"And that?" asked another officer from the back. "An A-4? That is what Jester flew in Top Gun, no?"

"Yes, a Skyhawk. A thirty-year-old movie and a sixty-year-old jet." Chack kept clicking through the clips. "This is an AV-8 Harrier coming head-on. An A-10 Warthog. Here is an F-106."

Faisson jerked upright. "Go back," he commanded.

Chack startled. "Yes, sir. Which one, sir?"

"The A-10." Faisson rose and neared the screen. "Why are you mixing a Warthog in with air-interceptors?"

"This film is from a Tigre," replied the lieutenant. "Warthogs operate in the same low-speed low-altitude regime as our helicopters. A-10s are their number-one air threat."

"Now go forward. Slow." Faisson followed the warbird's path with his finger. "There. Enlarge that." The general pulled out a mobe and scanned the videos stored there. "Here, I want you to compare this frame with the one on the screen." He tossed the device to Chack who brought up the two images on split-screen.

"They aren't the same," said Chack. "One is clean looking, the other is full of burns and duct tape."

"Zoom in on the nose."

"They have the same artwork?" noted Laval. "A white dog on a red doghouse."

"It is the famous World War I ace who is always trying to shoot down the Red Baron. It is Snoopy," said Chack.

"Snoopy? Why not a naked girl like all the other pornographic Americans?" asked a staffer.

"Maybe he has children. Maybe he is a grandfather."

"Are you thinking he is the same pilot, Général Faisson?"

"I know it is. Pilots personalize their aircraft as soon as possible, like a cowboy branding his steer."

"Where are the pictures from?" Laval asked.

"One is from an airstrike on a Leclerc brigade at Camp Ripley," replied Chack. "I recognize Général Faisson's video from a Eurocopter we lost a few days ago to some A-10s like these. It is a good thing both the pilot and WSO died in the attack. I would've been too embarrassed to show my face after being shot down by a grandfather in a duct-taped museum piece."

The room quieted. No one laughed.

"That pilot happened to be Général Felix Airiee, Commander of DAOS Special Forces Aviation," hissed Faisson, turning his back and clinking two polished metal spheres in his hand.

"I-I-I am sorry, sir. I did not know."

"*And* my closest friend from the Académie."

"Général, I'm quite sure he didn't mean anything," Laval offered.

"I'll be the determiner of that."

Brigadier Général Henriot, the young man's intel commander, came forward from the smoky shadows. "Sir, I will deal with him. Please leave him to me."

"How noble, Julian, but why aren't you dealing with Snoopy here, the rogue pilot that seems to be everywhere?"

"What would you like to know?"

"His name. His unit. His location."

"Général, we have no databases with that kind of information."

"THEN MAKE ONE!"

"To hunt down one man? How?"

"Read the paper," advised Chack.

Faisson whipped around to the sous lieutenant as Henriot sat him in a chair in the back. "No. I think he's right," said the brigadier. "The Middle States' papers love to report on SF victories, especially ones as major and as spectacular as these. They probably know him by name."

"You consider the American's victory *spectacular*, Julian?"

"Yes, based on this pilot's skill and valor, he has inflicted an inordinate amount of damage on us."

"Now this pilot is *valiant*, too?"

"I am not quite sure what it is you want me to say, sir."

"There is no such thing as a *skilled* American, general."

"But Commander Faisson, we already have record of him—"

"They are never honorable, they are never valiant."

"You are saying this pilot is just lucky, sir?"

"And reckless!"

Henriot's toes squirmed in his boots. Drops of sweat beaded on his forehead and dripped into his eyes. "With all respect, général, it would be detrimental to underestimate—" Before he could finish his sentence, something flashed in the air at him. Henriot ducked but not before two silver balls came at him, connected by a fine platinum chain that encircled his neck twice. Faisson gave a yank on its tether, sending a thousand diamond-hard nano-machined teeth racing around the garrotte and into the brigadier's flesh.

"Général, please, get this off!" The brigadier could feel the sting of the cuts. He choked as his fingers dug frantically at his neck.

Faisson jerked the ballistrae again, sending the links whirring like a dentist's drill. "*We* are on the offensive. The victories are ours, understood?" swore Faisson. Henriot's eyes bugged out. "Sometimes, one of their pilot is lucky, that's all." The chain tightened further, drawing blood. Henriot nodded spasmodically. "If you ever equate these Sovereign prairie-niggers with respectability again, I will sit you on a pole until you impale yourself." The intel officer fell to the floor as Faisson released the fetter. "Do I make myself clear?"

"Yes, Commander Faisson," croaked Henriot. "I will start immediately on the search for this pilot."

"Lieutenant, pack your duffle," Laval told Chack. "You will be very lucky to make it home with an honorable discharge."

Faisson drew up alongside. "Nonsense Phillipe. He is coming with me."

Laval recognized his general's grin. "No, sir. Please. I will see to his punishment."

"Tut tut," Faisson replied. "He just needs a finer grasp of the intricacies of the air war. I think a short tour with the Death Storks should do him some good."

"You mean a Rafale squadron?" grinned Chack. "Will I be able to ride in one?"

"Not *in* one," Faisson corrected, turning to the exit. "*Under* one."

CHAPTER 11
LETTER

The naked scientist stepped into the heated isolation tank for his first bit of rest in days. As he settled into the thermo-neutral saline, his brainwaves slowed from anxious beta to relaxed alpha, his limbs jerking involuntarily with each discharge of his tired nerves. Soon, he had drifted into a drowsy theta state, the time between meditation and sleep where daydreams stream by and the brain opens up to new ideas. Right before he dozed, he caught himself and pushed a thumb-switch, flooding the darkened room with the bright pulsating images of two-hundred television monitors hanging from the ceiling above him. Tanner had entered super-learning mode.

"IN WEST VIRGINIA TODAY THE ATF BROKE UP THE BIGGEST CIGARETTE RING IN HISTORY … HURRICANE AJAX JUST MISSED THE DOMINICAN REPUBLIC … MR. ANDERSON, YOU EXPECT THIS COURT TO LET YOU GET OFF SCOT-FREE … STIMPY, YOU EEDIOT … HOUSE SPEAKER LYNNDIE ENGLAND TODAY CHASTISED THE ADMINISTRATION FOR ITS ATTEMPT TO ABOLISH VISAS … ISRAEL HA CONVENIDO UN MES QUE SE REFRESCABA DE PERÍODO … RALPH, YOU COME HERE THIS INSTANT OR I'M NEVER GOING TO SPEAK TO YOU AGAIN … "

News, sitcoms, documentaries and quiz shows all competed for Aboud's attention in thirty different languages as concepts and projects and inventions started linking in his subconscious. He didn't know how the assimilation worked. He couldn't pick a program out of the cacophony if he tried. He just knew however the process operated, he owed most of his ideas to it.

"Hey Leper! You in here?" Spider banged on the door and barged in.

Aboud jumped up and flooded the floor with water.

Spider turned on the lights and gazed up at the overhead mural in wonder. "Wow! A jumbotron for the bedroom."

"I am not here."

Trent picked up a remote from one of the equipment racks and toyed with it until he got *The Simpsons*. "I've been sent to get you."

"Not now. I am in resting."

"Yeah, I can tell."

"Everyone is differing. This is how *I* relax."

"Well, relax later. You're needed."

"I have done all that General Woody told me to do," pouted the doctor. "The labs are stocked, the equipment fabricated and tested. All his projects are staffed and on-schedule. I am not needed anymore."

"Can you possibly get *any* more silicone into that lower lip, Angelina?"

Tanner pulled his lip, straining to see. "The general is not letting me fight. He just wants me for my mind."

"You sound like a jilted lover."

"I am not going to be used anymore."

"All right! I'm just saying—" Before Spider could finish, a knocking could be heard coming from the wall. It started as a faint tapping before crescendoing into a violent hammering. In seconds, the concrete block reverberated with a deafening thud as a hole exploded in the wall and TVs and glass came crashing to the floor.

Tanner barged dripping wet into the motor shop where soldiers from 122SCOUT were training on his equipment. He wiped a towel across his bleeding cuts before tying it around his waist. "Avaazi! Kar! Be tokhmam!"

"English please, professor." Captain Kim Smiling Bear had his head in the wall, inspecting the fresh hole. He was company commander of the scouts, a unit of Menominee Indians from Shawano, Wisconsin, that specialized in tracking and infiltrations.

"What are you doing? You are worsening!"

"Sorry, doctor. We're still trying to figure out the range." The other scouts crowded around peering at the damage and ribbing their gunner.

"Uh, oh. You're in for it now, Randy."

"Yeah, you blew up Haji's chemistry set."

"Watch out. Kato's going to start throwing his ninja stars now."

A modified HMMWV dominated the middle of the shop floor. Cables and test racks littered the floor as a four-foot POP array stood tall on its roof. Randy Shining Fox occupied the turret, beating his keyboard. "If you had made this like an Xbox, I wouldn't be having a problem, doctor. There's just too many knobs and trackballs and shit."

Aboud hopped up, nudging the native aside and taking over the effects director. "Six steps, remember? First, slew to your quad. Then, do a quick-acquire. Once the arc is mapped, designate, lase and fire. The computer does the rest."

On the far wall, beside the smoking hole, stood a line of target dummies. Tanner pivoted the turret so the large antenna faced them. "You need not aim the array precisely."

"I don't?"

"See your sergeant over there to the side? The signal can make it over to him. It is steered electronically."

A red laser-dot appeared on the man's chest as the effects generator began humming. "Hey, what are you doing?" Under the sergeant's shirt, a bubble of air appeared and ripped a hole in the fabric as it burst with a loud *pop*! "OWWW!" The noncom flew backwards and landed on his rear.

"Ha-ha," laughed a corporal. "Pershie showed you!"

Aboud twirled another knob. "The microwaves work on the nerves so you can vary the effects." He fired the circuit and sent an invisible bolt to the corporal.

"Hey stop! It's burning!" he yelled, falling to the floor beside his sergeant and fanning his bathing-suit area.

As the rest of the platoon gathered around the two men, laughing, they looked down at their legs where laser dots danced on their knees. "Hey, what's that?" They tried brushing the specks off as the array focused its beams. The weapon charged, then lurched, sending the soldiers to the ground with a sound that reminded Aboud of cracking knuckles. He powered down the device.

"Impressive," said Smiling Bear. "It not only engages multiple targets, but you can also tell it what parts of the body to hit."

"And the type of pain effect you want," added the scientist. "Heart attack, acid, numbness."

"Think you've got it down, Randy?"

"No way, sir. I'm going to get someone killed."

"Then why don't you take Doctor Tanner?" Spider inquired of the captain.

"Me?" asked the Persian.

"Yeah, you want to see combat, don't you? And you're the only one that can play this thing, aren't you?"

"That is a true statement but—"

"So you *have* to go." Trent slapped Aboud's bare back.

"You are right. Captain, I *have* to go."

"You know we can't let you do that," said Smiling Bear.

"Then I am done training you."

"There's nothing I can do, doctor. General Patterson would never allow it."

"Then your mission will not succeed."

Smiling Bear shrugged his brick-house shoulders. "I guess we'll have to take our chances then. Guys, load up."

His men moaned, rolled to their feet and retrieved their rucks. As they were about to open the Hummer's gate and throw in their gear, the vehicle disappeared into thin air.

"What in Chief Oshkosh?"

"Can I go *now*?" Aboud asked the scout. He held up the shimmer remote as the captain scratched his head.

"I'll see what I can do."

"OK, men. As you know, this mission has us going deep into bad-guy territory, eighty klicks behind the LOC. This will be the furthest we've ever gone. But that's the way we like it, right?"

"TWISTED SISTER!" hooahed the soldiers.

Our mission is to insert Major Trent here and his crew chief, CW2 Fredrick, onto Hinckley airbase and support the safe withdrawal of a squadron of A-10s."

Spider was busily tapping on Aboud's folio in the back. He waved to the room as he whispered to Wade. "What am I doing here?"

"What do you mean?"

"This sounds too dangerous. I'm going to get myself killed."

"That doesn't cross your mind when you're getting shot at in the air?"

"That's different. Up there, I don't have to look anybody in the eyes before they kill me."

Smiling Bear pulled out a map. "We'll night-march to Mora and lay up there until just after dawn. Once we've changed into civvies and camoed the vehicles, we'll head to Hinckley on I-35. The Freemartins will be waiting. I'll have the Super-Hummer and do the final reconnoiter. Use that time to erect your shields. Expect a mid-day launch to minimize shadows."

"TWISTED SISTER!"

"You already know this mission has Quarterstaff visibility and they'll be on high-warble throughout. Just remember, they could've picked the Ojibway or the Chippewas, but they didn't. They picked us because we *kick ass*. So do your best and make your tribe shine!"

"TWISTED SISTER!"

"OK, let's get down to details."

"What are you writing?" asked Aboud.

"My Last Will and Testament," responded Spider. "I'm leaving you my cheesehead hat."

"I am lactose-intolerant." Spider snorted and kept tapping. "You are letter writing?"

"Just keeping a record," said the pilot. "I've been keeping track of my missions ever since the boneyard raid. In case anyone ever cares."

Aboud continued reading. "Who is Laura?"

"This is cool," Trent said, flipping through the computer's polymer I/O pages. "Can I have this? We don't even have Etch-a-Sketches in the MS."

"Laura is John's wife," Wade answered for him.

"They write often?"

"They haven't talked in two years."

"Because they are estranged?"

"No. Because intercept makes messaging too risky. The SF has clamped down."

"John, does your home have satellite or does it have cable?" asked Tanner.

Spider thought a moment. "Satellite, last I knew. Why?"

"Come with me."

The three snuck out of the meeting and ducked outside where the air lay cool and still under the North Dakota stars. Spider and Wade struggled to keep up as Aboud bounded through the cattle pens and feed lots of the faux ranch that served as cover for the Leper Colony.

"Ahh, home," said Wade, inhaling the smells from a nearby herd of Black Angus. The two followed Aboud into a silo. "What's in here?"

Aboud flicked a switch floodlighting a hole that descended into the ground twenty stories. "Missile erector. This will be where we play around with new propellants, countermeasures and physics packages."

"We're going down there?" asked Wade.

"Nope, up here." Aboud navigated his way to a spiral stairway hugging the silo wall and started climbing.

"I'm calling OSHA." said Wade with his back against the concrete, ten steps behind.

Aboud led them up the tube. When they reached the top, they ascended through three levels of computer rooms and communication consoles before coming to a steel-webbed observation deck. Around them, equipment hummed and panels blinked as a huddle of satellite dishes peered skyward under the silo's rounded radome. The scientist sat at a workstation and began typing.

"What are you doing?" asked Wade.

"Looking up John's credit report. His satellite provider should be listed."

"Don't you need my address or social security number?"

"You are kidding with me, correct?" Tanner inquired, speed-reading the scrolling pages. "There you are. You are on GoogleSat."

"*They* have TV service now?"

"You don't get out much, do you?" said Wade.

"Their footprint has been steered to the coasts. But we will not be receiving tonight, we will be sending."

"Sending? What?"

"Your letter. Google has three commsats in geosynchronous orbit: GS9, GS10 and GS11. Only GS9 is active, the others are parked right behind as backup. By bursting your file up to a spare transponder we can bounce it back without anyone knowing. This is how I sent secrets to the SF."

"Yeah, but *you* got caught."

Aboud reddened. "I did not get caught. I just got lazy."

"Doesn't NSA monitor all satellites?"

"Not backup satellites. Their transponders are off. I will turn one on for a brief millisecond or two before we transmit your letter."

"But won't this go out to the entire continent?"

"Yes, your file will be broadcast to every home in America but since I know your setbox address only your TV will be listening for it."

Spider thought of his promise to Woody. "No, I can't."

"What do you mean?"

"It sounds nice but it's against opsec."

"But you command your own detachment."

"Only Quarterstaff can waive opsec and they'd never do it. Especially for personal communication."

"But—"

"Thanks a lot, but I'm going to have to wait until the war's over."

"But—"

"But what?"

"But it is too late, John. It is on its way!"

~ ~ ~ ~ ~ ~ ~ ~ ~ ~ ~ ~ ~ ~ ~ ~ ~ ~ ~ ~

"Come on down, Cody. Dinner's ready," called Laura.

"Not hungry. Going out," came the reply from the upstairs.

"It's *spaghetti*."

"Not a noodle guy anymore, ma, remember? *Vegan*."

"I know. I remembered. I made it with squash."

"Not hungry!"

"Where are you going? When will you be back?"

"Not until morning," said Cody, downstairs now.

Laura startled. "What on earth is that?" Her son was wearing a white shirt, blue tie and blue baseball cap with his tattered elephant jeans and untied sneakers. She covered her mouth, laughing.

"You've never seen me in a tie?"

"Yes. When you were in Cub Scouts."

"This is my Cadet uniform," replied Cody. "I joined."

Laura's face drained. "You joined? Joined what? I didn't give you permission."

"I don't need permission. I'm an adult."

"You're not an adult. You're sixteen. You're still a child"

"Not according to—"

"I don't care what the law says. This is my house, you're my child, that makes me judge, jury and executioner around here."

"Then I'll just turn you in for domestic abuse."

"CODY RICHARD! You are dancing on my very last nerve. Now march right up those stairs and take off those ridiculous clothes. You are beginning to be as scary as that delinquent freak-of-nature friend of yours."

"You mean me, Laura?"

Cody moved aside to reveal his friend, Darren Taylor. The boy was hideous. Half his head and face was shaved clean straight down the middle, the other half sported a shaggy purple-dyed mullet and goatee. Even the eye-shadow and spiderweb tattoo on his adorned side was purple. He took off his glasses to stare at Laura through yellow-slitted catseyes.

Laura threw down her dishcloth. "Did you talk Cody into this nonsense?"

"Yo, Code. This your mom? She's *kingbitch* foxy."

"What did you say?" approached Laura.

Cody stepped between the two. "Knock it off, delinquent. That's my mom."

Taylor spied down Laura's shirt. "I said, nice dairy cannons, Laura."

Laura reached behind the refrigerator and brought out a plastic broom. She raised it and smashed the boy alongside his head.

"OWWW! OWWW! OWWW! My eye. My eye. You knocked a contact into my eye!"

Cody stepped aside as Laura kept beating Darren as he ran for the door. "You disgusting little cockroach. Get out of here and don't you ever come back, you hear me?"

"Whoa, mom!"

"And you. You! What would possess you to join a group that would accept the likes of him?" The broom came down again and hit Cody square on the nose.

"Mom. MOM!" Cody shrieked.

"You wouldn't be doing this if your father were here."

Cody stood bolt-upright and grabbed his mother's broom handle in mid-arc. "Well, the loser's *not* here."

"How dare you."

"He's not here and he's never coming back. Can't you get that through your mind or has he fucked you over so many times that you enjoy it now?"

Laura wrenched the broom free from her son's grasp and swung for the fence, not caring a whit if she hurt him. She missed wide as he ducked under the barrage, picked up his hat and made for the front lawn. She chased him as far as the porch. "You leave, don't ever bother coming back," she yelled, broom raised.

"I won't, don't worry," he spit back.

Her son hopped into Darren's blue cart and disappeared around the corner. All along her block, the neighbors were out, watching from their steps. She wondered if they were going to report her. They were supposed to. Instead, they started cheering and clapping. The exhibition of parental justice had startled them but they liked it. They wouldn't report her this time, but they would keep an eye out.

Laura turned back inside where she flushed dinner down the drain, poured herself a glass of shiraz and hunched over the counter, crying. The war was closing in. It had taken her husband, it had taken a friend, now it was taking her son. She felt her heart beat through her blouse but didn't know what to do. She downed her wine.

At least with John it had been different. At least she had known what she was getting into. She had known he was a man of war. Heck, she even liked it a little, to be truthful. It attracted her as well as repelled her. But not Cody. Cody was her baby. The only thing she had left. She wasn't going to lose Cody, she determined. She wasn't going to let the war win him over, too. She sat down to watch reruns of *What Not To Wear* as she spooned fudge syrup out of a jar. She got half-way through it when the screen went black.

> HEY, PUNKIE. IT'S ME. JOHN. IF YOU ARE ALONE, TYPE IN THE NAME OF THE MOVIE WE SAW ON OUR FIRST DATE.

She picked up the remote and clicked it. Then again, but the message remained.

John? Who John? What John? *Punkie?* That's me. Her eyes filled with tears as bits of her old life, a life that had laid atrophying in her brain, came flooding back. She typed out the word *TOPGUN* then mashed the enter button.

> 0150Z21MAY1. DAY 598. TODAY, FACED DEATH AND WON. AGAIN. RIPPED PIERRE'S HEAD OFF HIS SHOULDERS AND SHIT DOWN HIS LUNGS. KILLED MANY SUNDRY DIRTBAGS. SINGLE-HANDEDLY SAVED THE MS.

Laura's mouth hung open as she put down her jar. It *was* John. He was alive and sending her a message. On the TV. Her John. She could tell because she could hear him as she read. How was it possible? How did he get in her TV? Was he back? There was more.

> FIRST SORTIE, DAWN PATROL: GOT TAPPED COMING OVER THE LOC. MIRAGES PICKED US OUT OF THE WEEDS. REALLY, THEY PICKED THREE OUT. OM STILL HAVING TROUBLE FLYING TREETOP.

Sorties? Mirages? Is he flying? "*Are you flying again?*" she railed at the set. "I thought you were training in Arizona. How can they let you fly? You're *fifty* for God's sake."

> ME AND TWO PUKED OFF OUR RACKS BEFORE WE GOT TO THE TARGET. WE COULD HAVE MADE IT BUT JUST AS WELL. CEMENT AGAIN. CLEARED THREE AND FOUR TO ENGAGE. THEY GAVE AN EYE-WATERING BAT-TURN AND LET LOOSE WITH

> THE GUN. MISSED BUT SHOOK THOSE FROGS
> UP. FOUR WAS OUT OF POSITION SO THEY PAD-
> LOCKED ON HIM. ONE OF THEM SAT THERE LIKE
> A GRAPE. SHANK TURNED INSIDE HIM TOOK HIS
> TIME AND GOT HIS FIRST MORT. HE DID GOOD.
> BETTER THAN ME.

Laura sat on the edge of her coffee table and read more, remembered his inflections, recalling the way he talked when the squadron came over.

> SECOND MISSION. GOOD NEWS! LIVE MUNITIONS. DE-
> CIDED TO GO FOR BROKE AND TAKE ALL THIS IRON
> INTO CAMP RIPLEY. THE BELLY OF THE BEAST. A TANK
> GARRISON. OM WAS STILL TOO HIGH BUT HE HAD
> GOOD BOMBS. WENT IN UNDETECTED. LECLERCS
> AND APCS. AT LEAST BRIGADE STRENGTH. TWO AND
> FOUR TOOK OUT A COMPANY EACH. I DID TOO. NICE
> TO SEE EXPLOSIONS AGAIN. MORE DEAD FRENCH-
> MEN MEANS AM CLOSER TO SEEING YOU AGAIN.

She aimed the remote and hit rewind. "You're what? You're killing people so you can see me?"

> NO TIME TO SWITCH TO GUNS BEFORE SAMS
> STARTED FLYING. I MUST HAVE BEEN MAGNE-
> TIZED. TOOK A HIT IN NUMBER ONE. HAD TO STEP
> OUT OF THE JET NEAR STAPLES. I AM ABLE TO
> WRITE YOU TODAY THANKS TO QUICK PICKUP BY
> PARARESCUE.

The scrolling halted.

"Staples? Camp Ripley? "Why you ass. You're in Minnesota? All this time when I'm thinking you're dead and you're not even a hundred miles away!" Laura's shoulders sank into feelings of betrayal.

> PS AM RISKING YOUR SAFETY BY SENDING YOU
> THIS BUT COULD NOT GO ANOTHER DAY WITH-
> OUT TALKING TO YOU. AM OK BUT MISS YOU

DESPERATELY. I KNOW WHAT YOU ARE GOING THROUGH ALONE. YOU ARE STRONG AND COURAGEOUS FOR KEEPING THE FAMILY GOING. BUT NOW YOU MUST THINK OF LEAVING. IT IS GETTING TOO DANGEROUS TO STAY. I UNDERSTAND YOUR REASONS FOR NOT COMING BUT NOW IS THE LAST CHANCE. THINGS ARE CHANGING FOR THE WORSE. PLEASE SAY YES. GO SEE ELIJAH ON HIS BIRTHDAY. PACK ONE BAG FOR EACH OF YOU. HIT DELETE WHEN YOU ARE DONE READING THIS. I NEED YOU.

"You're not thinking of going to him are you?" asked Cody.

Laura jerked up. Cody had been behind her the whole time. "How dare you sneak up on me."

"You're not going, are you?"

"I thought you had to be on patrol or something?"

"I had to take Darren to an aid station. I wanted to come back and tell you I was sorry."

Laura softened. "How much did you read?"

"Most of it," he replied. "Answer me."

"Am I going? I ... I don't know." Laura fell back into the sofa. "I'm tired, Cody. Tired of holding us together. Tired of being alone, of not knowing. Tired of this ... war."

"So why go to him if you're tired of the war? He started it. He's the one killing Peacebuilders. You'll reward him by going. He's a traitor of the world. A racist nationalist."

"Your father is *not* a traitor."

"But mom, you're the one who told me he was."

"I know. I know I did. That was before. Before all these ... "

"These what?"

"Demonstrations, news shutdowns, the night roamings. Sam, at work's been taken. The Gross' down the street, from the paper, gone. Mrs. Fredrick. The UN soldiers. The UN flags. YOU!"

"But that's all necessary. To keep the peace."

"Says who? Where are you learning this?"

"International news. School. There has to be support for the government or there'll be anarchy. If the Sovereigns take over the country, we'll be sent back to Stonehenge."

"He saw all this coming."

"He saw it coming because he created it." His mother stared blankly off into space. "Mom, tell me you're not thinking of going. Not after he left us."

"Honey."

"He abandoned us. He left you. Me. It's always been something. Something else more important. Flying. Moving. Unaccompanied tours. Staff schools. The farm. When did *we* ever matter that much to him? When was the Air Force or farming ever put on the back burner for us?"

"Cody."

"Well, you can go to him. You can leave me, too. I don't care. I've got my own duty now. My own family. The Cadets and the UN. At least they'll always be here. Not like my traitor father."

"I told you not to talk about him that way."

"That's the way you talk about your husband!"

Laura's chin quivered. John's parting had not gone well. The farewell had been acrimonious and bitter when he left and it continued to fester in her long after he had gone. It was the first time she had not followed him and it was the longest they had ever been apart. She hadn't known if he was alive or dead. She was angry he hadn't contacted her. She knew why now. She also knew he was alive. A blast of guilt blew over her and she cried into a cushion.

Cody made a move to his mother. He wanted to sweep her in his arms and comfort her, but was too young to know how to cross the gap that stood between them. Instead, he did what came natural, what he had seen his father do countless times before. He turned and left.

CHAPTER 12
BRAGGING

Cody sat stupefied under the copper glow of the National Guard Armory lights. Sitting alongside, Cody's sponsor kept playing with his eye-patch while a dozen bleachers below, Cadetmaster Andy Walsh roamed the auditorium floor, addressing his new recruits.

"There were twenty-three in my class when I came in," whispered Darren Taylor, playing with his new eye patch. "Now there must be a hundred, hundred fifty."

"Ssshhh."

"Welcome to Cadet Warren 507. My name is Andy Walsh and I am commander of this unit. We serve under Warren Colonel Lamirand who also commands Cottage Grove's border agents, gendarmes and Milice. Provost Marshal Déat in Duluth is responsible for all the warrens in Minnesota. He reports to the French-UN commander General Faisson who is part of UNIFUS Force Command. From this organizational chart, you can see just how much the UN relies on community; we are only a few levels away from Secretary-General Zzgn himself."

"When do we get paid," asked a seventeen-year-old with a tongue tattoo.

"Son, you don't get paid for training. That would attract a flood of applicants who have no intention of joining."

"Do we get guns?" asked another.

"I want a scooter. These cadet carts are gay."

"Please, let me continue. I know many of you are here because you feel appalled at the prosperity and affluence you were raised in. You feel a duty to give back to the world. I know some of you have been sent here by parents who wish to shape you up and instill some discipline. And I know still others that are here to satisfy conditions of your parole. No matter what your background or what your motivation, I am here to tell you we don't accept just anyone. There will be tests and there will be standards to meet and I will be the final judge. If you are accepted, after completion of training, I will assign you to a patrol of eight cadets. You will be the eyes and the ears of the mission in Cottage Grove and the surrounding townships.

"Now, a little about training. We will introduce you to your restraints and defensive devices and teach you how to use them when subduing others. There will also be classroom study in UN doctrine and regulations. You will also be required to know proper communication procedures and chain-of-command before being let out on practice patrols. All this should be in your packets."

"What do you mean, *subdue others*"?

"Your jobs will evoke strong reactions in people. You will be approaching firearm owners, collecting guns, listening in on WiFi and cellphone conversations, monitoring chat rooms. You will need to know how to defend yourselves in these situations until help arrives."

"Are you going to feed us?" asked a Lumpy a few rows up.

"Yes, the UN provides you with uniforms, meals and lodging during your training, which brings me to our next item, room assignments."

"You didn't tell me we were sleeping here," Cody said.

"It's just for two weeks," replied Darren as he counted females. "Ugh. What a bunch of arm-biters."

"We will be assigning you two-to-a-room. Due to your young age, there will be a larger than normal representation of homosexuals, transgenders and transvestites among you. I need not remind you these individuals are a protected class under the UN's new Dependence and Alignment policies. If there is anyone who objects to sharing accommodations, tell me now."

Nobody moved.

"Good. We'll start alphabetically then."

Cody raised his hand. "You can treat me for shock if you think I'm sleeping with any queers."

The gym fell silent but only for a moment as a whole slew of new hands went up.

"Me neither."

"Count me out, I'm not sharing a room with no rump ranger."

"Not no. *Hell*, no!"

The auditorium erupted in a mini-revolt as the cadet leaders ran around calming the applicants and recalculating room assignments. The commotion earned Cody and Darren three hours of detention in the video training room.

"That was stupid, Code."

"I got my roommate preference, didn't I?"

"Yeah, but it also earned us four DVDs worth of Sensive Dyn ... Sensitive Din ... "

"Sensitivity Dynamics for Under-Represesented Groups."

"Yeah. It was cool though. Wish I'd done that when I went through." Taylor watched as Cody fiddled with the TV remote. "Hey, Johnson's lab down the road just had pups. Wanna go tazer 'em?"

"No."

"What are you doing?"

"I'm trying to get the Discovery Channel."

"You're hacking their TV?"

"I've got an infrared emulator in my mobe. I'm trying to get the remote to teach it so I can get into the cable menu."

"Discovery Channel?"

"Yep, it's Insect Survivor Week. Tonight it's African Siafu Ants against Brazilian Wolf Spiders."

"You exceptional or something? You're beginning to sound like a prep boy."

"No, delinquent. You a faggot? You slept with one." Taylor dug at his new nose stud that was starting to turn green. "Hell with it," said Cody. "It's not working anyway."

"Yeah, let's get out of here and light up a bogie."

Cody checked the corridor then followed Taylor out the emergency exit. They wandered the periphery of the armory until they found a corner that was light- and camera-free.

"Let's get our tongues forked," said Taylor. "It's supposed to be really Blair-Witch with the ladies."

"Naw, don't have the money," answered Cody. "Maybe after I get a few UN paychecks under my belt."

"So what did you do when you went back home?" asked Taylor. "Eat a taco from Mom's Cafe?"

Cody stubbed his cigarette out in Taylor's arm. "Shut the hell up about my mom, camel-face!" Taylor swore under his breath as Cody got up to leave. "I'm out of here. I've had it."

"Why?"

"This whole thing is lame. The cadets, the training, *you*."

"Don't go. I won't say anything anymore."

"This is so stupid. Everybody's a bunch a no-minds. They bleat like little sheep and do everything these jerk-offs say. I'm a grown-up. I want to be treated like an adult. I mean, look at this uniform. It's for kids."

"Just stay for now. Tell me again what you did at home?"

"I went back to get some cash. When I got there, mom was reading a letter from my father."

"Your father? He's in the MS. Gonna report it?"

"No. Mom would get in trouble."

"Do you have it with you?"

"The letter? No. Somehow, he sent it over satellite. It was on the TV."

"Très cool."

"Yeah, he wrote about one of his missions. How he took out a bunch of French tanks at Camp Ripley. He got shot down, but I guess he ejected OK."

"Isn't your dad a near-dead? I thought he was old."

"He flew A-10s when I was little. They must be hard-up over there because they got him flying again. The Warthog. You know, those tank-buster jets. Took 'em all out. Capped their ass."

"You sound like you're getting off on what he did. Like you're bragging almost."

"No I'm not. I hate his guts."

"Why haven't you ever talked about him before?"

"We haven't heard from him in two years. He's a failure as a father and while he's murdering Peacebuilders in the MS, we have to live with the humiliation back here. That's why I'm joining the cadets. To make up for him."

Cody kept talking as another chain smoker appeared from around the corner. He was solidly built, wore tan pants, blue epaulettes and a blue beret. He sported a small soul patch on his chin and his nametag said *LAVAL*.

Cody blew out a long stream of smoke at the jerk and played tough for his friend. "Hey, trumpet-ears, you earjackin' us OK or should we speak louder for your hearing aid?"

The lieutenant looked the boys over as if they were scabs that needed to be picked. His face momentarily brightening in his cigarette's glowing ember and then he was gone.

"Fucking boy scout."

"You did it now, Code. That was an officer. You just jumped off on a lieutenant. *Now* we're dead."

From the window above, they heard men arguing. One yelling, the other pleading. There was a struggle and furniture crashing then a thud, like a bowling ball hitting the floor.

"I'm getting the hell out of here," said Taylor.

"Me, too."

They both puffed their cigarettes down to the filters, tossed their butts and ran around the corner and into Laval. Over his shoulder, they watched flounder-eyed as General Faisson exited the Warren Colonel's office.

"Do not disappoint me like Lamirand," he said, talking to someone inside. "You let one more spy through your crossing and I will put your head on a pike. Now clean up this mess."

"I've seen him before," whispered Taylor. "He's on TV. Look at his ribbons and those stars on his shoulders!"

"I know. It's Commander Faisson."

"So, Phillipe, which one of your little friends is the sympathizer?" Faisson queried, joining his aide.

Laval pointed to Cody. "This one, sir."

Taylor's lone yellow eye turned round in the dark as he broke free and made for the parking lot. Laval drew his sidearm and fired into the air causing the teen's baggy jeans to slide down his hips and tangle around his feet. The lieutenant walked over, picked him up by his purple hair and hustled him back to the building.

"I didn't do anything. It was him," Taylor accused. "He's the symp. His father's in the SF. I was just trying to get more information from him."

"Is this true?" asked the general. "Your father is in the SF?"

"Y-y-yes, sir."

"And he is a pilot?"

"Yes, sir. A-10s, sir."

"The one responsible for the loss of my tanks at Camp Ripley?"

Cody nodded.

"I just found out, sir," Taylor whimpered. "I was just getting ready to turn him in, Mr. Faisson. Honest!"

"And yet, despite this shameful travesty of parentage, you are still courageous enough to reject your upbringing and join the cadets, the side of Right?"

Cody stared, not knowing what he meant. He jerked his head.

"I admire your convictions." The general smiled. "What is your name?"

"Cody, sir. Cody Trent."

Faisson wrapped an arm around the teen's shoulders. "Well, Cody, I like you. I can always use a man of your abilities. I'd like you to join my security detail. Can I count on you to accept?"

"Is this something good? I … I don't know."

Faisson laughed loudly at Cody. "Why, yes. Frankly, it is very good. You get to skip the mediocrity of the cadets and climb right up to the rank of aspirant, one step below a lieutenant."

"Wow! Yes sir, I would."

"Excellent," Faisson said, taking his aide's FAMAS. "All of my guards are armed. Here is yours."

"What do I do with this?"

The general took hold of Taylor's hooped earring and ripped it out, a chunk of lobe coming off with it. "Your first act of authority? Show me what we do with venial backstabbing vermin like this."

CHAPTER 13
RAID

Twisted Sister had to hump it to stay on schedule. The team worked vigorously to convert four khaki-green HMMWVs into four colorful civilian H1 Hummers, but progress was slow in the dim quonset as. In the middle of the activity, a rickety hunched man in WWII dress stood blinking at the preparations around him.

"This is a bradley museum you got here, sir." Michael Broken Claw, the scout's radioman, marveled at the helmets and boots and uniforms displayed in glass cases lining the walls. He reached into one and hefted out a glittering golden dagger. "You really get this off of Goering?"

The man stood in his baggy uniform and medals and didn't answer.

"Corporal, you done checking the radios?"

"No, sir," Broken Claw replied to Smiling Bear. He replaced the weapon and turned to go back to work. "Why you doing this, old man? You can get in a lot of trouble if you're caught helping us."

The veteran said nothing and instead lifted a sleeve to reveal a blue 4356678 tattooed to the inside of his wrinkled translucent wrist.

The HMMWVs had come in dirty and wet after picking their way through the moonless swamps and watersheds of rural backcountry Minnesota. The men hustled, cleaning them and getting them in showroom shape for their undercover trip north to Hinckley. Wade unrolled a smoked-copper decal and applied it to a door.

"Wow! Looks brand-new," said Spider, polishing the hood.

"I took body shop in tech school. I was going to be a body-shop tech until dad needed help with the farm," Wade replied, squeegeeing out the bubbles. "What do you think?"

"Should look like any other Hummer on the road. Except for the crappy upholstery."

Finished, the soldiers packed away their fatigues and put on cargo shorts and Hawaiian shirts. A few of them hitched jetskis while Smiling Bear put on the finishing touch; *MSSUCKS* license plates and *Give the Middle States the Middle Finger* bumper stickers. "We're in the XUS. We want to belong, don't we?"

The convoy pulled out of the secluded hideaway, waving goodbye to their stooped host as they drove north on dusty, gravel roads. Within a half-hour, the commandos were on the interstate heading for their lake cabin just like the rest of the vacationers.

"Hey, hey, hey. A Mickey Ds! Aren't we going to stop? I haven't had a burger in months."

"How are you going to pay, Randy?"

"I still have dollars."

"Grab an MRE like everyone else."

"Awww, boss. There's no special sauce!"

Smiling Bear's vehicle led the convoy. Spider, Aboud and Wade—dressed like Jimmy Buffet, Apu and Magnum—occupied the cargo seat, while four riflemen sat in the back. In front, Broken Claw drove as Smiling Bear petted Radar, the team's mascot.

"I like the beagle," said Aboud, leaning forward to get his face licked. "Nice touch."

"Yeah, but why stop with the dog?" insisted Broken Claw. "If we're really on vacation, there should be women."

The scouts in back chanted, "Women! Women! Women!" while Smiling Bear reached over and snatched the cigarette hanging from his driver's mouth. He stamped it out with his sandal. "Keep it down, animals."

Wade stared out his smoked glass window. "We're home, John. Abby, Laura, the farm. They're only an hour back that way."

"I know, big guy, but we can't think about that right now."

"After the mission, I'm going back. I won't stay long. I just want to tell Abby I'm all right."

Smiling Bear turned. "We all have family here, Wade. You've just got to stay focused."

"But I never said goodbye."

"We do uncon behind the lines all the time," explained the native. "When someone decides to get homesick, that's when people die. We'll get home, but we have to do it the right way, by ganking the bastards first. Then we can see our families."

Wade appealed to Spider. "You don't really need me after this. I'll just be gone a couple of days. Then I'll be back. Promise."

"Knock it off, Chewie. You're not going anywhere."

"I knew we shouldn't have brought you three weak dicks along." Smiling Bear reached inside his shirt and pulled out his automatic, pointing it at Wade. Just as quickly, Wade wrenched the gun around while yanking the man's trigger finger backward. Smiling Bear and Wade continued to struggle until Wade managed to reach around the front seat and twist the Indian's head in the opposite direction. Smiling Bear screamed out in pain as Aboud put up his hands.

"Wade. Stinking Bear. STOP! You're going to shoot my dog."

"You going to be OK? Are you still able to lead?" the Freemartin inquired of Smiling Bear as he glassed Hinckley aerodrome from their staging point to the south. The resistance fighter was concerned. He didn't want the scouts captured and didn't want his network rolled up. While he wasn't in command of the mission, he could pull his men at any time if he thought there was a chance they'd be exposed.

"I'm fine," Smiling Bear answered, taping his finger and waving the Freemartin off dismissively. He stared across the farm yard at Wade. Wade stared back at him as he went about stripping the vehicles of their camouflage.

Bravo, Charley and Delta reported in. The teams were established at their staging points around the field and were proceeding with cloaking. Smiling Bear took the glasses from the partisan. "What about the control tower?"

"It's taken care of," the Freemartin replied. "The shift supervisor is one of us."

"It's too high. Won't they be able to see over our screens?"

"They'll never notice. They're too busy with traffic. Casino airports are the busiest in the world."

"What about the sliders?"

"In this overcast? You won't see them until they pop their chutes."

Aboud stood on his HMMWV, rigging the last of the eight-foot shimmer screens. When he was done, everyone crawled into their seats through the side slits. "Watch this." Tanner clicked his remote and the Humvee disappeared.

"Holy shit," swore the Freemartin. "Where'd it go?"

"We're still here," said Wade, from inside. "It's just see-thru, that's all."

The soldiers gathered around, feeling for their doors as Smiling Bear gave the *saddle-up* signal.

The Freemartin gathered up all the discarded decals and burned them along with the soldier's beachwear. He felt around for the vehicle, not sure if it had left yet as, in the distance, a dismembered hand waved to him from the air. The partisan pulled out his radio and made a call. "Rocky. This is Bullwinkle. Fight's on."

It took two nerve-racking hours for the cloaked vehicles to converge on the Hinckley airbase from their staging points in the surrounding fields. Though their approach left a definite path through the tall cornfields, the parting stalks were too indistinct under the cloudy sky for anyone to notice.

"We've got movement. Outside the fence. One hundred yards straight ahead."

"This is asinine," whispered Spider, his legs dancing a jig. "I'm sure they can see us."

The HMMWV stopped and waited. Trent had no idea what was going on. The screens blocked the view of everyone but the driver. Everyone was on edge, guns ready, waiting for the shooting to start.

"Awesome," said Broken Claw. "They're driving right by."

The radio sparked. "Bravo's set."

"Copy that," Smiling Bear whispered in reply.

"Charlie. In position."

"Delta's good-to-go."

The captain acknowledged them with a quick double-key as the

Humvee got rolling again. For the next several minutes, the team made steady progress until arriving just shy of the Perimeter Road. Sirens began to wail and Security Police vans fanned out looking for their position.

"What'd you just do, corporal?"

"I don't know," fretted Broken Claw. "We must've broke a beam or something."

"Alpha's engaged! Alpha's engaged! Go weapons hot!" radioed Smiling Bear. To his front, four black SP vehicles drew up inside the fence, disgorging their occupants. The captain turned and put a hand on Aboud's knee. "Is this the action you were looking for, doctor?"

Aboud hugged his pistol and nodded vacantly.

"Then get up there. It's your show now."

Aboud kept nodding and remained frozen to his seat.

Wade shook him. "Aboud. Doctor Tanner." He unbuckled from his seat and gathered up his rifle. "Damn. He's not made of very tough stuff. I've got it."

"You've got what?" moaned Spider. "You don't know how to work that thing."

"I've watched him enough times. I think I can shoot it." Wade climbed into the turret and raised the POP array. To the airbase policemen looking on from the tarmac, the weapon looked like a big black roadwork sign that floated in midair.

"You need to ram the fence," Wade barked. "The effects won't make it through the metal links. Ram the fence!"

"Gun it!" yelled Smiling Bear.

The SPs watched as their fence bent over as if hit by a heavy invisible squall. They waved their rifles back and forth, not knowing where to shoot. Wade powered up the effects director just as one of the shimmer curtains snagged on a fence post. It pulled away from the vehicle as it drove forward, revealing the commandos inside.

"Everyone out!"

The police opened fire as the scouts rolled into a drainage ditch.

"What's going on up there?" Spider bellowed as Fredrick pecked his way through the keyboard commands with his index finger.

Tanner pushed into the turret before the big man could answer and shoved him aside. He slewed the antenna to the knot of SPs as the processor computed its aimpoints. When the microwave elements had charged, Aboud fired, chopping the guards to the ground with a noise like snapping bubble-wrap.

The scouts peeked out of their revetments and cheered. "Tan-ner! Tan-ner!"

"Where the hell's air assault?" cried Smiling Bear, searching the skies for his paratroopers. He kicked his way through the heap of unconscious policemen and felt goosebumps on his neck. He turned in time to see Wade fire his M-16 at him from atop the turret. "I'm going to kill you, crazy-ass!" the Indian yelled, ducking and rolling as bullets folded the air over his head. He sprung up with his rifle ready to fire on Wade as a base policeman thudded to the ground behind him, an M-16 in his hand.

"You might want to tune that thing a little better," Wade told Aboud. "They're starting to wake up."

"Looks like the chief saved your life," Broken Claw reported to his captain.

Blood was seeping from the guard's ears. Spider bent over him. "This is a GI, Wade. We only kill our own guys if it's the last resort."

Wade walked up and took off the man's headpiece, a small dent pressed into its front. "Helmet shot. Just gave him a bad headache, that's all."

Smiling Bear saddled up to Spider and Wade as they prepared for the next stage of the raid. "I'd love to thank you and cry on your shoulder and everything, but we've got a job to do. Get to your plane and let's get cranking."

Wade waved as the officer walked away. "You're welcome."

Spider left the bickering soldiers behind as he made for the flightline. It had been a while since he had seen so many fighter jets in one place, so many fierce warriors, cast in iron and awaiting their orders. These were the 23rd Flying Tigers, a squadron whose bloodline stretched back to the Pacific, a pedigree filled with heroic exploits and glory. The 23rd was the Air Force's best-of-breed and the only unit entitled to sport the legendary shark teeth on their nose. Trent slowed as if on hallowed ground.

"Which one are we looking for?" asked Wade.

"I want the last Hog in the row. There."

"Why is it painted in all the fancy colors?"

"It's Gunnar's. The commander's jet." Trent entered the ramp with ease. With his flightsuit, helmet and g-suit, he looked just like any other squadron pilot walking to his jet with his crew chief. Over his shoulder, an SP van whizzed by, giving them no notice.

Two Flying Tiger pilots appeared up ahead. They were just returning from a sortie and were walking toward their operations building. They held up a hand barring Spider's way. "Whoa, sistah! Do we know you?"

Spider pulled out a badge. "Nope. I'm from 9th Air Force."

"You're here for the surprise inspection already? That's not supposed to be until *next* week."

"It wouldn't be a surprise if you were expecting it, now would it?" replied Trent.

The pilots looked at each other. "Wait right here while we call our opso."

Spider pointed to their name tags. "Martell and Jackson."

"Yes?"

He opened his checklist. "Says here you're not supposed to be evaluated until the end of our visit. But, hell, since I've got you here anyway, why don't we just fly your checkride now? Any problems with that?"

"Uhhh, no that's OK, major," said Jackson, looking at his wingman. "If we're not supposed to be tested until the end of the visit, there must be a good reason for it. Let's just leave it as is." The two pilots saluted and continued quickly on their way.

"You kill me," Wade said, following Spider to Colonel Gunnar's jet. When they had drawn near, they found a pilot just climbing down from the cockpit.

"This bird have any squawks I need to know about?" Spider hollered to the officer as he was descending the ladder.

"Nope, just a hot start this morning. I caught it before it overtemped."

Wade went around back to visit with the crew chief just as the flightline sirens sounded. Spider pulled out his Glock and pointed it at the pilot. "Now just be a good little zoombag," Trent ordered, taking the man's sidearm. "And I won't involve you in all this messy stuff. Just pick up your bag and head to the ops shack and don't look back."

The pilot nodded wide-eyed and started down the ramp.

"And here. Give this to Thor. Tell him it's from Spider."

Trent climbed into the cockpit as Wade hid the crew chief's body under a start cart. The security police were still at the perimeter engaging the four scout teams and had not yet discovered them.

"You ready to start?" asked Wade, on the intercom.

"Just get the override wired. I'll take care of starting the engines." Trent flipped on the APU, brought up a throttle and watched behind him as the fan blades slowly began to spin.

From the maintenance hangar on the far side of the airport, Spider eyed a contingent of SPs racing to reinforce the perimeter. Behind them, another wave of vehicles approached, colored white and UN-blue. "We've got company. I can't wait any longer. You done?"

"Yep, go!"

Spider gunned his engine and surged forward out of the row before swinging his nose left to aim it down the flightline. "Swine Ops, this is the Sovereign Forces. I am Major John Trent. Is your commander up?"

"Spider? That you?" came the radio reply.

"Hey, Thor. Long time. Welcome back to The World."

"What's this about, John?"

"Your SPs have surrendered and my UNCONs have sealed off the flightline."

Gunnar snorted. "You're senile, old man. What, pray tell, does the SF want with the Flying Tigers?"

"They want to ventilate your jets before they can be used against us."

Silence.

"However, since we're such good friends, you'll be glad to know that I talked them out of it," added Trent. "For the moment."

"I'm so happy. What's the catch?"

"We want you to defect."

"Defect?" repeated Gunnar.

"You and your pilots."

"*And* my jets?"

"Especially your jets."

"And you expect us to decide in just a few minutes?"

"Not a few. *One.*"

"One minute or what?"

"Or I vivisect your Hogs. Where they sit."

"I have thirty-two aircraft on the ramp. There's not enough time for your men to set charges on all of them."

"I don't need to, I've got a gun."

The commander laughed.

"Look out your window, Sven. That's me at the end. My finger's on the trigger."

"John, I know you've been out of the cockpit for a few years but the A-10 has a gun-override on the nosegear, remember? It can't be fired while the jet's on the ground."

Spider pointed to Wade underneath him. "That's why I brought my own crew chief. He specializes in rewiring squat switches." Wade waved to the pilots watching from the building.

"You're an ass."

"No, Sven, I'm your friend. I'm pleading with you. We need you."

"You're asking me to commit treason."

"You think I'm a traitor?"

"Of course, you broke your oath. All of you broke your oaths."

"Pull it out and read it again, my friend. Your oath of office requires two pledges," explained Trent. "First, to support and defend the Constitution against all enemies, foreign and domestic. And second, to obey the president. There's a reason one comes before the other."

"You're justifying your actions because of grammar rules?"

"The Framers knew man's nature. They knew men would come along who would try to usurp power. That's why they put the Constitution before the presidency."

"It's up to the president to determine who our enemies are," argued Gunnar. "And so far, he's considered the UN our friends."

"But what if *the president* is the enemy? What if he's *the domestic*?"

"Who's to say? Not me. Not you."

"The Constitution says. *That's* the vow we follow. And I'd argue we're following it more faithfully than you."

"I do what I'm told," said the spike-haired Norwegian said. "That's my job."

"Our job is to defend an idea, a country, a way of life. Not a person. People fail, ideals do not."

"You're losing me, Spider."

"Thor, you're going to be shooting your own people very shortly. Bombing your own citizens and friends. Have you thought that through yet?"

"*Et tu*, Spidey."

"The Sovereigns don't shoot their own countrymen. Even when they're supporting the Coax."

"Then why are two of my SPs dead?"

Spider strained to look behind him, to the fence where Smiling Bear should have still been fighting the SPs. "Shit, Sven. If they are, it was a mistake. We brought a device that was supposed to stun, not kill."

"Pretty stupid way to fight a war."

"That's probably why were losing." Spider scanned around. The base was unnaturally quiet. He checked his watch and swore. He had gone way over his time limit.

"You're on the wrong end of this, John."

"You going to give me an answer, Sven, or are you just running laps?"

"You're being way too idealistic."

"What's more idealistic than swearing to die for your county? Can't think of many professions that require your life."

"That's the same thing you said when they drummed you out the first time, isn't it?"

"Times up, Sven. What's it going to be?"

"The answer's *no*."

"Don't be a hardheaded Viking."

"Sorry."

"Don't do this, Thor. I've got a twenty riding on this with Woody."

"You should have thought about that when you talked him into this goat-rope."

"I'm serious, Sven. Once I pull this trigger, you can't change your mind."

"Do what you have to, Spider. Ops out."

Trent couldn't believe it. He had been wrong. He had misjudged his friend. For all the missions and beers and cigars and condos on the beach they had shared, he had figured Thor wrong. Woody committed to this mission based on his conviction. He didn't want to go back and face *that* humiliation.

Spider nudged his brakes and lined up on the parked A-10s. When he was sure he could hit both rows of aircraft with the minimum of steering, he grasped his stick grip and pulled the trigger.

Click! Nothing happened.

"Chewie! You sure you got the right wires?" Trent swept his instrument panel and rechecked his switches before trying again.

Click! Click! Click!

"What the fuck, over? What's going on?" Spider looked down for Wade and found him with his hands high over his head, a squad of SPs surrounding him. Just then, something tapped against his helmet. He turned to see a gun barrel pointed at his forehead.

"Sir, shut down your engine. You're under arrest."

Trent cut the engine, threw off his helmet and shook his fists to the sky. "*Disappointed!*"

Spider and Wade were ushered to the front wall of the auditorium where the scouts of Twisted Sister already stood. Everyone looked dejected with their wrists in bands and heads hanging. Gunnar and his entire squadron had shown up to witness the spectacle, reveling in the Sovereign's humiliation from the comfort of their high-backed theater seats.

"You'd rather fight side-by-side with the blueberries?" chided Spider. Gunnar passed a hand through his blonde flat-top as his security captain kept an M-16 trained on Trent. "You're just going to let them section us off piece-by-piece?"

"Don't beg them, major," spit Smiling Bear. "These chickenshits don't know the first thing about fighting. What good would they be to us in the MS?"

Gunnar laughed. "I'm not the one in handcuffs, bingo-monkey! Looks like you picked a bad day to stray off the reservation."

Smiling Bear's face went incandescent as he pushed off the wall and sprung into the air. He hung there for a moment, just long enough to jump through his handcuffs, before landing in a ball and knocking Gunnar to the floor. As he reached out for the squadron commander's neck, a hard metal object crashed into the back of his head, knocking him spread-eagle to the floor.

"So much for the Sovereign doctrine of brotherly love, Major Trent."

"Do I know you?"

The tall, sallow man holstered his gun and kicked the unconscious Indian down the aisle. Gunnar clambered back to his feet and introduced the new arrival. "John, this is General Faisson. He commands the entire French presence here in the U.S."

"So he's your boss, then."

Faisson ignored him. "No need to introduce yourself, major. Your exploits precede you."

"Oh, how so?"

"You seem to be everywhere in my dependency. You get around."

Faisson stepped up to the dais and offered his hand. Spider studied the man's face. He had a complexion like broccoli and his breath was garlicky and sour. Trent fanned the air with his bound hands. "Whew! Bad breath. You've really got to stay away from those urinal mints, general."

Faisson pulled out a folio and leafed through its pages. "John 'Spiderman' Trent. Fifty years old. Born in Racine, Wisconsin. Son of Paul and Jill. Last known occupation, farmer. Last known residence, Hastings, Minnesota. Married twenty-five years to Laura Paigle. Father of two sons, Jared and Cody."

Spider's smirk faded. "What have you told them, Sven? You give him my credit card numbers, too?"

The general continued. "A-10 pilot and commander of Hogsbreath Flight. Responsible for the murder of 127 unarmed Peacebuilders at Camp Ripley, Minnesota." Faisson turned and eyed Aboud. Aboud backed against the wall. "Abetting a known spy and assassinating a French multi-national commander in the process."

"How would you know that?"

"Oh, we know quite a bit about *Spiderman*. Most of it criminal and all of it contrary to the Geneva Conventions."

Gunnar raised his hands and showed Spider his palms. "I didn't tell him a thing, John. Honest."

"Unfortunately, that's true, major. But still, I need to know more."

"Treat me for shock if you think I'm telling you anything, toad-packer."

"No need volunteering. I employ special people for tough interrogations like this."

Spider reeled as Faisson approached. "You *really* need a Tic-Tac, general." The Parisian smiled then stepped aside, revealing one of his guards; an awkward shaggy-haired sixteen-year old. "Cody? What the hell are *you* doing here?"

"Hello, father."

"Faisson, you son-of-a-bitch!" Spider snarled then lurched for the Frenchman, but not before Gunnar shot him in the leg. The report made everyone jump as Trent fell, clutching his thigh.

Faisson turned back to the spectators and gave a single clap. "Colonel Gunnar! I am impressed. I have been testing your loyalties for some time now. Today you pass with flying colors."

Spider rolled on the stage in pain. "Cody! He hasn't hurt you, has he?" he rasped.

Cody instinctively reached for his father, then froze. "Are you OK, dad?"

"Touching," observed Faisson. "Now, if you will excuse me Colonel Gunnar, I will be taking the major and Doctor Tanner back with me to headquarters in Duluth. You may do as you wish with the others." A contingent of celeste blue guards marched in from the side door as the general grabbed his captives. He heard a gun action slam close from behind him and froze.

"Sorry, general. The major's staying here."

"Excuse me? What did you say?" Faisson turned to see Gunnar's pistol pointed at him.

"I need him. He's going to lead my squadron to the MS."

"Now you're going to take up his cause? You really think you'll make a difference? A couple dozen torpid A-10s against thousands of my SAMs. Against my Rafales and Mirages?"

"That doesn't scare us," deadpanned Gunnar. "What scares us is your women. They're hairier than you."

"You will not get far. I will have my fighters in the air before you can start your engines."

"Not if you're dead."

"Now why does that not surprise me, cowboy?" Faisson whipped out his arm sending a ballistrae out his sleeve and sailing toward Gunnar.

"Thor, watch out!"

Gunnar saw it sparkle and took a shot before holding his gun up for protection. The two spheres hit it, looping themselves around the barrel. He felt a yank and fought for control as the diamond-hard links sawed through the metal. "Get them. Don't let them get away!" The SPs raked the doorway with automatic rifle fire as the pilots ducked behind their seats for cover. The room filled with smoke. In one moment, Faisson was on the floor, bleeding. In the next, he and his guards were gone.

"What should we do, Colonel Gunnar?" asked the head of the security police.

"Take your men and hit the flightline. Try to head them off." Thor answered, bending down to cut Smiling Bear's bands. "Captain, can your men back them up?"

"The reinforcements need to be stopped first," said the Menominee, rubbing his head. Your men can back *us* up."

Gunnar turned to John Hampshire, one of his flight commanders. "Sleepy, get your guys suited up. We're going to the MS!"

At the front of the theater, Spider was still rolling back and forth, panting. "So, you were planning to defect all along?" he asked, through his clenched teeth.

Gunnar nodded, inspecting his lopped-off weapon. "We had plenty of time to think about it crossing the pond. Your little raid here just made it happen a little sooner than we planned."

"Then why this?" Spider pulled out a thick checklist from the thigh pocket of his flightsuit and fanned it to the page where his friend's slug lay.

"I didn't know how else to get the drop on Faisson without getting found out. His StanEval agents are everywhere."

"So you're really coming?" asked Spider.

"If you let us keep our shark's teeth," responded the squadron commander.

Trent rubbed his thigh, then hobbled over to hug his son. "You OK, Code? You hurt?"

Cody was in shock. He trembled and hugged back. "No dad. I'm OK. I think."

Spider looked up and combed the hair out of his eyes. "You've really shot up. Mom's been keeping you fed."

"Yeah, she has."

Trent took him all in and beamed. "We've got so much to talk about. So much to catch up on." Outside, on the ramp, gunfire erupted. "But, it'll have to wait. Let's get out of here."

On the tarmac, the Faisson's FUN troops were firing from their Sherpas, pinning down anyone who tried to leave the building.

"We're toast," announced Hampshire. "We're going to have to try and go around front."

"Wait, Sleepy. What's that?"

Just above the flightline, one-, two-, three-dozen white parachutes blossomed in the dreary sky like popcorn and landed behind the attackers.

"SLIDERS!" yelled Smiling Bear.

"What's a slider?"

"Single-Glider," bragged Aboud. "I designed them. They are paratroopers but fly like planes. They wear glider suits so they can be inserted at standoff ranges without arousing suspicion. They were dropped an hour ago out over central Minnesota."

Smiling Bear launched his counter-attack as the French turned to address the new threat behind them. "Twisted Sister. Now! Alpha and Bravo, follow me to the ramp. Charlie and Delta, take the SPs and provide security for the pilots."

The commandos poured out of the building as Spider addressed the pilots inside. "OK everyone, listen up. We've got five Blackhawks on the way. Two gunships and three slicks. Not much room. Thor, whoever's not flying a jet—maintainers, munitions, intel—we've only got space for your best. Pilots, I've got maps for each of you. Each four-ship will take a different route across the LOC. You won't be landing at a base. You'll all be landing at dispersed locations on interstates and highways."

Gunnar piped in. "Again, guys, remember, this is strictly volunteer. There is no right or wrong here. It's up to you and your conscience. But if you're coming, get your survival gear and let's beat feet. The president is sure to find out soon and he isn't going to pleased!"

As the pilots made a mad dash to their lockers, Gunnar turned to Spider. "No hard feelings?" he asked, patting Trent's thigh.

"Payback's a bitch, Sven."

"Thanks for hanging in there."

"Don't. I honestly thought you were going to hang us out to dry."

"Hey, I want you to take my jet," said the colonel.

"I can't."

"No, I'm serious. You take it. I'll go back on the choppers."

"I mean, *I can't*, Thor." He looked up at Cody. "*I'm* going back in the chopper. With my son. We've got a lot of catching up to do."

"I'm not going," said Cody, flatly.

"Yes, you are."

"Look at me," his son said. "I'm a French aspirant in a UN uniform."

"They put a gun to your head. You're not responsible for that."

"No, they didn't. I volunteered."

Spider's eyes narrowed.

"Is there going to be a problem, John?"

"No, of course not. Will there, Cody?"

"I hope all you fucking traitors crash on take-off!" the teen announced to the pilots. His father's fingers dug deep into his arm.

"How would you like a big fat steel-toed jump-boot up your ass?" Cody gave a wry smirk as Spider yanked him down the hall like a sock monkey and heaved him into the pilot's lounge. Trent slammed the door. "Who the hell do you think you're talking to back there? Your mall posse?" Spider put his nose into Cody's face and, for the first time he could remember, had to crane his neck upward. "What's all this backtalking crap? What's been going on these last two years? The last time I saw you you were designing your own weather station and playing all night with your chemistry set."

"Two years? Not two years. How about twenty-four months? How about seven hundred days?" railed Cody. "How about a million Christmas's and campouts and ball games and dinners? How about the state swim meet where I placed third and band where I got to play solo?"

Spider stared at the gangly teen in front of him. Where was his bucked-toothed chubby-cheeked Cody? The Cody who loved bobbing around the pool for hours in his water wings. His little science-nerd who would watch a show all day long if it had anything to do with insects? He turned, choosing instead to watch the battle going on outside through the bar's picture-glass windows.

"Tell you what," Cody continued. "These last two years, I've grown up. I've become a man. Without you. I have my own thoughts, my own ideas, my own direction and I'm not your slave anymore to move wherever you say or think whatever you think."

"I didn't raise you to be," replied Spider.

"You didn't raise me at all. Mom did. You only showed up once in awhile to make life difficult."

"Mom only raised you until you were five, when you were old enough for school. After that, you were mine."

"What do you mean?"

"Kids rely on their dads for different things than their mothers. We take you out into the world. We introduce you to new things, new people. We let you stub your toe and make you change your own tire. Moms don't do that. Dads do."

"Those are stupid things. Why would I care about them?"

"Because those are the things that make you just like me."

"I am not! How could I be? You weren't even there."

"A dad doesn't have to be there. Dads go out into the world to pursue careers, lead their communities, protect their families. *To fight wars.*"

"You make it sound admirable, but you're just a glory-seeker."

"That's what men do, Cody. They seek glory. From their family, their bosses, their coaches, other men."

"Not me."

"That's why men wear uniforms." Cody looked down at his. "It's my job as your father to be an example. To let you know who you are, what stock you come from, to give you your identity."

"But I *don't* know you!"

"Don't be stupid. Of course you know me. That's why you hate me. You can't hate what you don't know."

"I didn't say I hated you."

"Of course you hate me. You're a son. That's what sons do when they're your age. They rebel. They're contrarian. They reject everything their father stands for. Don't think you've joined the UN because you're some enlightened gift to the world. You're doing it because that is what every son since Cain has done."

Cody gawked at his father. "Don't pretend to know what I'm thinking."

"I know because I was the same way with grandpa."

"You love war. You love conflict. You love killing people."

"You're confusing love with ability," Spider answered.

"Well, I'm not you. I don't love those things."

"You're wearing a gun, Code."

"I'm a Peacebuilder. I keep the peace. We repair what you destroy."

"We're not the ones ripping apart Iowa, Germany is. We're not swamping Oregon with immigrants, Korea is. It's not me fencing off Miami, it's the Cubans."

"Alignment takes time."

"In my time, it used to be called OneWorld Government. And Alignment will be called something else when *it* fails."

"What will fail is you."

"You're a fool," Spider muttered.

"I'm not a fool!"

"Of course you're a fool! All children are fools."

Cody grabbed his beret and shook it at him. "Not here. Here I've been accepted. For my brains. For my ideas."

"I raised you better than this, Cody. I raised you to think for yourself. So that you'd know when someone was preying on you. What happened to your love of learning? Your love in finding the truth about things? Don't turn off half your brain just because you're mad at me."

"I'm the only Pax Cadet to be promoted this fast and this young. To General Faisson, I am a man."

Trent kept watching the progress outside. The Sherpas were retreating and the pilots were running to their planes. "Then stay if you're so happy," he said, grabbing his gear. "Best wishes. Just know you'll be alone."

"What do you mean?"

"Your mom's coming. She's joining me in the MS. She's leaving later this week."

"No. No, she's not."

"Yes, she is. I've made arrangements."

"You're not going to win."

"There's nothing to win, Cody. What are you talking about?"

"You always win. In the end, everyone caves in to you. Jared sold out to be your little college-preppy clone. Grandpa gave in when he helped buy your piece-of-crap farm. But you're not going to take mom. You're not going to destroy me and mom like you did everyone else."

"Son, I've got to go. You let me know what you decide."

Spider made for the door as Cody stepped in front. He put his hand on his holster.

"Now what are you going to do? Shoot me?"

Tears welled in the teen's eyes and he fumbled with his holster.

Spider laughed as he guided the boy's hands. "You need to pull that rubber tab down first, then lift the flap."

Cody pulled out the gun and with two hands, pointed it at his father.

"So, you aren't like me at all, huh?"

"No."

"Well, if old Faisson trusts you enough to give you a gun, he must have told you never to draw it unless you were going to use it."

"I will shoot you."

"I would. If I had the chance to shoot my old man at your age, I would've."

"I *will*!" Cody stared motionless into his father's hazel-flecked eyes.

"It's pretty intimidating to shoot someone face-to-face, isn't it? Here, I'll turn around. Is that easier?"

"I hate you."

Cody stared at the back of his old man's head. It was just like he had hoped it would be. So why did he shake? Why wouldn't the gun stay still?

"I don't have all day."

He couldn't believe what he was about to do. Cody watched himself like he was floating on the ceiling. He didn't recognize the boy below him but he wished he could make him put the gun back. Wished he could make him think this was all a mistake. Wished he knew of some way he could blame it on a joke.

He watched his trigger-finger twitch.

OHMYGODDONTDOITDONTDOITGOBACKGOBACKWAKEUPITSJUSTADREAMPLEASEDONTPULLITPLEASEJUSTPUTITDOWNANDCUDDLEINHISLAPHELLFORGIVEYOUHELLKISSYOUHEALWAYSDOESITSNOTTOOLATECODYITSNOTTOOLATE.

Click!

Spider turned and took the gun from Cody's hand, ejecting the magazine. "Just what I thought. It appears your Imperial Leader isn't so trusting after all. He didn't give you any bullets."

Cody quivered. He stared off into the distance while his father slammed the clip home and placed the pistol back into cold, clammy hands. Spider brushed past him on his way out the door, turning one last time.

"That makes two of us who think you're a fool."

CHAPTER 14
KRISTALLNACHT

The phone rang and Laura refused to answer it. She was certain in her decision. As certain as the suitcase by the door. She watched the caller ID flash as she sipped decaf from her mug. On the eighth ring, she snatched the phone off its base.

"Mom, it's done! I'm going. Now leave me alone!"

A soft, kindly voice replied. "Hi, dear. It's Frank."

"Oh, Frank. I'm sorry. I thought it was mom."

"Honey, I apologize for mom. She doesn't want you to get hurt."

"Is she there? Did she tell you to call?"

"No. I called on my own," Laura's step-father lied.

"Yeah, right. I can hear her in the background rasping from her web in the corner."

"We're worried, that's all. It sounds so dangerous."

"John assured me it's safe. He said thousands go every day."

"And what of Cody? He's so young." Laura sighed. "Hon? Is Cody going?"

"I don't know. I haven't seen him for a week. He's run off to join the Pax Cadets. He's sixteen and there's not much I can do with him anymore."

"How will we talk? How will we know you made it safely?"

"Oh, Frank. You'll hear. I'll call. I'll write."

"Unbelievable, Frank!" said a second voice on the line. "It's been less than a minute and already she's got you twisted around her little finger."

"Mother! Get off the phone. I'm not talking to you anymore."

Her mother goaded her with faux softness. "Don't do it, Laura. Don't put your family in harm's way. You've been its only protector."

"What do you care? You don't want me to go because you think I'm giving up my independence."

"And your power."

"Please. Your feminism is so hackneyed."

"Your power and wisdom are what's held your family together all these years, Laura."

"No, my husband's held us together."

Her mother's hardtack Bostonian Brahman returned. "Rubbish. He's a disaster."

"You should know. You're on husband number three."

"Exactly. That's why you need to listen. I'm an expert on losers."

"You think John's a loser because of the farm?"

"*Loser.*"

"And because he joined the Sovereigns?"

"*Loser.*"

"No, he's not."

"He's a loser as well as a misogynist, a symp and a hothead independent. And you'll be just as much a disappointment if you leave the university."

"Mother, it's just a job."

"It's not a job. It's your career. Your badge of honor. Your respect. It's the only thing you'll have left when everyone else has abandoned you. What will this be telling Jared and Cody?"

"It'll tell them that we need to be a family again."

"It tells them that their mother doesn't count."

"And what do you mean by *abandon me*? You really think John is going to leave me after twenty-five years?"

"Your father did."

"John is not my father!"

"But he's a man, damn it. Your husband only wants you there so he can control you."

"He wants me because he loves me. Because he misses me."

"Then why did he leave? I'll tell you why. He left because there are more important things than you."

Laura threw her cup to keep from crying. "Oh, mother!"

"Don't be beguiled. If you go, he wins. *They* win. It's not love, Laura. Love is nothing but a tire iron to them."

The front door jiggled, then opened. Laura turned to the sink to hide her face. "I have to go. It's Cody. He just came home."

"Don't hang up, Laura. Not until you tell me you're not going."

"Bye, mom."

"Frank, don't just sit there like a wet mop, stop her!"

"Bye, hon. Stay safe. We'll be thinking about you."

Laura hung up and picked the pieces of her cup from the sink. "Where have you been, Cody?"

"Hi, mom. I told you, I joined the PC."

"That was a week ago," Laura challenged, turning. "You said you'd be gone one night."

"I've been in training. Training took longer than I thought."

"I went to the school," recited Laura. "I went to the police. I went to the armory. Nobody knew anything. Apparently any student can waive their last two years of high school to join the Cadets. The Cottage Grove police won't interfere. Not even the warren colonel will give out any information. Especially to parents." The phone rang again and Cody picked it up. "Don't answer that."

"But it's grandma."

"I SAID DON'T ANSWER THAT!"

Cody jolted backward as his mother grabbed the handset out of his hand. She dropped it in the garbage disposal and turned it on, grinding the phone into tiny plastic slivers. She flipped the disposal back off and turned to Cody.

"What's this?" he asked, holding her suitcase.

"None of your business."

"You're going to the MS, aren't you? You're going to be with him."

"Why would I tell you? You'd probably turn me in."

"I saw him."

"What?"

"I saw dad."

"When? How? Why didn't you tell me, Cody? Is he OK? How does he look?"

"He's OK enough, I guess. He looks tired. Lost a lot of weight."

"And you weren't going to tell me?"

"He said you were following him to the MS."

"I didn't tell him anything of the sort. We haven't spoken."

"Then he *lied*."

"No. He just knows me."

Now it was Cody's turn to be upset. His mother *was* leaving. He picked up her suitcase and threw it into the living room, refusing to believe she and his father could still have a connection after being apart for so long. "How can you?"

"Don't start in with me again, Cody. I know your father and I have had our differences, but life's not black-and-white all the time."

"What if I wanted to go with you, would you let me come?"

"Of course, honey, of course." She ran to him. "What did he say to change your mind?"

"He didn't. He doesn't want me to go."

"Cody Allen, he would never say anything of the sort."

"He saw me in my uniform and freaked. He grabbed me and threw me up against the wall." Cody rolled up his sleeves as proof. "He called me a fool."

"Like you're taking me for?" Laura took his blank stare as a *yes*. "Your father told the Freemartins to expect both of us. He wants you with him, too."

"He's lying to you, mom."

"Or you are."

"Fine. Take his side."

Laura walked up behind her son and put a hand on his neck. "Why don't you start packing. We leave in an hour."

"Why should I? So you can both gang up on me?" Cody walked to the living room and opened the drapes a crack.

"Oh, just shut up for once Cody and do what I say. Get your clothes. I've told the U I'd be cashing in a week of sick leave and the Warbys said they would watch the house while we were gone." Laura drew closer and looked over Cody's shoulder and out into the street. "What's so interesting out there?"

"I don't know. There were some people here when I got home."

"Are the Bruins having another BBQ?"

"Not unless they're serving an entire cow." Cody went to the kitchen as Laura opened the curtains. Outside, dozens of young people were gathered, handing out signs and posters under the streetlights. Pax Cadet carts were parked across the street as a KARE news crew interviewed her neighbors.

"That isn't a party, Cody. They're in our yard with banners."

Cody went to the kitchen laptop and typed *WWW.MNROAMINGS.ORG* into the browser. A map appeared on their splash page highlighting that evening's events. When he clicked a pushpin centered on Cottage Grove, the screen zoomed in to their street where pictures of their house and his mother and father were displayed.

> ROAMING TONIGHT 10:30 PM
> MEET AT THE HOUSE OF JOHN AND LAURA TRENT
> 6520 DICKENSON PARKWAY, COTTAGE GROVE, MN
>
> JOHN TRENT IS A MAJOR IN THE SOVEREIGN FORCES AND HAS COMMITTED MURDER, ESPIONAGE, ASSASSINATION AND OTHER CRIMES AGAINST THE WORLD.
> HIS FAMILY REMAINS IN-COUNTRY AND MUST BE HELD TO ACCOUNT FOR THESE BARBAROUS ACTS.
>
> JOIN US TONIGHT TO HELP SEND A PEACEFUL MESSAGE THAT THE COMMUNITY STANDS UNITED WITH THE PRESIDENT AND NOT WITH THE SYMPATHIZERS DURING THIS TRYING TIME OF NATIONAL SCHISM.

"Oh, my God!" Laura covered her mouth. "Not a roaming. Not here." She looked at her son in horror and slapped the computer shut. "You. You told them."

"No mom. I didn't say anything. I swear."

"Those are *your* friends out there." She watched as her son raced back to the living room. "*Someone* gave them our pictures."

"Those are your URL photos. Anyone can see those. They're part of your NextWeb license."

"Then where's your picture?"

"I don't have one, mom. I wasn't *dumb* enough to register, like you."

Out the window, newsmen beamed their lights into the yard as war-roamers called for Laura to come out and eco-roamers demanded that they see her fluorescent light bulbs and dry-flush toilets.

"I'm putting a stop to this. People can't just terrorize whomever they want and expect people to sit and take it."

Thuds began hitting the side of the house, including a red paint balloon that splatted its contents across her picture window. She made for the front door.

"Mom, you don't understand."

"Understand what? They're just kids."

"This isn't homecoming," he said. "They aren't here to paper your trees." Cody stepped in front of her. "You've been pinned, mom. These people are scary. College students, union people, bluebirds. Once they've pinned you they won't be satisfied until—"

Cody covered his mom as glass from an upstairs window crashed to the floor. They heard a whoosh and Cody bounded up the stairs, firelight reflecting on his face. "Mom! Run! Now! Out the back."

"No. This is my home. I am not a criminal." She ran out the front and waved her hands to the street. "Stop. I'm not an independent. I'm not a sympathizer! I'm a professor!"

The crowd had grown to ten deep and cheered when they saw her. Another firebomb sailed through the air, crashing through her bay window and into her living-room. She screamed. "Not my photos!"

She tried running back into the house but Cody stood in the door blocking her way. He handed her her wedding album and suitcase and pushed her back into the yard. They both grabbed a hose and began spraying the flames as their next-door neighbors watched. "Bax! Suz! We need more water!"

Her neighbors ran for their hose and unwound it then began watering down their own house. Behind them, the mob chanted.

"These people kill Peacebuilders!"

"SF. MS. *Kiss my ass!*"

"These symps promote anarchy!"
"*SF. MS. Kick their ass!*"
"SO CAN THEY BE TRUSTED?"
"SF. MS. *KILL THEIR ASS!*"

Laura doused them with her hose while yelling to a nearby patrolman. "Stop these hoodlums. Aren't you going to arrest them?"

"I don't have any backup, ma'am. There's at least a half-dozen of these flash mobs roaming around tonight."

She grabbed for his shotgun. "You don't need backup! You've got a gun. USE IT!"

A klieg light hit her as a reporter stuck a microphone in her face. "Mrs. Trent? Can you please tell us what part you played in the two postal worker deaths last week?"

"What?"

"We've received audio of you off the Internet where you advocate treating postmen as *players* for spying on Americans. Do you deny this?"

"I've never said anything like that in my life."

The suit kept talking as Laura looked about her, dazed. Bright-pink flames roared from her home. "This is a dream. This isn't happening."

The crowd converged on her son and Cody began to fight. He held a pistol over his head and stared firing. The mob struggled to disarm him as Laura jumped in, slashing with her heels.

From down the elm-shrouded block, an amplified voice boomed from a loudspeaker. "Everyone clear the streets! This is an order by the French military."

Immediately, Dickenson Street erupted with booms and sparks as stun-grenades machine-gunned overhead and blue APCs parted the panicking crowd. Laura wrestled her way through the thinning rioters to her son who sat in the grass nursing a bloody lip. From the dark, a soldier appeared. He approached the mob's leader, snatched away his megaphone and hit him over the head with it.

"It's General Faisson!" announced Cody, lifting his head.

The general held up a hand and spoke into the horn. "OK, you little terrorists. You've made your point. If everyone leaves now you can just about make it home in time to watch yourselves on the news." The crowd turned back and gathered their courage.

"This is America, Eurotrash! We have freedom of assembly here."

"Yeah, we're not going home until justice is served."

Faisson laughed. "Yes, I can see from all the nice expensive Navigators and Suburbans parked here just how interested in justice you are."

"We came here all the way from the city. Light-rail doesn't come out this far."

"That is a shame," replied Faisson. "Because there are rather severe travel restrictions in place. You are going to have to find more earth-friendly ways of organizing your lynch mobs from now on."

"Travel restrictions? We haven't heard of any new restrictions."

"That is because I just instituted them." The general barked orders into his radio as the turret on his AMX traversed and thundered away at the vehicles.

"Hey, that's my LS!"

"No. Not my Z5!"

As the air filled with bursting SUVs and luxury sedans, more APCs rode in from the opposite direction, crushing the cars with their steel tracks. The crowd ran to try to save their vehicles, leaving the yard empty.

"Awesome, sir!"

"Why, thank you, Cody. It's not hard to look good when your adversaries have such soft underbellies."

"Mom, this is General Faisson, my commander."

She recognized him instantly from the news and celebrations on TV. She wiped the soot from her cheeks and welcomed him. "Thank you, general. You saved our lives."

"How did you know to be here?" asked Cody.

"When France sent me to oversee their protectorate here, I saw fit to bring our Information Warfare unit along, too. They saw the posting on the Internet and I came as soon as I could." He sheathed his radio and strode onto the lawn. "I am sorry we were too late, Mrs. Trent."

Laura came as close to the blazing house as she could, then fell to her knees. "My home! My things!"

"We have a place to put you up. A place just for families like yours," he said.

"But why? This is where we live. Tell me I don't have to leave."

"It is for your safety. You saw this mob. They are gone now but they can come back at any time. And often do."

A few houses down, a UN van turned onto the street. Laura watched it warily. "But I have to go to work. What will everybody think at the U? They'll think—"

"Come, come now, Mrs. Trent. You're not being *arrested*."

"No?"

"*I* would never do that to you."

"Tell me, does this facility also processes families for reunification with loved ones in the MS?"

"So you have heard."

"Thank you for the offer, but I think we'll manage."

"I beg you reconsider." Faisson walked up to some hedges and pulled a black suitcase and photo album from the foliage. Laura bounded after him and yanked them from his grip.

"A prominent citizen such as yourself. Head of a university department. Chairwoman of her city's Planning Commission. If it should ever get out that you collaborated with the resistance to join your husband in the Middle States, I would fear for your safety."

A crack rippled through the home as the front of her Cape Cod shuddered before falling into her living room. Through the maelstrom of sparks, she made out her kitchen and beyond that, her bedroom. This had been *her* house, purchased a few months prior when she could no longer handle the isolation of the farm. But in the big scheme of things, she had no great attachment here. No memories lost. Those would be on the other side of the frontier. In the arms of her husband. In his eyes were all her memories. In his smile, her life. She looked down to her suitcase and took the handle. "Come on, Cody. We've got an appointment to keep."

Faisson sent Cody after her. When he came up behind, he took her gently by the arm and tugged away her suitcase. "Sorry, mom, but that's something we can't let you do."

ACT
II

CHAPTER 15
MANDATE

The German field marshal prattled on and on, slathering himself with praise. He boasted to his French counterparts how fearsome his Leopards were against the Sovereigns. He scolded them about how his *Heer* had to pull back so the French could catch up with his blitzkriegs. Faisson let him crow. Today, he could be magnanimous. Today, France was going to get her mandate.

"In Iowa, we broke through at Camp Dunlap," rambled Field Marshal Karl Karlsruhe, commander of the German-UN contingent. "There was not a single Sovereign left to kill or capture. They all ran."

"That is because you are so feared!" Faisson's generals mocked, in typical French style.

"Of course. The earth quakes when our tanks approach."

"Marshal Karlsruhe, the SF is not scared of any armor."

"Is that so?"

"Their doctrine is mobility," explained Lieutenant General Papon. "It is mathematics. They simply do not have enough Abrahms and Bradleys to fight force-on-force."

Division General deBrinon leaned into the speakerphone, talking and smoking in the same breath. "They shoot their anti-tank Predators from concealed Humvees and four-wheelers then withdraw in the blink of an eye. It's tactics, that's all."

"And it's because of these fearsome ATVs your offensive in the north has stalled?"

From the far end of the hazy conference room, DG Giraud stood and muted the transmitter. "Sean, how much longer do we have to suffer this boor?"

Faisson winced as he adjusted his shoulder sling and consulted the clock. "I will check." He punched up the other line. "Wildfire, does the Secretary-General still want us to hold? It has been forty minutes."

"I am told he is now ready for you," sang the joyous attendant. "Please stand-by."

From half-a-world away, a towel-covered Burin Zzgn stood shivering under a hot Somali sun as he exited his penthouse's subzero cyrochamber. "Sean ... dear ... friend ... help ... you?" Zzgn chattered.

"Mr. Secretary-General? I cannot hear you. Are you OK?"

"Yes ... yes. I just finished my cyrotherapy. Going from minus 120 to plus 120 degrees is quite a shock but does wonders for your limbic system."

"One hundred twenty? Where are you?"

The small snow-white Ukrainian gave his mittens to the nurse as he scanned the crowded beaches below. "The Trieste Gardens in Mogadishu. I am among the world's elite here, pampered and coddled in wanton hedonistic fashion."

"Sounds like America!" snorted Faisson.

"Better. Lots of land, cheap prices. Almost all the immigrants are American retirees. Buying homes and gambling away their 401(k)s at the casinos." He laughed heartily. "They're like boat people."

Karlsruhe broke in. "Did you enjoy your rafting trip, sir?"

"What a marvelous time, Karl! Thank you for suggesting it. After whitewatering down the Juba I just had to try out the Speed-Demon at Gedo Preserve Water Park. That is why I am tardy."

Faisson continued. "Mr. Secretary? About our call." In the background, a blood-curdling roar erupted from the line. The general stood and yelled into the phone. "Secretary Zzgn! Are you there? We heard a lion."

"Sorry, that was Linus. Every suite comes complete with its own denizen of the African veld. Mine is an Ethiopian Katanga lion." Zzgn pet the beast as a tanned Australian handler adjusted its hypodermic collar.

Faisson continued. "Sir, we have a problem with the Americans."

"Isn't that why we are at war, Sean?"

Karlsruhe laughed.

"Not the Sovereigns, Mr. Secretary. I mean trouble with our American Coax units. Our allies."

A skinny three-year-old slave girl offered the SecGen a glass of juice, squeezed from the rooftop citrus grove. Zzgn took it and smiled. "I suspected they would have sympathies. Was I correct?"

"We have had our first defection."

"The Flying Tigers?"

"You know of it?"

"Karl told me."

"The German's have spies in my protectorate?"

"One need not be a spy to notice such a notorious debacle," offered the field marshal.

Faisson's lips shrunk, barring his teeth. "Secretary Zzgn, I requested a private audience. I object at having to share my concerns further with the Germans."

"Sean, I requested he join us. Your armies control over half of the eastern LOC. You are the real UNIFUS power there. Not the Spanish or the Serbs or the other third-rate nations. You and Karl are a unified front. Now what do you suggest we do about our problem?"

"I am removing all U.S. Coaxial units from my front-line operations."

Karlsruhe protested, angry he hadn't thought of the idea first. "You can't unilaterally redeploy a third of your resources on your own. That should be a decision left for UNIFUS Force Command."

"I cannot wait forever," Faisson argued. "I am moving my Americans to the rear. They will be used to protect our logistics train and patrol the border."

"Ridiculous," declared the marshal. "If the Americans cannot be trusted in combat how can they be trusted to seal the border?"

Zzgn petted Linus' thick mane and fingered its long fangs as the animal slumbered at his feet. Seated beside him, an ebony-skinned nurse opened a blood kit and began her daily battery of tests. "While the plan is not without its flaws, Herr Karlsruhe, I am intrigued by it. What ideas do *you* have?"

"The French will need our help. I am prepared to send in one of my heavy Leopard divisions," offered the German.

"No need, dear field marshal. We have ample forces," assured Faisson.

"If you pull back the Coax units, you will be losing thirty thousand American cavalry and aviation troops. How do you figure to replace them?" inquired Karlsruhe.

Burin Zzgn, Leader of the Free World, gazed out over the gentle swells of the Indian Ocean as his vein filled its fortieth vial. If he was going to change his body chemistry and live to be a hundred-and-fifty, each of his supplements and flushings had to be in balance. "Yes, Sean, that is a lot. Where will you get the replacement troops?"

"France, sir. If you grant us a mandate."

"*Unverschämt!*"

Zzgn frowned. "You've approached President Weygand about this?"

"She approached me," Faisson fibbed.

"And France is willing to leave her homeland unprotected?"

"Every country in the EU has signed a Declaration of Dependency, Mr. Secretary. France has no enemies anymore. Except America. *And* Germany."

Karlsruhe exploded. "Mr. Secretary-General! I object to this vile hate-speech."

"Sean, did you not agree to bury your past animosities when you joined the Dependency? I can assure you that an aligned state such as Germany has no intention of working outside the world consensus."

Faisson leaned back, juggling his ballistrae. "We know our neighbor to the east all too well. An empty France will tempt them. We want a full guarantee Germany will not invade."

"Sir, we do not approve of such a move."

"You already have your mandate, Karl. Why not the French, too?"

"Because we *earned* ours. We do not have a problem with our sister Coax units."

"You will," Faisson said to his contemporary. "It will just be a matter of time. We chose not to wait."

Zzgn agreed. "You have uncovered a disconcerting problem, Sean. This contagion has the potential of spreading if not checked. You are to be commended for your discernment and action."

"Thank you, sir."

"But I am equally concerned that it may be premature to grant France its own mandate at this time."

"Secretary Zzgn, we are not asking for anything special. We simply want to be treated like the other states who have mandates." Faisson refused to acknowledge Germany by name.

Karlsruhe protested. "Sir, France is taking their battlefield incompetence and turning it into an excuse to gain special dispensation. Be very suspicious of those who advance themselves by insisting on shortcuts."

"I am afraid Karl may have a point, Sean."

"But, sir—"

Zzgn put on his glasses and read from a report. "You have lost a sizeable portion of your mechanized forces by staging them too far forward. Furthermore, you let a valuable HVA spy slip through your fingers and you just recently lost thirty attack fighters to the enemy."

Karlsruhe corrected the SecGen. "You didn't just lose them, Sean. You allowed them to escape, *intact*, so they can be used against us."

"Secretary Zzgn. I am sympathetic to your concerns, but there are explanations. Let me come there to discuss this. I can be there in—"

"I am afraid I have made up my mind, Sean. I cannot grant France the mandate you seek."

Faisson pushed his fingers through his hair and yanked. It was he who had foreseen the American civil war as a way for his country to climb back onto the world stage. He who pushed his government to reclaim the political influence they had ceded to the EU and NATO and the U.S. this past century. The mandate would have given France relevance again, the strength to dictate her own destiny. If it meant he would have to rule as its governor, so be it. If it earned him the seven stars and baton of Maréchal de France, then he was ready to suffer the inevitable comparisons to Napoleon. And if he just so happened to get rich off the industry and resources of these northern territories, then it was a price he was willing to pay. "Sir, please."

Karlsruhe smelled blood and circled. "Then you will approve us sending German reserves north to reinforce?" he asked Zzgn.

"Karl, your magnanimity is wearily transparent," chided the Secretary. "UNIFUS needs a strong France if it is to rid the world of this last remnant of independence. To that end, I am granting them a provisional mandate."

Faisson looked up in shock as if he'd just been granted another week on American Idol. His commanders cheered and congratulated each other.

"A *provisional* mandate? Based on what?" Karlsruhe wanted to know.

"The preemptive disaffiliation of his U.S. units and those refreshingly inventive Reunification Camps. You would do well to emulate both in your own Peacebuilder zone, Karl."

"Yes, sir."

"Of course, the grant is temporary, Sean. There will be oversight," added Zzgn. "But your protectorate is, as of now, given the full rights and benefits of a chartered UN mandate."

Faisson pulled his lapels down and straightened his tunic. "I understand, Mr. Secretary."

Zzgn was growing bored of this little political skirmish across the globe. To him, the civil war in America was just another piece on his chessboard waiting for him to play it. He woke Linus and tried toying with him by tugging at his mane and tossing him grapes. The great cat ignored him and lugged himself to the corner where he returned to his napping. Zzgn was not pleased with his pet. He took the remote from the zookeeper and mashed a small red button in its center. When the pith collar received the signal, it sent a ten-inch hypodermic deep into the lion's cerebral cortex, splaying the animal out like a trophy rug, its eyes staring up unblinking at the secretary. "What will your mandate be called, Sean? Do you have a name?"

"*Terre du Lacs.* Land of Lakes."

"Very good, General Faisson. Or would it be too soon to call you, *Marshal* Faisson?"

"I am honored by your belief in me and my country, Mr. Secretary-General. You shall not be sorry for your faith."

"I have no faith in either, Sean."

"But, I thought—"

"Your history on the battlefield is an embarrassment and further failures will not be tolerated."

The mood in the room became somber. "Yes, sir."

"I am putting you under the microscope. As governor of this new dependency, you will now be subject to the jurisdiction of the General Assembly. No more will you be able to run unchecked. You will be held accountable and your every move scrutinized. You will not be able to so much as spill your coffee without getting a visit from a Hague ligate."

The public rebuke stung the Frenchman and he bit his tongue as Karlsruhe roared.

"Welcome to your global rectal exam, Sean."

CHAPTER 16
SCHISM

The room was intended to be a lunchroom not a courtroom. The gallery fanned themselves with whatever pieces of paper they could find. Light from the sole window shown down on the defendants, cutting their features with sharp dark shadows.

General Lynn Patterson presided over the chamber. Generals Foxworthy and Isham, the two other judges on the panel, flanked him on either side. Woody's stars drooped dully off his dress blues as he pounded the room to order and addressed the accused.

"We have heard the prosecution's case. Now it's time to hear your side." The five Harvesters smirked. Patterson whispered to them. "Gentlemen, if you've changed your mind about a lawyer, this would be a good time to mention it." The men continued their grinning. "Very well," he said. "Adjutant, you can begin your final statement."

Ronnie Mars, the young JAG lieutenant in charge of prosecution, gathered her papers and approached the panel. "Two months ago, Edward Thompson and his group, the Apsostle's Harvesters, stormed the United States Supreme Court Building for the purpose of murdering its justices. Although U.S. marshals eventually succeeded in fighting them off, five of the anarchists got through." She turned and pointed at the defendants. "These men coralled all nine judges into the Robing Room, lined them up ear-to-ear and, after a mock trial, shot them execution-style with a single bullet."

"You were hoping it would go through all nine?" mused Foxworthy.

"I refuse to answer on the grounds that it may tend to incriminate me," smiled Thompson as a head-ringing explosion ripped through the front of their building. He had reason to smile. His friends were coming to break him out.

Attackers, masquerading as soldiers, had forced their way onto base. They cut a path of destruction through the carnival and drove their Humvee into the lobby where it detonated. Scuffles and yelling and machine-gun fire echoed down the main corridor as the raiders marched closer to the make-shift courtroom. When a squad of UNCONs finally stormed the building to reinforce the guards, a final loud fulmination rocked the foundation. After a moment of panicked speculation, a panting sooty-faced MP entered the room and raised his goggles to brief the tribunal.

"Don't shoot!" he cried, holding up his hands as Woody, the judges and tiny Lieutenant Mars drew down on him. As did the rest of the room. "It's all clear! We think they were Theonomists."

Patterson addressed his five defendants. "So the Theonomists want to break you out, too?"

The men sat up in their chairs and exchanged glances, the smirks missing from their faces.

"Good job, chief," rejoined Woody. "Everyone, holster your weapons and be seated." He motioned the lieutenant to continue as one of the defendants stood.

"Your honor, I'm changing my plea. I'm innocent. I was just the videographer. They are the real killers."

His table erupted as the other Harvesters leaped for him. Two no-necked bailiffs waded into the melee and tasered the defendants back to their chairs.

"So, your rescue mission fails and *now* you want to cooperate?"

"I'm not a killer, sir. I don't want to die."

"You just wanted a really good snuff film to send to Sundance, that right?"

"I can tell you anything you want to know. The operation. Where the rest of the Harvesters can be found."

"Young man, we already know everything we need to know," said Patterson. "The orders you claim to have received from Jesus on YouTube, your mock trial to avenge 175 million abortion deaths, the Thorn of Christ you purportedly put in your bullet. It's all a ruse."

"We are here at Christ's orders," announced a dishevelled Thompson. "We are the Harvesters of the Revelation."

"That so? Name another book then," Patterson ordered.

"W-w-what do you mean?"

"You *do* know there are another sixty-five other books in the Bible, don't you?"

"Yes—"

"Name one."

"Uhhh, Moses? Abraham?"

"You've made my point. You're as Christian as I am Batman."

"You're a pagan. Pagans don't get to determine who's Christian."

"No, but I'm your judge and I've determined you are nothing more than a bunch of hoods too loony to get jobs with the mob so you thought you'd try your hand as Hitmen for Jesus."

"It's a divine calling. We are willing to die for Christ."

"You are anarchists trying to bring down the government."

"The same as you independents!" Thompson said, turning to the gallery. "That is why we came to the Middle States. We should be heroes here. You should be parading us down the streets. Giving us medals."

Patterson cracked his gavel against the lunchroom table and stood, firing back. "The officers and soldiers of the Sovereign Forces have nothing in common with gangsters like you! We are not overthrowing the country, we are defending it. *We* are not the traitors here. You are."

"Your judgement is coming. God will decide."

The general calmed and sat back down. "Well, you'd better get a stronger god. Your's only managed to kill four of the justices. The fifth is in a wheelchair at Walter Reed chanting Pink Floyd lyrics with a thorn lodged in her amygdala."

The panel listened to the rest of the lieutenant's arguments and after a short recess returned with guilty verdicts for all five defendants. As the court adjourned, General Samuel 'Corky' Davis, the Sovereign Ground Arm commander, got up from his seat in the gallery and approached the presiding judges. "The least you could have done is voice your dissent, you coward," he hissed to General Mattuck Isham, Davis' ally on the Quarterstaff.

Isham kept his gaze down. "It would have done no good," he whispered back. "I was outvoted."

"But it would have sent a message. The whole MS was watching."

Isham snarled "You want to send a message? Then you do it next time."

"I would have. I was out of rotation for this trial." Davis stepped back as Isham brushed by. He walked to the window and ran a thumb over his brow to iron out the deep creases furrowed there.

"You're not dreaming up another little prison break for those wingnuts, are you Sam?"

It was Patterson. Davis wheeled around. "If I was, it wouldn't be hard."

"Better make it quick then. Your boys are going to be room temperature by sunrise."

Davis picked lint from Woody's dusty epaulettes and reset them on his rounded shoulders. "You can't let people think what the Harvesters did was wrong, Lynn."

"How else are they to take a unanimous verdict, Sam?"

"The public doesn't support you. They support us."

"That doesn't make you right." Patterson picked up his binders and walked out of the room.

"It's right if it gives us victory."

"And just what part do groups like the Harvesters play in that?"

Davis followed him out. "You go to war to win, to dominate, to overwhelm. Groups like the Harvesters are ruthless, yes, but they need to be. They demoralize the enemy, shorten the war and in the end actually wind up being more humanitarian."

"A pity they won't be around to reap what they've sown."

"This isn't over," threatened Davis.

Woody stopped in the hallway where a crowd mingled by the window. "Oh, no?" Outside, a fusillade of shots rang out. Davis ran over to look down into the courtyard as a pile of hooded bodies lay collapsed and slouched against the wall. Across the quadrangle, a six-man firing squad safetied and shouldered their weapons. Davis exploded.

"Patterson, you dodering fool! What have you done? The Harvesters weren't going to kill anymore. They were a propaganda tool. They were our next recruitment poster." The beefy Green Beret towered over Woody. He was five-inches taller and twenty-five years his junior. He backed his elder into the window pane and pushed.

"Oh, they're still being used for propaganda," said Patterson. "The execution was taped. I let the media in."

Davis shoved a meaty finger into the pilot's chest until the glass bulged. Patterson heard a crack and dug his fingers into his attacker's solar plexus before he fell. Grabbing hold Davis' rib cage, Patterson yanked it out and up, lifting him off his feet and across the corridor. When he reached the room on the opposite side, Woody burst through the door and threw the younger man unceremoniously onto the table.

"Where'd you learn *that*?" marveled General Zachary Foxworthy, Woody's friend and commander of the Sovereign Provincial Arm.

"Vietnam. A little something I picked up from my hosts in the Hanoi Hilton."

"What's going on in here?" Command General Rodney McCombs barked from the doorway. He puffed and sweated from his run down the hall, his several-chins jiggling.

Patterson relinquished his hold and let the passivated Davis up. "Seems Corky's upset we didn't tell him his dirtbags were getting an early send-off."

"You look like two drunken sailors fighting over a lap dancer," McCombs admonished. "I can't have my generals brawling in public like that."

Davis took a breath, wincing as he talked. "Lynn told me the execution was filmed. That true, Rod?"

"I don't know anything about any taping. Lynn?"

"I ordered it," Patterson admitted. He opened a new pack of painkillers and lit one with a match. "As part of the sentencing."

Just then, an officer came in, whispered to Davis and handed him a video tape. The tape had been seized by Corky's men as the news crews were leaving the airbase. It contained footage from the Harvester executions. Patterson lunged for it as Davis tossed it to their boss.

"Sorry," McCombs said to Woody. "We're shutting them down."

"Shutting who down?"

"The press."

"You can't do that."

"We should've done it a long time ago," replied Davis.

"We need the press," said Foxworthy. "Even an opposition press."

"This isn't a democracy," declared Corky. "It's a war, remember?"

We can't fight with their constant sniping and second-guessing. Their criticisms of our every decision."

Patterson shuffled closer to his nemesis. "Did anybody ever spank you when you were growing up or were you raised by your momma?"

"We learn from those criticisms," agreed Foxworthy. "In a way, the press makes us better."

"They don't make us better when they lie," Davis came back. "Not when they distort and deceive. Then it's criminal. Then it's treason."

"But they also give groups like the Harvesters a platform," agreed Isham, the intel commander. "By knowing what whackjobs are out there, we can watch them better."

"Matt. Zip it!" fumed Davis. "Whose side are you on?"

Woody turned to McCombs. "Rod, he's full of shit. Freedom of the press is guaranteed in the Constitution. Tell me this meathead is not your constitutional scholar." He snuffed out his butt and pulled out another.

"That's what we're here for today, Wood. To vote on a constitutional suspension."

"A *what?*"

"A constitutional suspension."

"Without a constitution, what the hell are we fighting for?"

"Things have changed, Lynn," replied McCombs. "We're losing. We can't take many more setbacks without going nuclear?"

"What about our oaths? The vows we took when we first entered the service?"

"Lynn, if the motion passes, we will be issuing a new oath within a week. The men will have to revow or leave," replied the five-star.

"Have you all eaten paint chips for lunch?" Patterson knew the SF wouldn't revow. Maybe the young ones, the new recruits, but not the veterans sensitive to being seen as traitors. These prior-military formed the core of their cause and they liked their country. They had joined to preserve it not break off and start a new one. Patterson looked at the three generals as they stood together; McCombs, Davis and Isham. They formed a putsch he knew would split Sovereign loyalties and leave their forces in disarray.

"What does H. B. have to say about this?" asked Foxworthy.

"He's already drafting a model constitution," McCombs answered.

Patterson reached for Davis as Foxworthy held him back. "You egomaniacal son-of-a-bitch. When this war is done, history books will list you just below Benedict Arnold."

"That's fine by me," replied Davis. "Just as long as it's right below yours."

CHAPTER 17
DEBRIEF

"This is suicide, Spider," said Thor, a mile behind his flight leader. "We're going in *again*?" It was the third mission of the sortie and his newly recruited men were frazzled, hungry and dead tired.

"As long as we have bullets and gas," answered Trent.

"Eight's bingo fuel."

"Press Eight," Spider told him.

Gunnar broke radio-discipline. "Spider, he's min fuel. Let him return to base before he flames out."

"Treat me for shock, Thor. If he flames out, he can put down on Highway 10 back there. Sorry for the baptism-by-fire, but when we get a rescue call, we take it."

Spider and his wingmen were giving Thor and his flight commanders a live-fire orientation of ADAKs theater. On their way back to base, a search-and-rescue chopper had called requesting help extracting a family of dirty shirts from a farm outside of Perham. *Dirty shirts* was a derogatory term used by the French to describe anyone outside the uniformed military who picked up weapons to fight. This described most Minnesota farmers; they didn't want anything to do with the advancing UN but were too busy feeding their families to join the SF. However, when it came to their property and livelihoods, these hardscrabbled sympathizers refused to evacuate and stood and fought instead. They weren't going to surrender a single acre without a good blood-letting.

The chopper called in as Spider was bobbling his map trying to familiarize himself with the area.

"Hogsbreath, this is Jolly 23. There's a family's pinned down inside the hog barn. They won't come out. I had to pull out as the bad guys came out of the tree-line. Black guys, head-dresses, loin cloths. They must be Machetes. The same group that overran the field hospital up in Frazee two nights ago. I was there. When those zombies found out we had evacuated everyone, they went crazy and tore up our grave sites. They dismembered our dead, for Christ's sake."

"Jolly, is the township road wide enough to set your bird down on?"

"There's some wires, but yeah, I think I can put her down."

"Good. I'll call you. Until I do, stay out of the way. *Way* out of the way." In the background, Thor continued his complaining but Spider shut him out. Up ahead, he had to attack a dangerous enemy in unfamiliar terrain with no fuel margins while babysitting seven wingmen. Not to mention a SAR chopper to coordinate and a barnful of stubborn pig farmers to save. That's why they call me *The Legend*, he smiled to himself.

Trent plotted orbit points and egress paths on his map while thrashing side-to-side to death metal cranking in his helmet. He scanned the sky for bogies while, inside, checked his instruments, calculated fuel states and tabulated bullet counts. As the farm came at him at 350 knots, he swept his eyes across the spread, taking in the buildings along with the terrain, the sun angle and the wind direction. By the time he was zooming overhead, he had choreographed the attacks in his mind and was ready.

"Eight. Pull it back to max-endurance. Orbit north. You control."

"And just hover there? I'll be a grape."

"You'll also conserve fuel," radioed Spider. "Four, stack high and suppress. You'll support Eight."

"Four."

"Eight."

"Five, take your guys and follow us over the target, then orbit north. We'll stay south."

DEBRIEF 185

SCHOTTKE FARM

Legend:
- ◯ A-10 Orbits
- ⟶ FUN Movements
- –·–▸ Hogsbreath Attacks
- ······▸ Schottke Retreats

"I'm not visualizing this, Lead."

"The Haitians think the A-10 looks like a cross. They call us the Devil's Cross. Just make sure you make a lot of noise as you fly over. That'll fill their diapers."

"Hogsbreath, you going to be able to get them out?" called Jolly. "I didn't want to go to bed tonight thinking what might happen to this family if we left them."

"We'll do more than that," replied Spider. "Just watch."

"Lead, what are those round things in the field?" called Sleepy.

"Hay bales, why?"

"Are they supposed to be moving?"

"Hell no." Spider wheeled his Hog around and fired at the bales, his cockpit filling with the sweat smells of sulfur and cordite. From the pasture below, a flurry of Haitians scrambled from their hideouts and made for the barn. "Look at them mothers scamper! Good call, Sleepy."

"They're heading for the friendlies!"

"No, they're not," said Spider. "They're heading for the bunkers. Let them."

"Lead, I've got movement in the hay bales to the north," radioed Hooper. "They're running for the trees."

"Chase them back, Four. I want them all coralled into the bunkers."

Hoop rolled out of his orbit and strafed in front of the retreating Haitians. They stopped as the ground in front of them erupted in great geysers of dirt. They reversed course to join their comrades.

"Now they're right on top of the family and protected on each side by ten-foot concrete slabs," said Gunnar. "Who's side are we on?"

"The dirty shirts still aren't coming out," said Shank.

"All right, Two. Why don't you persuade them."

Shank came out of his turn and descended on the barn. He aimed into the feed alley separating the two groups and fired his gatling gun. He followed his shells into the target as close as he dared, then pulled skyward, rattling the rafters and obliterating the farmer's senses with the roar. "They're leaving!"

Spider called para-rescue. "Jolly, put down now. Use the driveway so they can see you."

"Jolly's got the fares."

"Hogsbreath, time to spring the trap," Spider announced.

"What trap?" asked Gunnar.

"See the feed bins above the bunkers? We're going to make our own little fuel-air explosive."

"Like a grain elevator explosion?" asked Gunnar.

"More like a small nuclear device," answered Spider. "Lead's in hot. Three, you're the only one with incendiary rounds left. Tuck in close behind."

"Three," acknowledged Om.

The Haitian legionnaires filled the sky with bullets as the Devil's Crosses attacked. When they heard the A-10's loud burps, the plastic storage bins above them disintegrated into shreds as a dark cloud of grain, dust and fertilizer rained down on their heads.

"Spider, Om's too close!" cried Hooper.

Trent snapped his head around to find his wingman shooting burst after burst into the maelstrom, trying to ignite the mixture. "THREE! YOU'RE TOO CLOSE! ABORT. ABORT. ABORT!"

Om's third salvo of incendiary rounds finally sparked against concrete, watering the pilot's eyes with a blinding one-hundred-kiloton thermobaric explosion. The overpressure wave shimmered out across the farmstead like a giant soap bubble, collapsing the Schottke's barn and farmhouse. In one second, forty-three Haitians were breathing 5400-degree air, in the next, their lungs had been sucked out their mouths.

Spider fought for control of his jet as the blast-front passed over his wings. He was dizzy and when he came to, found himself flying sideways through high-tension lines. He righted himself in time to miss a span then ducked to miss another. More wires appeared and he closed his eyes, jinking through them by inches until the sky was a criss-crossed tangle of them, forcing him to the ground.

ADAK headquarters took up an entire abandoned Wal-Mart just east of Fargo, North Dakota. There, the Army of the Dakotas communicated with their brigades and coordinated their battle plans against the FUN. General Patterson flew in from Minot to hold his meeting there tonight. He met under the *Sewing & Crafts* sign in back to debrief the Hinckley raid and to welcome his new fighter squadron, the Flying Tigers.

"So tell me again about the sliders," asked Woody.

"We're still missing three of them," replied Captain Smiling Bear. "Aboud?"

"General Woody, there was an embedded mezo-cyclone cell between the drop point and Hinckley that—"

"A what?"

"I think he means a thunderstorm," answered Wade.

"According to the other jumpers, there were updrafts and hail inside."

"So they're dead?" asked Patterson, puffing away at a lucky.

"Or maybe captured, sir," said Lieutenant Sloan, leader of the Bent Angels, the slider platoon.

"What about the wounded SPs? You told me the POP gun was only supposed to stun."

"The granularity of the conduction coefficients in the effects director was not fine enough—"

Patterson cringed. "If you mention granularity and conduction coefficients one more time—"

"When the microwaves hit a foreign object like keys or loose change, they were superheated," explained the scientist. "The same with sweat. One man had his contacts fused to his eyes."

"And the morts?"

Aboud legs danced under the table. He grabbed his knees to hold them still. "Motion. They were running forward too fast. The computer couldn't adjust and the beams intersected four-inches into their chests. It shredded their hearts." He looked over at Sven Gunnar. "I am sorry."

Woody paced the floor, thumbing through the pages of his report. It was then that Spider snapped awake from his nap and let loose with a blood-curdling wail. "AAAAAAAAAAAAHHHHHHHHHH!!!" The pilot fell backwards off his chair, panting and wall-eyed while everyone in the store peered over their cubicles, wondering what had happened.

"Heap waupum war cry for a white man," grinned Smiling Bear, giving a dazed Spider the thumbs-up.

Woody shuffled over to the cowering pilot. "You can't you even sleep through a debrief without fucking it up, can you, Trent?"

"It was the wreck, sir," said Spider, picking himself up.

"Boy, *you* are a wreck. Pick up your crap and get out of here. And take the rest of your hogs with you!"

Trent fumbled for his bag and humped for the front door, his entourage following close behind.

"What was that all about?" asked Wade, grabbing bags of candy from the shelves on his way out of the store.

"I don't know," said Spider. "He must've missed the breakfast buffet at Country Kitchen this morning." He took out his pipe and filled the bowl with a Black Cherry-Ibuprofen blend.

"Was it the wires again?" asked Hoop.

"Yeah," answered Spider. "I dreamt about the Schottke mission and somehow the wires got in there again."

"What wires?" asked Fredrick.

"Spider's got a history," explained Shank. "He hit some high-tension lines when he was a young whippersnapper like us and had to eject. He landed right into his own fireball, thirty-millimeter shells cooking-off all around him."

"And you still have nightmares about it?" asked the farmer.

"Some people are afraid of drowning. For others, it's being late for class. For the major here, it's wires."

Trent shook his head "I wake up and I'm in a pool of sweat."

"That's where Spider got his callsign," said Shank.

"Sorry, guys," said the major. "Didn't mean to get you in trouble. You can go back inside. I'm fine."

"I'm not going anywhere near Wood when he's like that," said Hoop.

"Me neither," said Wade, downing a bag of M&Ms. "Too much military mumbo-jumbo."

The group scrounged for scrap wood from among the surrounding bombed out businesses. The started a bonfire and hung out under the stars and a giant *Help Wanted* banner printed in Spanish.

"It is not like the general," said Aboud, coughing from the smoke.

"He's been like that ever since I've known him," said Trent.

"No, it is like he is giving up. He does not think the new A-10s will help."

"Leper's right," said Hooper. "Wood laid out a pretty bleak picture while you were nodding off. Said the Germans are putting on a huge push down south. He's talking about pulling ADAK back to the Red River."

Spider's eyebrows raised. "That puts the FUN right on our front door. What about the nukes?"

"Dismantletation," malproped Tanner. "He said he was going to move them to Wyoming."

Hoop kicked at the dirt. "What do we do? I've never been on the losing end of anything before."

"Nothing we can do," said Spider, feeling his headache wane. "Above our paygrade. The Quarterstaff knows what they're doing. We just have to play the good soldiers."

Aboud got up and walked back toward the entrance.

"Hey, Lep. Where you going?"

"He cannot give up. His trying is not hard enough. He must think systematically."

Spider patted him on the head. "You best stay buried in your test tubes and oscilloscopes, little guy. Wood's wound around the axle pretty tight right now."

"I do not care," replied Aboud. "He cannot turn his back on freedom. If the MS dies, then all the free men in the world are next."

"Come on back to the fire," said Wade. "I'll teach you how to roast marshmallows."

Aboud slumped. "All right, fine," he conceded. He looked behind the men and pointed. "Hey, what is that black-and-white stripped cat doing over there with its tail raised?"

"Shit! Where?" Everyone turned and searched the night as Tanner ran back into the store where Patterson was addressing Gunnar and his men.

"Well, I apologize for all this doom and gloom, but I do want to welcome you to the Sovereign Forces and to the Middle States."

"Don't be sorry, sir," replied Gunnar. "We're happy to be here."

"I understand you had an interesting orientation mission."

"Which one?" asked Thor, scratching his buzztop.

"The Schottke farm. I heard you stopped a horde of Machetes."

"Stopped, sir?" Sleepy Hampshire, despondent over the depressing picture Woody had been painting, perked up. "We sucked out their eyeballs and pee'd in their brains. You should've been able to feel the fireball from here."

"That is a true statement," agreed Aboud. "We recorded it on our seismographs all the way back at our lab."

"What are you doing here, doctor?" asked Woody. "I haven't invited you back."

Aboud walked behind Patterson and picked up a piece of chalk. On the blackboard he wrote the letters T-R-I-Z. "TRIZ. Theoriya Resheniya Izobretatelskikh Zadatch. It's Russian. An acronym meaning 'The Theory of Inventive Problem Solving.'" Spider stood in the back, gesturing rapidly with a finger across his throat. "I introduced it at 3M over a decade ago," Tanner continued, ignoring him. "It was responsible for all our major breakthroughs. The process revolutionized our entire product line."

Patterson looked at the board, then back at Spider. The pilot slowly sat down, head slumped. "Quite interesting," the general said, sarcastically. "*If you're making fucking Post-It Notes!*" He went through his crumpled cigarette packs, looking for another heater.

"TRIZ involves a process of over forty repeatable steps. It applies substance-field analysis to eliminate theoretical contradictions in order to solve any given problem."

"But we don't have a problem."

"Yes, you do. The UN. You are giving up. You are retreating."

The room hushed. Patterson felt eyeballs on him as the ADAK staff joined the proceeding and lined the walls to listen. "Doctor Tanner, we all appreciate your dedication, but we have thought everything through. We have brainstormed every possible option. We have to plan for the worst."

"Brainstorming is not good. It is random," said the Persian. "You need to think systematically. You have to innovate algorithmically. I implore you not to take any hasty action until I can demonstrate my system."

"Does this system also happen to involve Dungeons and Dragons?"

"No. A TRIZ session. I want to be allowed to call a meeting of all your generals and devote an entire day exclusively to overcoming our situation and turning this battle around."

"A day?" repeated Patterson. "My maneuver commanders don't have a half-an-hour let alone a day."

"General, please. A day is all I ask. A day in return for—"

"In return for what? Are you going to guarantee success? Are you saying this TRIX, or TRIBs or TRIZ thing is foolproof?" Aboud could not. Woody took the chalk and planted it back on the board. "Look, there are more things going on that you know. We have just learned the French have been given a mandate. If that mandate turns out to be anything like the Korean's or the German's, that means we'll be facing a shitload of new tanks and aircraft. And if they institute a draft, things will get even more lopsided."

"And the FUN has nerve agents," added Gunnar. "Crates of the stuff at Hinckley." He threw a handful of foil-wrapped packages on the table. Aboud picked one up and poked at it. "We found these in one of them."

"Sample swabs, to test on animals," Tanner mumbled.

"What else, Woody? You look like there's more," questioned Spider.

"We may have a mutiny on our hands. We may have to redirect our units to put it down."

"You mean the Revowers?"

"Yes, how did you know? They solicit you?"

Spider gave a nod. "Don't worry. My guys are tight. But I can't speak for the other DOLs, though."

"I can give you the antidote," Aboud interrupted.

"What?"

Aboud threw Woody a packet. "This is nerve agent. I can manufacture the antidote. If you let me conduct my TRIZ session."

Woody's eyes narrowed. "Are you stroking me, doctor?"

Tanner held up his hands. "Oh, no, no! I only was meaning to give you an ultimatum!"

"The French aren't going to drop this just on our guys," Gunnar tried explaining to Aboud. "They'll use it to leverage us by threatening to gas civilians. You can't produce enough of the stuff if you've got no pharmaceutical industry."

Wade crumpled another candy bag. "I can do it," he said, a Sour Patch Kid-shiver rippling through his body.

"Farmer-man, you've been spending too much time around Leper," groaned Patterson.

"It's called genetic manufacturing. If it's an organic compound, I can manufacture enough of that stuff to treat the whole country in a month."

"How?"

"Cows. A thousand cows is all I need. I've been selling ginseng serum to the Chinese for years. My cows get injected with the active ingredient, then *pfft*! It comes out in their milk. Gallons a day."

"Too risky," said Woody. "I can't base our planning on cow aphrodisiacs."

"If the SF loses this war, it will not be just the Middle States that is affected," said Aboud.

Things were moving too fast for the seventy-year-old. TRIZ. Cows. Revowers. Patterson's gut began to churn. He searched through his coat pockets for more smokes. Aboud continued. "Others are fighting for you also. Friends. The Australians, the British, my countrymen in Iran. If the UN is successful in stamping you out, then they are next." Tanner's voice cracked. "Do not retreat. Give me a chance to make a difference. Please." Patterson found an old mangled cigarette inside the lining of his coat. He lit it. It tasted like airplane glue. "America brought us freedom," said the doctor. "We Iranians did not have freedom growing up. But now that we have tasted it, we will never go back. Not while we are alive."

Patterson waited until he was sure Aboud's speech was over before giving him the bad news. "It's too late, son. The QS has already decided on the pullback."

"Then I would rather die than see such a great nation surrender itself." With a flourish, Aboud retrieved a chemical packet off the table, stripped away the foil backing and swabbed the compound onto his eye. Immediately, the agent took over his enzymatic processes, twitching his eye then rolling it up inside his head, as white as a newly washed golf ball. Spider leaped for him as mucus poured from his nose and bowels. He caught him just as he collapsed and railed at him as he jittered and convulsed.

"What have you done, you savant? Now you can't help anybody."

CHAPTER 18
PREGNANT

A crisp Canadian Nor'easter busily washed away the midsummer haze as it turned Lake Superior into a cauldron of boiling cleggy whitecaps. It dashed down the tony Minnesota Northshore to the FUN shipping channels of Duluth where it stopped, unable to bore through the hot, stewing coal wharfs dotting the bay.

Laura watched the distant blue waters out the window of her FEMA trailer. Duluth had once been her diversion, her playground. She remembered better times: murder novels in the white sand, kayaking amidst the fall colors, the fireplace-warm ski chalets, snowmobiling. The perfect get-away. Too far for the riffraff of the Twin Cities—and too expensive—the scenic bluffs and craggy shores provided a cushion of luxury for the Midwest's elite to flock together, build their mansions and escape the banality of the everyday.

The perfect place for a concentration camp.

She dabbed her eyes as a tattered-looking man leaned up against her neighbor's trailer and urinated. No one in town cared that a re-unification camp now stood inside their city gates. No one asked what went on here. She knew these people. These were the winners, the ones who would run by a collapsed racer at Grandmother's Marathon, the achievers who would step over a dying climber on their way up Mount Everest, the faux-concerned who drank fair-trade lattés while paying their Iraqi nannies five dollars an hour to raise their irky kids.

She knew they wouldn't be protesting the horrific conditions in the camp. She knew these people. She was one of them.

The laundromat in the camp's center looked quiet; the long waiting line, gone. Laura grabbed her overflowing hamper and made a dash for it. Still slim and attractive at forty-five, she felt the stares of the men as she went. She wore a hot flannel shirt and baggy, frayed sweats. She didn't wear makeup for fear of attracting attention. She quickened her step but didn't know why. Yes, the prisoners were dirty, their hair greasy and frames gaunt, but after a few weeks she decided they were nice men, decent men. They were just down on their luck.

She mentally grouped the prisoners into three cliques. First were the Questionnaires, the ones turned in by friends and family who eagerly filled out mail-in police surveys. Victims of snoopy neighbors with old scores to settle, wives whose husbands wanted divorces so they could marry their secretaries, pastors who dared preach out against homosexuality.

The Engineers were next. They were the professionals; the techies who built pirate WiFi networks and geneticists who refused to experiment on stem-cells. They were independent-contractors who failed to register as employees and entrepreneurs who sold on the sidewebs to save their flagging businesses.

The last were the Pianists. They were the artists. They included a documentary film-maker interred for exposing UN child-sex rings, the CSPAN president who demanded camera coverage of the General Assembly, and an author whose novel portrayed the French in an unflattering light. She passed a clutch of them now, playing chess on an overturned oil drum.

Inside the laundromat, water pooled on the floor as a mother rummaged the waste cans for used detergent and softener sheets. Every chair held a staring defeated prisoner while their children tear-assed through the aisles with piercing shrieks.

The machines were all taken except one with its lid open, but it was full of underwear and T-shirts. Laura was in no mood to wait. She reached inside and piled the clothes on a nearby dryer, removing the tiny brown pieces of lint as a favor. After she finished the transfer, she looked at the mound of lint and realized she had made a small heap of human feces instead. "Oh, my God!" she gasped.

"I'm so sorry," said an old man, stooping rummy-eyed in the doorway. "Those are mine," he croaked with embarrassment.

Laura scrubbed her hands off in the sink as a short pear-shaped woman waddled up to her. "What are you doing? That's our stuff."

"I'm sorry, but it's been sitting here over three hours."

"It has not."

Laura pointed to the timer.

"That's broken."

"People are lined up here twenty-four hours a day," she asserted. "You can't squat on a machine and make everyone else wait."

The woman, 350 pounds at Laura's estimate, produced another basket of clothes and brushed her aside. "Yes, I can. I waited so now you can wait," she said, dropping her clothes into the empty washer.

"I have waited. *Three weeks*," Laura railed. "And I'm not going to be pushed around by some inbred malted-milkball who can't even clean her own father's drawers."

"FATHER! That's my husband you piece of white-trash!" The woman hauled back a stubby arm and swung it, hitting Laura in the neck. Laura grabbed the fist to keep from getting hit again and saw poop under the woman's garishly painted fingernails. She gagged.

"OK! OK!" Laura welped. "You can have it!" She grabbed her clothes and ran out the back where she threw breakfast up in the dumpster. Pizza boxes, dirty diapers and her corn flakes stared up at her as its sour stench overwhelmed her senses. She was a hairs-breadth away from killing something.

"Laura? Laura? Is that you?"

Laura wiped her mouth and turned around to see Abby dressed in a Burger King uniform and beaming a wide ivory smile. "Abby?"

"It is! It is you!" screamed her friend, bouncing up and down and running to her, arms outstretched. Abby's excitement was infectious and Laura smiled from the heat of it. She reached out and they hugged each other tightly for minutes.

"You look great," Laura said. She pulled back to take her all in; bright red lipstick, fresh mascara, even new earrings. Laura had never seen her so pretty. "What's with the uniform?"

"It's just part-time. Something to do," she said, pointing to the burger joint further down camp center. "Not that it pays anything."

"How long have you been here?"

"A little over a month, silly. Don't you remember? You were the one who told me to come here." A pall crept over Laura's face. She had forgotten all about the farm. "No, no, Laura. Don't do that. Don't cry." Abby took Laura's arm and led her down the alley. "Why are you crying?"

"You've been in this stye for a month and *I* put you here."

"You didn't put me here. I wanted to come. This is how I'm going to see my Chewie again."

"You'd be there by now if I had told you the truth about this place."

"You didn't lie. It just takes awhile," Abby assured her. "I've been filling out paperwork and getting my records together. Things are getting closer everyday."

Laura took Abby's shoulders and shook them. She watched nearby as a convoy of Reserve Mining buses loaded up hundreds of grimy prisoners to work in the taconite mills. "Abby, we're not going anywhere. Look around you. There are at least thirty thousand people stuffed into this crappy little harbor. And hundreds more arrive every day. They're not shipping anybody out. They're bringing them in." Abby smiled so Laura shook her again. "We're going to rot here! While our husbands are out there marking their territory, free to do whatever they want, we have to live in this polluted swamp with no food, no family and no security. Why can't you see that? Why don't you react?"

Abby shook Laura back. "Because it's not so bad. Yeah, it's not the best. Yeah, circumstances could be better, but at least we have roofs over our heads, we're alive, we've got hope."

Laura wiped away the hair sticking to her face. Abby's calm was enraging. Her blind love for Wade, infuriating, as was her acceptance of her fate. Laura wiggled free from Abby's grip. "I just want to slap that shit-eating grin right off your face, you know that?" she sputtered.

Abby's eyes crinkled. "If it'll help, go ahead. Just don't slap very hard. I'm pregnant."

CHAPTER 19
H.B.

Patterson sagged with exhaustion, more than he had in years. His eyes were puffy, his spine curling, even his shuffle was getting heavy. He just wanted to rest, to go somewhere and sit and stare and think about nothing—fishing, football, Audrey in Boulder. Anything but combat losses and mandates and Corky Davis.

Summer evenings were cool in the Dakotas; the air too dry to hold the sun's heat after it set. Woody could see his breath. He left Command and walked toward home, a bottle of eighty-year-old Talisker awaiting him. Down the runway came a roar that filled the base. He recognized the rumble immediately. It was an old friend, an F-105 Thunderchief, spooling for take-off. Patterson turned toward the ramp. His scotch would have to wait.

The Thud was Patterson's first fighter. It was a long sexy Chuck Yeager-era rocket with the swept-back wings of a wasp and the streamlined body of a Cuban perfecto. He had flown them out of Thailand during Rolling Thunder and seeing them again, fifty years later, made him smile inside. A giant blue flame blossomed out the jet's tail as the afterburner exploded with a trademark *thud*! Patterson watched the fighter climb into the ink, the smell of burning metal wafting over him.

The Minot ramp bristled with the giants of U.S. airpower: Korean War A-1 Skyraiders, Vietnam-era F-102 Delta Daggers, even front-line

F-15s, F-16s and F-117 stealth fighters. They had been resurrected from aviation purgatory; the Davis-Monthan boneyard in Phoenix, Arizona. Though referred to derogatorily as the Cactus Air Force by their adversaries, if it wasn't for these neglected warriors, the Sovereign Forces wouldn't have lasted a week.

Minot served as the chop-shop for all ADAK aviation. When the DOLs ran out of duct tape, this is where they sent their aircraft. Here, the best aerospace engineers in the Middle States mixed it up with high school gear-heads, union pipe fitters and the occasional Harley journeyman to return these warbirds to battle, often in better shape than when they had rolled off the assembly line.

Patterson reminisced as he strolled the apron. Underneath the wing of an A-7 Corsair II, he saw a tiny shadow that didn't belong, a single-engined propeller-driven tail-dragger, an O-1 Bird Dog.

"Where the hell did they find you?" he asked, fingering the pitted aluminum wings.

The Bird Dog was a frail forward observer aircraft used to direct air strikes during the Vietnam War. Woody climbed in through the tiny door, the smell of sweat and tobacco taking him back a full half-century. The O-1 had been Patterson's first assignment out of pilot training and to this day he still didn't know why it wasn't his last. Despite being no more sound than a roll of aluminum foil, Woody had chalked up over a hundred missions in the prop-job, until the day he was shot down. He had taken an AK-47 round in the engine that morning and had to ditch in a rice paddy. The O-1 carried no armament so its pilots outfitted it with anything they could find: shotguns, revolvers, swords, even Tommy guns. The crash attracted the attention of a village-full of VC who attacked out of the jungle, wanting to make crafts out of the young Iowan. He fired and when his ammo ran out, he reached inside for the only weapon he had left, a dented and scuffed Louisville Slugger. When para-rescue finally arrived, they found a bloodied, broken and near-dead Patterson, swinging his bat wildly atop a pile of dead Viet Cong farmers. Word of the spectacle got back to his squadron who bestowed him with his callsign. Patterson was never without his lucky Louisville Slugger again.

The four-star continued his nocturnal walk. As he ambled off the flightline he patted for a cigarette, realizing he hadn't needed a smoke for the last hour. He kept walking north, past *Headbanger*, the base's very own training missile and past the Transporter-Erector-Launcher yard, until he left the base and came to a collection of retention pools known as the Duck Ponds.

The water shimmered gray in the waning moonlight as he climbed a berm and tramped across an earthen divider to the other side. Once there, he found a lone park bench and rested. Inside his bowels, a dull pain intruded on his thoughts. It was death. He knew its knocking. His doctor had acknowledged he couldn't operate and prescribed painkillers and experimental chemotherapy, instead. Patterson tapped out a nerve block, lit it, then fell asleep to the peaceful chirping lullaby of the prairie.

Behind him gears whirred and he heard the heavy crunch of a footfall. He pulled out his gun and mumbled into the night. "Corky, you come to take me out?"

He made out a shape, but it wasn't a man. Something that bounded up the ledge toward him like a deer. He took a shot then ran for the pump house next to the pond. Crouching at the water's edge, the general held his breath as an oxygen regulator cycled nearby. He looked down at his glowing butt and tossed it into the water.

A giant seven-foot boogeyman walked by, carefully scanning the night. It blanked out the stars and bulged with pads and armor. Images danced across its wrap-around helmet, washing the insides in an eerie green glow. Patterson jumped up and shot.

"No!" cried the robot, in a metallic, transmogrified voice. It lashed out an arm sending Woody cartwheeling into the reservoir. Patterson popped up, gasping. He thrashed for his weapon in the foot-deep water as he waited for the monster to come crushing down on him.

"Edwards, I can't move. Get over here and help me up or I'll rip off your arm and beat you with it!"

Woody wiped water from his eyes and climbed up to where the servo laid on its back, its limbs thrashing wildly. "HB? That you?"

Harold 'H. B.' Budd, ailing billionaire and founding father of the Sovereign Forces looked up from his mechanical shell and smiled at his progeny. "Well, it's half me, Woody. Say hi to NGWE."

"What's *nug-we*?"

"Next Generation Warrior Ensemble," replied Brian Edwards, jumping out of a black Toyota Mega Cruiser and helping Budd to sit up. "Fully-sensored, networked and armored." The tech replaced Budd's air bit as the old man drew a deep long breath.

"Then why did it die?"

The portly jean-clad technician pulled wires out of the machine's backpack and connected them to a suitcase of diagnostic equipment. "It's the batteries. You shorted the plates when you shot him."

"Where are the batteries?"

"In the armor," said Budd, pointing to his chest.

"As long as he insists on armoring himself with plate batteries, this is what will happen when he takes a hit," complained Edwards.

"It saves weight," Budd replied, motion returning to his arms.

"That was you running?" asked Woody. "You covered those last fifty yards in just a few steps."

"I thought that was pretty cool, too," replied Budd. "It's like I can finally do the things I've always watched everyone else do. Only better."

"Diesel-fired stilts," said Edwards. "A computer-modulated spark system fires the plugs at the moment of push-off to give a soldier a ten-foot stride." The aide finished his repairs and stuffed the cables back into his boss' switching unit. Before bottling it back up, he double-checked the readouts. "Sir? You're O2 is—"

"Brian, push me up. General Patterson and I need a moment."

The young tech gathered his tools and loaded them into the SUV. He returned with a contingent of bodyguards who took Budd by the arms and lifted him to his feet.

Woody shivered and began wringing himself off. "I hope you're here to tell me you're changing your mind, because I haven't changed mine."

"Change my mind? About what?" H. B. began leaping in the air and bounding up and down the dike like an Olympic triple-jumper.

"Cut the crap, HB. The president's got consultants all over gunning for your ass. Even in the MS. You didn't come out of hiding tonight to get your Astronomy merit badge." Woody jumped in front of the old man to block his way. "You came here to tell me you're reneging."

"On what?"

"On your promise not to secede."

Budd walked over to the pump house and battered it with his fists.

He came down on it with his arms, crumpling the roof. "My only promise has been to win. I trust you still share the same sentiment."

"Not if it's the same way Corky wants to win," answered Woody.

"And which way's that?"

"He wants to start fighting POTUS troops. He wants to change the rules-of-engagement to include shooting Americans."

"Well, they're shooting at us!" Budd motioned to Edwards who returned with a basket of yellow rubber ducks. The tech threw them into the middle of the pond as H. B. tested NGWE's integrated sighting system. Budd aimed and fired at the bath toys with a .50-caliber Desert Eagle; each one of them giving a little squeak as he blew them from the water one-by-one.

Woody shook his head at the billionaire, wondering if he had built the suit for the troops or himself. "We start killing U.S. soldiers like we do the UN, then discipline goes out the window."

"Sam's a good man, Wood. He's got heart."

"That's not true. If he did, he'd be trying to find a way to win."

"He is."

"No, he's not. He's trying not to lose. That's fear."

"It's also practical. A third of our losses are due to XUS units."

"Quit calling them that, damn it. They're U.S. They're us."

"Well, *us* are killing us! We have to fight back. If we kill them then we have a chance."

"We will have *no* chance," barked Patterson. "Not only will we be fighting a new enemy but we'll lose the moral high-ground. We'll reverse years of growing sentiment. You think we have problems now, wait until you give the economies something to fight about."

"Whatever they throw at us, it won't be much."

Woody wrung water out of his pack of cigarettes and threw them to the ground. He pulled out a pipe and prepped it while regarding Budd. "This isn't like you, HB. You don't usually pick a plan based on metaphysical conjecture."

"The XUS is a toothless lion," Budd explained. "A shell of its former greatness. The president slashed their manpower, replacing his soldiers with a few high-technology tanks. He's closed all their installations and consolidated his divisions into five super-bases. He's mothballed half his squadrons in favor of a few overpriced toys and now they're without their ICBMs. Earle is an incompetent, an idiot commander-in-chief."

"Now it's starting to make sense," said the pilot. HB stared down at him from his mechanical turk. "You don't want to stop a president. You want to *be* one."

"If that's what it takes to win."

"And what will you have won?" sneered Woody. "The MS has no industry, no sea ports. It will be a Third World country with no freedoms or ideals. The country will be protected by an army of hypocritical traitors and ruled by a government made up of your own hand-picked sycophants. That won't be a democracy. That'll be tyranny."

"That would never happen. You know that, Wood."

"I agreed to join the Ex-Nihilos because you made me believe you'd never give up your fight for this country," said the airman. "That's why all those kids are out there fighting for you now, fighting the world."

Budd's suit wavered and his eyes flickered. Woody heard him wheeze. "It's for those kids I'm doing this," coughed Budd.

"Or is it for Davis? He's the man behind this. I know what he's offering is tempting. Visions of power. Maybe your face on Mount Rushmore." Patterson moved closer. "It won't end there. Not with him as second-in-command. Wake up. Take charge of your senses before it's too late."

LEDs flashed inside Budd's helmet as the prototype shuddered and went limp. Edwards and the guards ran up, catching Budd as he tottered.

"BP's 200 over 120. Heart rate is in the red. Go get his wheel chair, hurry!" Edwards ordered. They unstrapped Budd from his Goliath suit and pumped white goo into his IV lines as they hoisted him into his chair.

Patterson put a hand on his arm. "I'm not angry with you, HB. You're like a father to me. I know you'll do what's right. I love you to death."

Budd opened his mouth, but could only manage a raspy reply. "I'm putting Davis in charge. He makes the hard choices. He's got the heart of the SF. They want strength, not idealism."

Patterson hung his head as Budd closed his eyes. When his aides had packed up their gear, they wheeled him to his car.

"Even if I'm the only one left, HB, I'm sticking to my oath. It's all I have."

CHAPTER 20
THUMPERS

Verhagen fought for the microscope, banging heads with Aboud in the process. The major winced as he nudged his boss back, trying to keep the spaz away from the equipment. "This agent isn't like Sarin or VX."

Aboud nodded.

"Its effects are the same, but the mechanism is new. Atropine and 2-PAM chloride can't touch it." Verhagen rubbed his brow then wiped up a pool of Tanner's spittle from the bench top. "With no organophosphates jamming the neuro-receptors, it's got to be something blocking blood flow to the nerves."

Aboud fumbled for a test tube rack. His assistant caught it before all their work crashed to the floor. "Are you wanting to try Wade's serum?"

The Persian nodded. "Doowhedoowhedoowhe—"

"Do we have enough? I'll go see," replied Verhagen. "How are you feeling, doctor? What are your symptoms now?"

"Pain. Lotta pain. I feel on f-f-fire but cannot perspire."

Verhagen shook his head "I still don't see how you're still alive."

"The s-s-swab was for testing animals," the little man replied. "The concentration was too small to kill a human."

"Maybe, but it was still a boneheaded stunt."

Aboud glared back at the assistant, his eye twitching.

A nerve in Tanner's arm fired, sending the microscope to the floor. Verhagen fumed as he stooped to pick up the pieces. When he came back up, Aboud was in the process of stabbing himself in the arm with a syringeful of cow serum.

"Doctor Tanner. No. We haven't tested it yet." The hypodermic went wide, imbedding in the table. "It's poison by itself. It could kill you."

"I have to. I cannot t-t-take this anymore. My mind is going out." Aboud ran his hands along the lab's white walls, searching for the door in his dimming vision. He found the handle and pulled it open, looking for Wade.

Fredrick sat on a stall gate in his newly constructed dairy, quaffing milk from a pail. He rummaged through a stack of well-worn magazines while his new herdsmen read over his shoulders.

"Nice rump," Wade said.

"E'yep. Tight and firm."

Fredrick rotated the page. "Great legs!"

"E'yep. I like their shape. Nice and long," his men agreed. The farmer kept twirling it. "Somethin' wrong with the girl?"

"Her tits are too low."

"Tits are low! Course her tits are low, they're huge!"

"E'yep, they're big 'uns all right!"

"I thought you liked 'em big, boss."

"Yeah, I like them big but not if she's going to be stepping all over them." Wade threw the catalog on the pile. "Then they're no good to me. Keep looking guys. We need to double our herd size in a few weeks but not with inferior genetics."

Fredrick jumped down off the post and finished stripping one of his test cows. He dumped her milk into a large stainless can. Up ahead, he could hear lowing as Tanner and Verhagen pushed their way through his herd.

"Hi, Will," he said. "I've got another sample for the centrifuge." Verhagen didn't answer. He was holding Tanner up by the arm. "Is it getting bad?"

"He tried injecting himself with the plasma concentrate."

"Then it works!" beamed Fredrick.

"No," said Verhagen.

"Yes," Aboud came back. "The galactosidase you are manufacturing has an affinity for the accumulating glycoidlipids. I n-n-need it to restart cell meiosis. To hydrolyze the acetylcholine that is firing my synapses."

"What the hell is he talking about?" Wade asked Verhagen.

"If the serum hydrolyzes, he's cured. If it oxidizes, he's dead."

"I *guarantee* you it will work," Aboud stammered.

Fredrick hoisted his pail and took a swig. "Well, you look peaked just the same. Why don't you have some milk?"

"How c-c-can you eat at a time like this?"

"No, I mean *have some milk*." Aboud slapped at the can as Wade put it to his lips. Verhagen held the doctor still as the milk went down his throat.

"Don't worry," said Fredrick. "The aGal A in this sample isn't concentrated enough to be fatal. Yet, if it does bond to the protein, we should be able to see some change."

"I'm impressed," said Verhagen. "You stay at a Holiday Inn Express last night?"

They dropped Aboud to the cold barn floor and got half the warm cream into him. The rest ran down his neck and clothes.

"Oh, you should not have done that," Aboud said. "I do not feel well." His eyes fluttered and Verhagen grew concerned.

"Look, it's working," said Wade.

"His heart's stopped," reported the major.

"At least he's not twitching all over."

"I've got to get to a defibrillator. Where's a defibrillator?"

"We don't have one. This is a barn. We don't give CPR to cows."

Verhagen began searching the walls around him. "I've got to call the CP. I've got to get the medics."

"Relax," said Wade. "It looks like he's coming to." At their feet, Aboud began coughing and gagging as a curious heifer nuzzled the scientist with a hairy sopping nose. "Get it away. I am better. I am better!" Tanner batted the animal convulsively as he pulled thick strings of mucus from his hair.

"I'm not worried about you," grinned Wade. "I'm worried about my cow," He backed the spurned animal away and scratched her between the ears.

For a few more minutes, the two watched as Tanner went from

a jittering and frothing invalid to his timid, reserved self. "What are you feeling, doctor?" asked Verhagen.

"My symptoms are gone! We have discovered the right mechanism!"

Wade looked up close at his friend's drooping eyelid. "Tell me again why it had to go in your eye?"

"To get it into my system quickly. To force General Woody to give me my TRIZ session." Aboud fingered his face. "Maybe I should have just rubbed it on my arm."

Outside, gunfire sounded.

"What's that? Are the guards target practicing again?" asked Aboud.

"I don't know," said the farmer as a side door burst open. In the archway, First Lieutenant Howard McCord stormed in, his black-and-green pixilated night camo glittering in the dark.

"Chief Warrant Fredrick, where is Doctor Tanner?" he panted.

Wade pointed to the ground where Aboud was struggling to get up. "Why? What's going on?"

"Probably nothing. Dragon squad's got some activity outside the fence that set off a wire. Probably just a wolf or two checking out the menu in your calf lot."

"That all?"

"Or a spy."

"A spy?" whispered Aboud. "Can I go out and help? I'll get my gear."

"Thanks, doctor," McCord replied, grabbing Tanner's collar. "We've got a whole company of Devil Dogs assigned to the colony. You just stay by my side for now."

"Echo-Hotel. This is OP1," crackled the radio.

"Go ahead, OP1," McCord replied.

"We've got infantry approaching. Platoon strength."

"Shit! Bravo Team, you hear that? Get north and back them up. OP1, any vehicles?"

"No vehicles, just riflemen. Wait ... HOLY BALLS!"

"OP1, report."

"Where'd they go, Hooch? Echo-Hotel! Echo-Hotel! They're gone."

"Who's gone?"

"The bad guys. They're inside the perimeter. They ran by so fast we couldn't get a shot."

"They *ran*? Why didn't you engage?"

"They leaped by just like antelope. They didn't even mess with us. They made straight for the—"

"OP1, this is Papa-Yankee. We've got a Stryker in overwatch on your position."

"Give me a report Papa-Yankee," radioed the lieutenant.

"Smitty, you got anything up there? Smitty? OH, JESUS GOD!"

Outside the door, Wade, Aboud and Verhagen heard more gunfire.

"Echo-Hotel, where are you now?" crackled a new voice.

"Captain Bennett, I'm in the research barn now. I've got Leper."

"Mutt, I'm sending you Angel Team," replied Bill Bennett, the company commander. "Secure the target and get him under cover."

"What's going on, sir? How can twenty dirtbags make it through a company of armored cavalry?" McCord grabbed Aboud, but didn't know what to do with everyone else. He flipped down his optics and opened the door to get a fix on his commander as a bullet entered his NVGs and erased the back of his head. Aboud's face glistened red with the lieutenant's blood.

"Wade? Will? Have I been hit? Am I hit?"

Wade snapped up McCord's rifle as three young Angel Team riflemen and their sergeant rushed in, firing grenades into the black.

"D'ya get 'em, Stall?"

"How the fuck should I know? I couldn't see nothin'."

The soldiers bolted the door and reinforced it with a steel cow gate. "Where's Top, Stall?"

Outside, a man screamed.

"GOD DAMNED ANIMALS!" yelled Buzz Stallings, now the company's new first sergeant.

The four stood fixed in their sweat and stared dumbly at the wall as the door began bending and folding on its hinges. The GIs filled it with rifle fire until their magazines were empty. Then the lights went out.

"Come on," said Wade.

"Where we going?"

"The milk house. It'll be easy to defend. There's only one way in." Fredrick grabbed the men around the shoulders, yanking them from their spot. As he led them through his herd, boots pursued them along the roof. He popped his head up from among the swishing tails. "Quiet!" he ordered. "Listen." Above them, a hole opened in the metal roof as red laser beams played across the dusty air, searching for them.

"Hit the dirt!" the dairyman yelled, as bullets rained down on them, snicking into cowhide and bone. About them, a dozen of the animals fell and the rest scattered, leaving the group exposed.

"There they are," hollered the Alpha Team soldiers, firing a volley into the eaves. The barn's diesel generator powered up and the lights came back on revealing black birdlike shadows dropping down from the rafters and into the surrounding stalls.

"Did you see that? What the hell are they?"

The group used the nearby carcasses for cover as they crawled for safety behind a cement water trough. Wedged between the tank and a stack of writhing Holsteins, the gritty-faced gunners grabbed their clips and began to reload.

"We're surrounded, Stall. And there's more coming," cried Corporal Jake Eerdmanns, firing bursts blindly into the beams above.

"Hunker down beneath the cows," the NCO replied. "Until it's hamburger, we should be all right."

"I can't," his assistant said. "Someone's already there." Between two sixteen-hundred-pound mamas lay Aboud. Still dripping with the brains of Lieutenant McCord, he had found an air pocket in which he had hoped to avoid detection.

"Wade! Where's Wade?" cried Tanner. "Did he run? Did he leave us here?"

Fifty yards away, at the far end of the feed alley, the dairy's eighteen-foot retractable door buckled and came crumpling down as Fredrick drove through it with a new green-and-yellow John Deere tractor. "The Honey Wagon's here, kids!"

"Manure?" repeated the first sergeant, gawking at the shiny four-thousand-gallon New Holland manure spreader Wade was pulling behind him.

"It's manure on the inside but half-inch plate steel on the outside," yelled Wade. "Get in!" Muzzle flashes lit up the shadows as the men climbed the hitch and rolled into the thigh-deep muck. They came up shooting as rounds ricocheted off the outside.

Fredrick gunned the engine and lowered his bucket, plowing a path through the bovines as the shadowy apparitions followed them on all sides. After a few seconds, his motor lugged as the cows started piling up in front. That's when he saw a commando scramble up his hood and pull out a knife.

The raider looked slight up close, almost skinny, with wild eyes and flared nostrils. From what he saw, Fredrick had no explanation for the attacker's power, speed or acrobatics. They were more like circus animals on crack than men.

In an instant, the man was on him like a velociraptor. Wade fired, lifting him off his feet and somersaulting him under his front tires. Behind him, the assailants surrounded his wagon, climbing up the sides. Wade shot two but couldn't see the others. Neither could the soldiers inside.

"Hold your breath," he yelled to Stallings.

"What?"

"Hold your breath!" Wade puffed his cheeks and pinched his nose to ready the team before opening the rear effluent chute. Liquid manure poured out the back, sweeping the men out with it as the black-clad commandos jumped inside trying to figure out where they had gone.

Fredrick shut the chute door and powered up the wagon as a shadow loomed over him. He grabbed a pitchfork from the back of the cab and turned just in time to catch his assailant in mid-air. He stuck the tines deep into the thing's chest and tossed it over his shoulder where it fell onto its comrades in the spreader.

The attackers slipped and slid on the slick, wet metal as the wagon's augers and chopper knives and flailing blades leaped to life. The hopper screws turned and cut them down at the ankles then the knees and hips. Next, the counter-spinning rotary shears chopped their torsos into clean six-inch chunks. Flailing plates whirled underneath to beat the slabs into tiny pebble-sized pieces of bone, skull and joints before the spreader sprayed the final mess across the barn walls like homemade salsa.

Aboud pointed to the rafters. "There is more still up there!" Wade took his bucket and rammed a nearby support post. The barn shuddered as the timber sheared and dropped the roof six feet. The raiders fell to the floor in a knot.

Angel Team leveled their M-203s and fired grenades into the tangle, only to watch the attackers dodge out of the way. Stallings had never seen anything like it. His team backed up as laser dots danced on their uniforms and one of his enlisteds went down. "I'm hit, sarge!"

Wade jumped off his Deere and pulled the boy to safety only to discover he was dead.

"Damn them. Damn them fucking freaks to hell!" shouted Stallings. "What the hell is going on?"

"I don't know," replied Fredrick. "But they sure aren't Imperial Storm Troopers. These guys don't miss."

"Can we still make it to the far door?" Stallings asked as he rammed home a new clip.

The research barn had four free-stall wings that formed an *H*. They were cavernous and open so the animals could roam and relax between milkings. In the center, a large rotary milking parlor connected the free-stalls together. The operational hub of the facility, its construction provided tighter, snugger and concrete-reinforced security. Wade pointed to a cow ramp fifty yards away. "Head for that gangway. It leads to the milk house. We can hold out there until help arrives."

Stallings held up his broken walkie-talkie. "What help? We're all that's left."

The team sprinted for the ramp, Wade in the lead and bullets following them. Verhagen was hit, then Stallings. They reached the incline and scrambled into the milk house one man short.

"Goddamn civilians," cursed Stall, running back for Aboud who had slipped on a grate. He bent down to grab Tanner's arm as a commando popped around the corner. Stallings raised his M-16 but saw it slapped away. He pulled out his knife but watched it twisted from his grip and used against him in a flurry of thrusts that sounded like beating wings. The brawny Chicagoan looked down at his intestines and fell motionless atop Tanner.

"They got Stall," Eerdmanns screamed.

The team fired from their hips as the ramp filled with black shapes. The attackers were almost on them when, behind them, a manure-encrusted skid loader roared out of the black and flew airborne down the ramp. "It's clobberin' time!" yelled Wade. The dairyman worked his controls with the finesse of a videogamer, shoveling the boogeymen into his bucket as he drove through them. When he had them up against the wall at the bottom of the gangway, he raised the scoop, scraping its edges along the concrete until he could hear their banging and pounding to get out. "Cat got your tongues, boys?" He spit out a plug of Copenhagen and put in another as the loader started moving backwards. "NO!"

Fredrick stomped on the brakes but still the tires skidded backwards. Legs and arms and heads began peeping at him from the scoop as muscle overpowered hydraulics. Wade raised the Bobcat up on its rear wheels and shoved the gas forward until the handle bent. Slowly, the contest abated as the added weight resealed the bucket to the wall and arms and legs and heads popped off bodies and fell to the ground.

While Wade battled on the ramp, Aboud gathered the bleeding, battered remnants of 1222CAV Devil Dogs inside the central pod. He could sense the commandos slithering soundlessly close behind but didn't know their number. Realizing they would not be safe until Wade returned, Tanner herded his group into a hay-covered calving pen and hid them behind an expectant heifer that lay panting in the corner. He turned out the lights then jumped into the veterinary therapy pool nearby.

Sniffing. Something was in the room and it was sniffing. The men held their breath and didn't dare move, not even to shoulder their weapons.

Aboud hid underwater, floating as stealthy as a big fat manatee. Suddenly, a raider peered over the side and looked straight at him. He was dead. He knew it. The creature turned his head left then right and gave him a drugged leer before turning toward the others with his rifle blazing.

Tanner squeezed his eyes shut trying to block out the strobe-light flashes of the machine gun. His lungs screamed for air as he weighted his options; stand up and get shot or inhale and drown. He remembered Stallings and the way he had died before deciding drowning wasn't such a bad way to go.

One quick inhale and that would be it. It's not so bad. I've had a good life. It was time to go.

Tanner accepted his fate and for the first time in his life, his mind finally found peace. A constant companion since birth, his fear dissolved as hopes and expectations no longer held sway. He felt strong and sure as his body poised for the shock of the water. He thought of his parents and his brother then smiled and took a long deep pull.

Verhagen and the two infantrymen felt their pregnant shield quiver as bullets peppered her flanks and insides. They waited for the commando to stop and reload but the shots kept coming, turning the cow's flesh into ground round. A spitzer penetrated the carcass, lodging in the major's thigh. The two enlisteds screamed as they too were hit, when Aboud vaulted out of water like Flipper and fired his M-16 into the raider's back until the attacker fell silent.

Tanner doubled-over. He bucked and hacked as water left his lungs. Verhagen crawled over to administer a Heimlich.

Eerdmanns attended to the fallen commando, rolling him over with the muzzle of his weapon. "This thing's still alive, doctor. And he looks like you."

Aboud walked over on his hands and knees, wiping the grime and blood from the man's face. "Oh, no. What have I done?"

"You saved our asses," responded Verhagen. "Don't tell me you're feeling remorse for this thing."

"He is not a thing. He is Iranian. He is my friend. This is my boyhood friend."

"Who is there?" the infiltrator called out in Farsi.

"Zahra, it's me. Aboud."

"Aboud?"

"Yes, Aboud Geha." Tanner threw down his M-16. "How could I? I am so sorry. Not you! Not Zahra!" He opened his friend's tunic to try to stem some of the bleeding. "Why? Why are you here? Why are you trying to kill us?"

"We came to help you. The Guardian Army is here to join your cause. Iranian soldiers to fight for freedom."

Aboud took off Zahra's helmet and ran his hand over the man's shaved head. Dozens of donut-shaped bruises speckled his scalp. Zahra muttered to Aboud before trailing off. "The UN. The French—"

"They captured you? They tortured you?"

The raider shook his head and coughed blood. "They heard of our plan to smuggle into the Middle States. They intercepted us on the frontier. They put caps on us. Magnetic coils that thumped in our heads."

"TMS," Aboud mumbled to Verhagen.

"Yes! That is what they called it. They had it on night and day and night and day. We could smell our skin burning."

Tanner continued checking the man's pupils and pulse. "Do not talk, my friend. Rest."

"The machines did things to us. Gholam could see in the dark. Nadir could navigate without a map or compass. All of us have not slept in a week yet we ran here twenty-five miles and are not even tired."

Aboud tried ripping his shirt to pack the man's wounds. He knew it would do no good and cursed to himself.

"I'm a sniffer. I smell. I can tell a broken birch twig from a crushed milkweed stem. I can smell a week-old cigarette. I can smell blood."

"But your eyes," asked Aboud. "You looked right at me in the pool."

"I am blind now, yes. They blinded me so there would be more room in my brain for my nose." Zahra's chest gurgled as he fought for air. He felt for Aboud's hand. "I smell tears, my friend. They had better not be for me."

"How can they not be?" questioned Aboud. "I murdered your parents now I murder you.

"You were a boy. A pesar. They had a gun to your head."

"I am ashamed for my cowardice. For my treachery."

"And yet today you protected your friends and killed the enemy."

"But you are not my enemy!"

"Today, I was. You did right. I am proud of you."

Tanner bundled his friend up and tried to lift him. "I am taking you to my lab. Hang on. Do not die, Zahra."

"To die in the company of a friend is a feast. Khoda-hafez, Aboud," and Zahra closed his eyes and breathed his last.

As Aboud bent down to kiss his cheeks, sounds of a struggle could be heard coming from the ramp. Aboud remembered Fredrick. "Where is Wade?" With the others, he hobbled through the dark lanes of the parlor to find Wade standing up against the wall being pummeled by the last remaining thumper. Drawing near, they saw that Wade had broken one of its arms and had pulled the other out of its socket yet still was being kicked and struck ferociously. Tired of wrestling, the stout dairyman laid all his weight against the thing's hip, grabbed a thigh and pulled with a powerful jerk. The bone popped out of its hip like a freshly butchered chicken's and the thumper crumpled to the ground.

"What kind of animals are they?" he asked.

"They are not animals, they were made that way," answered Aboud.

"Drugs?"

"Transcranial Magnetic Stimulation." He reached down and took off the attacker's helmet then pointed to the many circular bruises that dotted the commando's head. "Magnetic pulses. Aimed to destroy selected parts of the brain like tiny air-hammers."

"Then shouldn't they be retarded?"

"The parts of the brain that the French doctors killed are the parts that cause us to stop and think, that cause us to hold back before we do something. Without these natural inhibitors, the remaining senses are free to perform at superhuman levels." Aboud examined the positions of the man's bruises. "Your's was an agile."

"Good thing they didn't give them steroids," added Fredrick as the savant continued to kick and spit and flail at him despite its broken limbs. "And what makes them do that?"

Aboud pointed behind the man's ear. "The anterior cingulate cortex. They thumped their pain processors, too."

From the bottom of the concrete gangway, Angel Team returned carrying the limp body of their sergeant. "It's Stallings. He's dead."

Aboud slumped. Stallings had died defending him and it was this thumper that had probably killed the sergeant. He watched the shape as it writhed and continued to lash out with its bloody stumps. As a fellow countryman who had come for the cause of freedom, Tanner pitied him. But now the man was something else, something defying description. With his new-found courage, Aboud stood straight up, pulled out his automatic and took aim. Wade held up a hand then lifted the thumper by the shoulders and gave it a quick violent jerk, breaking its neck.

"A bullet's too good for him. This *is* an animal and he deserves to die like one."

CHAPTER 21
MESSAGE

"Sir, the junior officers are ready to do this," Ajax Dunn told his boss, washing down a carnival dog with a can of Tab. "We just need to educate them a little more. They're still pretty jumpy about revowing, especially if they have to go against their commanders."

"What's so damned hard about it?" the other said. "You raise your hand, you vow to defend your country and uphold the constitution, and you swear to God. The only difference is it's a new constitution and the country is the Middle States."

"There's a new constitution? You didn't tell us about that?"

Dunn was talking to Corky Davis. They were meeting in the anonymity of the carnival to get an idea for the amount of resistance their impending putsch would have to overcome. In the distance, they heard guns, low and throaty just as the base sirens went off.

"Air raid?" asked Davis.

"Not against a nuke base, sir," replied the lieutenant. To the south, fireballs appeared on the horizon as tracers reached for a black dot they couldn't yet see.

"Mirage!" yelled Dunn, who grabbed Davis by the shoulders and pushed him into a hedgerow. Over the runway, the air tore with a shriek as the French fighter released its munitions and pulled vertical to escape retaliation. Around the field, specially-designed HMMWVs armed with customized air-air Sidewinders slewed their turrets to follow the attacker. When the seekers locked onto the aircraft's IR signature, all four SLAMRAAM batteries emptied their tubes at it. As the missiles chased the jet vertical, their processors were sensing closing rates and calculating lethality almost as a single unit. When the computers figured the probabilities for a rear-quadrant kill too be low, the SAMs disengaged to pursue a front-hemisphere shot. The missiles split apart and accelerated ahead to an altitude of twenty thousand feet where they waited, hovering like vultures. When the enemy fighter arrived, its airspeed gone, the missiles flipped on their sides and converged near-horizontally, their plumes tracing a beautiful multi-petaled pattern through the sky that exploded in the middle like a giant yellow sunflower.

"They're attacking a nuke base?" Davis bellowed in anger.

Wing spars and bits of fuselage rained down on carnival vendors as a sun-bleached Dunn peeked his head through the cedar shrubs waiting for explosions. "Didn't he drop any bombs?"

A block away, a crowd was gathering around the side of the SAGE building. The two ran for the throng, parting it to expose a cratered wall and four round asterisks of blood. At the base of the building, a medic kneeled, attending to a pulpy mass that lay on the ground.

"What is it, corporal?" asked Davis.

The medic answered through a handkerchief. "It's bodies, General Davis. Four bodies." He poked through the heap, trying to separate fingers from ribs and arms from legs.

"How were they killed? I didn't hear an explosion."

"From what I can tell, they weren't killed on the ground. These came from the air."

"Say again," said Dunn.

"They came from the air. The plane dropped them. They're human bombs." The medic reached into the goo and pulled out a shiny metallic lug. It was clamped around a human spine. "They must have been dead before they were hung from the wings. At least, I hope they were."

A piece of hotdog rose up into Dunn's mouth. He ran around the corner before hurling up the rest. When he had coughed the last chunk free, he took out his peer phone and called the Leper Colony.

Peer phones contained the relay and switching electronics of a cell tower. The Sovereigns had been forced to invent them since their cell towers were under constant attack. By routing calls through other peer phones, the MS had found a way to communicate again that NSA could not intercept. But the technology was new and required the phones in your chain to be no further than three miles apart. This topology was not well suited for sparsely populated states like the Dakotas. Dunn didn't get an answer. He decided to let it keep ringing. You never knew when people were traveling through your chain.

"Who are they?" asked Davis.

The medic separated the flesh into four piles. "These three are SF, sir." He grabbed a patch of clothing and wiped off a spot, revealing a blue-and-green Bent Angels patch.

"212PARA," mumbled Davis. "These are my boys. The three sliders that were lost in the thunderstorm."

"This one's French, sir. Nametag says *Xavier Chack*."

"Who would do this?" asked Dunn, back from the bushes.

"Someone's sending us a message," said Davis.

"To humiliate us? To revenge the Hinckley raid?"

"To tell us we aren't safe under our nukes anymore. To warn us."

"Warn us? Warn us about what?" Just then, Dunn's phone rang. He dug it out to of his pocket to answer it.

"Who is that? Who are you calling," asked the general.

"The Leper Colony. General Patterson's R&D lab. The doctor there is some kind of Einstein. I thought he might have a way to keep another attack like this from happening."

Davis snatched the phone from his lieutenant, broke it in two then stomped it into the sidewalk. "Don't ever let me ever catch you talking to Patterson or any one associated with that zoombag. Understand?" Dunn nodded and took a step back. "He is a loyalist and is doing all he can to fuck up the revowing. We need that kind of thinking silenced. Especially now."

"I don't follow, sir. What do you mean?"

"We need to quicken our pace. The French are going nuclear."

CHAPTER 22
DEAL

A dark July storm boomed overhead, drenching Skyline Drive in rivers of rain. The driver took care with his passenger, negotiating the hairpin turns with prudence as he climbed out of Duluth's gridlocked administrative tranche to Pétain Airbase above.

"Where are you taking me?" squawked a reedy Laura Trent to her two mute escorts. "The infirmary?"

The van's midnight blue finish carried the waves and fleurs-de-lis of the new French mandate of Terre du Lacs. The paint scheme turned heads as the vehicle entered the base's main gate and drove through the picturesque residences along the Lake Superior bluffs. A solitary two-story limestone estate stood at the end of the drive: their destination.

"Nice place," she said. "But you're not going to get me to eat here either." She tried wiggling free from her guards' grasp but not before they threw her into the home's chandeliered entranceway. Inside, Sean Faisson greeted her with a bow.

"Not even if we offer you a bowl of chestnut pheasant soup, Mrs. Trent? Or perhaps a beef bourguignon salad?"

Laura sneered at him. "You. What is this place? What am I doing here?"

"You are my guest. I heard you have been under the weather and unhappy with your accommodations at the processing facility since you arrived."

"You should know, you built it." Laura looked up a ten-foot-wide grand staircase as it swirled around the foyer's rotunda. It led to a second floor wrap-around balcony encircled with ornate wrought-iron railings. To her right, a bright, airy parlor room awaited important guests while, to her left, a post-and-beam great-room unfolded to expose rough-hewn heart pine timbers and a wall seemingly made out of glass. The general's men ushered his guest inside.

"I *am* sorry for that," Faisson said, referring to his guards. He dismissed them with a tilt of his head. "As I am for the delays in getting you processed so you can rejoin your husband in the MS. But it doesn't mean I am not above being hospitable. Please sit down and join me." Faisson sat down at the table and began tucking in to his meal of soup, stuffed wild boar leg in onion marmalade and hare pudding.

"No thanks," she answered. "I'm not really in the mood for taxidermist cuisine today."

"Then how about some fettuccine alfredo and a glass of lambrusco? You always were an Olive Garden freak," came another voice from the kitchen.

Laura turned from the window vista. "Cody!"

"Hi, mom," he said, bending for a hug. She pulled away.

"So you're the one behind this!"

"Do not be so harsh on the boy, Mrs. Trent. He is concerned for you, that is all. When he said you had stopped eating and had refused to let him see you, I became concerned, too."

Laura eyed her food as Cody placed the plates before her on the table. "If that's true, then let me go," she said.

"We cannot. Your safety would be compromised." Faisson toasted her with a charge of Domain Vacheron 2003.

"I'd rather be stoned by my neighbors than go back to your sty."

"How can you rightly say that?" asked the Frenchman. "You have everything you need; free shelter, food, security."

"I live in a swamp, have to wait in line for cold mashed potatoes and am surrounded by a bunch of coughing smelly hobos."

"You paint a very bleak picture."

"How would you know? You live on Skyline Drive."

"You've got it all wrong, Mrs. Trent."

Laura walked to the picture windows and pointed to the trees. "The hell I do. You can't even see the camp from here."

"No. You are wrong about the house," Faisson said. "It is not mine. It is yours." Laura put her hands on her hips and opened her mouth, but nothing came out. "This can be your residence. If you'll have it."

She regarded the opulent appointments, the floor-to-ceiling fireplace, the industrial-strength kitchen, the lap pool, the Finnish sauna. Her mind did somersaults.

"I have read your file," continued the commander. "You are a very impressive woman. Master's degree. College professor and administrator. We could use your talents to improve our reunification centre; streamline operations, improve collaboration, cultivate community acceptance."

"And how would I do that? I live in a concentration camp. I would need an office. And staff," she said. "You're not about to give me any of those."

Faisson arched his eyebrows. "That is why I am offering you this house."

Laura did not trust the smooth-talking Faisson. She looked to Cody for direction only to find his attention focused on a dish of tiramisu. "What you ask is impossible," Laura replied. "The city doesn't want you here. Nobody likes the French. The mandate, the tranche, the camp. Americans won't take this for very much longer."

"But Duluth is a progressive municipality," replied the general. "That is why I picked it for my headquarters. They are very supportive of liberal causes."

"It's a very *wealthy* city with business people who don't want to be looking at refugee tents from the windows of their favorite restaurant. To win acceptance for your plans, I would need access to the community. Freedom to meet with leaders. You aren't about to let me out."

Faisson threw a set of keys onto the table. She stared at them warily.

"It's a Towncruiser, mom!"

Laura picked up her glass of wine and emptied it. "You're setting me free? I don't have to go back to the camp? I won't be followed around by your goons?"

Faisson nodded.

"I thought you were worried about my safety. Won't I be in danger here?"

"This house is on the airbase. It is the old commander's residence. You will have around-the-clock patrols."

"And my husband, John?"

"Yes, what of him?"

"I still want to go. To be with him," she tested. "I will still be doing all I can to expedite our reunion."

Cody recovered from his reverie and slammed down a hand. "I don't believe you! The leader of the world's newest dependency has just offered you a job and all you can think about is dad? Treat me for shock, mom, *he's* the one who put you here."

"Your dad did not put me here," asserted Laura. "He just ... he just ... "

"Now, now Cody," chided Faisson. "Do not be disrespectful to your parents. I asked for your mother's help expressly because of her principles and morals. We need more people like her and I would be disappointed if she didn't do all she could for her family."

"And you're OK with that?" Laura asked. "I run your Reunification program until my emigration comes through and then I can leave?"

"And, from time to time, supply me with reports."

"Reports?"

"On the activities of others. Any information that might be of interest to the mandate."

"What kind of information?"

"Just trivial things," he replied.

"You want me to spy?"

"Spy? No. More along the lines of *community relations*."

"I don't like the sound of this," she said.

"I want you to gather opinions and give them to me in the form of suggestions or comments. In order to tap the collective wisdom of this new nation, we need someone who is willing to rub shoulders with ordinary people, to fraternize with their leaders, to let me know what the *buzz* is, as you say." Faisson got up to look out over the harbor. "So what do you say, Mrs. Trent? Does what I offer you sound attractive or should I call for your driver to take you back to your trailer?"

Laura stared at him, framed by the departing storm clouds. She felt the effects of the wine and poured herself another glass. She didn't like this man. He was inherently untrustworthy and what he offered, immoral. How could she turn the tables and still keep her freedom? Still keep these opulent quarters?

She would trick him. She would use this job against him. She would gather information and either turn it over to the authorities or use it as leverage to get her to the Middle States that much faster. If he wanted her to rat someone out, she would make up a story and lie. Anything to avoid betraying people. Anything to keep her out of the camp. She gave a curt "*Fine,*" then dove into her fettuccine like a starving Biafran.

Faisson stooped and kissed her hand. "Thank you, Mrs. Trent."

"You can call me Laura, I guess."

"Laura? Yes, Laura." He reached into his chest pocket and handed her a cellphone. "Please call if any problems arise. Anything that would lessen your comfort in any way."

Laura pushed aside her empty plate and inhaled the rest of Cody's dessert. "I will."

"And now I must be on my way." As Faisson turned to leave, his two guards entered with a bright yellow bracket in their hands. They bent down and began attaching the device to Laura's ankle.

"Wait a minute. What's this?" she yelled after him.

"Do not mind the bracelet," Faisson replied.

"You conniving bastard! I knew this was a trick."

"An unavoidable precaution we must take. It will allow us to respond quickly should anything happen to you while you are outside the base. I could not forgive myself if I did not do all I could to protect you while in my employ."

"How can you?" she shrieked, kicking at the men. "How can I go out with this showing? What will my friends say?"

"Tell them it is the newest fashion from Paris," he smiled.

Laura fumed as she tried to pull her sweats over the bulging contraption. She grabbed the keys to her Lincoln then stormed out of the room in a huff.

"Where you going mom?"

"To Coldwater Creek. If I'm starting a new career, I need a new wardrobe. As well as a couple of full-length georgette skirts."

CHAPTER 23
NUKE

"Good morning, sir. Uneventful night, I trust?" Lieutenant Colonel William 'Devo' Donovan asked, holding out the morning's tasking reports and a cup of coffee.

Patterson entered the bright lobby and brushed past him on the way to his fourth-floor office. "What else do you have for me?" he barked over his omni-present pre-dawn headache.

"Yesterday's BDAs and SITREPs."

"And?"

"And?" replied Donovan, returning the question.

"And where's my *New York Times*, shit-for-brains?"

The LC searched his stack for the week-old paper. Woody pointed to it tucked under his arm. Donovan handed him the tabloid with a grimace.

"And where's the goddamn puzzles?" Patterson demanded, entering the elevator.

"Puzzles? What puzzles?"

"The *sudoku* puzzles. The ones with the numbers and shit on it. I do them everyday with my granddaughter and now the fucking page is missing. Where is it?"

"We cut it out, general."

"Cut it out?"

"Yes, sir. The page contained some content we decided was too … too derogatory in nature."

"Too derogatory, huh?" The elevator shushed open on the general's floor as Patterson stubbed a cigarette out in Donovan's fire-retardant flightsuit. "Colonel, you're screwing me into the ceiling. If you still want a fighter recommendation, you had better deliver my papers in one piece. Starting now."

"Yes, sir," replied Donovan, producing the rifled page. The aide took his place at the reception desk as Patterson shuffled into his office and slammed the door.

"Good God," he said, sitting down.

> UTICA, NEW YORK. TODAY, THE ARMED FORCES CRIMINAL TRIBUNAL SENTENCED GENERAL LYNN PATTERSON TO DEATH IN-ABSENTIA FOR HIGH TREASON AND CONSPIRACY TO OVERTHROW THE GOVERNMENT OF THE UNITED STATES. GENERAL PATTERSON, A FOUR-STAR GENERAL AND FORMER COMMANDER OF CENTCOM IS A HIGHLY DECORATED VIETNAM WAR VETERAN AND IS THE FIFTH SOVEREIGN FORCES OFFICER TO BE FOUND GUILTY BY THE COURT. "WE ARE NOT GOING TO WAIT FOR THE END OF HOSTILITIES TO BRING THESE TREACHEROUS SNAKES TO ACCOUNT," PRESIDENT MILTON EARLE SAID OF THE DECISION. "THESE MEN BETRAYED THEIR COUNTRY AND WE WILL USE WHATEVER MEANS NECESSARY TO STOP THEIR SABOTAGE OF WORLD PEACE." WITH THE FINDINGS OF GUILT, PATTERSON WAS STRIPPED OF RANK AND WILL BE EXECUTED BY FIRING SQUAD UPON HIS CAPTURE.

High treason. Betrayed. Guilty. Conspiracy. Firing squad. The words held no import in the Middle States but they stung nonetheless. Patterson stared until the text ran together in a thick black blob. He wondered if his wife in Colorado had read it this morning over her morning muffin. He wondered if his granddaughter saw it next to their puzzle. His phone rang. He didn't pick it up until the sixth ring. It was Foxworthy.

"Wood? This is Lobo. We've got a breach at *Headbanger.* Someone in the launch control center just hit the panic button."

"No other silos? Just the training tube?"

"So far."

"What do you think?"

"It could be the president."

"Why would he attack just one launcher? One smack-dab in the middle of an airbase?"

"I don't know. You want to up the DEFCON?"

"Let's get everyone together first. You call the rest of the Q?"

"I tried, sir. So far, only McCombs and Isham are available," said Foxworthy.

"And Davis?"

"Can't raise him."

"Fuck!" Patterson swore. "That nutjob has finally made his move."

"Who? Earle? What move?"

"It's not Earle. It's Davis. Davis is going nuclear."

~ ~ ~ ~ ~ ~ ~ ~ ~ ~ ~ ~ ~ ~ ~ ~ ~ ~ ~ ~

Minuteman U01 sat inside Minot Silo City just a quarter-mile from Quarterstaff HQ. From the surface, everything appeared calm with just a few more men than usual guarding the facility. Deep underground, activity buzzed as Corky Davis orchestrated reprogramming of *Headbanger's* guidance and launch control computers from his perch atop the upper-most equipment deck.

"What's that readout?" asked Davis, genuinely interested. "A counter? Why did it just stop?"

"That is the code generator," replied Aboud, rechecking the cabling between his briefcase decryption panel and the warheads. "The logic feeds the wrong codes into the guidance unit until it gets a reaction from the CPU."

"The *wrong* codes? I sent for you to get me the *right* codes."

Tanner's eye twitched back at the general. "I am using a side-channel attack. By watching for current spikes and clocking response times, I can tell how the processor is thinking and therefore, how close my guesses are. From that, I can derive a lock code in minutes instead of days."

"I wish we had this when we took over two years ago," said the army general. "We could've reprogrammed all the president's warheads instead of ripping them out and replacing them one-by-one."

"Where is General Woody?" Aboud asked, watching the busyness about him. "He needs to know I am not at the lab. That I am here with you."

"He knows. I told him. Now how much more time?"

"Five minutes more for the first warhead, then I will start on the last two," answered Aboud.

Soldiers sped hurriedly by as they carried equipment to and from the long launch control center tunnel. They wore a uniform Tanner hadn't seen before; gray BDUs with gray subdued patches and black armbands.

"When will he be here? You said he was going to meet us," the scientist asked again. "I generally take my orders from him."

Just then, Davis' radio cracked "General, Big Bird's secured."

Davis rogered him, then slapped Aboud on the back. "It'll be awhile, goat-ranger. It sounds like General Woody just got himself all tied up for the moment."

~ ~ ~ ~ ~ ~ ~ ~ ~ ~ ~ ~ ~ ~ ~ ~ ~ ~ ~ ~

"Devo, call the SPs and secure the building. Don't let anyone in. Especially Davis and his—" Before Patterson could finish, Donovan burst through the door, his teeth stained red and a small wet hole dotting his chest. The aide thudded to the floor as two thickly-built soldiers dressed in gray scanned the office and entered, stepping over him. Outside, in the lobby, a third man closed the door behind them.

"So, you're Corky's new elite," exclaimed Patterson. "Davis' best and brightest. I thought he might pull something like this." The sentries remained mute, monitoring their radios with their earbuds and taking up stands in opposite corners of the office. In between them, hidden between two walnut-stained bookcases, an escape lift led to the emergency combat operations center one hundred feet below the building. Patterson made a break for it as fast as his corroded joints could move.

"It's best you just have a seat, general, and sit this one out," Guard Number One said, barring his way with Guard Number Two. "You'll be free to go when we get the word."

"Go where? You let that head-case general of yours launch a missile and Minot will be nothing more than twenty-five square miles of fused silica." The soldiers eyed each other. "You look surprised. Guess the general didn't think enough of you to tell you he was starting a nuclear war."

The men pushed him into his chair.

Patterson scanned the room. Davis was showing himself to be unpredictable and Woody didn't know where it was leading. He looked down at his dead aide and thought fast. "Do you have family in Minot?" Patterson held up his phone. "You might want to think about giving them a call. Just in case the president gets a burr up his ass and decides to retaliate."

G2 looked at G1, then took the phone. They conversed with each other as Patterson reached inside the lighted display case behind his desk and pulled out his Louisville Slugger. He came down with it hard on the outside of G2's ankle, rolling it inward. The guard screamed and fell to his knees, meeting the bat's upswing with his nose. He rolled over backward, silent. Woody switched hands and swung for G1 who caught the stick in his palm. The feather-weight general sailed backwards into his leather chancellor's chair, where he had stashed a streetsweeper under the arm rest. He pulled it out and shot G1 dead with a load of buckshot to his face.

G3 responded from the lobby, throwing in a concussion grenade from the reception area. It colored the office magnesium white and filled the room with a fine cloud of glass and debris. When he entered, he sprayed the room with his M-4, emptying his clip. As he reloaded, Woody stepped out of his lift and shot him in the back with a belch of flames from his Tommy gun. "Honor your elders," advised the septuagenarian. "Especially the ones who have been waiting for you."

~ ~ ~ ~ ~ ~ ~ ~ ~ ~ ~ ~ ~ ~ ~ ~ ~ ~ ~

Aboud copied down the lock code onto a pad and began moving his jumpers to the next connector on the vehicle bus. Above him towered the three matte-black reentry vehicles, the solemn cones dominating the space. Despite the names *Serandon*, *Baldwin* and *Penn* stenciled on their sides, everyone gave them a wide berth as well as their respect.

"Well, doctor?"

"Here is Alpha's PALs," replied Aboud, handing Davis the codes. "I will start on Beta next."

"Won't be necessary." Davis motioned for his technicians to reattach the missile shroud. Over his shoulder, Tanner watched as three dead missiliers were carried out the tunnel and piled nearby onto the metal-grate flooring.

"What is happening? What is going on here?" he asked.

"The SF is undergoing a small change in management," Davis replied, folding the codes into his pocket. "A shift in focus."

"And these officers? They are Woody's men."

"An unfortunate consequence of their opposition to our initiative." Davis grabbed Aboud around the neck and brought him close. "Are you going to be disagreeable, too?"

Aboud's eyes hopped in his head as the man's gargantuan pores, nose, and smirk hovered inches from his face. A giant mechanical shudder echoed through the tube as the silo's blast doors began opening.

"Sir, we have to go. Now!" yelled Lieutenant Dunn. "There's action up top."

"Well, doctor? Are you with us or against us?" asked Corky.

"General Woody is not with you," Aboud declared.

"Oh, *he'll* be with us. And so will the rest of the SF once the troops see we mean business."

"No. If General Woody is not here, it cannot be good."

"Wrong answer!" snarled Davis. He squeezed the Iranian's throat as Tanner let loose a well-placed crescent kick that connected with the officer's jaw. Tanner was thrown to the floor as bullets hailed down from above.

Davis and his men retreated to the tunnel. "We can't leave Tanner," yelled Dunn. "We need him to run the colony."

"Fuck Tanner," Davis spat, rubbing his chin. "The world's a better place with one less rug-peddler." The general locked the bolts to the blast-proof hatch and dragged Dunn to the launch console where they entered their codes and activated their launch switches. Locked inside the silo, Aboud clung to the grating in fear as the missile shook, billowed smoke and belched fire.

~ ~ ~ ~ ~ ~ ~ ~ ~ ~ ~ ~ ~ ~ ~ ~ ~ ~ ~ ~

Patterson exited the lift and shuffled unannounced into the dark ECOC command center. McCombs and Isham were already there, astonished to see him.

"Well, hello, Rod, Matt. You look surprised to see me."

"W-w-we got a call from Lobo," answered Isham. "Something about trouble at the training silo."

Patterson walked up and slammed their table with his fist. "TROUBLE?" he bellowed, startling the technicians in the room. "Davis just commandeered a Minuteman and launched it to God-knows where!"

"Launched it? Here?" exclaimed the intel commander.

"You're an ass with ears, you know that Isham? What did you think just shook this building? One of Rod's farts?"

"We didn't know a thing, Woody," nittered McCombs.

"Don't play stupid. You're all for his revowing and breaking away."

"Maybe," admitted the Quarterstaff chief. "But not this. He did this on his own. We had no idea."

"Then that's worse," Patterson spit. "That makes you nothing more than a pair of passive greasy weasels."

"I still don't see what he hopes to accomplish," said Isham, typing on his laptop. "He doesn't have our PAL codes."

"He certainly doesn't have mine," said Patterson. "Rod?"

"Mine neither."

Isham put his pencil down and leaned back. "Then it's inert. He's sending up a dumb missile to send a message. To tell General Faisson to back off for sending that Mirage into our airspace."

"And how will the president know its a dud?"

"Davis knows Earle won't retaliate," answered McCombs. "The president signed onto the MAD Compact. He has to wait for a damage assessment before launching a second strike."

"All he's doing is bluffing then," Isham reassured.

Patterson turned to the Early Warning screen on the wall. A red dot appeared in the middle of North Dakota and began moving eastward. The air commander put a hand through his hair and rubbed furiously. "Either that or he's found a way around the locks."

~ ~ ~ ~ ~ ~ ~ ~ ~ ~ ~ ~ ~ ~ ~ ~ ~ ~ ~

The Sovereign Forces' anti-satellite detachments operated the only F-15s still flying for the air arm. These mission-critical fighters camped underneath common orbit paths in order to shoot down enemy Keyhole and Lacrosse spy satellites. They did this by racing skyward and launching their ASM-135 missiles to precise intercept points in space. By the war's second month, the ASAT units had destroyed so many enemy spacecraft, the president ran out of money trying to replace them. Their early victories brought clear skies for the Sovereigns but also idleness for their unit.

"1st ASAT, William Tells," answered Lieutenant Colonel Nate 'Spanky' Beatovich, picking up the phone.

"Spanky? This is Woody. I'm here in the Batcave and need your help. Do we have an alert bird ready to go?"

"Alert bird?" he echoed. "We've got no squadron. You deactivated us, remember?"

"Something's come up," pushed Patterson. "You have to have something airworthy. What about missiles? How many ASATs do you have?"

"One. You know that," replied the pilot. "Jesus Christ, Wood. What's going on? If the U.S. just put up a bird, we've got enough time to slap something together."

"We *don't* have time."

"We always have time. A bad-guy satellite will take an hour before arriving here."

"It's not theirs we're shooting down. It's *ours*."

"Say again?" Two crew chiefs ran in from the ramp, panting and pointing up. "Colonel, look outside." Beatovich went to the window and gaped. Out of the western sky, a thick plume was rising into the blue like a brilliant snow-white candle. "Holy shit."

"Spanky, you're looking at a Minuteman and it's *live*," said Woody.

"Is this a general exchange?"

"No, it's one-way but we've got to stop it before things degrade to that point."

"Where's it going?"

"If I had to guess, FUN Command in Duluth."

"If you had to guess? You mean our guys didn't cook this off?"

"No."

"Then who? How?"

"Nevermind," Patterson said. "What about a jet?"

"We've got one Eagle left. Mine, but the radar's inop."

"You can see the missile, can't you?"

"Yes."

"Then you don't need a radar. What about fuel?"

"I couldn't even guess what's in the tanks."

"They're not topped off?"

"Get off my case, general. We don't have a mission! You took my pilots and took my jets because you said they were needed elsewhere." Everyone in the pilot shack waited for Woody to reply.

"You're right, Nate. I've put you in a bad position. But you're the only hope we've got to stop this thing. Even if we only look like we're trying to shoot it down, our efforts might convince Earle not to retaliate."

"Maybe."

"How soon can they strap on that ASAT?"

"Less than a minute," replied Beatovich. "I've already hit the alert."

"Spank, you know this will put you over hostiles."

"It beats pounding mud in an A-10, which is where you were probably sending me next anyways."

"You know me too well," softened Patterson. "Good luck. The Quarterstaff thanks you and will be listening in."

"No charge," replied Beatovich. He hung up and ran out to his already-idling Eagle. In the cockpit, his crew chief handed him his helmet as he tried connecting him to the ejection seat.

"Sir, you forgot your harness."

Beatovich looked out the hangar door as the smoke totem climbed halfway overhead. "It's OK, Harley. I've gotta go."

"No, sir. I can't let you. Let me go get it. I'll be right back." Anderson leaped off the crew ladder and ran to his commander's locker. Spanky let him. The ASAT light on the cockpit annunciator panel came on, indicating his missile was mated. He gunned his throttles and blew out of the hangar with his parachute unattached.

Beatovich raced down the taxiway as the Minuteman plume towered above him. It was breathtaking, glowing in the sunlight as straight and white as the Washington Monument. He didn't wait to get to the runway. He lit his afterburners and took off from where he stood.

At forty thousand feet, Beatovich's radar warning receiver picked up a handful of French SA-17 Grizzlies climbing for him. At seventy thousand, his tanks went dry and his engines flamed-out. He needed to be at eighty thousand feet for an intercept. As his airspeed bled off and the SAMs almost on him, Spanky did the only thing a pilot without a chute could: he kept his nose on target, fired his weapon and died in flames.

CHAPTER 24
EARLE MEN

Marine One whipsawed over the Carolina coast, its rotors cutting a wispy halo through the steamy swamp air. Inside, President Milton Earle finished his SpaghettiOs lunch, licking the can clean.

"Sir, the pilot's going to have to put down soon," said Chief-of-Staff Laird. "He's running low on fuel."

"I don't care, Peter. We're going to keep orbiting if it hairlips every steer in Texas. Do I make myself clear?"

"Please, Milt. Just let your father enjoy his birthday party in peace."

"Ol' Jerkey-Face? Not a chance," replied Earle, wiping his mouth with the back of his tie. "He is using his birthday to endorse my brothers run against me for the White House. I call that war, not peace."

The aide persisted. "Number one, your father is a Republican. It's only natural he would endorse his Republican sons."

"He didn't when *I* was a Republican."

"Number two, you can't run for office anymore so they can't possibly be running against you."

"They're running against my policies and bad-mouthing my accomplishments. It's the same thing."

"Number three, you weren't invited."

Behind the pair, Secret Service Agent Russell Hendricks whispered into his cufflink. "They're wheeling out the cake now, sir," he relayed.

"Good." Earle walked to the cockpit and pointed to the Pickney House below them, the ancestral home of the Earle dynasty. "Major, put down north of the summer house," he said, pointing to a small redbrick in the rear of the plantation. "But let's do a fly-by first. I want to make sure the press gets a good shot."

As ordered, the green-and-white helicopter flashed across the bucolic lawn party, sending hats scurrying and sprinkling the festivities in a drizzle of white dogwood petals. Clifford Jameson Earle, the president's father and former vice president of the United States, scowled as all ninety candles on his birthday cake blew out.

The chopper landed seconds later and a husky-throated brunette from CNN International hailed the president as he climbed out. "Sir, weren't you scheduled to be in Camp David today with the Chinese?"

"Yes, I was. We made very good progress."

"Then the build-up of Red Chinese troops on the Korean Peninsula is not a threat to the Taiwanese?"

"What's that asswipe doing here?" asked Clifford, jilted, as the media rushed to get video of his son's landing. He pushed his wheel chair away from the mutiny and formed up with his boys. "Did any of you know about this?"

"Not me, father," replied a dark-haired Clive Earle, a two-term senator from the Piedmont State.

"Not me," replied Congressman Cassius Earle, the president's other brother and the Robert Redford look-alike of the three.

"Look," said the president, preening to the cameras. "Asia is a complicated place. The UN is just as concerned about them as we are and has the tools to handle the situation, so maybe we should let them hash this out." Out of the corner of his eye, the president caught sight of the slim, petite Celeste Penn-Earle, his father's 29-year-old wife and his newest step-mother. He buttoned his coat and waved good-bye to the reporters. "And now, please let me honor my dear father on the occasion of his nonagenarianism. Thank you."

Cassius bent over Celeste to help her relight the candles as Clive strode out onto the lawn to head off their little brother.

"Good to see you, Clive," greeted Earle, trying to get around him.

"Nice hairpie," he said. He looked down upon his sibling's raven black toupee and pulled out a few of his brother's gray ear hairs. "You really ought to match it better with these, though."

Clive rubbed his ear. "Look, you're not here to make a scene, are you?"

"Are you, *who*?"

"Are you, Mr. President?"

"That's better."

"Because if you are—"

"I just came to wish that smelly ol' crawdad of ours a happy birthday and to enjoy the company of my brothers." He pushed Clive aside and walked over to the cake where he swept his blonde step-mother off her feet and gave her a kiss. He put her down as she giggled.

"How are you, Milt," greeted Cassius. "I mean, Mr. President."

"Cass. How you been, bro?" Earle winked at him and pulled him close. "Been diving into any of that yet?" he said, nodding to Celeste. Penn-Earle colored and retreated to her husband's side.

"How dare you imply—" said Cassius.

Clive came over and poked a finger in Earle's chest. "Get out of here, now!"

The oversized commander-in-chief clasped his brothers close and posed them for a photo op with his father.

"Celeste is my wife and your mother," growled his father through his coffee-yellow teeth. "You will show her respect when you are at my home."

The president bent over to kiss his father on the pate. "The same respect you showed *my* mother when you put *her* away?"

"He had no choice. She was falling apart," said Cassius.

"Or was it because he had all the sons he wanted and I was going to mess up his plans?"

"Our father was seeking the presidential nomination."

"You mean *losing* the nomination," Earle snarled back.

"Which wouldn't've happened if she'd aborted you!" Clive goaded.

"Silence! Enough!" shouted Clifford, bursting the party's calm. The attendees watched on in awkward silence.

Clive held up his hands and pleaded with his brother. "For the love of God, Milt. This is going out for all the world to see."

Earle rapped him in the head with his knuckles. "You got *any* corn in that crib of yours, bubba? Take a look." Behind them, the press corps had turned off their cameras and were packing up to leave. "I'm their darling. They'd rather pee in their milk than make me look bad."

"Then why has the Wall Street Journal called for you to resign?"

"Hell, for arresting Glenn Beck?" shrugged Earle. "Everyone applauded that. He's as loopy as a bow-legged snake."

"And why is the Tennessee governor calling for a special prosecutor?" chided Clive. "Is it because you sent U.S. Marshals to keep his legislature from recognizing the MS?"

"He can call for grits to be rib-eyes, that doesn't mean it'll happen."

"Face it, Milton. It's not just us," said his father. "America hates you, too. You've handed your own country over to the UN. You've lost control of your own forces."

"Who cares about one country when you can be adored by the whole world?" belly-laughed the president.

"The whole world didn't elect you," replied Clive.

"Then run against me," Earle dared. "Run against my record, my accomplishments, my administration. I'd *love* to see that wreck again!"

"We will. But we're going to impeach you first."

The president bit his lip. "You wouldn't dare. Father might hate me but he would never do anything to let the Earle family name be tarnished."

"You've already seen to that," said Clive.

"What would be the charge?"

"That's the hard part. Which of the hundred offenses do we pick?"

Earle dumped out a champagne flute, filled it with Maple Hill from his flask and downed it. He didn't like being outflanked. Ever since birth he had been sent away, bought off, ignored and each time he had battled back and survived. By wits alone he had managed to overcome his father's shunning and cling onto the powerful Earle birthright. Even in his mother's womb, they couldn't flush him away and he wasn't about to let them now. "Which one of you is behind this?"

"I'm the one who's going to introduce it in the House," said Cass.

"It wouldn't go anywhere if I didn't get the Senate behind it," argued Clive.

"Shut up, both of you," their father reprimanded. "I'm the one who cooks the chicken here!"

"The people will see this as a political play for the presidency," said the commander-in-chief. "It'll backfire."

"What do you care? You're not running. You're a lame duck," replied Cassius, before pausing for thought. "Unless you're planning on running for a third term." Earle downed another glass of bourbon. "Milt?"

Clive recognized his brother's expression. It was the same look he gave their father when he had set fire to the neighbor's cat. "If Milt can change parties to win one election and sign the Declaration of Dependence to win another, what would be so outrageous about running for a third term?" he wondered out loud.

"Because he's a scandalous, no-talent, buffoon," said Clifford.

Earle slammed his drink to the table. "A buffoon who's eclipsed and obliterated every pissant accomplishment *you've* ever made, father. A buffoon who's managed to become the goddamn president of the goddamn United States!"

"*Was* the United States," corrected Cassius. "Seems your little vendetta against us has also started a civil war."

"So Miltie, how *are* you planning to get your third term?" asked Clive. "Your wife? Is Belle running?" Earle stared at them through the bottom of his glass. They were getting too close for comfort. "Or will you run as VP then sprinkle arsenic in your running mate's grits?"

"Neither," shushed Clifford. "It's the 22nd Amendment. They're suspending it. They're going to install him as monarch."

Earle choked on his whiskey.

"Who are they?" asked the boyish Cass.

"His blueberries. The UN."

"On what grounds?"

"Oil, nuclear proliferation, the war. They'll come up with some pretext."

"You mean he won't even have to run?"

"Not ever," gloated POTUS. "Not until the three of you have been bagged and sold as mushroom compost."

"It won't hold up in Congress," said Cassius.

"Think for once, boy," scolded his father. "Congress ratified the Declaration. You voted for it!"

"You ... you told me to!"

"To save your seat," added Clive. "We both would've been out on our ass with all the other Republicans."

"And the Court?"

"The Supremes base their opinions on international law," replied the president. "They side with the World Court ninety percent of the time."

Cassius thought a moment. "Wait a minute. If they can suspend the 22nd Amendment, what's stopping them from suspending Articles of Impeachment, too?"

"Nothing," said their old man. "Unless we announce it first." The vice president wobbled to his feet and tapped his glass to get the press' attention before they all departed.

"Ladies and gentlemen, I have an announcement to make."

"Stop this right now, father."

"Like hell I will," the VP whispered. He addressed the reporters. "Tomorrow, at 8 a.m., my son Cassius will introduce a bill in the House of Representatives calling for the immediate—"

Before Clifford Earle could finish his sentence, a pained look passed across his face as he ripped at his shirt. A gasp rippled through the gallery as fell back into his chair. "Dad, what is it? Are you going into A-Fib?"

Spittle flung from the patriarch's mouth as he tried to sputter a reply. He arched in the air like a porpoise before flipping backwards onto the lawn. "UNNNGGGHHH!"

"Better check his implant," said Earle, pulling a small black key fob from his pant's pocket and dangling it in the air.

"That's dad's pacemaker remote!" shouted Clive Earle.

"No, this one's mine," smiled the president. "The doctor gave me an extra one just in case dear dad couldn't restart his heart on his own."

"You bastard!" Clive coiled and lunged at his brother. Before he could get there, the president sent another shock to his father's heart. It slammed into his chest like a semi.

"UNNNGGGHHH!"

"Stop it, you're killing him!" cried Cass.

Clive and Cass launched an attack on their six-foot-five-inch brother, punching him in the stomach and tackling him to the ground.

"Give me that remote, you misopatrist."

"Then call off your impeachment or I'll make him squeal like Ned Beatty again."

Above them, Richard Varney, the senator's Secret Service agent, jumped on the president and put him in a wrist-lock but not before Agent Hendricks stuck his Sig Sauer into Varney's temple. As all three Secret Service agents began throwing Krav Maga strikes at one another, Peter Laird appeared and leaped into the scrum.

"ENOUGH! ENOUGH! Stop, all of you, you dysfunctional, megalomaniacal, narcissistic rednecks!"

Earle rolled in the grass to get away from his brothers. "Peter, call the Marshals. I want these two arrested before they can go anywhere near the Capitol."

"That can wait, Mr. President. Something has come up." From behind the plantation house, a peepish officer ran up in Air Force blues, carrying a heavy black briefcase. Peter Laird whispered in the president's ear as Marine One began spooling up in the back.

"What is it, Milt?" asked Cassius, dabbing at a cut lip.

Earle rolled over and pushed himself up. "If you truly don't think I have presidential material, then pray for us all," he replied, dusting himself off. "Because it seems we have an ICBM heading our way."

CHAPTER 25
SHAKEUP

Corky Davis lay hooded and shackled outside *Headbanger's* flame-scorched ranch house, the silo's above-ground security and administrative center. Around him, papers and maps littered the dirt as investigators rifled his belongings trying to piece together that morning's events.

"You've had a pretty busy day today," Woody Patterson remarked, pouring over Davis' journals and files.

"Making anything out of all this?" asked Lobo Foxworthy. Woody unfolded a map. "Was he trying to take out Duluth?"

Patterson hitched his shoulders and looked down at the man. "He's making this hard. Try his handcuffs."

Foxworthy crouched down and took off Davis' wrist bands.

"Tell me about the PALs, Corky. We can't figure out how you deciphered the Permissive Action Links so fast." Davis was mum and offered no reply. "We'll find out, you know. We're rounding up your lieutenants as we speak."

A Humvee entered the pad and pulled up alongside the two men. Two medics got out, took off Davis' hood and checked for a pulse. Shaking their head to Woody, they loaded the body onto a stretcher and put him inside. Patterson stood and called after him. "Your warheads never made it, Sam. Thanks to a very brave pilot." Behind him, Foxworthy's firing-squad readied for another volley as Patterson directed his attention to the condemned. "Dunn, you're next on deck," he announced.

Ajax Dunn, shiny and bronzed from the California sun, looked more the laid-back surfer than a Davis ruffian. He and the other gray-clad lieutenants stared manacled and crying as the SPs locked and loaded their next rounds. "No trial? No chance to give my story?"

"This is a war, young man. No one's interested in hearing quibbling when you're trying to kill them."

"Yes, sir."

"I'm sure you're not surprised," Woody mused. "You weighed your options. You knew a firing squad was a possibility if you joined up with Davis."

"Yes, sir."

"He didn't force you or threaten you. You knew what he was attempting and you still followed of your own free will."

"Yes, sir."

Patterson lit a Pall Mall and held it to the lieutenant's mouth. "I don't smoke, sir."

Patterson stuck the jag in anyway. "There's something doubly-sad about being executed," he continued, lighting a cigarette for himself. "Being shot by your own side. Death *and* shame."

"Yes, sir!" Dunn shouted, fighting away tears.

"I've got just one problem, son. I don't know who all revowed."

"Yes, sir."

"I don't know how many of you Paladins there are; how deep Corky's army went. I need somebody who does. Somebody who will tell them what's gone on today and to stand-down."

Dunn took a puff. "Yes, sir?"

"We've rolled up his network. We're telling them the same thing I'm telling you: either help us and live or resist and be frogmarched in front of a blood-spattered wall."

"Sir?"

"Will you help us, lieutenant?"

"Yessiryessiryessir—" Dunn sputtered, his cigarette flying out of his mouth and across the pad.

"Very well," said Patterson, nodding to the guards. "You're free to go."

Dunn rubbed at the red marks on his wrists as the other lieutenants followed his lead and agreed to disassociate themselves from

Davis' splinter group. Foxworthy returned their pistols, rifles and ammo. Before the general returned their knives, he turned the blades on them and cut off their rank.

"All of you are being stripped of rank," Patterson explained. "You will finish out the war the lowest of the low. You will be digging ditches for corporals. You will be saluting privates."

"Sir, we didn't know Davis was actually going to launch—"

"This isn't punishment for the millions of lives you almost took. That will hang on your hearts all your days. This is punishment for your disloyalty and lack of judgement. Patterson watched as the junior officer's faces lengthened. They looked straight at the horizon, preserving what little respect they had left. "*Questions?*"

"No, sir!" When their knives were returned, the branded soldiers hefted their gear and made for their vehicles, their gaits stiff with rage.

"Will we be having any more problems with you, Dunn?" Woody asked after him.

Lieutenant Dunn turned and snapped a sharp salute. "We'll be happy to fight for a man like you, sir." He pivoted and walked away.

Foxworthy sent his firing squad detail back to their barracks and began cleaning up Davis' paper trail. "Will HB approve of all this, Wood?"

"It's done. He'll have to."

"We've been fighting for two years now," remarked Foxworthy, wiping his brow and squinting into the empty maw of the Minuteman silo. "We still don't know what we're doing, do we?"

"I've never started an army—a country—from scratch before, Lobo. When you're flying by the seat of your pants, all you can hope for is to hold the moral high-ground."

"Which brings us to McCombs and Isham. What are we doing with them?"

"They're resigning," answered Patterson.

"*Or else?*"

"No *or-else*. They'll know."

A heavily armed SP scampered out of the ranch house with a message for Foxworthy. "General, we found something I think you should see." The policeman led the two inside the darkened launch facility and down the crew elevator where blackened walls and twisted metal testified to a great searing conflagration. Lieutenant Colonel Herb Batcheller, Gravehauler commander, Minot's missile squadron, waited at the tunnel entrance for them.

"We found them in the corner, under the equipment racks." He led the four-stars to the corner and pointed to what resembled a black pile of rags.

"These are men?" Foxworthy asked. The bacon smell made him cover his mouth and turn away.

"These your's, Herb?" asked Woody.

"This is probably them, but at four thousand degrees, it will take a while to confirm."

"Why do this right under our nose?" asked Foxworthy. "Davis could've commandeered a silo in the middle of Wyoming and we would've never caught up with him."

"This is a training facility," said Batcheller. "It's not tied to the squadron opsnet. It's the only facility that could launch without approval from my other ten silos. Davis knew what he was doing."

More medics arrived with liters and body bags as they delicately separated the cremated goulash of limbs, joints and flesh. From deep inside the pile, a muffled voice called out. "General Woody. Is that you?"

The corpsmen yelped and fell backwards on their rumps. "Holy shit! One of them's alive!"

Patterson pushed the men aside and, in sickly pops and crackles, pried the heap apart. What he saw made him recoil. "Aboud? *Dear God!*"

From inside the glistening mass, the charred scientist sat up, his face red and swollen. Where his lips were supposed to be, there were veins. Where his nose should have been, there was a thin pulsating flap. His eyes were lidless and there was white fat dripping where his ears should've been.

"What? What are you looking at? You are scaring me," said Tanner, unable to blink.

Patterson didn't want to tell him he looked more Garbage Patch Kid than human. "Slow down, doctor. Take it easy and tell me what happened."

"These men were dead. Shot dead. General Corky brought them from the tunnel and piled them there. When the missile launched, the blast was rolling us all into a corner. I was at the bottom. I escaped harm because of these dead men. After that, I am not remembering."

Patterson regarded the bloody mess then looked to the medics for help. "He's got to be running on one hundred percent adrenaline," they said.

"Are you going to be shooting me?" Tanner asked.

"Why would I do that?"

"I launched the missile," Aboud blurted.

"*You* broke the PAL locks?"

"General Davis had me do it. He said you approved it. That you were going to be here. I am sorry I did not wait. I should have told him *no*. I have to pay. I have killed millions of people."

"How did Aboud hack the PALs?" asked Foxworthy.

"I don't know," shrugged Patterson. "I don't even ask anymore."

The medics poked at Tanner's bloody face, confused as to why he was still alive. "Doctor, you're pretty badly burned. We need to take you to the hospital and get you looked at." As they pulled him out of the goo, everyone breathed a sigh of relief as Patterson removed the piece of skin that had been adhering to the scientist's face from one of the other dead men. Aboud took a look at the gruesome mask and passed out into the cauterized bodies.

"Sergeant, lower the winch. We've got a Code Blue."

Foxworthy and Patterson walked back into the topside sunlight as the medics raced the Iranian to the base hospital.

"Lobo, I'm making you interim SGArm commander," said Woody.

Foxworthy stopped. "So, you're usurping power. Just like that," he asked, rhetorically.

"Yes."

"Without deliberation or counsel or vote?"

"Did I need a vote to have Davis shot?"

"I don't have field experience," replied Foxworthy. "I'm civil affairs. I command police, judges, lawyers, not war-fighters."

"I need you to go out and check on the troops," said Patterson. "Visit the maneuver commanders. Find out who's loyal and what morale is like."

"You're making this up as you go," accused Lobo.

Woody wobbled. "Everything we do from here on out is a precedent."

"I can't support this. I'm sorry, Lynn. Things are moving too fast. This power grab has got my spidey-sense tingling. You seem a little too eager to be Command General."

Foxworthy puzzled as Patterson turned white, doubled-over then threw up on his uniform. "AHHH! What the hell was that for?" he cried, wiping coffee and eggs off him. At his feet, Woody rolled in the dirt, grabbing his stomach. "Woody? What do you want me to do?"

Patterson made a puffing motion.

Foxworthy searched Patterson's flightsuit pockets. He found a pack in each one. "PKT? Doxil? Taxol? What kind of brands are these?" Woody grabbed the Fentanyl prescription, stuffed three into his mouth and lit them all at once. Foxworthy sat beside him in the dirt as he watched his friend recover. "That's quite a secret you've managed to keep to yourself," Lobo observed. "How long you got?"

Woody inhaled deeply, tasting the metallic tang of the anesthetic. He uncoiled as he felt it gird his pancreas and organs. "Long enough."

"Morale is already low due to our ceaseless retreating. If the line commanders find out their new Quarterstaff chief isn't going to be with them for long, there'll be a rift again. You know that, don't you?"

Woody propped himself against the wheel of his Hummer, nodding in a gray opiate haze. "But you won't tell them that, will you?"

"What *should* I tell them?"

"Tell them we're going on the offensive."

CHAPTER 26
CAMP SNOOPY

Hearty laughter erupted from the laager amidst the heavy smells of smoke and diesel and fern. Spider, Wade and the others sat in the warmth of the fire, chasing the night chill with a jug of raspberry wine.

"Well, paint *Goodyear* on my side and float me over a stadium," thumped Wade. "I'm impressed."

"Yeah, boss. I'm stuffed," dittoed Hoop. "That was great corn."

"Good," burped Trent. "Because we'll be eating it for another month."

Ochre flames beat back the encroaching dark as the men slumped into their chairs. At Wade's feet, an orange-and-white tabby named Pumpkin scrounged for leftovers while Spider lit a pipe and Hoop burnt the coffee. Beak Brucato laughed as a coarse-tongued calico licked at his fingers. "Punk only cares about the butter."

"I was *hoping* you could put Daisy to good use," said Fredrick. "She's past her peak, but she can still put out enough milk and butter to put some fat back on you guys."

In the trees across the bivouac, a rifle shot rang out. Everyone leaped up, chairs flying and weapons drawn, as a wide-eyed black-and-white Holstein crashed through the brush and jumped over their fire. Corporal Lawrence Cragg, the DOLs armorer, emerged from the snags in hot pursuit. Fredrick stuck out an arm and clotheslined the corporal as he ran by. "I didn't bring her here so you guys could *eat* her."

"It's meat, sir," replied Cragg. "I just wanted some meat. If I have to eat another mystery MRE, I'll gork."

Spider stomped on the boy's ear and snatched away his M-16. "You go off on our meal-ticket again, Jar-Jar, and it's no ice cream for you. Now get up and go bring her back."

Over at Chesty Wright's dimly-lit tattoo hootch, Aboud screamed as a buzzing ink gun dug into his arm. "Guys, you've gotta see this!" yelled Brucato. The group sauntered over as Aboud flexed his scrawny biceps, showing them his *Starship Enterprise* tattoo. "What do you think?"

"What's this? No skull-and-crossbones? No girlfriend's name from back home?"

Wright shrugged. "Don't look at me, I'm just the artist."

Wade laughed, gagging on his chew as the mob took turns yanking and poking Aboud's arm. "Is that Picard or Kirk inside or just a mole?"

"Kirk, of course. Why?" he replied.

"What on earth possessed you, boy?" Fredrick roared.

"We used to watch reruns growing up. That is sparking my interest in science. What is so funny about that?"

"Don't get him mad, I hear his phaser charging!" Hoop snorted.

Aboud rolled his sleeve down and departed the tent. "*Asspipes.*"

The clique cackled several minutes more before finally joining Aboud at the fire where he was tuning its thermodynamics with a stick.

"Sorry," said Wade, slapping him on the back. "What did you mean by *we* anyway?"

"Me and Zahra. We loved Star Trek. He was my friend from the earliest time. That is why I wanted the tattoo. Not for bragging. For his memory."

Wade got up and put some more oak on the fire. "I brought you guys something."

"Another cow?" asked Hoop.

"No, these." The pilots leaned forward to see six green test-tube-sized ampules glisten in the farmer's hand.

"So that's why you quit being my crew chief?" asked Spider.

"They're injector kits," noticed Shank. "We've got those already."

"Those won't protect you from the French agent," interjected Tanner.

"You mean that crap you rubbed in your eye?"

"That crap has a heavy-metal radical," explained Tanner.

Wade handed out the kits. "Which in simple terms means once the agent attaches to the glycotriasylceramide receivers at the end of your nerve endings, it'll never let go."

"*Receptors*," Aboud corrected.

"Yeah, receptors." Wade held his injector to the fire and shook it. "This stuff is stronger than what you carry now. It'll form a stronger co-valiant bond with the agent and make it let go of your nerves." He looked to Aboud. "Right?"

"Co-*valent* bond," smiled Tanner, inspecting his tattoo. "Good!"

Spider inspected his vial.

"It is a gel," said Aboud. "Chewie's idea. For more concentration."

"How is gel going to get through a tiny needle?" asked Hoop.

"There is no needle," answered Aboud. "These are pyro-injectors. A shotgun shell primer forces the gel out in a tight jet. It cuts through clothes and skin as it is delivered into your muscle."

"That's going to leave a mark," said Beak. "How long after exposure do we have?"

"Forty-five seconds from the first symptoms."

"Which are?"

"Tremors, drooling, *rhinorrhea*," replied Aboud.

Wade hoisted his wine jug. "Runny nose!"

"That is a true statement," said the scientist, holding his eye to keep it from twitching. "But this is all we have been able to manufacture so far. So the first batch goes to the pilots. Two each."

"Just the pilots? Well, stick that!" said a voice from the shadows.

"Who said that?" Aboud swung around from the firelight, scattering the camp cats that had gathered in his lap.

"That's Gopher, our resident fighter-groupie," announced Spider, pointing to his A-10 parked just out of the fire's glow.

"He looks like a boy."

"I'm *sixteen*."

Wade squinted out into the gravel apron where the jets sat in inky silhouette. "Your parents let you out here?"

"My parents are freaking liberals. They left for the XUS months ago. I gave them the slip at the frontier. Spider took me in. Probably because I reminded him of someone."

"You let him in your cockpit?" asked the farmer.

"Oh, he does odd jobs for us. Tonight, I have him stenciling kills."

"Hogsbreath leads ADAK in all categories," boasted the teen as he stenciled tick-marks along Spider's fuselage. "Tank, truck *and* APCs."

"How many does Spider have?"

"Spider leads the flight. 194 kills," said Gopher.

"You never told me you were good at anything, John. After all these years, I thought you were just another dumb farmer like me." Fredrick was slurring now.

"I'm not any good," he replied. "Just bloodthirsty."

"He won't let go," agreed Shank, stirring the embers. "He doesn't give up. He drives us harder than anyone."

"And we love it," said Beak.

Spider relit his bowl. "Nothing but the best for my hogs."

Hoop marched over and snatched the wine jug from Wade before it was empty. "Speaking of love, Spider, don't forget you gave me and Shank conjugal leave this week."

"I did? I don't remember that."

"What is *jungle* leave?" asked Aboud, picking up one of the returning strays.

"Time with the wives. Every month, Spider gives us four hours. We meet at the Star Light in beautiful downtown Jamestown, North Dakota."

"Booya!" toasted Hooper. "A pleasure-seeking pool-side pump-fest!"

"Ah, I see. And when do you see your wife, John? Doesn't she need pumping, too?"

Trent felt a hitch in his throat and didn't look up. Everyone picked up their sticks and stabbed at the fire for a while.

"Incoming!" yelled Gopher, from his perch.

Out on the runway/interstate, a pair of blacked-out headlights appeared and sped into their camp. It was a HMMWV with 1121AV stenciled on the doors: their squadron. The driver checked in with Camp Snoopy's guards before stopping at their fire.

"Let me guess. It's our new squadron commander," said Hooper.

"Keep your hole zipped, hear me?" threatened Spider. "I'll handle this homo."

"Well, hello, John," said Om McCardell, waiting for his driver to come round for his door. "It's so good to see your crew getting their rest for the next day's missions."

"Hello, Noah. Nothing better to do than harass the worker bees?"

"I like to get out often and visit my men. I find it helps morale."

"We find it gives us diarrhea," whispered Hooper.

"What did you say, *slug*?"

Trent looked at his watch and yawned. "Look, I'm too tired for this. State your business Om and let my guys go to bed."

"*Om*? What is an *Om*?" asked Tanner.

"It's the callsign we gave him," said Shank. "It's short for Oscar Mayer."

"You named your commander after a wiener? Why would you do that?"

"My callsign is not *Om*! It's changed. It's Viper now and you'll call me by my proper name and rank."

"That's why," pointed Hooper

"What's your point besides your head?" asked Trent.

McCardell pulled out his briefcase and produced a folder. "This is for you." He gave Spider a sheaf of papers.

"This is a list of charges. You're court-martialing me? For what?"

"The incident at the Schottke farm."

"Schottke farm?" asked Hooper. "You mean the part where you fragged yourself or the part where you kicked the mother out of the rescue chopper to make room for your fat ass?"

Trent sat down at the fire and leafed through the charges as his wingmen kicked dirt on Om-Viper and called him a pencil-neck. "This wouldn't be a personal vendetta now, would it, Noah?"

"Your little fuel-air stunt almost got me killed, John."

"And it also got you promoted, didn't it?" spit Hooper. "If I knew you losing a jet was a qualification for squadron commander, I would've held my tongue and let you auger in."

Spider thumbed through the docket some more and ripped out a page. He sprung to his feet and stuck it under McCardell's nose. "What is all this legal mumbo jumbo? It reads like a lawyer wrote it."

"These charges refer to your excessive use of force in violation of all international norms of measured response."

"International norms? You sound like a UN ambassador."

"That mission displayed your lack of concern for our responsibilities as military professionals. How it risked our limited assets and endangered our relationships."

Spider rolled up the folder and jabbed it in Om's chest. "Tell me more about these *relationships*."

"You have no idea what's going on above you," replied Om. "What we're trying to do at the negotiating table."

Spider grabbed McCardell's arm and squeezed. He could taste blood as he bit his tongue. "Treat me for shock, *colonel*, but we're here to kill the Vichy bastards, not negotiate with them."

"Killing doesn't seem to be good enough for you, John. You have to maim and humiliate and castrate. That's your style and it's gotten you noticed."

"By you or them?"

"You have a reputation, John. A reputation that is frankly embarrassing in the eyes of the world."

"I do my job. The attack was effective."

"Your attack was *bedlam*. The UN transmitted video of the aftermath to the whole globe. The bodies where piled up like cordwood. Their eyes were gone and their lungs sucked inside-out. The Security Council is calling your attack racist and an act of Haitian genocide. They're accusing us of using an illegal WMD."

"And it's your thinking that by taking my wings, we can make happy with the Secretary-General and be back on his Christmas list?"

"We have very delicate deliberations going on with the French over the return of some HVA prisoners. Your name came up."

Spider turned to the dying fire and sank back in his chair. He liked brawling with toads like Noah and fighting bureaucracies like the Air Force but never had he taken on a government. He had never taken on the world. He threw the papers at his feet and ran fingers through his dirty, salty scalp.

"Everyone, this is Captain Cuddloe," announced the lieutenant colonel. "He's new to the squadron and I'm assigning him to Hogsbreath flight. He'll be your new flight lead."

"How? We don't have enough jets," said Spider.

"I'm giving him yours. You're under arrest."

"Like hell I am." Trent spun back around and charged the colonel as a muscular SP bolted from the back of the Hummer and leveled his M-4. Before he could shoot, a shotgun blast lit up the night above them, silencing the melee.

"Spider's not going anywhere," said Gopher, from the cockpit above. He held a sawed-off 12-gauge and had a bead on the guard. "Put down the gun, brain dead!"

Om nodded to his man and everyone took a step back. "Fine. You can stay. But you'll be confined to DOL Yankee pending the outcome of your trial. Jacoby here will make sure you don't leave. Not even to fly."

"You're grounding me? Does Woody know you're doing this?" demanded Spider. "Because if he doesn't I can guarantee—"

"—that he will back his own squadron commander in whatever decision he makes," McCardell completed.

"Give it your best shot," warned Trent.

Om's vehicle swarmed with cats. He kicked and shooed at them before getting in. As his driver started the engine, he held out a binder for Spider. It read *LISTE DE DÉTENTION DE CAMP.*

"Now what?"

"A little reading material while you await your sentence. I know you've been heartsick over your wife missing her rendezvous."

Trent reached through the window to clutch Om's windpipe. He fell to the ground as Jacoby hit him in the kidneys with the butt of his carbine. McCardell croaked a few times, then dropped the folder in the dirt. "Don't worry. She still loves you. I think. Turns out she's been interred at a French reunification camp in Duluth."

McCardell tapped his driver. As the HMMWV turned to leave, the LC stuck his head out the door and waved.

"And yes, she *is* one of the prisoners they are willing to bargain for."

CHAPTER 27
TRIZ SESSION

Looking grim in worn leather boots, tattered vests and eyeQ riding glasses, a lumbering earthquake of Patriot Guard motorcycles boomed through the wind-blown town of Parshall, North Dakota. The ride captain, an intimidating bear named Ox Platner, rode point on a metallic blue custom-chopped Harley hard-tail. To his right, one of his novice riders veered his bike too close for comfort and he kicked it away. "Damn it, Bruno, learn to steer that damned thing or keep the hell back!"

The Patriot Guard was a motorcycle gang of big-hearted tough-looking Vietnam and Gulf War vets. They had originally formed out of sympathy for fallen soldiers and their families, riding around the country to protect them from anti-war protesters. The UN invasion changed all that. Now they served as a volunteer militia fighting alongside Sovereign Forces regulars. Normally formidable and fierce, today they were babysitters, escorting a bunch of doddering SF generals on a classified top-secret picnic to the lake.

Platner hooked a right at the Quality Grain elevators and headed west to Lake Sakakawea Park. Once at the entrance, he forked onto a small pockmarked road that said *Pavilion 200 Yards.* When he came to a stop at the reservoir's edge he was promptly rear-ended by sixty-eight-year old Bruno Hochmuth. "I told you to be careful," bellowed the three-hundred-pound giant. "These are forty-thousand-dollar bikes!"

Behind him, a dozen more riders skidded and swerved on the loose gravel before falling over each other into a pile. Platner's lieutenants waded through the wreck to help untie the knot.

"We'll pay for this," said Woody, carefully unfolding himself from the dirt. "Just like we agreed."

"Just go have your meeting," Ox huffed. He righted his bike with a yank, fingering the dents. "We'll set up guard and take care of the rest."

"Tell me again why we're not on base?" asked Hollywood-chiseled Bill 'Double-O' Bond, Woody's XI Corps commander.

"To get away," he replied. "To have our first quiet day in years, free from distractions."

XII Corps Commander Brutus Atcheson, gaunt as an Auschwitz ghost, pried himself out from under a red-spackled Electra-Glide. He stood, rubbing his artificial knee. "Damned you to hell, Woody. I think I popped a screw."

"And tell me why again, all the cloak-and-dagger stuff?" asked Bond.

"POTUS consultants. If they knew we were all gathered here together, they'd have a turkey-shoot. This was the only disguise I could come up with on such short notice."

"Not very effective," said the handsome Bond, watching as Atcheson tried dusting off his leathers. "Don't know many Hell's Angels who wear helmets and ride around with their chaps on backwards."

"I'm here under protest. You know that, don't you?" he grumbled.

"Yes, Kelly, I'm well aware of—"

"The Germans are making probes into our southern flank. I'll be damned if I'm going to be stuck here at some worthless team-building exercise making origami while my guys have to fight the French *and* the Germans."

"Your presence is most appreciated," gritted Patterson. "Now get in there, have a beer, and shut up."

"Or what? You're going to shoot us like Davis?" Atcheson hissed.

Woody waited for his commanders to gather their bags and head for the shelter. Nearby, a load of teens from the Bismarck Screamin' Demons Marching Band stepped out of their bus and retreated as far away from the outlaws as possible.

Aboud waited inside the pavilion. "Welcome," he said in a heavy

Mideastern accent. He wore a thick stand of fake biker whiskers and a tattered jean vest. He dug into the cooler and offered them an ice-cold Rattlesnake.

"This your doctor?" snorted Bruno.

"Yes. Doctor Tanner, meet Generals Bruno, Bond and Brutus, my ADAK corps commanders."

"Tell me, son. You aren't going to be giving us the Quarterstaff's boiler-plate rapport-building toejam, are you?" asked Brutus.

"This will not be like that, General Brutus. I can guarantee. This session will be used to eliminate bottlenecks to innovation. Today's activities will result in a concrete, immediate solution." The generals stared at him, then at Patterson. "I promise," he added.

The generals muttered and stalked off to their chairs as Patterson shook his head. "I know you have faith in this TRIZ stuff, doctor. But I don't think it's going to fly. I may have jinxed things with my reorganization."

"General Woody, trust me," said Tanner. "They need this. To be outside. Away. Relaxed. It is necessary for creative thinking."

"Tell me, Aboud. None of your creative activities include origami, do they?"

"That is a true statement!" he said, picking up a blank piece of paper. "Want to see my Persian dung beetle?"

Woody rubbed at his temples hard as someone tugged his arm. "That ride was kick-ass, Lynn. Like a second childhood," commended Simon 'Bollweevil' Buckner, Army of the Dakotas commander. He gave Aboud an easy smile and claimed his beer. "Nice tattoo, son."

Patterson was encouraged anew. He thanked his friend and headed into the pavilion to start the session. "Men, I can't tell you how important it is that you're here. We are at a crux. A crossroads. We are at the essence of losing our freedom, our sovereignty, our country. Not for any lack of spirit or motivation but for a dearth of men and weapons and room." He tamped a Fentanyl on the picnic table and lit it. "For the last two years, we have tried to trade space for time, hoping the Coax would run out of will and resources. This delaying tactic hasn't worked and since the introduction of mandates, the UN's forces have grown in both size and contempt. Today, it ends. Today represents a turning point. Today, we go on the offensive."

Double-O raised his hand. "How, Wood? We've lost over a half-million square miles. We're outnumbered four-to-one."

Patterson planted his hands on the table. "I don't know, Bill. That's why we're here. It'll take innovation to overcome our handicaps. That's why I brought Doctor Tanner here. Doctor Tanner runs the Leper Colony. That's the unofficial name for our new R&D Lab. In the few months since he's arrived, the colony has been instrumental in a number of key battles. I call upon him now to lead us in our greatest battle, the battle for the Middle States."

Aboud bounced to his feet, introduced himself and immediately launched into a joke about an imam and his camel. He forgot the punchline. He followed this with a round of tongue-twisters and in-place calisthenics that fared no better. "Let's get this happy-horseshit show on the road!" the Army of the Sierras commander barked.

Aboud picked up his chalk and wrote *T-R-I-Z* on the blackboard. "Teoriya Resheniya Izobrotatelskikh Zadatch. This is a Russian model-based tool for problem formation and advanced system analysis to reduce random idea generation and remove technical contradictions."

The generals all threw down their pens and crossed their arms. "What the hell?"

"Doctor, we're simple men here," explained Woody. "We either have political science degrees or run shoe stores back home. Give us something to work with here."

"TRIZ is Russian for Theory of Inventive Problem-Solving," Tanner stuttered. "A Soviet patent officer invented the system when he noticed the inventions coming across his desk had many principles in common. By comparing thousands of applications, he distilled these laws down to a list of forty Methods of Invention."

"For instance?"

"One is called State Transition. To solve a problem, you try changing the state of a substance. For example, in order to drill an accurate hole in a rubber tube, freeze the material first to keep it from tearing or distorting. Or, if you are a diving coach and do not want your divers to get hurt, you soften the pool water with gas: air bubbles."

"We're not engineers, doctor. We're soldiers."

"TRIZ isn't restricted to engineering problems," Tanner answered.

"It is interdisciplinary. People use it to solve social dilemmas, psychiatric disorders, cultural issues, even military strategy."

The men stared back at him blankly.

"One TRIZ principle is called Matreshka."

"Like the Russian dolls that nest inside each other?"

"Yes." Aboud typed on his laptop and projected an image of a Leper Colony research vehicle onto a white screen up front. "This ATV is too top-heavy. The rocket launchers and armor keep tipping it over. What would you add or remove to keep the vehicle upright?"

"Lower the center-of-gravity," offered Bruno.

"Then the frame would be too low to clear terrain," noted Aboud. "What else?"

"Deflate the tires," offered another. "Or use outriggers."

"Walk," someone joked.

"Add weight."

"Yes," said Aboud, writing *MATRESHKA* on the board for emphasis. "Be thinking *inside*."

"Inside the tires?" Woody pondered.

"Good! How?"

"Ball bearings?"

"Too noisy," someone answered. "You'd be as stealthy as a glockenspiel."

Aboud wrote *STATE TRANSITION* on the board.

"Change the phase," said Bond.

"Water. Instead of air, fill the tires with water!" offered Patterson.

"That is a true statement!" cried Aboud. "Actually, we filled them with a lead-based self-sealing foam. But good." He handed Woody a box of candy. "Take one."

The new command general pulled out a wax bottle with red liquid inside. "Wow! Nik-L-Nips!" he exclaimed, biting off the top and sucking out the juice. "I haven't had this since the fifth grade."

Brutus Atcheson grated. "I hate to ruin your reminiscing, but tricking-out a bunch of ATVs is not going to win us a war."

"Then how about this?" said Aboud, tearing down the sheet with dramatic flourish. Behind it, a large shimmer array hung from the rafters, rewired to project multi-media images from Tanner's computer.

It was eight-feet high and wrapped around the commanders like a horseshoe.

"What are we looking at here?" asked a hairy-necked two-star from the Army of the Mississippi. He scanned the screen from left to right as satellite imagery and traffic-cams and closed-circuit security video jerked by haphazardly in dozens of individual frames.

"What is the biggest problem the SF faces?" Aboud asked back.

"Manpower," replied General Keith 'Kip' Ware, Woody's new bookish replacement for SGArm commander.

"Something bigger," prompted Aboud.

"Ratty old jets," said Woody.

"Old fart generals," Foxworthy deadpanned.

"Bigger. I am looking for force multipliers."

"Eyes. Eyes and ears," muttered Bob 'Tweety' Silvester, the incoming intel chief. He sported a long gray ponytail and bushy handlebar mustache. He was fresh from a field operation. "We have no satellites, no reliable SIGINT platform, no C3I to tell us what we're walking into." He leaned forward, staring at a video feed. "Doctor? Is that Fort Bragg?"

Aboud called up his database. "Yes."

"That's the Special Ops School. I taught there. How can you be receiving images inside a POTUS installation?"

"And look there," pointed Double-O. "That's the Pentagon. It's inside the Metro Entrance. There's Earnie, the gate guard. Remember his little girl, Brutus,? The one who always called you General Scarecrow and ran away every time you walked by?"

"No, I *don't*."

Tanner clacked away at his keys as the generals kept up their commentary. He called up an aerial shot of the Virginia coast and, in particular, a French carrier steaming into harbor for repairs. Outside the pavilion, Ox and his men dropped their BBQ duties to chase away a crowd of curious children. "That's a live satellite feed of Norfolk," said Tweety. "Woody, do we have space assets you haven't told us about?"

Patterson took out his bifocals and walked up to the LED matrix. "What carrier is that?"

"It's the *Richelieu*," said the spook. "What's it doing at Norfolk? Can we get any better resolution?"

Tanner tapped and typed some more. "Like this?" In an instant, the satellite image disappeared, to be replaced by an interior angle from the ship's bridge. Inside, French naval officers dressed in white uniforms looked out onto the flight deck below.

"Whoa, we're inside? Is this real-time?"

"Those are Frogs. We're seeing inside their walls."

"We are not inside their walls, General Brutus, we are inside their network."

"Matreshka!" shouted Bond. Tanner threw him some wax lips.

"What you are seeing is a vger," explained the scientist.

"A *veeger*?"

"Yes, it is a spybot I designed. I named it after a *Star Trek* episode where Captain Kirk discovers a long-lost space probe that is actually—" Patterson canted his head and looked up at the scientist through his eyebrows. "Yes, anyway. Vger is a simple spybot, a class of worm that crawls any number of public or military Internets. Only instead of looking for Web pages, mine looks for programs. Programs with backdoors."

"You hacked these nets and backdoors all by yourself?"

"No, I bought them on the black market."

"Whoa. Black market? I'm not Donald Trump," Patterson reminded him. "How much is this costing me?"

Aboud explained to the officers and staff how backdoors gave unregistered users access to proprietary military software. U.S. military and IT systems had been outsourced to software companies in China, India and Malaysia since the nineties. During this time, intelligence agencies paid to have these foreign contractors add secret portals to the software so their military would have access in time of war. When the U.S. service branches decided it would be cheaper and easier to connect these systems to the Internet rather than secure industrial-strength milnets, it made classified military data vulnerable to common everyday citizens. Even organized crime was in on the business; the Mafia, D-Company, the Triads.

"So what are we talking about? Millions?"

"About a hundred million dollars," replied Tanner.

"I don't have money to fix my Strykers," said Ware. "It would be suicide to invest more in computer spybots than basic weapons systems."

"But vger *is* a weapons system," replied Aboud. "Watch carefully."

The boy wonder went heads-down on his laptop and in a quick succession of commands, sent the *Richelieu*'s sailors scrambling by turning on its sprinklers, lifted and lowered Ft. Bragg's entrance gate on the base commander's car and accelerated the Pentagon's x-ray machine so fast, the conveyor spewed purses and briefcases all over the checkpoint.

"Wow," said General Rayburn 'Slick' Brady, Woody's Sovereign Air Arm replacement. "If you can do that to the bastards, can you turn off their SAM radars?"

"And change the firing sequence on their tank engines?" wondered Buckner.

Aboud listed the equipment he could control: "Refinery valves, traffic lights, Microsoft Windows, even coffee-makers. If it can be on the Internet, we can take over control."

"Can they do the same to us?"

"No," said Tanner. "Our equipment is too old; we are still on secure proprietary networks."

"I knew my crappy Windows 95 would be good for something some day," remarked Bruno.

The gathering became animated. Everybody had a new idea. Tanner tossed out Pay Days and Bit-O-Honeys and candy necklaces for every new one he heard. In the back, Pierce McDougall, LIII Corps Commander, padlocked on one of the feeds. "Those are my guys."

Patterson watched him walk up front. "What did you say, Hawkeye?"

"I said, those are my guys. One of my CAV units. I can tell from the Hummer markings."

On the screen, in night-vision green, six SF soldiers ate breakfast and rough-housed in a shallow mountainside gully. On the sides of the image, instrument readouts, written in a Hangul, flickered and moved about. In the middle, crisp white crosshairs bounced back and forth between the men. "Where is this?" he asked, pushing past Aboud.

Woody recognized the readouts as a pilot's heads-up display. "Those are GPS coordinates there. Forty-eight north. One-sixteen west."

Tanner typed them in. "Washington. Western Idaho, I guess."

"Am I watching a Korean gunship range my own men?" asked

McDougall. "Is this fucking shit for real?" he shouted. "Can't you turn off their camera? Shut down their engines?"

"I am sorry, sir. There is nothing I can do," replied Tanner.

Aboud shook his head as the display turned bright white with cannon fire. One by one, the exploding shells turned the unsuspecting soldiers into watery splashes. In seconds, the men were gone.

"Those were my guys," whispered McDougall, fingering the screen.

"Doctor, you can turn off the feed," said Patterson.

The session ended in silence and broke for an early lunch. Aboud tried handing out clue cards for his lunch-time scavenger hunt, but no one showed interest.

"You can put those away, son," said Woody. "I think they're all on board."

The officers walked to the beach and filed onto five party boats. Each pontoon carried a radar, a cache of missiles and a detail of Patriot Guard, who also had lunch grilled and waiting. They took off at a slow idle, fishing and puttering and laughing just like any other group on the lake. When they returned to the beach, they found Aboud putting the final touches on a giant fifty-by-thirty-foot sand table of the Middle States.

"Wow," said Bruno Hochmuth. "This is bigger than my garage back home." The generals circled the map, marvelling at the colors of the missile fields and the detail of the hand-sculpted Rockies.

"Inside each of your BZs, you'll find a toy tank or APC," said Tanner, handing out remotes. "These represent the position of your units and will be used to visualize scenarios. Please handle them responsibly."

Double-O Bond thumbed his controller, nudging his miniature tank into Bruno's battle zone. Bruno pushed him back. Soon, the entire Sovereign Forces was in a riot. "I also took the liberty of installing overrides," said Aboud. He tapped his tablet as the battlebots obediently returned to their starting places.

Woody stepped forward. "Gentlemen, as you can see, our backs are up against the missile fields. Soon, we'll have nowhere left to retreat." He poked in the sand. "Our troops are the best trained, most highly-motivated soldiers in the world. Each time one of them die, he has already taken with him twenty-seven Arabs, seven French and three Germans. Despite these kill ratios, the Coax keeps flooding the front with more and more reinforcements. What are our options?"

"What's the next TRIZ principle?" asked Hochmuth.

Aboud scratched his head. He wrote *SEGMENTATION* into the sand. "How can we kill each one of them individually and finally?"

His elderly students thought for a moment. "Remove their oxygen?"

"Stop their hearts?"

"Let's keep going. Separation. Can we remove the dangerous things?"

"Bullets from their guns?"

"The primer from their bullets?"

"How about Merging? Can we neutralize them by pulling them together?"

"If they ever got that organized, we'd *really* be in trouble."

"How about Asymmetry? Get them off-balance?"

"We can feign a penetration," said Bruno.

"Overload the LOC? Good," said Aboud. "Where?"

"It can't be in the center. They'd pinch us."

"Up north or down south," answered Leslie 'Tank' McNair, Army of the Plains commander. "Use our northern and southern borders as free flank protection."

"Won't Mexico and Canada attack?" asked Tanner.

"They're so small they're insignificant," said Patterson.

"Then why doesn't the UN attack through their borders. Aren't Mexico and Canada dependencies?"

"Mexico and Canada don't want anyone meddling with their sovereignty. They've told the General Assembly to stay out. That they can handle things on their own."

Aboud leaned forward, studying the table again. "Our next method is Intermediary. Can any other countries fight for us?"

"We have Japan, Britain, Australia. But they're technically non-belligerents, not allies," offered Tweety. "They're triangulating because they don't know which side will win."

The doctor scratched at his itchy beard and looked up at the sun as it filtered through the willows. "That leaves us with Matreshka again. Can we put anything inside?"

"Can we get more U.S. units to defect?" Buckner asked Woody.

"Not anymore. The UN has pulled them. They're in the rear now, performing border patrol and guarding ration points."

"How about the Freemartins? The Southern Actors?"

"I am thinking of something more radical," said Tanner. "Outside our sphere." He poked nine dots into the sand, arranged in three rows of three. "Can anyone connect the dots with just four lines?"

Foxworthy, a math teacher by profession, tried first.

"That is five lines," Aboud declared. He pointed to three others who tried their luck with an assortment of squares, hourglasses and bowties. "There is only one way to do it." Tanner took his stick and etched up, diagonal, across and back in an arrowhead pattern. "Notice the lines have to extend *outside* the box to solve the problem." The officers looked at him with glassy stares for a few moments when a frisbee floated across their beach and sailed into the water. A huffing lathered yellow lab plowed through Aboud's gameboard after it.

"Boulder! No! Come back!" yelled a skinny freckle-faced eleven-year-old from the next camp over. The retriever, frisbee proudly in tow, obediently complied and trudged back across the remains of Aboud's sand table, stopping long enough to shake lake water on everyone.

Tanner stared at the mess, trying to figure out another way of getting his point across. He heard laughter and shouts from across the parking lot where a major multi-family tug-of-war tournament was being held. Tanner walked over and introduced himself. When he asked if his friends could join, the players all dropped their ropes and backed away as the hairy forbidding bikers strode up from across the way.

"I only need fifteen of you," Aboud told the officers. He tied five of the ropes together then laid them on the ground like a starfish. "You five here are the U.S., you five, the UN. Three more over here are the SF and I need one each on the remaining points. You'll be Canada and Mexico." The generals grabbed their ropes, trying to look tough. "The team that pulls the knot over their own starting line wins." Aboud removed his red, white and blue Middle States bandana and dropped it. "Ready. Go."

The teams huffed and strained against each other for a minute before Team USA pulled the knot over their line.

"Unfair weight advantage," wheezed Team UN.

Aboud let them rest before starting again. This time the UN won.

"What is this proving?" asked Foxworthy. "The bigger teams are always going to win."

"True, *if* you play by the rules." Aboud ran around the star, pushing the one-man Mexico team and the one-man Canadian team together so their ropes formed up alongside Team SF. Now the star had three points with five men to a side. He dropped the flag, but this time the sides fell exhausted in a draw.

"*No one* won this time," said Hochmuth.

"But the enemy was neutralized," Aboud pointed out.

"You're saying if we can get Mexico and Canada on our side, we just might pull this off?"

"That is a true statement," Aboud nodded.

"That will never happen," said Brutus. "The greasers and the maple-suckers hate us."

"That brings us to Heterogeneity," prompted Tanner. "Do these countries all act as one? Do they have *no* pro-American groups or rightist parties inside them?"

General Brubeck from Pecos Division thought a moment. "The LULAC in Mexico are pro-American. They live in the border states. They're tired of the corruption and decay of their government. They're constantly jailed and killed for demanding reforms. *American*-styled reforms."

"There's the Freepers in Canada. The Canadians for a Free Republic," offered Buckner, in a thick Alabama drawl. "They're rural, poor, tired of the lefties taxing them to death. They're good soldiers. We have a lot of them leaking across the borders to fight with us."

"So, some groups *are* sympathetic to our cause." Aboud smiled. A plan was coming together and everyone was beginning to see it.

"And they're close to the border," added Bond.

"So what? They're just civilians," wrangled Bruno.

"I am not thinking about their fighting strength," replied Aboud. "I am thinking they can cause diversions to get us across the border."

"You want us to invade?" asked Patterson.

A picture was beginning to form in Kip Ware's head. "Yes, just long enough to use their countries so we can hit the Coax on their flanks."

"Good," said Aboud, giving him a bubble gum cigar. "Can we not then surprise the Coax by sneaking behind their lines so as to come down into their rear?"

"Not if the UN finds out. Then they'll come across, too," challenged Brutus.

Tanner kneeled down and formed a line of pebbles in the dirt. "Our last principle: Porosity. A border that lets us through but not the enemy."

Woody crouched and pointed with his cigarette. "Like Cambodia and Laos. When Charlie needed safe-haven, that's where he would go. He knew the U.S. didn't have the will to follow them there."

Tanner got jittery and his leg started bouncing. "Good. The UN cannot cross the border because they have to play by the rules."

"And if they don't play by the rules?" challenged Atcheson.

"They have to," said Aboud. "They made them."

Brutus Atcheson, the wrinkly bean-pole, stood up. "Woody, you can't be seriously considering such a thing," said Brutus.

"Yes, I can."

"Basing our existence on such a weak supposition? That Canada and Mexico will let us invade their countries while keeping the UN out? We'd have better odds playing slots."

"We only need a twenty to thirty mile strip," said Ware.

Atcheson glared at Ware. "I would expect *you* to defend Lynn. He's the one who installed you as his puppet."

Woody stepped between the two. "Where is this going, Art?"

The scarecrow pressed his hooked nose into the new five-star's face. "You start a coup, you execute the competition, you stack the Quarterstaff with your toadies and now you want all of us to sign off on this schlock? Who takes responsibility when your plan does a face-plant?"

Patterson ground his molars as if he were eating glass. "I did the things I needed to do to keep this army together."

Brutus sneered back. "How convenient you are now its Command General."

Patterson's backbench gathered behind him as Brutus' faction joined around him. The groups circled and regarded each other. Woody looked into their faces. If he did not have the backing of all his commanders, he could not expect his orders to be carried out. He couldn't be in every unit with a gun to every head. A feeling of dread washed over him as he realized he had lost. "What are you going to do, Brutus?" he asked as his men saddled up their bikes for the long ride back.

"Despite how far you've set us back with your new Quarterstaff?"

"Yes," Woody replied, wearily.

Atcheson cinched up his helmet and had Platner kick-start his bike for him. "We're going to make this work, Lynn. It's the only thing we've got left."

Woody craned his face to the sun as his generals packed up and rode off. I should've stepped down after Davis, he thought. They're never going to forgive me for taking over the Quarterstaff myself. He sucked his lucky down to the butt, wondering how their new offensive would turn out when Bollweevil Buckner strolled up from behind and stuck a three-by-five clue card in his face.

"I won the scavenger hunt, Wood. Where's my prize?"

CHAPTER 28
BETRAYAL

Laura horsed her black Towncruiser onto the interstate. Every quarter-mile, tiny European hybrids and specks swerved in her path, diving like kamikazes for roadside recharge stations before their batteries ran out of juice.

"Damned *diebrids*!" Laura screamed into her OnStar, stomping on her brakes.

"What's going on?" asked her friend, Hayley Dobson, on the other end.

"I'm just not used to these French drivers. Where are they coming from?"

"Ha! You've got *Le Road Rage*. Good luck with that. We're up to a thousand new imports every month. They work in the tranche. Now what were you saying about dessert?"

Laura accelerated back to interstate speed and resumed her train of thought. "Why don't you bring dessert? I'll have Bethany do the salad and Zoe do the fondue."

"Honey, it's too hot for fondue. I'm in the mood for sushi."

"Good idea. I'll get to use my press for the first time."

"What's the theme?"

"Theme?" Laura asked.

"The theme! We've got to have a theme. Remember the zoo benefit when we all came in the same zebra costume?"

"I don't have a theme. What do you have in mind?"

"Let's do the Flintstones," remarked Dobson. "A skimpy leapordskin would be a great way to show off my new tae bo legs."

"That's not going to work for me," said Laura, itching under her anklet. "How about a wig party with a prize for the most outrageous."

"Better yet, let's do Marie Antoinette! We can all dress as French aristocracy to celebrate the new mandate. Maybe you can get some of those French pilots up there on your base to join us. That Marshal Faisson's pretty cute. You don't know him, do you?"

Laura coughed into her steering wheel. "No."

"It's so good you're back in town, Laura. It's been years since we've seen you and John. Matt can't wait to see him. He doesn't have anyone else to sneak cigars with anymore."

"Oh, don't count on seeing John this summer," Laura offered quickly. "He's pretty busy with the farm."

"Oh, well. Guess it's just summer with the girls then."

Laura changed the subject. "Duluth is so big now. It's grown since we were here last."

"It's the camp. We love it," said Dobson. "The jobs, the businesses. Having this flood of workers and guards move in has really turned Twin Ports around."

Laura looked out as the sprawling internment facility sped by her window. "You're not concerned with what goes on in there? The beatings? The disease? The executions?"

"OMG! Where have you heard that?"

The sun glinted off the camp's razor-wire as vagrant souls loitered the rows of FEMA trailers. "What if it was your son in there? What if your smug oily neighbors turned on you and burnt your house down and made you wash your clothes in shit-water?"

"Laura, you're scaring me. Have you been surfing the freenet?"

"I've got to go," mumbled Laura. "I'm pulling into Kowalski's now. I'll decide on a theme and call you later."

"I can't wait to see what you've been up to these past two years."

"See you on Tuesday," said Laura.

"And I can't wait to see your new mansion on Skyline. Woo-Woo, girl!"

Laura drove the rest of the way in a daze. She played back the mess she called her life and wondered how she could keep it all a secret. Pulling into the grocery parking lot, a paunchy bagman walked by. "Afternoon, ma'am."

"Hello," she replied, as he made his lunchtime swing for grocery carts. The August cicadas chirped from the trees, crying in pain as if frying in a pan. In two steps, the heat hit her and she cursed as perspiration wicked through her new St. Johns silk blouse. Inside the store, air conditioning blasted up from the floor, lifting her skirt.

"Look mommy," pointed a corn-rowed three-year-old riding in her mother's cart. "That woman's got a bracelet on her ankle, just like the bad people on TV."

Laura pushed her skirt back down as the woman harrumphed and clip-clopped away. She wanted to flee as others gawked at her as well. Turning to escape, the bagman burst through the doors with a column of carts, blocking her way. She grabbed one of them and sped inside instead.

After a moment of shopping, her insides calmed. She warmed at the thought of her upcoming soiree and could see her beautiful house filled with the mindless banter and gentle laughter of her friends. She approached the seafood bin. It was empty.

"Can I help you?" asked Bret Robillard, the bagman.

Laura started. "Yes. Sushi. Where is your sushi?"

"What kind?"

"Tuna."

"You mean niguri?"

"Yes. I think so. Are you out?" she asked, sneaking a second look at the man as he finished stocking the shrimp.

"Unfortunately, yes. Can I suggest the niguri-toro?"

"What's that?"

"It's excellent, a fatter cut of tuna. From the belly. Would you like to take a look? We just got some off the truck. It's in back still on the pallet."

She stared at him again, then agreed. He led her around the butcher case and through a slatted plastic doorway to the loading dock.

"This is it here," he said, taking a knife to carefully slice through the polywrap. "They're twenty-five dollars a pound."

"Do I know you?" she asked.

"I don't think so."

"Yes, I do. I've seen you here before."

"Maybe at another store. We have a few in the Cities. But it's not possible you saw me here."

"Why do you say that?"

"You've been to our Cottage Grove store, but you've never been here before, Mrs. Trent."

"Now I remember you!" she said, the fog lifting. "I was there with Abby Fredrick, but how do you know my name?"

Before he answered, Robillard was on her. He put a hand over her mouth and a knife against her rib cage. Opening the meat freezer, he forced her inside and shut the door. When took his hand away, he put a finger to her lips and pointed to her anklet.

"Hi mom!" yelled a baggy, mopish Cody. He burst into the backyard unannounced, devouring a tub of Edy's Raspberry Chip Royale.

From the far side of the pool, Laura popped her head up from amid the crocuses and irises and snapdragons of her flower garden. "Cody, you butt! You scared me half to death."

"What are you doing?"

"Cutting flowers. And you?"

"Eating your ice cream." Laura disappeared back into the hot fragrance of her alyssum as Cody ambled closer. "Did you know there's gelatin in ice cream?" he said, reading the label.

"Interesting."

"Gelatin is boiled animal ligaments, bone meal, pig skin and cartilage."

"Yum."

"It's also in your makeup."

"It's nice to see you're still interested in science."

"Where you been?" Cody asked again.

"I've been out. My first full day by myself. Away from the office."

"I see you got some new clothes. You look pretty."

"Thanks," she said. "Where's your general?"

"I don't know. Around."

"I thought you were one of his men. Joined at the hip."

"I'm his guard, not his butt-wiper." Laura regarded him. "Where else did you go?"

"I don't know. Shopping. Around. Are you *my* butt-wiper now?"

"I saw some grocery bags."

"Then you know I was at Kowalski's. What else did you find in my garbage?"

"I don't know. Nothin." Laura went back to digging. "Are you having a wig party with the Dobsons?"

"What did you say?"

"I said are you having a party. I saw all the wine in the kitchen."

"No, you didn't. You said *wig* party."

"Well, what I meant was—"

"Where is he? I know he's here." Behind Cody, framed by the open French doors, stood Faisson. Laura rose and dusted herself off. "General Faisson, how dare you!"

"It's *Field Marshal* Faisson," corrected Cody.

"That is very nice of you, Cody, but I haven't been knighted yet. I am still just a general until the prime minister commissions me."

"Can it, Cody. He's been here the whole time, hasn't he?"

"Mrs. Trent, yes I have, but no need to take it out on the boy."

"I'll take it out on him when I want. He's *my* boy."

"But, of course," Faisson apologized, sweeping his hand and bowing.

"I thought you said this was my house."

"It is."

"Then what gives you the right to tramp in anytime you please?"

"My apologies. I should have called."

"You're not sorry. This never was my house, was it? What else are you reneging on? I've held up my end of the deal, haven't I?"

"Yes, you are doing a wonderful—"

Laura threw her flowers to the ground and took a step forward. "Then why are you following me? Why are you barging into my house without telling me? Why are you monitoring my phone calls?"

Faisson took her by the shoulders to show his sincerity. "I can tell you with the utmost honesty we are not tapping your phone."

Laura shook him off and stepped back. "Then how does Cody know I was talking to my friends? That I'm having a party?"

"It's your anklet," he said, pointing.

"You're bugging me?"

"For your own good, remember?"

"Then why send my son out here to weasel things out of me that you already know?"

"Things don't always work perfectly," the Frenchman said, taking a rose from her pile. "Take radio signals, for instance. They have a hard time going through metal."

"Like a car door?"

"Thicker." He sniffed at the blossom. "Where might you have been today that could've interfered with our electronics?"

"Nowhere. I went to a clothing shop, a grocery store, then home."

"Hmm. Whom did you meet?"

"I met a friend, Zoe, at Coldwater Creek. We got latte at Caribou Coffee, then I finished the rest of my shopping on my own."

"There was no one else you talked to? No one else who introduced themselves to you. Gave you something?"

Laura lied. "No."

"Anyone in the grocery store?" Laura's brows knotted. She turned and went back to her digging. "Mrs. Trent, I cannot tell you how much I have gone out on a limb to provide you with such opulent appointments. You, a person the UN sees as a dangerous sympathizer. You are sure nothing happened in that store?"

"Nothing."

He walked over and waved a hand folio over her ankle. She pulled her foot away. "What are you doing?"

"I am interrogating your environmental sensor. It has recorded a reading of minus five degrees. That is ninety degrees colder than it is now." Laura twisted her ankle, inspecting the gadget. "Now either you tell me what happened in that grocery store or all this goes away," he said, lifting his arms to the house.

Laura resumed her digging while struggling to maintain a calm demeanor. "I met a man. He said he knew my husband."

"Have you ever met this man before?"

"No."

"What did he say?"

"Nothing."

"Nothing?"

"Nothing much. He said my husband knew I had been interred." Faisson waited for more. "What do you want?" she protested. "He shoved me into a meat freezer for God's sake!"

"Seems a little heavy-handed for a greeting, don't you think?"

"He said John wanted to know I was OK."

"Is this the man?" Faisson flipped his folio to its database page.

Laura stared at the face. "Look, I don't know him. He seems like a nice man, with a family."

"Mrs. Trent, I fear for your safety," Faisson said, turning and admiring the home's century-old limestone construction. "If he can penetrate our security so easily in public, I am concerned what he may do once he finds out where you live. We may have to put you back inside the camp."

"I don't know," she cried. "It was dark. Things happened fast, then he was gone. Look, he's not a Southern Actor or a Founder or Freemartin if that's what you think. He didn't *do* anything!"

"That is why we are interested in talking to him. So many independence groups are ready to assassinate and destroy. How refreshing to finally come across someone level-headed. We want him to convince others that violence doesn't help."

"Why me?" she asked. "Why do you need me to do all your dirty work? Isn't that what your vaunted Milice are for?"

"We cannot haul in everyone from the grocery," said the Frenchman. "We are a nation of laws, after all. We are just going to talk. Maybe even have him join your office as a consultant."

"This is your matter, not mine."

"You could be saving hundreds of lives, Mrs. Trent."

Laura didn't buy it. She knew contact with a Sovereign would earn the grocer a trip to The Hague. She knew what the court would do to him once he got there. "Yes, that's him."

The general smiled and held out his device. "Good. Now just put your thumb print here."

"What for?"

"He is an American. We cannot detain an American without authorization from a U.S. citizen. Formalities. Until we are officially a mandate." Faisson held the page under her nose. She glowered at him then pressed in her thumb. He inspected the print, then tapped the SEND button. As if on cue, Faisson's radio sparked to life.

"We have authorization," cracked a voice on the other end. "Squad One, seal the front entrance. Squads Two and Three, take out the freight doors and converge on the employee quarters. On my mark. GO!"

Laura threw dirt and roses in Faisson's face. "YOU BASTARD!" Cody ran over to wrestle his mother away. "You said you just wanted to talk to him," she cried. "Why are you sending in a SWAT team?"

"Mom, you can't do this. You'll get in trouble."

"Nonsense, Cody. You're mother's just a little upset." Faisson wiped the dirt and stings from his face with a white handkerchief. "She doesn't understand we need to protect the public in the event this man overreacts and tries to take hostages or some other unpleasantness."

"Get your hands off me, Cody. They should be on him."

"Come Cody, your mother has a party to prepare for. We are just in the way." Faisson barked commands into his radio and waved without turning. "Thank you, again, Mrs. Trent. You are a wonderful addition to our cause. I will see you again soon to inquire on your other friends."

Cody turned. "Sorry, mom. You going to be OK?" He bounded after his boss without waiting for an answer.

Laura watched the two depart before falling on her knees. "I better not hear about his body being found in some tailing pond, *general*!" Laura hunched into a ball and hyperventilated into her palms. After a minute, she took her spade and dug into a fresh mound of dirt. When she got to the bottom, she reached in and pulled out the two glass vials of green iridescent gel Robillard had given her. She pressed them to her lips and whispered to herself.

"Oh, John. What have I done now?"

CHAPTER 29
SNEEZIN

The crowd in Dependence Hall could not get enough of Burin Zzgn. He continued to wave and smile under the kliegs as his standing ovation went on another five minutes. He stepped down from the podium to mingle with the crowd. When his StanEval agents arrived to meet him, he was gone.

Backstage, the Secretary-General put on a wig, hat and sunglasses and slipped into the night. Inside the glasses, an apatetic projection device was housed, a high-tech spy gadget used to digitally disguise the wearer with, in this case, old age. He clicked a button behind his ear as a computer-generated glow bathed his face in subtle wrinkles and sags that made the 42-year-old look sixty-five. Zzgn stepped out onto the rain-slicked cobblestones of Old City, Philadelphia and turned for his hotel, unobserved. Under his coat, his phone rang. "What is it, Wildfire?"

"It's your guards. They want to know where you went."

"Tell them to leave a message."

"Should I let them see your GPS coordinates?" she asked.

"You know better than that."

"It's 9 o'clock. Is the ceremony over?"

"Yes, what does the opinion cloud look like?" he asked.

Wildfire perused thousands of news sites, chat rooms and political blogs, consulting the Internet for reaction to his appearance. She returned a millisecond later with the results. "Early projections are trending up. Over fifty-two percent favorable. Do you want me to scan cellphone chatter, too?"

"Thank you, no. I am off to dinner, then bed." The SecGen pocketed his phone, relieved to be free from the crowds and his agents. He knew what could happen with well-wishing throngs and loyal guards; they could morph into mobs or even assassins. These weren't the fears of an irrational mind but real childhood engrams from his past. They explained why he hadn't ever employed aides and despite being outgoing and generous, never had friends. It was hard being an extroverted sociophobe.

Turning onto Market, Zzgn backtracked down 4th Street before ducking through the gold-plated doors of the Trump Bourse. From across the palatial lobby, four-year-old Joss Vann instantly recognized the leader by his bulldog strut and terrier fierceness and pointed at him with one of his chubby fingers. "Look mom, it's him!"

"It's who, Joss?" his mother, Jami, asked.

"It's him. The man on TV. Sneezin."

"*Sneezin?*" Jami Vann turned and saw an elegant elderly gentleman in a black Borsalino dress hat and sunglasses walk toward them.

"Well, hello little man. You are pointing. You must think I am somebody important." Zzgn removed his disguise and held out a hand.

"See mom, it's the president. Hi, Mr. Sneezin. My mom voted for you!"

"OMG! OMG!" Jami Vann repeated over and over. "Ericc? Ericc? Look. It's the Secretary-General." She tugged at her husband who was absently typing away on a Blackberry. "Huh, hon?"

Zzgn executed a dapper bow and kissed her hand. "Honored to meet your acquaintance."

Ericc introduced them. "Mr. Secretary-General! My gosh, what an honor. I am Ericc Vann. This is my son, Joss and my wife, Jami."

"OMG! OMG!"

Zzgn laughed. "Mrs. Vann, I am not a policeman. I am not going to fine you if you say the word *God*."

"OMG! OMG!"

"What brings you to Philadelphia, Mr. Secretary?"

"He's here for the Declaration of Dependence, dad. He's dedicating it. See, he's on TV." Joss pointed to one of the monitors hanging on the wall.

"Technically, son, when we display historical documents like this at World Heritage sites, it is called enshrinement, not dedication. You weren't able to be there?" Zzgn asked his father.

"No. I'm here for a board meeting. I'm president of a defense company."

"We came along cuz mom says we never see dad anymore," Joss said. Ericc had turned back to his Blackberry again.

"I see."

"Where are your guards, Mr. Sneezin?"

"They are not here. Once in a while, Mr. Sneezin just needs to be by himself."

Jami flashed an embarrassed grin. "It's not *sneez-in*, honey. It's *zeech-gin*."

"Awww," said Joss. "I wanted to see an agent. I heard they have those new Beretta rail guns. The one's that shoot spinballs around corners." His mother gave him a pinch. "*Ouch! Mom*!"

"Joss. It's not nice to talk about guns. Guns hurt people."

"That is all right, Mrs. Vann," said the SecGen, looking across the crowd. "It looks like Joss will have his chance to see one of those guns now." Across, the hall, at the lobby entrance, a handful of StanEval burst through the doors and cut a path to the Secretary. The atrium clogged with onlookers as the guards surrounded him in their black coats and ties.

"Secretary-General! Secretary-General! Will you sign our Declarations?" The throng parted as eleven-year-old Berty and Hanna Herron ran up, holding out their pens and programs. Behind the bouncy stick-thin twins, their harried mother followed.

"Hello, Burin. Zzgn. *Mr.* Zzgn," Linnette Herron stammered. She grabbed his hand and shook it.

"No formalities, please. You may call me Burin."

"Wow! What are the chances of this?" said Trey, her husband. "Can I get a picture?"

"Better than that," said the Secretary. "How about both your families eating dinner with me? I am famished."

"Dinner?" The Vanns looked at each other. "We just ate."

"And we've got friends waiting," said the Herrons.

Zzgn threw his arms around the families. "I insist. It is not often I have time to spend with friends. Real people. You *are* my friends?"

"Yes, well, sure, but—"

"Oh, daddy, oh daddy. Can we?" asked the girls. "Can we please? We'll finish our plates this time. *Please?*"

"Well, I don't—"

"Excellent!" said the Secretary-General and with a smile, swept the group into the dining room.

"Why did you make us sign the Declaration of Dependence, Mr. Sneezin?" asked Joss. His mother yanked at his precocious little arm.

"Joss, he didn't *make* us sign anything."

"Then why are the Middle States people mad at us?"

Zzgn held up a hand. "That is quite all right, Mrs. Vann. Your child's curiosity is disarming and quite refreshing," he said. "America is a good country, Joss," he said, bending down. "But some people think they are too good. That is called nationalism. Do you know what that means?"

Vann shook his head.

"It is like bigotry. Racism. That's bad. That's hate. The Declaration of Dependence teaches that all cultures are good. That all cultures are equal, not just one."

Joss wrinkled his nose. "They are? Even cannibals?"

Zzgn's eyes narrowed.

"But why here?" asked the Herron girls. "Why are you keeping the Declaration of Dependence here where *independence* started?"

"Because your founding fathers actually based the Constitution on the international laws and customs of the day. America's birth was dependent on other nations. So America doesn't just belong to you, America belongs to the whole world."

The hotel's manager strode up to introduce himself. "Mr. Secretary-General! How kind of you to visit our hotel. If we had known you were coming we would've—"

"I am having dinner for eight in the Garden Room in back."

"Yes, well, tonight, we are hosting a wedding. I can arrange—"

Zzgn motioned his detail to begin clearing the revelers. "Bring us menus and a wine list. We will be ready to order in a few minutes."

The UN guards entered the room. When the best men confronted them, a sunglassed agent took the groom by the neck and pushed his face into the bruschetta. "Oh, my!" Jami Vann put a hand to her silicone-enhanced lips as bodies thudded to the floor.

"Mr. Zzgn, this isn't necessary," said her husband. "We can do this some other time, perhaps the next time you are in Philly."

"But I'm hungry *now*, Ericc."

The agents ushered out the bloody wedding guests as Linnette Herron looked close to tears. Trey held her close. "Mr. Secretary-General. Burin. We really have to be going. You must have much more pressing matters to see to than to entertain us."

Zzgn ushered his guests inside and pulled out chairs for them and sat down at the head table where he emptied his pockets of numerous pill bottles and vials. The waiters presented menus as the busboys cleared the dishes.

"What are those, Mr. Burin?"

"Those are my vitamins, Joss. I take two hundred and fifty different kinds everyday."

"Two hundred and fifty! Wow. I only have to take Flinstones. Where are your Flinstones?"

"Come on, Jossie," his father said. "Let's let Mr. Zzgn eat dinner in peace. We've got a long drive ahead of us to the shore."

Zzgn's screwed his face into a ball as he slammed a fist to the table. "I am World Leader! I *will not* eat dinner alone!"

At the sound of the crash, Jami started crying. The Ukrainian led her to a chair. She looked at Ericc as she sat down. "We'll have the duck," he told the maître de.

"And we'll all have the salmon," dittoed Trey, seating his family opposite them. "Eeeewww!" shrieked the twins.

Candles and wine were summoned as family chatter warmed the room. The singsong banter of the children and absorbed gossip of the wives reminded him of the palace dinners of his Ukraine youth. He crunched handfuls of supplements as he watched the men out of the corner of his eye.

"Where is your family, Mr. Sneezin?"

Zzgn turned to Joss. "My parents were killed when I was your age. And my sister." The table hushed. "Right before my eyes. A mob broke into our palace one night, took our possessions and shot my family."

"You were a prince?" asked the twins, excitedly.

Zzgn nodded. "Did you know that, Mr. Herron?"

Herron spit his spinach phyllo into a napkin. "Me? I'm sorry, no. I really haven't been paying as much attention as I should to current events," he said, offering an elastic grin. "Politics. Congress. The war. I just don't have the stomach for all that contention."

"He really *has* been busy," added Linnette. "Working. Travelling Supporting our family."

"How did you two meet?"

The twins jumped up and down in their seat "Oh, it's to die for," exclaimed Hanna. "My father's a motivational speaker and mom was in the audience one day."

"Yeah," Berty cut in. "Mom was talking to a friend and wasn't paying attention to dad so he called her up front."

"And he proposed to her to shut her up," finished Hanna. "And she said yes to shut him up."

"I proposed because of her *beauty*," corrected their father. He toasted then kissed his wife.

"My mom and dad met in a bar," declared Joss. His mother kicked him under the table. "*OOOWWW!*"

"And what do you do, Joss, when you're not causing so much trouble?"

"I go to school in Malvern. That's a suburb. I used to go to pre-K until the UN teachers came. Dad pulled me out saying my brain would rot so now I go to Phelps Prep."

"He's an exceptional child," Jami smiled. "We just felt he wasn't—"

"Yes, aren't they all," remarked Zzgn.

The waiters brought the food. The SecGen pounced on his Chicken Kiev as the adults picked at their plates. A cellphone rang. "Ah, duty," said Zzgn. "I knew it would call sooner or later." He took one more bite of his broccoli rollantine before clearing aside his dishes. Zzgn's mobe was also his cellphone. It looked thick, like a portable shaver. He sat it on the table and unlatched the detachable top. Pulling on a telescoping support, he extended the lid twelve inches above its base where a red laser projected a video feed of his caller and a virtual keyboard onto the tablecloth to his front.

"Cool! What's that?" asked Joss.

"A new mobe cellphone. Very high-tech from India. I doubt you will ever see one like this in the U.S."

Ericc Vann put a hand on his son and got up. "Burin, you've obviously got matters of state to attend to and we're really intruding here. We will leave you to them."

"No, I insist," he said, typing on the keys. "You are my friends. I have nothing to hide from friends."

"If it's all the same, we really must be—"

Zzgn looked up at him. "Sit down, Ericc. *I insist.* I am conducting this business in public so you will perhaps have a greater appreciation for what the UN is doing for you and your families."

Jami tugged his coat, urging him to sit. He did.

After a few seconds, the phone booted up and a face flickered across the table. It was Faisson's. "Mr. Secretary."

"Yes, Sean. You have something monumental I take it."

"Yes, I do. Do you have a moment?" Zzgn listened on as Faisson told him about his capture and interrogation of a Freemartin spy. "So, these spies were using the grocery chain as their cover?"

"Yes, an open public venue where they could network and pass messages without having to call meetings."

"What fine work, Sean. What was he able to tell you?"

"They are staging a prisoner break at our reunification camp."

Zzgn leaned back and filled the room with hearty laughter. "Grocers will do this? How? By shooting donuts at you?"

"With all due respect, sir. The prisoner admitted ADAK would be supporting the escape."

"The Army of the Dakotas is willing to penetrate three hundred miles into your mandate just to repatriate a bunch of hoodlums?"

"Apparently there is also to be an ADAK offensive."

"An offensive? What offensive?"

"According to our spy, the Sovereigns are massing along the Canadian border."

The Secretary-General took out a blue horse pill, slipped it into a stuffed mushroom and popped it in his mouth. "I thought you told me they were withdrawing."

"That was Karlsruhe. I never believed for an instant the SF would pull back without a fight."

"So you're telling me you trust this one little grocer more than one of your own contemporaries?"

"Yes."

The Secretary checked on his guests. Everyone pretended to not be paying attention; Ericc was back on his Blackberry as Trey entertained the women. "General, standby while I talk with my aides."

"Aides?" asked Faisson. "You don't have any aides."

Zzgn typed on his tabletop keyboard, summoning his StanEval captain who hefted over a large black dufflebag. Ericc Vann watched them over the top of his PDA.

"Burin, with all this military talk, you must need time alone with your staff, don't you?" asked Herron.

"Today, you are my staff," he replied to both men. "You are successful and accomplished. I regularly seek advice and counsel from my global citizens on a wide range of matters."

"Staff? I don't understand. Where are yours?"

"I do not have much luck with staff."

"But what advice can I offer? I've never been in the army," said Vann. "This is way over my head."

"It is not intelligence I seek," replied Zzgn. "It is loyalty."

Two StanEvals walked up behind both Vann and Herron and attached black plastic collars to their necks.

"What are those?" asked the four-year-old.

"These are pithboxes," Zzgn answered.

"We pith frogs in biology lab. We paralyze them with needles in their heads so they don't jump around while we look inside their stomachs."

"They teach you a lot at Phelps," said the Secretary. To either side, Vann and Herron tore at their straps as their wives looked on in disbelief. "Are you mad?" gasped Ericc. "I thought you wanted our help."

"I do. These devices will simply help insure the quality of that help."

"You can't do this. My husband has done nothing wrong."

"Maybe not in his deeds, Mrs. Herron, but certainly in his neglect."

"What do you *mean?*"

Zzgn allowed the waiter to bring dessert. He cut himself some cheesecake and washed it down with a demitasse of Jamaican espresso. "Your husbands represent what is wrong with America. The affluent who are concerned only with their own personal comfort and safety."

"What's wrong with that?" grunted Vann.

"Nothing, Ericc, except when your attitude disregards the struggles and conflicts the rest of the world experiences every day. Then such selfishness characterizes willful neglect."

"You make us out to be symps or independents. We're not. We support the UN."

"Your disinterest make you accessories."

The towering Dutchman wrenched at his collar as it started humming and vibrating. "What is this? What's it doing?"

Zzgn walked over to inspect. "That's the palpatator. It's mapping the base of your skull to compute the proper angle into your brain stem."

Jami Vann shrieked then passed out into her son's lap. Her husband grabbed the featherweight Secretary by the turtleneck. He pulled back a fist to pummel him as StanEval agents fired spinballs that tore through his jacket and embedded in his ribs. Zzgn watched him fall to the floor. "Secretary Zzgn. I run ContraTech. I make elastomeric flak vests for you and your troops. Please!"

"Where are a man's loyalties when he sells out his own nation? When he plays all sides for money?"

Linnette Herron took a cellphone from her purse and began dialing 911. "You're insane or something, right? I think you took too many pills. I'm calling the police now before this gets out of hand."

"It's OK, honey. I'm all right," her husband soothed. "Nothing bad'll happen. This is just a test or something. The UN does this a lot. Right Mr. Zzgn?"

Zzgn smiled and sat down to his coffee. "Interesting. I have two *virtual Americans* here. One, Mr. Multinational who spurns his homeland by awarding jobs to foreigners while he moves his headquarters overseas. The other is Mr. Happy Days who pretends everything is butterflies and rainbows even though civil war rends his country and invaders circle round for the spoils."

"I'm not playing," said Vann, straining to get up. Zzgn showed him his remote control and pushed a small blue button. Vann felt a pinprick on his neck and he slapped at it.

Zzgn rose to address the men, his hands raised to the chandeliers. "This war is an epic battle, gentlemen. One that will decide the history of the world. It was your types that sat out the Revolutionary War. It was your people who watched the Civil War from the sidelines. Consider tonight a chance for redemption."

Faisson looked up impatiently from the tablecloth. "Mr. Secretary, are you still there?"

"Yes, Sean, I am back with you."

"I am informing you that I am massing my forces to the north in anticipation of the Sovereign buildup there."

"Congratulations on breaking their code, general, but you will not veer from the plan. The Coax is to make a lightning push across the entire eastern LOC as a single integrated unit. No exceptions."

"I must humbly dissent, Mr. Secretary-General. This threat requires special dispensation. I am asking that you allow me to answer it on our own terms."

Zzgn didn't answer. He looked at Vann and gave a cursory nod. "What is your advice, Ericc?"

"He's your commander," the CEO replied. "You put him in command for a reason. He has more knowledge of his opposition than anyone else. He must know what he's talking about."

"He's *French*, Ericc. *I* hate the French. *You* hate the French." Zzgn typed a response into his mobe. "I am disappointed you chose political correctness over your gut reaction."

Faisson continued arguing. "If we do not honor this information, ADAK will overwhelm my entire northern formation."

"Then you must hold them, Sean."

"And you must convince the Canadians to help. Make that ass Morgan realize he's going to have to commit to UNIFUS at some point."

Zzgn looked to Herron next. "What? Me?" Herron asked. The Sec-Gen held up his remote and dangled it for him to see. "I would agree," stammered Trey. "To ... to fight independence, all alignees must join in and help. So the war is over sooner."

Zzgn shook his head and typed some more. "Wrong answer. The war must be dragged out. Everybody must be engaged and busy until the time is right."

"You *want* the war to go on?"

Zzgn downed his last handful of pills. "Sean, why are you putting so much faith in just one spy? What is so special about this man?"

"He was brought to me by a most improbable source. He is unimpeachable."

"And you are willing to risk your entire command on his word?"

"I have complete faith in our tactics."

Zzgn put Vann back on the hot-seat. "He sounds confident," said Ericc. "He sounds sure. There's a harshness to his voice that says he doesn't mess around. I would believe him."

"Oh, I believe him," Zzgn agreed. "I just don't want him upsetting my plans."

"Your plans aren't to win?" asked Herron.

"There are bigger fish to fry than the U.S."

Jami Vann rustled from her son's lap. Ericc took her by the shoulders. "Look, I'm learning way more than I need to know. Way more than I *want* to know."

Faisson continued speaking from the table linen. "Tell the PM to put his heaviest units on the U.S. border. Between Walhalla and the Red River."

"Sean, the Canadians have problems of their own in Quebec."

"Then let us fight ADAK on our own. We can strike before they assemble."

Zzgn put his mobe on mute. "What do you think, Ericc? Do I let my little Napoleon run his own show or do I put his forces under German authority? I am so close to stripping him of command."

In all of his forty-two years, Ericc Vann never had to look at death before. Hadn't even broken a bone. Hadn't ever been mugged or been in a crash. If he didn't drop the bullshit now, he was dead. "The French are too proud. Their panties are still burning from World War II. If you threatened them with German rule, they'd have a stroke and tell you to blow your mother."

"Bravo!" Zzgn rose and gave a standing ovation. "Finally some good red-meat American counsel."

"You're going to change your mind?"

"Heavens no," said the Secretary. "Both the Germans *and* the French have big heads. If I sic them on each other, that will slow them both down a bit." Zzgn spoke into the phone, giving his final orders; Field Marshal Karlsruhe was to be Supreme Commander of the eastern line-of-contact and Faisson was to take orders from him. Faisson launched into a bitter tirade that Zzgn cut off with a slap to his phone.

Herron leaned over to Vann. "He seems to have liked that. Think we can go home now?" Vann shrugged his shoulders and resumed counting the guards.

"What's that, Mr. Herron? You don't approve of my methods?"

"What? Me? No. I mean. Yes. I mean. I don't understand."

"You don't understand what? Why I would sabotage my own war? Set back the Dependency movement? Throw World Alignment into chaos?"

"Y-y-yes, I guess."

"It's very simple. Overwar."

"Overwar?"

"This American War, this US-UN War, this War of Grudge between the coasts and the flatlanders is a throwaway. A side-battle. A backwater skirmish compared to the real war, the Overwar, my true passion."

"But this is the biggest war in history," remarked Herron. "You're saying it's unimportant?"

"It's pivotal. It's taking out the EU, most of the Third World and the number one superpower all in one fell swoop."

"You've planned this?"

"And the China-Taiwan conflict. And Britain-Russia, Japan-Korea, Australia-New Zealand." Herron's mouth gaped open as Vann slapped his hands over his ears.

"But what about OneWorld—" Linnette asked, scratching her head.

"Only you Americans believe this global oneness dung. Nobody else does. Certainly not the UN. We never did. More than anybody, we understand nationalism. Why else is the General Assembly so eager to slice your country into pieces for themselves? You don't see them opening their borders to each other, do you? You don't see them sharing resources with their neighbors." Everyone listened except Ericc. Ericc squeezed his eyes shut and rocked back and forth. "The French will always be French. The Germans, German, the British, British. Everyone knows this. Everyone accepts this. Except you. The very people who invented freedom in the first place."

"But if you don't believe in Dependency and Alignment then what is your goal?"

Ericc stood and slapped Herron across the face. "Stupid! Shut-up! Are you a total buffoon? Can't you see what he's doing? You're going to get us killed!"

"And what am I doing, Ericc?"

Ericc Vann knew exactly what was going on. He had read enough Clancy and Turow to know a plot twist when he saw it. "*He's* a nationalist," Vann continued. "An independent. He wants to eliminate the superpowers because *he* wants to be one."

"And?" Zzgn prompted.

"And he'll bulldoze the UN when he's done."

Zzgn clapped again and bowed with a flourish. "Capital! Quite capital, Ericc. You are a quick study. But tell me." He bent over and stared into Vann's eyes. "Tell me, which country is mine? Which state will I use to rule the world? Is it Ukraine, the country of my father? Is it Russia, the country of my birth?" He stared into Herron's eyes. "Could it be China or Taiwan, who are both itching to invade each other? Chechnia, who is ready to sweep across the Trans-Caucasus to capture her oil fields. Or will it be Jamaica, where it's sunny and warm all year round?"

"Why are you telling us this?" asked Trey.

"As I said before, you are my friends. Even a world ruler needs friends." He slapped their backs as small smiles flickered across their wives' faces.

"Does that mean you're going to let them go now?" asked Jami.

"Alas, while they will remain my good friends, they failed my test as aides. I am sorry," he said, folding up his mobe. "My search must continue."

"W-w-what does that mean?" asked Linnette.

"It means you will have one minute to say your good-byes."

Ericc Vann immediately picked up a butter knife and began slashing at his leash while Zzgn gathered his guards and strode to the exit. Linnette Herron ran after him, beating on his chest and pleading for her husband. She buried her nails into his neck just as a spinball sent her to the floor. "You can't to this," she screamed. "This is America! We are Americans!"

"Maybe on paper," Zzgn replied, aiming his remote and turning the men stiff as pine boards. "But certainly not in character."

CHAPTER 30
PRE-STRIKE

The brown scrubby knob of Old Baldy glowed in the rays of the early morning sun as it stood guard over the banks of the Pembine River just six miles south of the Canadian border. At its top, a ghillie-suited UNCON sniper scanned the horizon for trouble.

A meeting had been called. Canadian Freepers wanted autonomy from their socialist Prime Minister in Ottawa and his bosses in the European Union. The Sovereign Forces needed a protected avenue of approach to surprise and encircle their French foes. The two striving parties agreed to synergize their efforts and they picked this secluded site to negotiate an annexation.

"I don't want to hear it, Lobo. That's not an option," Patterson said.

"They say if we don't help them take Winnipeg, the deal's off."

"We don't have the fucking manpower to fight their war."

"They said they have the manpower to take out the Mounties, Woody. We just have to provide security to prevent the Canadian army from reinforcing."

"I don't have titty-squat for that either. *Jesus.*"

Woody shook off Foxworthy as the younger man offered to help him climb down the loose talus to the river. Tom Brennan, leader of the Minnesota Freemartins, was already there and yelled up to them. "That's them!"

Foxworthy panned his binoculars across the frothing rapids below. He spied two lemon yellow Zodiac inflatables rounding the bend toward them. Brennan waded out into the chilly waters and hauled them in.

"They're ready to go, General Patterson," said the Freemartin, hiking over to them. "What do we tell them about Winnipeg?"

"That we can't take on a third front right now," answered Woody.

"We've been cultivating these guys since the war started, sir. They've helped smuggle our families across. They've fought for us. In some ways, with their government, they've been under the UN's thumb ten years longer than we have."

"I appreciate that, but we just need to get in and get out."

"Well, I'll just let them know they can go back home then."

"We can't cross the border without their help," replied Lobo. "And they can't take on the Land Force without ours. They're not going to risk their lives if we can't protect them."

Fishermen lined the stream. They were Brennan's men and were armed with fly rods and nine-millimeter British Sten submachine guns. He watched one of them hold up a trout, wondering what to do. "Most of their population is located in Winnipeg," Brennan continued. "They want their city annexed into the Middle States along with their rural municipalities."

"Our offensive will have a better chance if the Freepers hold the main metro center," Foxworthy added.

"Then you do it," argued Patterson, tossing a butt onto the wet river rocks.

"We're not soldiers. We're police. What do we do if their army counter-attacks?"

"Write them fucking parking tickets. Christ, I don't care."

Foxworthy crossed his arms and propped his chin up with a fist. "OK, we'll do it," he told Brennan. "Tell them I'll send all my northern troopers." Brennan saluted then turned to join the delegates in the meeting tent. "How are you doing, Woody?"

Patterson shrugged. "I'm shitting sunbeams and lollipops out my ass. How do you think?"

"You've got to let someone else do this. Sit this one out. You're in too much pain."

"I'm fine," Patterson softened. "It goes away when I cuss."

"One more thing," said the policeman. "They want a formally signed treaty."

"Who do they think I am? The president?" he replied. "We don't have a government. Hell, they don't have a government. They're just as ragtag as we are."

"That's what I thought you'd say," said Foxworthy.

"When they've ironed out the details, I'll give them a firm handshake and warmest regards. That's what I'm giving the LULAC in Mexico. That's all I've got." Patterson pulled a pouch out of his pocket and hand-rolled a smoke. He was into fatties now.

"Are we going to pull this off, Lynn?"

Woody counted: "Three armored brigades, nine foot brigades and a division of irregulars? We don't have a snowball's chance in hell."

"Irregulars? Where'd you pull them from?"

"Prisoners. Australian mercenaries. A couple of companies of combat amputees." Patterson licked his paper shut. "We're scraping the bottom of the goddamned barrel."

"What about air?"

"More boneyard rejects. P-51s for escort, OV-10s for airlift, A-1s for close air support. Maybe even a couple of B-52s if we're lucky."

Foxworthy inhaled the chromatic aroma of Patterson's medicated tobacco. Above them, a rust-colored dust devil swirled across the barren plateau. "I don't see how we can keep this quiet. NSA is bound to notice we're out of ASATs. If they launch another Keyhole, we'll lose our element of surprise."

"Aboud has all that worked out. That's where I'm going next."

"We'll get this done, Wood." Foxworthy saluted and walked away.

The five-star made for his Hummer and strained a few steps up the slope before stopping. "Lobo? Mind helping me up? I seem to have forgotten my walker."

Frank Corriston pulled through the gates of Cavalier Air Station bypassing the traffic jam of idling troop carriers and mammoth HEMTT cargo transports. Code-named Camp Cougar now, the base served as the staging ground for Operation Downpour and its main armored fighting brigades. In the middle of the melee stood PARCS, the giant

200-foot-high early warning radar that had guarded America's northern approaches during the Cold War. It now lay half in rubble, a giant hole scorched in the antenna's side, a testament to the fury of the opening days of the war and a French SCALP cruise missile. "Pull over here," said Patterson.

The driver obeyed, pulling up alongside a huddle of lab-coated engineers. They bent over Aboud as he taught them how to spray-paint the grass.

"What the sam hell is my prize scientist doing in the dirt finger-painting?" cried Patterson, scanning the fields and parking lots. Around him, the scenery was awash in randomly planted multi-colored squares as far as he could see. Even vehicle and tent tops were mosaics of easter-egg colors.

"I am aliasing your staging grounds," Tanner replied.

"You'd better not be."

"It spoofs satellites."

"All these squares?"

"That is a true statement."

"What's wrong with camo netting?"

"Six hundred acres of netting wouldn't work. It would look like six hundred acres of camouflage and would attract attention. Besides, this way, we don't need to cover the entire camp."

"This is the big idea you wanted me to see?"

Aboud blinked away a twitch. "You are not liking it?"

Patterson slapped his thigh with his hat. "I'm sorry to have to play the dumbshit again, but can you tell me how you can hide all this activity by turning my camp into a chessboard?"

"These squares may look big here, but to a satellite twenty-three thousand miles away, these squares are just dots. Pixels."

"I thought satellites could read my license plate."

"No. Spy satellites in geosynchronous orbit are too far away and their optics are too small. They fill in the fine detail by using equations called fractals. When the signal is beamed to earth, they are actually transmitting an equation of an image, not *the* image."

"And let me guess, you know the equation."

"I can make this field look like a lake. I can rearrange the pattern to resemble Times Square. By knowing how fractals work, I can make any picture I want just by planting fake pixels in the right places and with the right colors."

Patterson felt a pinch in his insides. He winced and walked back to his Hummer to sit down.

"You do not trust me, General Woody?" Aboud asked, following. Patterson who shook his head. "Have I before done something to let you down?"

"Not a once," Woody managed. "And that's not good because then we just wind up piling more and more impossibilities on you. The Canadian negotiations are folding, the new recruits aren't trained. This is such a long shot. I'm afraid we're setting you up for failure."

Aboud gave his equipment to one of his engineers and wiped his hands on his coat. "It doesn't matter if you succeed or not, only that you did good." He sat beside Patterson. "In my country, we have a story about a dog who saves a child by biting a desert cobra and killing it. When the dog gets home, the father sees the dog's bloody mouth and, thinking it has eaten his child, kills the dog before finding out the truth."

"Who am I?" asked Patterson. "The father or the child?"

"You are the dog."

"Then who is the father?"

"Uh, I don't know."

Woody looked pale and drawn. He was exhausted and the cigarettes were losing their effect. But in the face of this little gray man, he saw hope. "You sound like this will work."

Aboud nodded. "Everything is going well, sir. I have recruited a team of complexity scientists from Santa Fe who have analyzed all French battles for the last six hundred years. We have input all their tactics and strategies to come up with a list of responses. We have even designed an algorithm that predicts when they will retreat and where."

"Well, maybe Downpour will work," said the general. "You haven't let me down yet. If your polka-dot trick works, we may be able to preserve the element of surprise and buy us some extra time to do this right." Patterson pressed his hat with his hand. "We just might pull this off yet."

From the concrete rubble of the bombed out PARCS, an olive-drab Gator sped out of the base CP and skidded to a stop in front of them. "Sir, it's the French Navy. The *Richelieu* just entered the St. Lawrence."

"Great, more fighters. What else are they bringing?"

"France's last brigades of tanks and infantry," replied the officer.

Woody threw his cap on the ground and stomped it. "SHEEIT, Aboud! Haven't you been monitoring the fleet with your vger thing?"

Tanner's eye began twitching. He swatted at it as if it was a gnat. "Vger cannot be used like that. If used continually, NSA will detect and block it. We have to be saving it until needed."

"How much time do we have, major?"

"A couple of weeks, sir. If we're lucky."

Woody smacked his lips several times and stuck out his tongue. "I'm beginning to get a bad taste of desert cobra in my mouth."

CHAPTER 31
GUILLOTINE

Laura was buzzy and bloodshot but excited to be finally showing off her new castle. She scrubbed the last few feet of baseboards and wondered if she looked like she had spent the last twenty-four hours cleaning. No matter. She was dressed for the part: a dirty, disheveled Bastille-era French peasant.

Her old boating friends arrived first; Hayley Dobson with big red hair and loud extravagant personality, heavily painted to divert attention from an overdeveloped nose; Zoe Radcliffe, tiny and mousy and Laura's favorite; tall Bethany Wimmer, neurotically cheerful and incessantly dispensing blessings in God's name. Laura shrieked as they stood in the door. She hugged them and led them to her kitchen where she poured them all Mojitos.

"This is Madison Gates everybody," said Dobson, introducing her friend. "Say hi to my marina-whores." Like an evil twin, Gates considered them through her dark mascara before giving a little leer and extending her hand.

Zoe sipped at her drink. "Looks like Hayley's already primed."

"What on earth are you wearing?" asked Bethany, staring at Dobson's fishnet stockings and push-up apron.

"I'm a French maid," she replied, kicking up her stilettos.

"We're supposed to be dressed like we're from the French Revolution, not the Lido."

"Whatever works," declared the redhead. "It managed to get the gate guards all in a lather, didn't it?"

Laura led them on a tour of her chateau. "Wow! That's the biggest fireplace I've ever seen," said Radcliffe, stretching her neck to the roof.

"It's made from river rock from Gooseberry Falls. There's two more in the master bedroom and bath."

"Woo-Woo! A fireplace in the bathroom. You two have got everything covered here, don't you?" said Dobson, helping herself to another drink.

Laura shook her head. "Anyway, here's the view." With a flourish, she pulled open the drapes to expose an entire wall of glass filled with an expansive view of the Duluth harbor and Lake Superior behind it.

"OMG, Laura!" exclaimed the round-faced Wimmer. "You and John are so lucky." She looked around for the posts. "What's holding up the ceiling?"

"A steel beam. Watch," she said as she flipped a switch and retracted the panes into the ceiling like a giant see-through garage door. The clique followed Laura through the opening and out into the back.

"What's the hole in bottom of the pool?" asked Bethany.

"A tunnel. In the winter you can swim up from a tunnel in the basement."

"Where *is* John by the way?" asked a suspicious Dobson.

"Yeah. Are we going to get to see him today?"

Laura bit her lip realizing she had forgotten to make up a story. "No. Not tonight. This is harvest time. I don't see him for weeks when he's out in the field."

Dobson stabbed a toe in the burbling brook and took in the manse's towering limestone facade. "Honey, he has to be harvesting opium poppies to afford this place."

Laura dug into her peasant's frock and pulled out a pack of Gauloises. She lit one and held it up. "Not poppies, tobacco," she answered. "Even better."

"They let John grow tobacco?" Everyone grabbed a cigarette from the pack and started smoking.

"I work for the UN, remember?"

"Girl, you *do* live dangerously."

The front doorbell rang. Laura left her friends coughing around the pool while she left to entertain her other costumed guests for a while. When the house was full and the tours completed, she refilled her glass and returned outside.

"Laura, where did you say you're working again?" asked Wimmer.

"I work in the tranche. I'm running the FUN Public Affairs Office."

"Well, where can I sign up 'cause I'd like to get me one of these!" She opened the garage door wide to reveal Laura's shiny black Towncruiser.

Dobson peered in. She was starting to build a grudge. "My, you *do* have perks."

"They're not really perks. This is my company car. I need it for my job."

"Honey, my pink Mary Kay hybrid is job-related." Dobson swept her arm across the yard. "*This* isn't. You sure you're not sleeping with that General Faisson?"

Laura sipped at her highball as a new guest in boots and a black hood joined them out back.

"And who are you supposed to be?" squeaked Zoe.

"I figured everyone would come as Marie Antoinette, so I came as her executioner."

Madison Gates laughed and perked up from her ennui. "Shit. What day is it?"

"Tuesday?" answered Wimmer.

Gates got up and bolted for the living room. "Come on everybody, the executions are on."

Laura choked and could barely clear her throat before Gates had found the remote and had turned on the TV. The afternoon's socializing dissolved as everyone gathered around the screen.

"No," said Laura, holding out her hand. "Give me the remote. This is a party. I really wish you wouldn't."

The young blonde gave Laura a dismissive one-liner and everyone laughed. Laura googled for a sympathetic eye but all were enraptured instead by the show. She withdrew to the side as the screen flashed to four black men tied to poles who were being menaced by long-robed executioners with scimitars.

"What's going on? Who are they? Americans?"

"They're Vice Lords," said Gates. "They raped a thirteen-year-old last week downtown."

"How come they're not being guillotined?"

"Because the girl was Muslim, therefore the French Shia get to decide the punishment. Now, shhh. Quiet."

The guards on the scaffolding approached the criminals and put hoods over their heads when the screen went blank. "Booo. Hisss," protested the guests as Laura stood to the side with the plug in her hand.

"Come on, everyone. This is really a downer. Let's eat." Her guests pleaded to let them watch.

"Just a little bit."

"It'll be done in a couple of minutes."

"It's not like they don't deserve it."

"These things are done tastefully."

"We need to know what's going on in the world."

"I wish our judicial system would be this quick."

Laura saw it was too late to go back. The women were piqued. Real death was sexy and a guilty pleasure they seemed none too interested in resisting. Madison smiled and plugged the screen back in as a young lieutenant read his orders to the sun-baked crowd at the camp.

"Come on, Laura," offered Zoe. "Let me help you with the sushi."

~ ~ ~ ~ ~ ~ ~ ~ ~ ~ ~ ~ ~ ~ ~ ~ ~ ~ ~ ~

Weekly executions were broadcast from Clough Island, one hundred acres of swampy meadow and pea-gravel fill at the abandoned end of Duluth's South Channel. It was the last stop for Reunification Center internees before they were to be shipped to the Middle States. In reality, people sent to this isolated wasteyard were seldom seen again, executions being one of the reasons.

"Maréchal Faisson, sir?"

"Not now, Laval."

"But, sir, you told me—"

Faisson held up a hand as the bodies of the four Vice Lords were dragged backstage while their blood was scrubbed from the decking. "In a minute. I have a head to take."

"You told me to tell you when Madame President came on the line."

"Is it Weygand?"

"No, she refuses to talk to you. This is the Defense Minister."

"Tell them to go to hell unless I talk to Weygand."

"I'm afraid it's they that want to talk to you now," replied the lieutenant.

Faisson tugged at the sleeves of his dress uniform and brushed at its gold piping. "Take over for me, Phillipe." He snatched away the phone. "Minister Touvier, this is Maréchal Faisson. Is this true the president will not be here today? What is the delay?"

"There is no delay," the DM announced. "She is not coming, ever."

"But why? As a Maréchal de France, I am to be knighted. I demand my presidential accolade."

"Then I guess you won't ever be Maréchal, so quit referring to yourself as one."

"But *I* have won France her richest colony. *I* have returned France to her former glory. No one but me and Napoleon can make that claim. *I* deserve her greatest honor. I demand a seventh star and my baton."

"*Napoleon*! You have not won France anything, my petit empereur. You may have just lost her."

"You talk in hyperbole. Let me talk to Weygand."

"The Germans are readying to invade, Sean. They are crossing into Strasbourg as we speak." Faisson stared into his mouthpiece. "They have petitioned the Security Council and want to claim us as a protectorate."

"A protectorate? Why? How?"

"Because we are defenseless, *you fool*! We have sent you all our homeland forces and now can't protect ourselves."

"Zzgn will never stand for—"

"Your faith in the Secretary-General is profane," she rebuked. "The Germans want to reunite the Frankish empire. By bringing back the First Reich, our common ancestry will be resurrected and our national identity wiped out. This appeals to Burin's philosophy of dependence. He has endorsed the action."

"What has this to do with me?" Faisson blustered. "With Terre du Lacs? This is a new country. I have a right to govern. I am its prince."

"The mandate has been rescinded, général."

"You talk rubbish. You have no jurisdic—"

"Zzgn intercepted your war plans. It seems you are about to launch an attack into North Dakota that violates his orders. He has just finished presenting Madame President with the evidence."

Faisson swallowed hard, as if gulping a stone. On the platform, his spy stood staring at him. Laval was staring, too, waiting for instructions. The guards, the prisoners in the yard, all staring, seemingly mocking. Like he was small and naked.

"The SecGen has lost faith in your ability to command," continued the minister. "He is putting FUN forces under Field Marshal Karlsruhe's control. You are the prince of nothing, Sean."

The phone rustled on the other end. They were arguing, debating. The ancient Hun was at the gates again. What would they do? He listened and waited for them to ask him to defend France's honor and save them.

"Enculer de poulet, petit con." Fuck a chicken, small idiot.

"Madame President?"

"Was your brain optional for you, Sean? Shut up. This is Darnand."

"Madame Prime Minister. I am expecting the president. She gave me her word I would be dubbed today. That she would give me reign as maréchal over her army."

"Zzgn told me everything. How you let personal animus cloud your judgement. How you are hot-headed and take undo risks. That you disregard orders and are prosecuting your own campaigns."

"He lies."

"That is his prerogative. As it is his prerogative to shove you down a jet intake and use your entrails as butterfly food."

"Let me speak to the president."

"She trusted your expertise. She sent our entire National Defense Reserves at your request."

"She was right to trust me," he snarled. "I am the only one who cares about France's interests. She needs to hear my side."

"Parliament is asking for the president to step down. She wants me to tell you to go masturbate in the corner."

"Is there no one in government who has a spine? Let me talk to a man!"

"Reality and you don't really get along, do they general? The president will not be taking the fall for this. I will. I am the one who will be offered up. I am to be the sacrifice for your incompetence, your misconduct, you son of a cross-dressing whore."

Faisson sank to his knees. "We are so close, Madame Minister. In just a few days we can punch through the American's lines. We can be in Dakota. We can roll up the Sovereign Forces, claim the missile fields for France and for once, prevail over Germany."

"You will have to do your freelancing without the fleet. I am turning them around. I am also negotiating with the Secretary-General to bring our troops home. We need them to defend the homeland, dependence be damned."

"I will not permit this cut-and-run!" Faisson yelled, his stomp echoing across the stage. "My men won't go. They will fight for me, not for a ménage-a-trois of hairy-assed lesbians."

"I wish I could be there to vomit on your head," Darnand deadpanned. "Good luck with your endeavors, Sean. And with that friend that is inside your head."

Faisson kept the phone to his ear a full minute after it went dead, pacing the stage in lazy figure-eights. He recalled the last fast few months of his life; the accomplishments, the promises of victory, the grand expectations of Empire. This was the foundation he had constructed, stone by stone, of a life of great renown and honor; a grand commander, the next Emperor, the revered saint, the Savior of France. Now the stones had all come down. Not one by one, where he could have easily repaired or replaced them, but all together, as if by one titan convulsion. One epic earthquake. He didn't know where to start rebuilding. He didn't know if he could.

~ ~ ~ ~ ~ ~ ~ ~ ~ ~ ~ ~ ~ ~ ~ ~ ~ ~ ~ ~

"OMG, Laura! Look. You're on TV!"

Laura walked over from her ki press to see Beth pointing excitedly at the screen. There she was, inset at the bottom of the monitor all black-haired and curly, the photo taken from her UN security badge. Above the text chyron was Bret Robillard, standing alongside a dark-stained maple guillotine, his face downcast and his shoulders slumped almost to the ground. Laura dropped her glass on the granite flooring, shattering it.

"What's wrong," said Zoe, stooping to pick up the pieces.

Gates raised the volume. "Quiet everybody. They're getting ready to execute this symp." The room quieted as a ticker ran across the bottom of the screen.

> BRET ROBILLARD OF ST. PAUL, MINNESOTA IS LEADER OF A LOCAL FREEMARTIN UNIT. HE IS SENTENCED TO DEATH FOR PLANNING THE ASSASSINATIONS OF AMERICAN AND UNIFUS PERSONNEL. BECAUSE OF THE PATRIOTISM AND COURAGE OF A LOCAL CITIZEN, THIS SPY AND HIS MEN HAVE BEEN STOPPED BEFORE THEY COULD DO HARM TO THE GLOBAL BODY. THANK YOU, LAURA TRENT. MAY YOUR DUTY AND VIGILANCE BE A MODEL FOR US ALL.

Hayley pumped her fist. "All right, girl. You rock!"

"Our own little Mata Hari," toasted Madison.

The two led the group in a round of applause as Bret Robillard looked into the camera right at Laura. "Oh, no. Please no."

The women stopped cheering and returned to the TV as the headsman led the Freemartin to the guillotine at the center of the platform.

~~~~~~~~~~~~~~~~~~~

"Bret Robillard. You stand convicted before the body for crimes against Dependence and being found an Enemy of the World. Your sentence is death by beheading. Do you have any last words?" asked the lieutenant. Robillard didn't answer. The headsman pushed him down but he wouldn't budge. "Get him down," Laval whispered in French.

"I'm not kneeling," Robillard said.

The executioner tried again but to no avail; the American was too big. Laval jabbed his finger to the ground. "I said, *get him down!*" The henchman hit Robillard behind the knees with a whip. The Freemartin stumbled and folded into a half-crouch before rising again. He collapsed as he was hit again and again. He touched the scaffolding to steady himself but managed to rise back up.

Faisson stormed onto the stage. "You will get down!" He took the Maréchal baton he had made for himself and hit the Freemartin hard across the back of his skull. The baton cracked in half and sailed into the gaggle of prisoners. Robillard wavered but still stood. The prisoners cheered and began chanting.

"I broke," the big man said. "I gave up the names of my men because I broke." The camera's zoomed in on his face. "I wish to die standing."

Laval stuck his nose in his face. "You can't stand, you insolent independent. Now kneel."

"I will not bend a knee to France," Robillard shouted. "I will not honor the dishonorable, in life or in death."

Faisson's eyelids fluttered with anger. He stepped away and fingered his ballistrae. "Tie him up," he ordered.

Laval turned as the general strode away. "We can not do that, sir. It would make a mockery of the proceedings."

"Tie him up, I said."

The blood-drenched executioner joined in the discussion. "Sir, I don't even think the blade will function. What if edge bogs down before—"

"He wants to die standing then let's give him what he wants." Laval and the headsman stared at each other. Faisson's teeth ground and his fists drew into white balls. "Damn you. I'll do it myself." He stomped over to the apparatus and kicked over the bascule before undoing the man's shackles. Then, taking a section of rope, he stretched Robillard between the uprights and tied his wrists to the rails.

Laval bent over to help but before he had finished fastening an ankle, Faisson yanked the release cord bringing the blade down with finality. Laval fell backward, the steel just missing him but not before swallowing a mouthful of blood. He wiped his eyes to see the spy splayed apart like a freshly opened book as he curled to the floor in two halves. The lieutenant coughed then vomited all over himself.

The Clough prisoners started a riot. Shots rang out and gas grenades burst as the soldiers brought the tumult under control. Faisson wiped his hands with a handkerchief and strode the podium.

"This is what awaits anyone who is thinking of doing the same. The world is tired of American tyranny. Our global village has had enough of its conquests, coercion and intimidation. For anyone who continues to believe in the myth of its power, its virtue, its exceptionalism, let him look no further than this blood-splattered canvas."

~ ~ ~ ~ ~ ~ ~ ~ ~ ~ ~ ~ ~ ~ ~ ~ ~ ~

Laura heaved all the way to the bathroom. When she got there, she locked the door and kneeled on the floor. She bowed over the toilet and stared at her reflection. Everytime she got revolted by the image staring back from the bowl, she would flush then flush again.

"What's wrong, Laura? You all right?" asked the others, banging on the door. "Don't cry. You were just doing your duty."

Laura looked around her, the Hulya Turkish towels, the Finnish sauna, the garden Jacuzzi. Then she thought of the grocer again. The one who gave her word of John. The one whose battered face stared at her from the camera. The one whose body laid open on the scaffolding, cleaved like a deli ham. The tiny traitress yetched bile again and again until she pulled all the muscles in her back. After the waves of sickness passed, she brushed her teeth and opened the door.

"We're proud of you," said the crowd. "We could've never done what you did."

Laura was ready to cry again when the front door rang. Hayley ran to answer it. "Hey, the hunks from the front gate are here," she squealed, peeping through the peephole. Laura tried to stop her but was too late. Dobson opened the door revealing a contingent of cameras and pool reporters.

"Mrs. Trent, in recognition of your service to the world community in your apprehension of a Freemartin spy, you have been selected to be the Secretariat's latest inductee as a United Nations Goodwill Ambassador." A young aspirant presented her with a poster-sized certificate for the cameras.

"How exciting," said Dobson, sticking out her chest. "Wow."

"I'm here to bring you to the tranche, said the soldier. "A big celebration is planned in your honor. How do you feel?"

Hayley rubbed up against him "Hey cutie! You're a little young, but, you'll do."

Laura pushed Dobson aside and slapped the boy. "How dare you enjoy this, you blood-thirsty little savage! *You* may have enjoyed that carnage but how dare you think I would be a party to it."

Behind the reporters, a squad of black-shirted Milice, the French Gestapo, surged forward and began clamoring for her. "She's not coming. Grab her!" The men bolted through the news crew, shoving the women aside and knocking the young soldier into the bushes. The house filled with shrieks and sounds of things breaking as Laura's pursuers ran out the back after her.

"Hey, you better leave her alone," managed Cody, picking himself up from the yews. "That's my mother!"

CHAPTER 32
PIMP MY RIDE

Spider, Hoop and the rest of the men of Camp Snoopy took a rare hour off to sit in their lawn chairs and cheer the vintage warbirds as they floated down their interstate runway. The bombers and fighters that were flying in sported other-era names like Diamond Lil' and Sizzlin' Liz and Fifi. With war going on at their doorstep, these battleworthy aircraft were no longer content to live out their lives on the airshow circuit. Their owners were patriots, too, and they came from all corners of the MS to fight. They were here to be part of the upcoming offensive: Operation Downpour.

"This the rest of your Ghost Squadron?" Trent asked of the frail veteran beside him.

"A-yep," he replied.

"They're beautiful planes."

"A-yep."

Trent looked at the pilot's bony hands and see-thru skull. "You're not scared of going back into battle?"

"A-nope."

Spider checked off each plane as it taxied by. When the aircraft got to the end of the runway, he barked orders to the marshalling crews, telling the men where they should be parked.

"All right, a B-14!" clapped Hooper.

"There's no such thing," said Spider.

"A P-49! Yeah, man!"

Beak shook his head. "You don't have a clue, do you?"

"About WWII planes? Why should I?" snorted Hoop. "That's old crap. I want my jets."

"Yeah, we want jets!" cheered Shank.

Spider apologized to the old-timer for them. "Forceps deliveries."

"Pudknockers," said the warbird commander.

Hooper had a new friend, a shell-shocked shitzu he had found roaming their camp one night for scraps and who he now carried around with him inside his flightsuit. He fed the war-stray a few dabs of MRE peanut butter from his lunch while Shank held up score cards made of white cardboard and charcoal scratchings. He graded the airframes for appearance, originality and how hard a landing they made. The burbling roar of a pair of Korean-era MIG-17 Frescos approached next.

"All right, jets," hooped Hoop. Give them a *nine*."

"Where are these all coming from?" asked Shank.

Spider consulted his list. "Mason City, Iowa. Just a bunch of hick dentists and lawyers. They bought them from the Ethiopian Air Force a couple of years back and put them together on the weekends. They don't have a lick of combat experience. Been flying them around for fun."

"Things are that bad?" asked Beak.

Trent nodded. "Frescos are tough little buggers. Tight turning. Hard to see … what the hell?" Spider rose out of his chair as a rogue HMMWV drove onto the interstate oblivious of the landing fighters. Trent called the jets to go around as the pilots lit their afterburners, barely clearing the vehicle.

"Yeehaw! Roadkill!" yelled Hoop as Shank held up a *ten*.

"What the fuck, over?" radioed the pilots. "We almost bought it back there."

Spider keyed his mike. "Sorry about that, guys. We're getting him cleared off now. Reenter the pattern and try again."

The Hummer departed the pavement heading straight for the lounging pilots. It disappeared down a swale and re-emerged, airborne, scattering everyone like a shot. When the vehicle pranged back to earth, it drifted sideways and skidded to a stop ten yards away. Spider walked over and ripped the door open. "Are you totally insane?"

"Hi, John."

"Chewie? What the heck was that? You came within inches of killing yourself and two pilots."

Hoop fingered the dent in the roof. "Make that millimeters."

"How about I take your keys and send you home?" threatened Spider.

Wade handed him the keys. "I was hoping you'd say that."

"You're supposed to be at the colony with Aboud."

"I want to go home."

"We all want to go home."

"Abby's in a concentration camp."

"So's Laura," said Trent. Then: "Weren't you supposed to be working on the serum?"

"I'm done with the antidotes. The last batch was today," Wade said, dabbing blood from his head where the roof had caved in.

"So why come here? I can't do anything."

"You're going to Duluth."

"We're going to Duluth to bomb it not have brunch."

"The camp's there. Just outside the base. I want to ride with you. I want to get her out."

"The commander's put Spider on double-secret probation, remember?" said Hoop. "He doesn't even have a jet."

"Then I'll fly with you," Wade told him.

The pilots laughed. "Wade, they never made any two-seat A-10s. The Hog only has one seat."

"Fine. I'll sit in your lap."

A growl emanated from inside Hooper's flightsuit. "Watch out. His name is Snuffy and he *will* take your head clean off."

Behind them, in the advancing shadows, a four-ship of green OV-10 Broncos landed, their sonorous propwash filling the glen like a lullaby. Wade watched as they pulled off into the median further down the interstate. When they had parked, their tailcones opened and a dozen paratroopers jumped out the back. "What are those?" he asked.

"Broncos."

"I'll go with them, then."

Trent grabbed his friend's arm. "Look, Wade, you're not going to Duluth. Woody's got it covered. The Freemartins are running the breakout and UNCON is backing them up. Abby'll be fine."

Wade startled John by snatching his collar and pushing him up against the Hummer. "Yeah? You so sure? Sure Laura's going to be OK? That she won't get caught in the crossfire or left behind or gassed or tortured?"

Wade's fists felt like two manhole covers. Spider didn't struggle. "I'm just a soldier, Chewie. I can only do what I'm asked to do. It's my duty to obey."

"Well, I'm not," replied Fredrick. "I'm just a dumb farmer. Who milks cows. Who's lost a part of his family and isn't going to lose another."

Spider put his hands around Fredrick's wrists to try to get some air. "If I—we—put our orders aside and follow our own interests, then we lose. The war *and* our families."

Hoop and Shank took an arm each and began prying Wade off their major. "Come on, chief. Let go."

Spider felt the big man let up. "I'm sorry, Wade. We're fighting for our freedom. Something bigger than ourselves. Something that demands our ultimate sacrifice."

"Tell that to Laura, Mr. I've-Got-It-All-Together." Wade took a step forward and stuck out a calloused finger. "Tell that to her face. When you can do that, maybe then I'll believe you."

Captain Steve 'Gumbo' Bennett flew Bronco's for the Marines. He had gotten out after the first Gulf War, all but relinquishing himself to a career with Edward Jones. That changed when H. B. Budd took an interest in him. Bennett had been called to USAFA headquarters for an interview the same time as Spider. Since then, the two pilots had lost track of each other. They spent a few minutes catching up.

"What's your mission?" asked Spider.

"We're in the second wave of the strike package," answered Gumbo. "We're coming out of Canada behind the bombers. After they soften up the landing zones, we're dropping grunts and equipment along the French supply lines."

"And what are the rockets and gun pods for?"

"After we've puked out the paras, we get to swing back and kill bad guys."

"Nasty break." Trent walked around the aircraft and looked inside. "You took out the back seat?"

"Yeah, the extra room lets us fit in a couple more bullet-catchers."

"How do you get the jumpers out?"

"You just pull up vertical and shake and out they come."

Two Bronco loadmasters pulled up alongside, towing a wagon. On the wagon squatted a brand-new Kawasaki Ultra 250X, freshly painted a camo blue. "A little help, sirs?"

"What's this?" asked Trent.

"Our new amphibious landing craft."

"A jet ski?"

"We load two anti-tank troops on the seat, drop down a foot or two above a lake, cut them loose and voilà! we've got a navy."

Trent played with the controls. "I like it. More mobility."

"I think it's stupid," replied Bennett. "It makes us water-bound. These things can't go on land."

The officers grabbed hold of the skis and wrestled it into the Bronco with the enlisteds. The boat barely fit, its rear-end hanging in the air. "It needs to go in another foot or so." The men laid into it with their backs and heaved again.

"OUCH!" cried a voice as the jet ski lunged out of the hold and dropped out the back. The crew retreated and drew their weapons as a dark shape emerged from under a tarp inside. It was Wade.

"Who the hell is this?" asked the Cajun. "And what's he doing stowing-away in my aircraft?"

Wade looked at Trent. "I told you, John. I told you I was going to—"

"—take a nap," Spider finished. "Next time, before you down a whole gallon of raspberry wine by yourself, make sure you can find your way to a tent."

"You've got raspberry wine?" inquired Bennett, holstering his weapon. "Enough to go around?"

"You're as sad as a prison blanket," complained Spider, huddling around the fire. "What's the matter with you?"

"Tell me again about the puddle rockets," Fredrick inquired.

"The jet skis were Aboud's idea, I guess. The Broncos drop down over a lake or river and skim a foot or so above the water. When they're as low as they can go, the pilots cut them loose and fly away."

"And the soldiers?"

"The soldiers ride the jet skis like they were freshmen coeds on orientation week," said Hooper. "In four years, it'll be an Olympic sport, you watch."

"You need snowmobiles," Wade offered.

"Stick to cows," replied Trent.

"No, it's called watercross."

"It's got a name?"

"Me and the boys, we'd skim the ponds around the farm when were bored. We were too poor for jet skis."

"They don't sink?" asked Hooper, putting Snuffy down to pee.

"The record's one hundred miles."

"What about land? It's summer," wondered Beak. "There's no snow."

"Snowmobiles do fine on land. The skis and belt and belly plate won't last much more than a couple of days, but—"

"But they don't have to," smiled Spider. "This offensive will be over by then." Spider's gears were turning. "What kind of modifications are we talking about?"

"Adjust the suspension, pressurize the fuel system, tape off some ports. Why?"

"I'm thinking we need to tell Woody," Trent answered, walking over to one of Gumbo's Broncos and rooting around the cockpit. "Right away."

"You mean I've actually thought of something Aboud hasn't?"

"Are you going to call the old man?" asked Hooper.

"You call him," ordered Spider. "I'm going airborne. Tell him I'll be there by 0300 Zulu and that I'm bringing the Middle States Watercross Champion with me."

"You've flown props before?" asked Shank.

"Yeah, an assignment with a Bronco squadron got me out of flying a desk at the Pentagon."

"But Spider, you're grounded." Hoop looked over his shoulder at the guard shadowing them. "What about Mr. T over there?"

"That's where you guys come in," he answered.

Dusk descended on the camp as Hooper did a quick walk-around of the aircraft and Spider and Wade buckled in. When he gave the all-clear, Trent started the left engine and the Bronco shuddered to life. Without checking his gauges, he gave a quick salute and exited out of the glade before the OV-10 pilots woke up.

"You didn't kill him, did you?" asked Spider, taxiing by the supine Sergeant Jacoby lying passed-out inside his guard hooch. "He doesn't look so good."

"Wine and hydraulic fluid. I mixed it just like you told me." Wade's helmet barely covered his ears. He pushed it down to get the chinstrap to fasten as the pickled Bronco pilots stumbled from their campfire after them. "We've got company."

Spider started the number-two engine to try and pull away. "Are we going to find enough snowmobiles for this to work?" he asked.

"There's been no snow," replied Fredrick into his headset. "The dealers were up to their eyeballs before the war. There should be thousands still in their crates." Fredrick gave up on his strap and turned to look behind. "Hurry, John. They're shooting at us!"

Spider was rusty. He fumbled for the controls as the Bronco's cockpit layout came back to him. He goosed his engines and swung out onto the concrete. "Hold on!" The propellers grabbed at the air fast, much faster than an A-10. His tires screeched around the turn almost running them off the pavement. The struts bucked and bounced making Trent think he had a flat. He scanned behind him, inspecting the rubber. When he turned around, he saw an A-10 on final. It flared for landing and came right for them.

"JOHN! We're going to crash. I'm ejecting."

"No, Chewie. Don't." Spider aborted the take-off and stomped on the brakes. He threw the props into full-reverse and drifted to a stop as the A-10 tank-killer squeaked to a halt above them. Trent shut down the engines and opened his canopy as the livid Bronco pilots caught up and tried to pull him out.

"Making new friends?" called down Om McCardell, from the Hog's cockpit.

"Sorry, Spider," said Beak, running up from the camp. "I told him to land on the eastbound lane. He must have directional dyslexia."

"This is an emergency," Trent yelled up to his commander. "I've got to get CW2 Fredrick to Camp Cougar. It's a matter of military urgency."

The A-10's turbines spun down as McCardell stepped onto his ladder. "Have you ever heard of the chain-of-command?"

"It's my fault," confessed Fredrick. "I knocked out your guard. I made the major take me."

"Yeah, he made me fly him."

"Spare me, chief."

"You only forbid me from flying Hogs," Trent reasoned. "This is a Bronco." Spider waited for his wingmen to come to his aid. Instead, they walked around Om's jet, admiring it.

"Tits jet, Colonel McCardell," said Shank.

"Yeah, who'd you backstab for this?" chided Hoop.

Spider joined his officer's walk-around, his eye catching on the fighter's paint job, a new camouflage of sweeping green-and-gray patterns laid out in small squares. "Pixilated?"

"It's called matrix camo. Based on fractals."

"Sweet," said Beak.

Shank stared at the new smaller engines and pointed at the set of polished metal burner cans sticking out the back. "This thing's got *blowers?*"

McCardell nodded. "Courtesy of the boneyard dogs. They cannibalized them off an F-15. Fifteen thousand pounds of thrust each."

Spider tried to look non-plussed. "Speed?"

"Combat load? Close to 450 knots. They didn't beef up the airframe so there's no telling where it'll overstress."

Hooper gawked into the air-to-ground missile slung under the wing, its detector following him as he moved. "This Maverick's on backwards."

"The missile is captive. It has no warhead," explained Om. "But the camera works. It's a cheap way to check-six. Like a backup camera on a car."

"Sick!"

"What else?" asked Spider.

"We have prismatic glass chaff for protection against heat-seekers. And the speedbrakes. They're asymmetrical." McCardell thumbed a switch on his right throttle-lever, sending a signal to the aileron on his right wingtip. It commanded the flap to split into halves. The upper-half flexed straight up big as a barn door until it extended ninety-degrees to the wing. The bottom-half did likewise, extending below the wing and whacking Hooper's skull in the process.

"You can choose which side to open?" asked Shank.

"Pop one open in the direction you want to go and the bat-turn will roll your socks down."

"Well, it's certainly a nice jet," said Spider. "Congratulations."

"It's not mine," McCardell said. "It's yours."

"What?"

"Hey, Spider. Come look see."

Spider put on his specks and shuffled to the nose where Beak and Shank pointed to a freshly painted scene of Snoopy locked in battle against the Red Baron from atop his doghouse. The artwork was well detailed, even down to the dog's cartoon grimace. "You're *giving* this to me?"

"What, you want a fucking dental plan with it?" McCardell threw him his helmet bag. "Yes, the jet's yours."

Trent stared at his nemesis, trying to read his expression. "What's wrong with it? Are the wings ready to fall off. Am I supposed to be the guinea pig?"

"This isn't my idea. It came straight from Woody. Personally, I feel if you auger in, the world instantly becomes a better place," he spat.

"And the court-martial?"

"He refused to convene one."

Spider ripped a loud "YYYEEESSS!" as he jumped in the air and threw out his back. He shrieked in pain as his wingmen lowered him to the ground.

The colonel laughed. "Enjoy yourself while you can, *Spiderman*. Because after the offensive is over, you're mine again."

CHAPTER 33
GIZZELLE

A flash of morning lightning bleached the Rochester downtown in stark white. Its report cracked in the distance only to be swallowed up by the storm's low gray scud. Inside the Mayo chapel, a tall handsome brunette stood and approached a stained-glass Virgin Mary. The woman stared as streams of rain flowed down Mary's cheeks like never-ending tears. After a moment, she returned to her Bible and flowers, gathered them up and walked out the door.

Margeaux Murphy's age could not be guessed. She had been a beauty since birth. To all who cast a glance at her aquiline cheeks and full lips, it was obvious she would carry her gift through to old age. She wore a sleeveless yellow dress dotted with petite pink flowers. It came down tastefully just above her knees while a white pillbox hat balanced gracefully on her head. She was the kind of woman who could still wear a hat.

The overcast scattered and she felt the welcome heat of the sun. Across the grounds, on the bank of the Zumbro, a woman and small child stood, holding umbrellas. Murphy walked over to them, heels clicking with each step. "Hello, little princess," she said, barely above a whisper. "It's mama come to see you. Happy birthday, mademoiselle." The woman and girl stepped aside as Murphy knelt in the drenched grass and laid her flowers at a small non-descript gravesite. Hidden in the clouds above, a helicopter flew by, scattering the umbrellas with its gust. The mother and her daughter ran after them, leaving Murphy alone in the Mayo Children's Field.

The wet and chill soaked into her stockings. So cold, she thought. What kind of mother leaves her child alone and in the cold like this? She scraped the dirt with her fingers, wanting to reach her little girl. Instead, she slumped into a crying heap at the foot of her red granite gravestone.

GIZZELLE FAISSON
BELOVED DAUGHTER OF SEAN AND MARGEAUX
QU'ELLE REPOSE EN PAIX

"Margeaux?"

Murphy froze. "Sean. How did you find me?" Faisson wrung the beret in his hand. He stared at her back. "Do you have the DGSE after me or have you assigned me my own little satellite to follow me around?" She got up, brushing the dirt from her dress.

"I've been watching the airline manifests," he admitted. "With Gizzelle's birthday coming up, I thought you might come and visit."

"How often have *you* come, Sean? You live in America yet I don't see your boot prints here." He looked down at the flowers. "You still cannot bring yourself to see her, can you?"

"How can I?" he asked. "You are the one who wanted her here. You are the one who said they could help."

"And what did her *French* doctors say, Sean? They said there was nothing they could do."

"But they didn't kill her," he hissed. "It was the Americans who killed her."

"At least they tried, Sean. At least they had the courage and the intellect to try."

She took a step toward him and his nostrils filled with jasmine. Her sable-brown hair glinted in the sun and her burning gray eyes blurred his vision. He stood mesmerized and fought for air as his heart swelled against his lungs. He was a slave to her gaze, just as when they had first met. God, I love her. Why did this have to happen?

"You are always their apologist, no?" he said.

"I told you about this place a full month before her coma," Margeaux stated. "I told you these doctors could help."

"But her French doctors were not done with their tests."

"Her French doctors were *imbeciles*," she snapped. "They kept giving her the same tests. They did not want to admit they didn't know what she had. They just watched her die."

"As if the Americans knew?"

"We will never know, Sean, will we? She had already slipped into a coma by the time you brought her here." Margeaux put a hand to her husband's chest. "I don't know why you despise the Americans so. But they didn't kill Gizzelle. You did and your insatiable hate."

Faisson barred his teeth as he wheeled around to strike her.

"Go ahead, general. Give her a good one, she deserves it." Across the walk, not far away, a man in coat-and-tie sat watching them while eating his lunch by the river. "Since this is practically France now anyway, hitting women is probably legal," he added.

Faisson approached the man, waving him away. The suit flipped him his middle finger. "Do you know who I am?" Faisson said, knocking the man's sandwich to the ground. "You will leave this place immediately."

"Last I checked, it's still a free country, Froggy." The man smiled up at him and pulled his jacket away, revealing a silver City of Rochester detective shield and the butt-end of a .40-caliber Smith & Wesson service revolver. "Now why don't you leave the pretty lady alone and get the hell out of my city."

In a flash of rage, Faisson pulled out his knife. The detective stumbled backward with a look of disbelief and went for his gun. With eerie calm, the Frenchman took his blade and drew it across the policeman's knuckles, severing the tendons. The hand gushed blood and went limp. "JESUS CHRIST!" The detective jumped to his feet and stuffed his hand in his armpit while grabbing for his gun with the other. Faisson's guards stopped him, one pistol-whipping him in the head, the other applying a hammerlock. The three struggled as Margeaux ran up and kicked Faisson in the shins.

"Sean, you monster! Stop this," she yelled, flinging hair and spit. "Stop this right now!"

Faisson took her by the wrists and held them over her head. When she had run out of energy and blows, he nodded for his soldiers to lead the injured detective to his helicopter.

Faisson embraced his wife as she sagged in his arms. He put her down on the bench and sat down beside her. "I've missed you," he said. "Terribly."

Margeaux cried. "I've missed you, too."

Faisson brushed the brown stains off of her knees. She let him. He knelt down to the ground to get closer, touching her smooth white calves again, caressing her ankles. "I can't get you out of my mind, Margeaux. You obsess me during my days. You haunt me during my nights." He reached for her face and tilted her chin toward him.

"And Gizzelle, Sean?" she wondered. "Do you ever think of our child?"

"You and Gizzelle both. That is why I haven't been able to come back here. That is what has kept me away. I still see her when I wake. I can still hear her voice. It's like trying to live life with half my organs. Half my body. Half my heart." She looked down at him and brushed his cheek. "I howled like an animal the night you left," he continued. "I dropped onto all fours like a wolf and all night unbearable pain poured out." He looked into the smoky deep of her eyes. "You haven't lost a bit of beauty."

She sniffled. "Not even with these wrinkles? Not even with these gray hairs?"

"I'm sorry," Faisson said.

"Sorry? About what?"

"I still don't know if Mayo could've helped cure her. But I needed to give our little girl all the resources that were available. I needed to let them try to save our baby. I didn't give them that chance and it's haunted me ever since."

"I've never known you to be sorry before, Sean."

"Gizzelle knows."

"Then you're done?" asked Margeaux. "Done with your obsession? With your mania? Against the Americans?"

"Yes. That is what I'm saying."

"Promise? Promise this is all over?"

"Yes, I promise," he lied. "If you promise to come back to me."

Margeaux brushed a lock of hair from her face and stared at him, dry-eyed. "I can't. I've remarried, Sean. You must have known."

The words fell on him like a house. He was sinking. He watched the ship that had been his life get smaller and smaller as he sunk to the bottom, weeds wrapping around his head and limbs. He slowly untangled himself from her hair and let go of her leg. "Who? Who did you marry?"

"His name is Alex. Alex Murphy."

"*Murphy?*"

"That's right. An American. I married one just so I could see your face when I told you."

Faisson seized his wife by the neck and plucked her from the bench. Shaking her head violently, he reached inside his waistband and found his holster empty.

"Looking for this?" she croaked, pulling his FAMAS out of her handbag and shoving it into his chest.

Faisson squeezed his wife harder. He didn't care if she shot him. Right now, he would welcome it. She mumbled something unintelligible then he heard a shot. Before he could react, a thousand hands fell upon him. Something like a hammer hit him at the base of his skull. Within a moment, he was on the ground looking up.

"Sir, you can't do this. Not here." It was Laval. The guards were all around; some on him, some on his wife.

Faisson patted himself. Mon dieu, she had not shot him. She had shot in the air to draw attention then thrown the gun in the river. How had she taken his gun? While intervening for the American? Had the policeman been a trap? To protect her knowing he would snap?

His wife shrieked as she was led away. "Let this be a lesson, Sean Faisson. You will never win me back. *Never.* As long as Gizzelle is in the ground, you will always be to blame. Do you hear me? She will always be between us!"

Overhead, a 4NewsNow chopper hovered as a parade of Rochester squads encircled the park. Police ran past the Mayo Brothers statue as they retrieved their detective and whisked away his Margeaux. In the distance, Faisson heard a familiar willowy voice. The voice from his past. The voice from his nights. His Gizzelle.

"Daddy? Daddy? Don't cry. I'm not mad."

He rolled over on his stomach and gawked at her headstone, her mother's flowers, the pictures she had perfectly arranged. Faisson ripped a clump of hair from his head and buried his face in the dirt as Gizzelle repeated the same words she had said the night she died.

"Don't worry, daddy. I forgive you. I will always forgive you."

CHAPTER 34
BOSSE

Laura sat sweating at the end of her cot picking through a canvas clothes bag stenciled *UNITED NATIONS HIGH COMMISSIONER FOR REFUGEES*. Stripped to her underwear, she pulled out a red wool coat, corduroy pants, yellow sorrels and began putting them on.

"You've got the wrong bag," admonished Cody to the frazzle-haired aid worker. "You've given her winter clothes."

"That is all we have," the helper replied. "Maybe you want I send it back to the good-hearted people of France?" She jerked her head to the other similarly attired prisoners. "It is more than they deserve, no?" She zippered the bag shut and dragged it out the door.

Laura picked at the fuzz in the fur lining while she gauged her emaciated tent-mates. "Why am I here?" she asked, wiping her tears.

"This is Clough Island. The out-processing point. *You* wanted to be here. You wanted to be back with dad."

"I killed that man!" she bellowed. She struck the ridge pole, raining tiny drops of condensed perspiration back on the women.

"Mom, he was a Freemartin. The worst of the worst. They kill Peacebuilders. He would have thought nothing of killing me."

"I tried so hard," she said, continuing to pick at her clothes. "So hard to keep my family together. Me. You. Your father."

"Quit using me and him in the same sentence."

"I hated it when he went off to war. Libya. Grenada. Iraq. When he left this time, I hated *him*."

"The whole country does, mom. He's a hothead. A traitor. An embarrassment."

"At first I thought he was wrong. Now, everything he warned about is coming true."

"Treat me for shock, mom!"

"I had to be right. I had to be the leader. To pick up the slack because he wouldn't."

"Then why go back to him?"

Laura ignored him. "I blamed him when the UN came. Hell, I even welcomed them. Them! The very people who are shooting at him even now."

"Who else but the UN can stop independence? The United States can't police themselves."

"As long as I didn't hear from him, I was fine. I could keep us together." Laura scuffed her boots in the dirt. "I could pretend nothing was happening."

"Mom, are you listening to me?"

Laura searched Cody's face. Beneath his shaggy bangs and baby fat, she saw John. The baleful stare. The exasperated mouth. Oh, John, how have I survived all this time without feeling your hands on me? Without seeing your scowls? Without hearing your forgiveness? Her chin quivered and she twisted around to avoid Cody's glare.

"Mom, I need to know. Has dad been in contact with you? Have you talked to him? Has he given you anything?"

"Why do you keep asking me that? So Faisson can hunt him down? So they can put him in this stink hole, too?"

"What would be so bad about that. At least you would be together."

"CODY! PEOPLE DIE HERE!" The shriek woke the tent out of its stupor. The prisoners stared at the sallow woman in the funny red Santa coat before turning back to their own troubles. Laura returned their stares and addressed the fifty-something waif beside her. "Why aren't you outside?" she asked. "Why are you all just sitting on your beds looking like a comet's going to hit? It's still daylight out."

"Laura!"

Both Trents turned. It was Abby. She stood small in the door wearing farmer's coveralls, a gaudy sweater and a bump in her stomach.

"I can't believe I found you!" She dropped her overnighter and ran to them with arms raised.

"Abby? What are you doing here?" asked a surprised Laura. "You are supposed to be at the Reunification Center."

"Not anymore. They sent me here to the Clough Terminal for out-processing."

Laura shook her head. "No."

"Yes! Ever since you got your job in the tranche, everything's been clicking; a better job, a trailer upgrade. Now I'm on my way to the MS to see my Chewie!"

"I didn't have anything to do with that."

"I thought you did. I figured you were the one who was finally getting my papers in order."

Laura snapped at Cody. "Did you know of this or is Faisson going to lay this on me, too?"

"What are you talking about, mom?"

Laura turned Abby by the shoulders and shoved her out the way she came. "Get out. Get out of here, now. Do you understand? Get back on that bus and go back!"

Abby dug her heals and spun around. "Laura, I don't understand. This is where families are taken to the MS. This is where I get to see my husband and show him Wade, Jr. This is where you get to see John."

Laura twirled her head, her curls splaying out like a figure skater. "This is where you're sent to work the taconite mines. This is where you get sent to fight on FUN suicide squads. This is where you get beheaded on TV or shot in secret and dumped in the forest."

Cody twisted his face. "That's not right, mom. What proof—"

"Me. I'm proof. I've been working in their offices. I've been poking in their files," Laura said. "Not one person has made it to the Middle States from here. Not one person has left alive, *period*."

"You're insane," said Cody.

"The French want our land. Faisson wants our industry. And the world wants us dead. This is how they are going to do it." Laura released her grip on Abby and turned to Cody. "And you knew. You knew all along," she said, flattening his nose with her finger.

"Knew what?"

"You pulled a gun on your father, now you've put a bullet in your mother's head." She popped him backwards and returned to her bunk.

Cody wrung his hands. He hoped what his mother had said wasn't true, but he didn't have access to her kind of information, either. He looked at the grim faces around the tent and felt dread. "Mom, I've given up trying to keep you from dad. I brought you here so I could say goodbye. To wish you well. General Faisson's letting you go. He's giving you what you wished for."

"I'm here because I'm no longer of any use to him."

"If that's true, then why am I still here? Why am I still one of his guards?" Cody cradled her face in his hands. "Mom, nothing's going to happen."

The setting sun beamed in through the shelter's open flap. Around them, women started moaning as a half-dozen African girls in shaven heads and dirty diapers entered the tent. The girls went jerkily from bed to bed, bumping into each other like cockroaches looking for bacon grease. They poked at the prisoners and looked under their covers until they found a plump high schooler with blue-dyed hair hiding in the corner. Three of the slave girls yanked the distressed teen to her feet and led her out the door. Another slave looked into Laura's mouth and squeezed her breast.

"No you don't!" she huffed, slapping the hand away.

The three collaborated in Gabonese and, with fantastic speed and strength, hauled Laura up by her wrists. Abby and Cody responded by pulling her back. Laura felt her arms were going to pop out when Cody let loose with a boot and punted one of the toddlers out the door. The others let go and ran outside, chanting, "*Bosse. Bosse.*"

A monstrous form filled the opening. It was a huge man. He had on a pure white T-shirt and sleeveless safari vest. He wore neatly pressed gray trousers tucked into black shark-skin jack boots. A golden machete hung over his shoulder and his bald black pate shined with dozens of black-and-blue rings. He smelled strongly of sex and rum.

"Heh, heh, heh. Waat haav you done with my leetle keettens?" The Bosse ducked his head and strode into the tent toward a prostrate Laura. The roly-poly slave girls huddled close to his feet, pointing. "Ahhh, yaes. Goood." He reached down and lifted Laura by her black curls. He looked into her hazel-green eyes and pinched her sunken cheeks. Laura could feel an electric abandon about him. She could see his breath as he snorted. Her body shuddered and she started kicking and scratching to get free.

"This is Laura Trent," screamed Abby, hitting and pulling at his arm. "She works for General Faisson at the tranche. Put her down this instant!"

Bosse's brows raised. He dropped Laura. "*Faissssson?*" he hissed.

"Yes, that's right," said Abby. "Now leave us alone."

He came over and sniffed Abby and poked her plump side. "Mmm, piggins!" he said and snatched her by the waist as if she were a puppy who had just piddled.

Laura rocked on the ground mumbling as the Bosse headed outside with her screaming friend. Cody looked at his mom for a moment, then launched after Abby. As he cleared the door, the flat of Bosse's machete slapped against his face. The boy heard a sickening squish as his eye ruptured and teeth broke against his cheek. The force of the blow sent him high into the air. He did a skateboarder's roll as he hit the ground and came up with his gun cocked and ready.

In an instant, the Bosse had closed the distance but not quickly enough. Cody aimed for his chest and got off two shots. In a blur, the agile caught the bullets with his blade and sent them sparking harmlessly off into the dusk.

"Preeetee boy," the Bosse said, slapping the gun from Cody's grip. He bent down to pet his hair before yanking him into the air by it. As he drew back his steel, Cody pinched his eyes closed and emptied his bladder.

"I changed my mind. Take me."

Cody opened his good eye to see his mother embracing the African and kissing him full on the mouth. The beast began to soften and put a hand on her hip. "No, mom. No!"

"You said I'd be all right, Cody. You said I could trust the UN."

"Mom!"

"Shut up, Cody. Go. Take Abby *and go.*"

The boy looked in the dirt for his gun and lunged for it as the thumper's heavy leather boot caught him by the ear and pinned him to the ground.

"*I SAID GO!*" yelled Laura. "I don't care anymore. This can't be any worse than what I've already done."

Bosse walked Laura to his Gator and chained her to the back with the rest of his harem. Cody patted his skull for fractures as a familiar vehicle approached from the gate.

"Well, hello, Leonardo," hailed Faisson. "Gathering some new wives for your nightly entertainment?" The general exited his PVP and sat on the hood, ballistraes rolling in his hand. "You really should try TiVo some time. So you don't catch a disease."

"Yooo sahd all er mine."

The Frenchman marched up to his camp commander and watched the man's eyelids and cheeks twitch uncontrollably. "Going overboard with the magnets, don't you think, Bosse?" He walked over to the women and brushed the hair from Laura's face. She looked away but he took her by the chin and stared at her in the sun.

"Yooo sahd."

"Not this one. This one's special. This one is my child. A beautiful princess."

"Ahh dunt wark for Frenchie. Ahhm Secretariat."

"Yes, how *does* Zzgn manage to find perverts like you?" Faisson asked as he spun his hips and loosed his ballistrae at Bosse's neck. The balls glinted briefly in the setting sun as the African ducked and sliced upward with his machete. The stroke cut the chain and sent the spheres sailing harmlessly across the camp. Bosse's smile beamed wide as he laughed and rose up from his crouch.

"Now Frenchie dice."

Something sharp stung the Gabon's stomach as he felt a tug around his midsection. He looked down at his belly and watched as a second chain whirred into his vest and cut through his shirt. "Huh?"

"Ah, ah, ah," scolded Faisson as Bosse clawed at the device. With each *ah ah*, the general yanked the controller chain further, causing the tiny diamond-coated nanoteeth to cut into the man's stomach a fraction of an inch more.

The Bosse stood riveted as blood wicked into his shirt. He looked up with pleading eyes as Faisson sauntered closer. "Pleeesa?"

"Not today, my friend. Today, you've gone too far." He took the keys from Bosse's pocket as the razor-sharp links bit deeper and deeper into his flesh. "I've looked the other way long enough. Now I'm saying *no*." Faisson undid Laura's shackles then returned the key to Bosse's pocket. "You're a disgusting pig and your debauchery has no place in my mandate."

Faisson watched the man for a signal, his pupils, his nostrils, his pores; any inkling the man was about to attack. The black man smirked and when the twitching in his cheek stopped, Faisson yanked his chain. Blood, organs and bits of bone sprayed onto Laura, Abby and Cody as the top half of Bosse tipped backwards into the dirt, his machete still poised high above his head.

The Frenchman wiped his ballistrae clean and pocketed it before walking to his vehicle to retrieve a straggly yellow teddy bear. As his aide kicked at the Bosse's stout black legs to knock them down, Faisson offered the bear to Laura. "Here you go, sunshine. Don't cry. Daddy's here and he's got Ronsard, your favorite." Laura took the toy, wondering at Faisson's lost stare as the general carefully wiped the blood from her face.

Cody gave his commander a hostile glare and, stepping between them, put a protective arm around her.

"Come on, mom. Let's go. You've had enough creepiness for one day."

ACT III

CHAPTER 35
ESCAPE

Sergeant Mark Lee checked his watch. He was running late. In an hour it would be midnight and if he didn't have his Stingrays stabilized and in place by then, the breakout would be compromised. *Not* the way Command would want to open up the offensive.

At twenty feet below the surface, the water's murky detritus limited his vision to that of a sandstorm. He took a swallow of oily fetid air and felt what it must be like to be a carp. A concrete pillar appeared out of the gloomy harbor bottom. Lee steered his light toward it and read the lettering. It was the Blatnik High Bridge, the roadway connecting Duluth to her Twin Port city of Superior. At least they were on course. He clicked three times on his cricket. The team gathered around his light to be counted. Killer Squad. Dagger Squad. All accounted for. He stuck a finger into the thick brown water and gave it a whirl; final approach, form up and move out.

Lee twisted the grip on his inhaler and felt the turbine yank him off his feet. The machine hummed in his hands and dragged him down the channel horizontal. He tasted the oxygen freshening in his mouthpiece as the compressor blades pushed more water through its breather. For a moment, he let the turbo corkscrew him like the tail of a kite before throttling back so his formation could catch up.

The team circumnavigated the estuary for five miles before coming to the Clough. They split off into four Teams; Dagger One and Two forked south to the backbay on the Wisconsin side; Killer One and Two kept heading straight ahead toward the marshes to the west.

The Clough Terminal Annex lie quiet and asleep under a quilt of black sky and singing stars. Lee surfaced through a thick film of petroleum and coal dust and pushed his inhaler into the weeds. He wiped the scum off his face, removed his mask and scanned the shore with a pair of NVGs. "It's a thirty-foot climb to the top," he whispered to Assistant Team Leader Rod 'Gooch' Sickli. "And it's mined and wired."

For most of the island's existence, Clough had been a farm. More recently, a golf resort until the UN had halted development to protect the endangered piping plovers living there. Now, it was a steamy rathole of silt, tents and trench latrines barricaded by fifteen-foot-high bunker-panels and guarded by towers at all four corners. Bosse's men guarded the camp and occupied the bombed-out remnants of the Best Western just to the east. To the west, a small detachment of FUN soldiers guarded the guards from their bivouac along the shore.

"Stingray, check."

"Killer Two is holding at Objective Willow."

"Dagger One's ready at Pinecone."

"Dagger Two's good-to-go at Cactus."

Lee sent the men a double-click over the radio as he batted away a heron that was hungrily pecking at his wetsuit. "Well Gooch? You sure this is going to work?"

"It worked in the lab."

"OK, then. Let 'em fly."

Sickli produced a plastic flask from his webgear and shook it, waking up thousands of slumbering lightning bugs trapped inside. "Rise and shine, guys. It's Miller Time." The flask glowed green with activity as he opened the cap, sending the insects into the night. For a moment, the fireflies didn't know where to go and hovered in an undulating cartoon-bubble over the men's heads.

"Shit! They're giving away our position."

"Give 'em a minute, sarg. Let their training kick in."

The glittering swarm spun and throbbed as the insects tasted the air for traces of C4, nitrites and other explosives. Slowly, they picked up a scent and one-by-one, headed for shore where they descended on

Clough Island

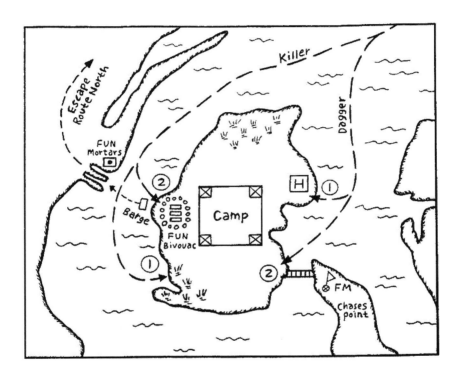

the mines buried there in dim but visible patterns. "Well spit fire and call the dogs," whispered Lee as he watched the sniffers gather on the sand. He looked at his watch then keyed his mike. "Stingray. We go in five minutes. Ready. Ready. Hack."

Corporal André Girard lit another joint and slapped his young mistress on the rump as she climbed out of his cot and into her underwear. "Ouch!" she yelled, stumbling backwards in the dark, giggling. "Don't do that unless you mean it. That turns me on."

"Mais qui diable êtes-vous?"

"*Make we dibble?*" She wrinkled her nose. "Talk like that some more. That turns me on, too."

He shook his head and when she was half-dressed, pushed her outside with the others. "Sors de là!" Get out of here!

The townie brushed herself off as more soldiers and girls emerged from the camp's shipping-container barracks. "Oh, look. They're taking us back to the club!" said the shapely teen to her friends. She was checking her lipstick with a lighted compact when her lover slapped it to the ground with a snarl. The boys all laughed as they tucked in their shirts. "Putains des merde!" they mumbled as they corralled the girls down the walk.

The sodium-glow of the tranche twinkled from across the channel as a taxi boat bobbed in the hidden cove below. The men led, feeling their way down the bluff. When the group reached the beach, Girard swiped a card through a reader and turned off the mines. The women waded out to the launch, but needed help to get in. Girard whispered to the slumbering driver, "Wake up, you wanker." The man didn't move.

Girard cursed. He flicked his joint onto the beach and waded in to wake the man up. When he gave his friend a sharp smack, the man's head flipped backwards off his neck like a Pez dispenser. "Maudit!" he screamed and the soldiers went for their holsters.

"Looking for these?" The three blonde Freemartins pulled the soldier's FAMAS pistols from their bags and screwed on silencers. In back of them, out in the bay, the hulking black shapes of Killer Two arose out of the water and brushed past the stunned Frenchmen on their way to the beach.

Girard raised his hands and backed away. "You want me to set free the prisoners? You want breakout? I know security. I know the codes.

I can help you. Just tell me what you want."

"I want you dead," Christine Robillard said, her eyes welling.

"No. Don't."

"I want to stomp your brains into the fucking sand, you French smudge mark!"

"Please. I beg you."

"Good. Go ahead, plead some more," Robillard said. "Because I'm going to feed you to the fish like you did my father." She raised her silenced gun and fired.

Christopher 'Doc' Anderson hitched a leg over the precipice of the Best Western and hiked himself up onto its roof. Anderson served as Dagger One's hospitalman and was more used to cleaning up after an assault than leading one. But here he was, shimmying up the side of an enemy barracks and sneaking up on a sentry simply because he knew how to handle a blastblade.

Blastblades yielded a quick and silent death and was the UNCONs preferred weapon for covert ops. The business end of the knife consisted of a short three-inch hollowed-out titanium blade while the grip-end contained a cartridge of compressed CO_2 gas. When inserted precisely between a victim's forth and fifth ribs, the weapon sent a blast of pressurized gas into the thoracic cavity, percussively inflating the diaphragm and collapsing the lungs. Anderson watched the weapon work now, the blade making a muffled *pffft!* into the sentry's back and swelling the African's chest like a beach ball. He arched backwards into the dust and gasped for air but, unable to inhale over the deadly pressure, asphyxiated in seconds without a sound. Anderson sheathed his weapon and threw his ascender over the side, signaling the all-clear for Dagger One's sniper to clamber up and join him.

Dagger Two crouched quietly under the cart bridge on the eastern side of the island, their leader, Carl 'Ping' Kollmeyer, waiting patiently for the Freemartin's signal from the other side. The Freemartins were amateurs but since they had the contacts and knew the neighborhood, they were running the escape. The Stingrays were there only to take out the FUN, something the FMs were not equipped to do.

Two French soldiers guarded the bridge. One, above them, lazily cast a lure into the water attempting to catch a fish. The other, on the mainland side, was about to meet his demise. Kollmeyer caught sight of a laser flash from the far bank. Now there was only one guard to worry about.

Ping took a deep breath and snaked his way up the rocky incline to the thick lilacs and low-lying sumac above. On the opposite side of the bridge, he heard a branch snap. Shit.

"Charles? Quel était celui?" What was that? The thick crewcut guard grabbed his Minimi machine gun and took a few steps onto the bridge; calling again. "Charles? What is wrong?"

Shit. Shit. Shit, Kollmeyer said to himself. He took out his cellphone and began dialing as the guard turned back to his post and radioed his commander for advice.

"Hello, this is Fifty-Three. I hear sounds from Chases Point. Charles won't answer."

"Yes, Fifty-Three. Standby," the clerk replied. Laughing erupted in the background as the man's commander came on the net. "Bear making off with your fish again, Felix?"

"Ah, what the fuck do you know?" the guard retorted. "I'll take care of it myself. Fifty-Three, out." He clicked off his radio as a cellphone rang from his pants. From the caller ID, he saw that it was his wife; the shrew was calling from Grenoble, probably to tell him his paycheck was late again. He flipped the phone open and put it to his ear. "Le Christ. Didn't I talk to you last week?" the Frenchman barked to his spouse. "Where are you? Out drinking again?"

"Not tonight, *Kermit*," came Kollmeyer's reply. "Tonight, I'm right behind you."

The guard turned as the Stingray's two great hands seized his head and held it like a vice. He unsheathed his knife and stabbed the UNCON in the side but Kollmeyer's elastomeric body armor stiffened from the impact and blocked the blow. A piece of tape went over the Frenchman's mouth as a pair of powerful gritty fingers dug for his jugular, ripping it away from his neck. He felt a painful pinch as blood stopped flowing to half his brain. By the time the American had hold of the other, the executioner dropped to his knees like a Catholic and went to sleep for a very long time.

"Mom, we've got to get out of here. Now!" Cody's voice urged over the sound of machine guns and explosions in the distance. Laura didn't wake.

"She's been like that for days," Abby said, rousting from her cot. "What is it, Cody?"

"The Freemartins are here. They're pulling down the walls. They're breaking us out. We're free!"

Abby reflexively grabbed her stomach and watched the tent walls flash around her. "No, no. That can't be. They'll ruin everything. How am I going to find my husband?"

"Mrs. Fredrick, they were never going to let you go. Surely, you know that by now."

Abby ran to look out their tent flap. "No, no! They're wrecking it. They're wrecking everything!"

"Mrs. Fredrick. Abby. People are getting killed out there. We've got to go. We've got to get mom out of here. Now."

"Where will I go? What will I do?"

"I don't know, but I'm sure the Freemartins' plan will be a lot better for us than Faisson's."

A mortar shell whistled from high in the sky then lanced into the refugee tent behind them. Yells turned to screams as the blast sent shrapnel into the dark. Cody caught a metal splinter in his shoulder as embers and smoke swirled around them and started their tent on fire. "AHHH!"

"Cody, are you OK?" Abby cowered from the flames, her face covered with soot.

"Jesus, holy—" Cody ripped open his shirt but couldn't see the wound with his bad eye. He felt for the sliver instead and yanked it out with his fingers, the steel still glowing. "Come on! Get mom. Let's go!"

More shells rained down. They landed indiscriminately among the tents and sounded like massive canvas sails being ripped from top to bottom. Abby dressed in their flashes then she and Cody dressed Laura and dragged her outside. "No. No. I won't go."

Cody stopped. Above them, soldiers dangled out of the guard towers, dead, while bulldozers and loaders toppled the walls underneath. A stream of threadbare prisoners brushed past in their winter coats, clutching bags of papers and clothing and food. They made for the channel only to run into another mob going in the opposite direction. Laura turned for the tent. "We're all going to die. Leave me alone."

"We will if we don't get off this island," Cody railed.

"You're a UN soldier," said his mother. "Protect me. Stay with me."

"Not anymore I'm not. Faisson took my gun and now I'm a symp just like you."

She wrenched her hand free. "I'm not going anywhere! This is where I deserve to be."

"Mom. You have to."

Twenty yards away, a bald-headed FUN soldier backed out of a tent door. He yelled for everyone to come out. Men emerged, then their women and children. As he herded them into the yard, Laura made her break. "Take me with you, too! I don't want to be rescued!"

The soldier leveled his rifle and fired, the muzzle lighting up the row. In a fifteen-second burst, his magazine was empty and the prisoners had all folded to the ground.

"MOM!"

Laura held up her hands as the soldier reloaded. "Well, hello Mrs. Trent. Fancy meeting you here!" The boy turned around to face her, revealing purple hair and a purple spiderweb tattooed on the other half of his head.

Cody gasped. "Darren! How did you get here?"

"You're not the only one who's ever been promoted out of the Cadets, *buttrag*." Taylor placed the weapon on his hip and yanked back the bolt.

"What are you doing?" bellowed Cody.

"I'm doing as ordered. We're fragging all the prisoners so they can't escape. Including you." On Taylor's uniform, a laser dot appeared just above his sternum. He watched it dance around for a second before a 25-millimeter grenade exploded against his armor and blew his chest open like a cherry blossom. Laura howled into her hands as the boy flew backwards into a trench latrine. She crumpled into a wad.

"Everyone's heading to the channel," Abby pointed. "They're loading onto barges but they're filling up fast."

Cody ran to Laura to pick her up. She was flaccid and kept falling out of his arms. He grabbed her wrists and started dragging. "Leave me," she whimpered.

"We're not leaving you."

"I can't face—"

"You can't face who?"

"Your father."

Abby ran around to grab Laura's ankles when she stopped dead in her tracks. "Cody. Don't move." On the teen's uniform, a red dot hovered. She turned and watched as a black figure strode out of the smoke and glided toward them as if on skates. A full foot taller than her, he had bear-like arms and pecks. Shin guards and knee pads girded his legs and camo-paint covered his face. The green glow of his riflescope lit up his nametag: *LEE* it read. "No. Don't shoot. He's American, he's not UN. He's with us!"

The sergeant brought his head up and considered the three. He gave Cody's blue armbands and blue scarf another look.

"This is Laura Trent. Her husband flies A-10s for the Sovereign Forces. This is Cody, their son," explained Abby, rapid fire.

Lee saw something he didn't like and snapped back under his scope to fire. He flipped his selector from DIRECT CONTACT to AIR BURST, sighted in his laser rangefinder and pulled the trigger. Cody went deaf as the round blew by his ear and sailed over a sandbagged foxhole behind him. When the shell had traveled the pre-programmed distance, it fuzed and exploded in the air, sending hot spall into the hole and osterizing the machine gunner inside.

Lee dropped his rifle to half-mast. "I don't know how long you're going to survive in that get-up, son," he smiled. "But you'd better strip to your undies. Unless those are UN-blue, too?"

Gooch Sickli returned from the shore. He charged up the narrow alleyway like a bison and yelled in Lee's ear. "The mortars are coming from across the river, north of the marina. They're targeting the prisoners. Nothing else."

"That's why the FUN didn't reinforce the compound," Lee said. "So they'd have an excuse to blow them all away. What about the barges?"

"The first is almost full. The second one's under fire and sinking."

"Then they'll have to swim."

"Take my mom," said a bleeding and half-naked Cody. "Please. She's in bad shape. She'll never make it."

"Her husband is John Trent," Abby yelled. "He's a hero."

"I'm not going," Laura said, standing. "I'm staying. Take her. She's pregnant."

"So what," said Abby, indignant. "I'm fine. I can swim."

Laura started to walk away. "Cody, take Abby and make sure she gets on that boat," she said, over her shoulder.

Abby grabbed her. "Sergeant, do something! You can see she's not right."

Laura shook her off and swept her arms around the camp. "This is my doing! I've done all this," she said. "If I hadn't betrayed that Freemartin, these people wouldn't have died."

"What are you talking about, mom?"

"I spied. I turned someone in." She was slobbering on herself now. "A brave man who was defending his country. Who was defending me. I gave him up just so I could go back to a nice home. Just so I could pretend for another day everything was fine. That things weren't so bad."

Lee reached out his hand. "Come on, ma'am. You can shoot yourself later."

Laura slapped the hand away. "*Fuck off,* slab-chest!"

"I wish there was something I could do," the Stingray said to Abby. "But I can't make her go." He smiled and started making for the channel as Abby bunched up a fist and slugged Laura solidly between her eyes. Laura's knees buckled as Lee snatched her before she fell.

"What do you think?" Abby grinned. "I haven't hit anything that hard since me and Wade went cow-tipping sophomore year!"

Lee and Sickli exchanged grins. "That'll work!"

The foursome ran for the barge, Lee leading with a semi-conscious Laura flopping over his back. The half-naked Cody trailed, stopping to pick up a sweater and a pair of galoshes. They reached the top of the dropoff as searchlights scrolled the harbor sky. To their front, pillars of rocket plumes paraded overhead as mortars sent more flares and shells their way.

Lee watched the barge pull away and raced down the slope after it. "Hold on! Hold on! Just a few more," he hollered. He passed Laura to her son and waded into the channel with Abby hiked over his head.

"There's no room!" squalled one of the escapees. "We're full up!"

Lee reached up and, grabbing the man by the collar, flipping him into the drink. The horrified prisoners gawked down at the menacing soldier then took the pregnant mother and set her down beside them.

Beating blades sounded from the north as the prisoners were hit with a searchlight. Someone cried out, "A rescue chopper. It's coming to save us!" The boat people waved wildly as the French gunship sent five-inch Zuni rockets sizzling over their heads that exploded in giant geysers behind them. Muzzle flashes followed as a line of bullets erupted in the water and started walking toward the beach. The mob screamed as Lee ran for Cody and Laura. He landed on them in a thud as the slugs cut across the sand.

The Gazelle flew over the shore and disappeared behind the island as Cody felt for his ribs. "Mom, you all right?"

"You're bleeding," said Laura, still dizzy. "What happened?"

"I'm not bleeding. It's him." Cody rolled Lee over carefully as a team of commandos came running down from the bluff. Doc Anderson arrived first. He checked Lee's pupils and hammered on his chest while Laura sat in silence, blinking uncomprehendingly.

The medic ran lines and administered injections as rest of the Stingrays tried in vain to seal the holes in his side. Anderson checked Lee's pupils one last time, then closed his eyes.

Laura looked at the man's sleeping face for a long time and felt a crushing grief. This man was dead and he wasn't coming back. He died not for his family, not for his men, his country or for his desire to kill the enemy. He had voluntarily laid down his life—no, *sprinted* to lay down his life—so death would not touch her nor her son. Laura's mouth crumpled and as she put a cold finger to his lips.

"Why did he saved me?" Laura asked. "Why? I'm the last person that deserves saving."

Anderson put away his gear while showing Laura his back. "Lady, he didn't save you because of who *you* are. He did it because of who *he* is."

"Cody. Laura. Come on. Hurry!" It was Abby, calling out to them from the drifting barge.

"Mom, let's go."

Cody led his mom to the raft just as the Gazelle popped out from behind the trees for a second pass. Atop the hotel, Hawkeye Caban was waiting. He picked up the gunship as it flew into the open and swept his sniper scope just ahead of the cockpit. As the pilot's heads lined up, one beside the other, Caban squeezed off a round, killing them both instantly with the same bullet. The helicopter rolled inverted and crashed, setting fire to the bay's ever-present slick. From the safety of her barge, Laura watched through the flames as the Stingrays covered the body of their fallen leader with her red wool Santa coat.

CHAPTER 36
DESCENT

Laval sat in the corner pouring over the SITREPs: pipelines cut in Clearbrook, a man captured in a giant bat-suit in Black Duck, software glitches with RAPSODIE in Bemidji. Yes, indeed, the Freemartins were having themselves a busy night. He had to admit, they had the TOC humming.

"What's that?" asked General Schueller, stubbing his Gauloises into a heaping ashtray. "Put it on the touch-table." The signalman pounded his keys as the radar display flickered to life in front of them.

"This is what RAPSODIE showed in the Canadian sector about a half-hour ago."

"So."

The tech turned on the animation. "These are the radar returns just before it went off-line." The staff watched as a gaggle of eastbound green dots made a ninety-degree turn and started coming south for the U.S.

"Geese," dismissed General Papon, the FUN air commander.

"*Really*. In September, Maxime?"

"I've seen it all the time. Tight cluster, rapid course reversals. These returns are too small to be aircraft."

"And they turn in such a perfectly square angle?"

A radioman interrupted their conversation. "General Schueller, it is the Germans. They have broken our southern demarcation line at Worthington. Their Leopards are engaging our reserves. What are your instructions?"

Schueller coughed up his coffee. "The nerve." He looked to Laval. "Where is he?"

"Resist the Germans. Those are General Faisson's orders," the lieutenant bade, not answering.

"In direct violation of the Secretary-General's orders? Fine!" Schueller tapped commands onto the table and called up a battle map of his Le Sueur formation. "Air Force, what can you give us?"

"I can give you shit," Papon declared. "Faisson has all our attack squadrons committed to the northern push."

"Then the Navy will support us. They are not yet committed."

A portly Admiral Darlan answered from across the room. "They are not committed because they are still half-way across Lake Superior, you fool."

Schueller took over the table, evaluating blue-force scenarios, threat assessments and sensor feeds. "I don't like the looks of this."

"Then turn south into Karlsruhe and counter-attack the cabbagehead," replied Laval. "See how *he* likes it."

"With what? Fondue forks? Our Leclercs are in the north with Faisson's super brigades."

"I don't care if you have spitballs, *Fight!*" hammered Laval.

"Who do you think you are, lieutenant? We take orders from the général, not his *bitch*." Papon threw an empty pizza box at the aide and pointed a pencil. "Now clean this place up before I stab this in your neck."

Laval grabbed a bag and began filling it with butts and cans and coffee cups. He whispered to his clerk. "Where is that whore, Douvet? Get her on the phone."

"That's who I am talking to now. *She* called me."

"Then tell her to get in here. She has five seconds!"

"She says she can't, sir. She wants to talk to you."

Laval snatched the phone. "Private, you are AWOL, do you know that?"

"Lieutenant, I am trapped. I am with somebody and he won't let me go."

"You little prostitute. I don't care if you're fucking Faisson himself. Put your legs together and get your ass down here. Now!"

"Then come down here and get me yourself because it is your general who is holding me captive!"

It took Laval five minutes to reach Tent City at the far end of the base. The conscripts lived here, testified to by the broken bottles and fluttering tent flies. Pulling into the laager, Laval's headlights caught a half-naked man stealing women's underwear from one of the clothes lines. "Hey! You there. Halt." The aide dove out of his vehicle and sped after the golem as he tucked the clothes under his arm and disappeared into a shelter. The lieutenant followed him to the private's quarters and knocked on the door.

"General, it's Phillipe. May I come in?"

Laval dove for the ground as a shotgun blast blew the door off its hinges and covered him with splinters. Inside, Faisson sat cross-legged on Douvet's bed, painting his toenails and listening to a strange high-pitched moaning on the stereo. "It's whale music, Phillipe. Do you like it? I'll 'tooth it to your mobe."

Incense permeated the space and votive candles flickered all about. Behind a footlocker, Private Douvet, dressed only in panties and a bra, cowered in the corner. When Laval appeared, she grabbed her clothes and bolted for the door. "Freak!" she yelled at Faisson as the general lunged for her pantyhose. She wrestling him for them for a second before giving up and leaving without them. "Lesbian!" he shouted after her.

Laval stared at his commander, the tousled hair, the kabuki eyes, the Robinson Crusoe stubble. All about him, pictures of Margeaux and Gizzelle littered the bed. "Sir, you're needed. There's been explosions in the camp."

"Phillipe, this is my wife. Would you like to see her nude?"

"Karlsruhe's tanks are in Worthington. He's trying to take command by force."

"I'll 'tooth it to you. She is really quite beautiful."

"And the Canadians are invading."

Faisson pulled up a foot and blew across his toes to dry them. "They have no troops. It is Zzgn. He is trying to sabotage the push."

"I think it may be the SF," offered Laval.

Faisson stopped his blowing. "Impossible."

CHAPTER 37
OPERATION
DOWNPOUR

Fresh troops and equipment continued to flow north to fortify Faisson's super brigades, against Zzgn's orders. Task Force 70, Task Force 82 and Task Force 92 were two days from achieving operational readiness. Armor-heavy and commanded by his best officers, they were poised to go forehead-to-forehead with ADAK's massed buildup in North Dakota.

The redeployment left the de Lacs and Le Sueur commanders with virtually nothing; twenty thousand infantry and eighty tanks were all they had between them. These generals regarded Faisson's ploy as a desperate way to save face after being stripped of command. But they would follow their leader no matter the consequences; if not for desire to be a part of history if he succeeded, then to spit in the eye of the Germans in the event they failed.

Division General Marcel de Brinon, commander of Formation du Nord, was put in charge of the Task Forces. He had taken over the town of Grygla in northwestern Minnesota just hours before and had erected his battle center on the high school baseball field. Hiking his large pants over his large belly, he dumped cold coffee on home plate and gloated. What better way to start a day than desecrate an American hallmark as revered as a baseball field?

The battle had been going well. M1 Abrahms and M2 Bradleys still lie burning in the streets from the previous day's battle. Fifteen miles ahead, however, the Sovereigns were digging in. He had sent up a Sperwer unmanned vehicle to circle the battlefield. It was promptly shot down but not before his intelligence officers got a peek into the enemy's rear; half their tracked vehicles were on fire and a massive reinforcement was underway.

Faisson had been right. This was to be the place for the American's last stand. De Brinon smiled. This will be a good week. Even with ADAK's massed armor, he knew he outnumbered his foe seven-to-one. What he didn't know was Winnipeg had fallen three hours before and he would be out-flanked in another three.

The Canadians for a Free Republic swept out of their homes in the early morning hours while Winnipeg still slept, capturing the police stations and setting up roadblocks. They cut the city's fiber backbone—the pipeline carrying all of Manitoba's phone, data, TV and digital radio communications—triggering a news blackout. A handful of freepers attacked the TransPower electric grid at three strategic soft spots—a spindly 500-kilovolt transmission tower near Vasar, a diesel fuel tank at the Silkirk backup plant and a DC bus bar at the Dorsey Converter Station. The six-thousand-mile network toppled as, one-by-one, the utility's hydroelectric plants flipped off-line to protect themselves from the province's heavy night-time air-conditioning load. When the last generator went dead, Saskatchewan and Ontario opened their ties and the middle fifth of Canada was plunged into darkness.

It took hours for word of the coup to reach the government in Ottawa. The first signal to leave the besieged city was a cryptic message received in Morse Code by ten-year-old Charlie Elwick. He and his buddies had picked it up on to their shortwave radio during an overnight sleepover in his treehouse. He woke his parents and gave them this odd passage:

> EXPLOSIONS IN WINNIPEG.
> TANKS AT TIM HORTONS.

Lynn Patterson's aerial circus was already filling the skies of lower Manitoba by the time the government had been alerted. His strike package of bombers, cargo planes and fighters crossed the border at Walhalla and wheeled overhead Canada's slumbering frontier before

Operation Downpour

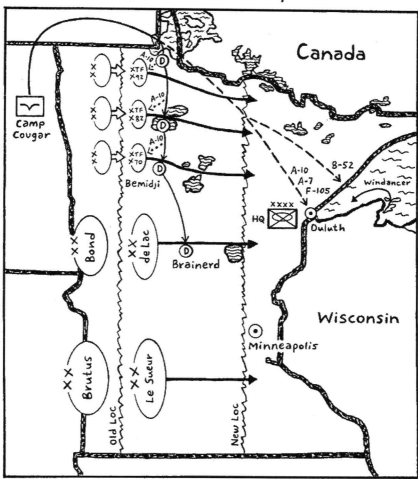

⇨ Main Armor Attack
⋯▷ Supporting Attack
Ⓓ Drop Zone
→ 'Drop and Shock' Strike Package
(C-130, OV-10, B-52)

→ Avenue of Retreat
∿ Line-of-Contact
⇢ Operation Testify

entering FUN airspace at the Northwest Angle, Minnesota's 'chimney stack.' From there, the Sovereign Air Arm poured out of Lake of the Woods like a cloudburst to deliver a brigades-worth of Drop and Shock troops into Faisson's unsuspecting rear.

A detachment of SGArm engineers landed at the grass strip outside of Angle Township and erected Forward Arming and Refueling Point Exxon in just under an hour. The depot provided bombs, bullets and go-juice for the Apaches and A-10s harassing the French from the rear while the main ADAK armored force charged them from the front.

The pilots of 00BOMB spearheaded Operation Downpour. The squadron, composed of B-52 BUFs and RB-66s, were flying their first mission since the Vietnam War. Sixty-five year old Lieutenant Colonel Robert 'Stumpy' Hymel led the mission and had nicknamed his unit the 'Bald Eagles' in respect for his crew's long years. Their mission: take out the FUN's highly maneuverable Rafale fighter jets while they were still on the ground, napping.

The bombers came in low with bunker-buster bombs and cut the runways first at Baudette, then Bemidji. The mission went perfectly during the first strike but at the second, one BUF and three RBs took SAM hits. Too low to bail out, the aircraft crashed into Bear Swamp Christmas Tree Farm with the loss of all hands. A-7 Corsairs from the Sioux Falls Lobos retaliated by setting the Roland missile batteries afire with cluster bombs while F-106 Delta Dart and F-101 Voodoo escorts bounced the French pilots as they tried taking off.

Brainerd's Escadron de Chasse 01 was the last Rafale fighter base to be targeted. Sliders from 122PARA 'Rotting Vultures' arrived first. The unit was unique in that it was made up entirely of combat-amputees. Only the smallest and most experienced were selected for the mission. They flew new Leper Colony-improved wingsuits that were warmer, instrumented and flew twice as far. When combined with the special shock-absorbing titanium prosthetics Aboud had designed for their stumps, the Rotting Vultures became the first jumpers ever to be able to land without parachutes.

After their release over the skies of Breckenridge, Minnesota, the paras sailed undetected through one hundred miles of troposphere to their target in the lake-resort town of Brainerd. Alpha Squad sent out two teams to take out the AAA crews while Baker Squad assassinated the pilots in their bunks with blastblades. Still, news of the attack got out when a dying pilot cellphoned the alert-birds to take off before the Vultures could neutralize them. The two Rafales intercepted Hymel's formation south of Leach Lake and loosed a flurry of Mica air-air missiles at them. The -106s and -101s engaged and in the ensuing furball, one lone B-52 emerged. The bomber expended its ordinance across the flightline as fragged, sending perfectly shaped black orange fireballs blossoming into the dawn. The Stratofortress lurched into a bank and headed for homeplate, the only BUF to return and it wasn't Hymel's.

When the bombers were finished, they had cleared an alley straight down the middle of Minnesota. The lane connected four bodies of water along its axis: Lake of the Woods, Red, Bemidji and Gull Lakes. Aboud's complexity scientists calculated the French lines of retreat and identified these waterways as being the best locations to set up choke points. These became the dropzones where Woody would unload his new amphibious forces.

OV-10s carried the skimmers; two infantrymen and four Predator anti-tank missiles each, riding herd on a militarized open-water snowmobile. Each water-mobile team could take out four APCs and forty enemy soldiers on their own. At 75 miles per hour, the propeller-driven Broncos swooped down to the wave-tops. When they had dropped their teams onto the lakes, the pilots zoomed back overhead, securing the dropzones with their rockets before returning to the FARP to reload and refuel.

C-130 cargo planes lumbered in next. The aircraft came in low to avoid radar and deposited paratroopers and combat ATVs on the surrounding shores and lowlands using dangerous low-altitude low-opening drops. LALO drops gave the soldiers only one swing under the canopy before they hit the ground. When they had landed, the paras formed up their vehicles and missiles into four-man Dragoon teams and scampered across the swamps for cover.

In all, sixty-five hundred high-mobility amphibious anti-armor troops lay in wait for their prey in the marshes and flowages of central Minnesota. Drop and Shock was in place.

Not all drops were pretty and not all the paratroopers were seen as liberators. At the Red Lake drop, eight men from 1002INF 'Rusty

Needles' landed in the barbed-wire fencing of seventy-year-old David Fanning. Fanning was a white technical, the town's warlord. He and others like him throughout the country were borderline-felons who used the UN's advances to terrorize their enemies and enrich their bank accounts. Seeing the Sovereigns return after enjoying a year of unrestrained violence and intimidation meant his neighbors would be back; the ones from whom he had taken land and herds and homesteads. Shit, they would probably hang him. Fanning and his sons hopped in their '74 Datsun pickup, drove up to the foundering soldiers, manned their bed-mounted .50-caliber and, in what would later become known as the Woodrow Slaughter, murdered them in cold blood. Fanning and his sons would hang a week later.

Reports of the attacks were sketchy. De Brinon read them as they came into his BC; skirmishes with a supply convoy in Shotley, snipers harassing his patrols in Wilton, a blackout in Canada. As his techs finished tapping into the high school's T1 line and were booting the servers, his aide rushed in with a TV. "It's a newsfeed from the CNNUN station in Brainerd." He clicked the remote as scenes from a school bus accident appeared.

"Officer, can you tell our viewers at home why the bus driver drove off the road like this?" asked a comb-over blonde as she stuck a mike in the face of a TSA trooper.

"From as near as I can tell, he was forced off the road when a huge plane with large wings flew over. He said the aircraft was so low it almost hit him."

The camera panned around the accident site, revealing skidmarks, broken glass and an overturned school bus. Just then, a new convoy of planes flew by low overhead, disgorging paratroopers and equipment along a lake that looked to be less than a mile away.

"What's this?" asked de Brinon.

"I don't know," said the clerk. "The media has been playing this feed for the last half-hour."

"And I have to hear about it on TV?"

The reporter kept talking as her crew packed up their news van and raced for the dropzone. When the vehicle arrived, hundreds of Sovereign soldiers were assembling their packs and securing their perimeters. The cameraman bolted for one of the squads as the GIs leveled their rifles. The high-heeled reporter pushed him forward. "Get your ass in gear, Frank. This is going out global." The infantrymen started their ATV and began backing away.

"Excuse me, who is in charge here?" asked the reporterette, trotting after them. "Can you tell me what unit you're from and what you hope this mission will accomplish?"

Before the woman could ask the men if they were fearful of their personal safety, the team opened fire, putting a neatly-grouped triple-tap through her sternum and a double-tap into her in the forehead. After he was sure everything was on tape, the cameraman ran but not before he took a round to his cerebellum. The camera continued transmitting from the dirt as a half-dozen HE grenades ripped through the van and tore it off its chassis.

De Brinon broke out into roaring laughter, spitting his croissant across the room. "Well done! Oh, how I've wanted to do that!" In the distance, a faint earthy burp echoed from the east. De Brinon stood. "QUIET!"

"What is it, sir?"

De Brinon slapped the aide for his stupidity and walked out onto the baseball field where he heard the belch again. A PVP from his reserve armor battalion veered into the lot, its driver hanging out the window. "A-10s! A-10s!"

De Brinon swore. He turned back to his command post and was almost inside when the trailer exploded before him like a small sun. The blastfront burned his clothes off him and sent him wheeling through the air and sliding into second base. He could smell his hair char. Through the blades of grass, the general made out the courier's jeep lying on its side in flames. Downtown, cannon fire boomed as disabled M1s came back to life after a nighttime of playing possum. Across the street, a resurrected Abrahms rocked as an HE round cracked into his compound, splintering another of his tracks. American tankers poured out of their hiding places inside to extinguish the small decoy fires they had started on their hulls the night before. As the men crawled back into their turret, the tank's main gun traversed de Brinon's way and depressed. DeBrinon blinked as the last soldier paused to wave before the general's long accomplished life turned to black.

CHAPTER 38
WINDANCER

Bruno Hochmuth shivered uncontrollably as he paced his makeshift headquarters. Why, of all places, did his XO have to choose the Thief River Falls Curling Club to set up their combat command center? Across the rink, one of the division radio nets popped and crackled. As he ran to answer it, he slipped, executing an ass-plant on his pack of Kools in the process. He swore as he clambered up. He had had enough of the rear and mustered his Bradley crew to take him on a tour of the battlefront.

Already five hours into the operation, Hochmuth was eager to see how his opponent was responding. He ordered his track down County Ditch Number Fiftyone and raced for the front. "There's that bath-skipping crouton," said the two-star. "De Brinon's Leclercs are taking up positions around Goodrich." He handed the goggles to his executive officer as mortar and artillery rained down on the barley fields around them.

"They're almost ready to come across," said the XO. "How long?"

"The A-10s just started their attack," replied the general. "I think the French will probably keep hitting us for another few hours before we see any effect."

"Then why are their turrets pointed backwards?"

Hochmuth took the binoculars again, putting on his glasses this time. "I don't fucking believe this," he said. "Charge."

"Charge?" asked the aide. "We're not ready to—"

"I said *charge*, dammit. Those garlic-shitters are retreating already!"

~~~~~~~~~~~~~~~~~~~~

"What are you doing?" cried Faisson, bursting into the TOC.

"We are withdrawing. What does it look like, you ass," ripped his generals. Smoke and chaos laid thick in the room, everyone doing five things while shouting commands to three others. No one was leading. He strode into the mayhem.

"No. Stop the withdrawal. Launch the push."

"Commander Faisson, we have twenty-five thousand SF guerrillas in our rear conducting raids and cutting our supply lines."

"Two division's worth? Ridiculous. Where would they get them? Stem cells?"

"Are you saying our sensors are lying?" challenged Julian Henriot, the French intel general.

"I'm saying your sensors are easily confused. If we had four different units overcount the same enemy platoon, we'd soon have a battalion."

Schueller called from across the room to one of the IT technicians. "What is going on at Red Lake? Has our artillery cleared the bridge yet?"

"Not yet, sir. Our artillery does not appear to be having any effect. Our detectors have reported zero hits while our side is taking heavy losses."

Faisson leaned in. "And what of the Germans? Is our marksmanship as sad in the south?"

"Eighty-five percent artillery effectiveness in Le Sueur, sir."

"Impossible. How can our batteries have such wild differences in results?" asked Henriot.

"We have a spy," replied Faisson.

Schueller looked around the room. "A spy? Where?"

"Not here. In the system," said the five-star. "Stop the bombardment."

"How can we?" argued Schueller. "It is the only way we can clear a path back to our logistics base."

"We have a virus in our battle management system," Faisson announced. "It has corrupted the ballistics modules. We are shelling ourselves! Halt all barrages until our batteries can switch to manual targeting." Faisson jabbed a finger at a Harry Potter network tech. "You. Drop everything and start intrusion countermeasures. Sniff this thing out and find its source."

The tech looked to Schueller for approval before proceeding. Schueller nodded.

"What's going on here?" Faisson asked his army general. "Are you forming a coup against me?"

"General Faisson, I am sorry to inform you that you have no real function in our operations any more." Schueller straightened to his full six-foot-five. "It is best you leave."

"You will address me as maréchal or I will bust you to corporel!"

The clamor in the TOC deadened.

"You are not a field marshal, Sean. You never will be. You have brought shame to France and most probably you have lost us the war."

The indictment kicked Faisson like a boot in his stomach as the words woofed in his brain in Sensoround. He felt old and struggled to regain control over his officers. "Do not retreat, men," he commanded, walking to the front of the command center. "The Sovereigns have a small force. Get your status reports over the radio instead of using datalinks. Talk to the men at the front. Talk to de Brinon."

"De Brinon is dead. His HQ was wiped out over an hour ago."

Faisson bit his lip.

"Sean, please," Air General Papon said, trying to usher the commander to the back of the room.

Faisson pulled out his pistol. "This is mutiny!" He held the gun to Papon's temple. "I am Maréchal Faisson, General of the Army! Governor of Terre du Lacs!"

"It is not a mutiny," replied Schueller, coming forward and pushing the gun away. "It is orders. Zzgn has put me in charge. UNIFUS is here to take you into custody." Schueller tilted his head to the door where an out-of-place StanEval agent stood guard in black coat-and-tie.

"I've found the bot!" cried the tech. All ears steered to his station. "It's coming from a sideweb. A new one."

Schueller hunched over the boy. "Send the signature to NSA. Maybe they can help."

"I have. The bot is in the GPS registry," he said to himself. "Standby

". . . I've almost got it." He pounded on his keys like Chopin then swore as the servers crashed and the room went black. "It pulled out! I had the file quarantined, then it was gone!"

Schueller tried calling up the touch table. "Where is the terrain overlay? I *need* that terrain overlay!"

"Where is my moving target indicator?" added Papon. "I can't prioritize my fighters if I can't sort targets."

Activity in the TOC ground to a halt. Henri Schueller held up his hands. "Everyone, until the servers come back up we are going to have to use maps and markers. Just like the old days." He pointed to a female non-com. "Sergent, where are they?"

"Sir?" she asked.

"The maps. Where are the maps?"

"We don't have maps anymore. We haven't carried them for five years. The BMS made them obsolete."

"Who told you to get rid of our—" Schueller's hands tightened into fists. *Faisson*. He was going to knock him straight through the wall. He turned to grab his has-been prince but the general had vanished. In the rear of the conference room, a glass window shattered onto the pavement below, Faisson going with it.

~ ~ ~ ~ ~ ~ ~ ~ ~ ~ ~ ~ ~ ~ ~ ~ ~ ~ ~

For the forth time since sunrise, Aboud came to the boat rail and urched into the lake. His stomach coiled then wretched, as if ridding itself of a yellow parasitic alien.

"I couldn't see any breakfast that time," said Nick Nedeau, Windancer's captain. "You must be feeling better."

"That is not a true statement." Aboud scrubbed at his mouth with a filthy sleeve. Ahead, a pack of thirty colorful racing yachts tacked their way out of Apostle Islands Sound and heeled southwest for Duluth. "Why are we last? Don't we need those other boats for cover?"

Nedeau spun his wheel to port and yelled for a brawny Stingray to haul on a halyard. "I'm doing my best here considering you replaced my crew with landlubbers and overloaded my hold with twenty thousand pounds of computer equipment."

The seventy-foot Santa Cruz racing yacht had won many regattas in its forty years on the Great Lakes. But it was the boat's size Tanner valued more than its speed, for it was the only vessel on the lake able to hold all the computer and radio equipment he needed to run Vger Control. Racks of servers filled the galley below him while routers and transceivers occupied the staterooms and head forward. Graphics processors lined the hull as projection screens hung on the bulkhead. Windancer was normally a sailor's dream but today, it was a rolling, yawing hacker's heaven.

Aboud staggered forward. He had positioned his WiFi antennas along the foredeck and shrouded them with canvas so they wouldn't arouse suspicion. He checked their connections as a cold spritz from the bow sprayed his face, refreshing him. When he returned back to the pilot house, he plopped down at his console with a thud. "Ready to join the living, Leper?" came a voice from blacked-out salon down below.

"Yes, let's bake and shake."

Tanner's cyber-squad consisted of fifteen teens and twenty-somethings he had recruited from the top three professional gaming teams in the world: Team NiP from Sweden, 3D from Willowcreek Baptist Church in Chicago and Boy Scout Troop 40 from Grafton, Wisconsin. These kids knew Aboud. He had been beating them at Ghost Recon, Halo 5 and Counter-StrikeUN for years. When Aboud had first solicited their help, they hesitated to sign on. When he told them danger was involved and smoking encouraged, they were in.

The gamers didn't know much about spybots or wireless bridges or the seven TCPIP protocol layers; Aboud would handle the techie side. What the scientist needed was their quickness and agility and proven adaptability under fire. That was why he had created the matrixed game-world they were now playing in. It was the one environment they excelled like no others in the world.

"I'm getting pinged!" cried ins, in charge of fire-control.

"Where?"

"The main fire control server at the TOC. Those snail-snorters must've finally figured out they were shelling their own guys."

"Can you back out?" asked Aboud.

"Nope, some geek is shutting down all the ports."

Aboud orchestrated the operation from a tactile desktop he had assembled from his perch in the pilothouse. To keep up with the machine-gun tempo of the gamer's missions, a keyboard and mouse would not be enough. Tanner needed all his senses, most of all, his sense of touch.

The desktop he sat at contained a number of specially designed haptic devices that converted motion and position into computer inputs. The objects resembled the size and function of common articles of office productivity: a pencil, highlighter, appointment book, Post-It Notes, a family album. But when Tanner donned his computer graphics visor, the objects disappeared and became computer-generated 3-D symbols representing the files and programs and images in his computer.

Multi-colored sticky pads lay in a neat pile on the far corner of the desk. Tanner hefted it and as he picked his way through the pads one-by-one, a sheaf of open applications flashed by his CGI visor. He plucked the pink pad, his fire control program, and thumbed through the pages as lines of computer code and subroutines flicked by his eyes in rapid succession. When he found the page representing his trojan module, he tapped the pad with his finger to maximize the program in his glasses. Scrolling down with his pen, Aboud highlighted a snippet of self-destruct code, tore off the page and stuck it to moto's inbox.

Moto was the team's transporter. He took Aboud's vgers and delivered them to the other players by sneaking through the paths and alleyways of the enemy's netcentric battle systems. Moto took the mines from Aboud and, with his game controller, hunted and pecked his way through the enemy frontier as dark nameless figures shot at him from the hills.

Tanner followed the Baptist's progress on the bulkhead monitors below, as a server farm appeared on the horizon. He watched as moto entered the installation and followed a lighted path to a GPS antenna array. Isn waited inside and placed the mines alongside some satellite dishes before hopping into moto's virtual HMMWV.

"Don't blow the shack yet," hollered Aboud. "If we do, we can't use it again. Wait until you are sure the daemons have found you first."

Isn took his finger off the detonator and went back inside where he continued to feed skewed artillery coordinates to the French batteries. He didn't have long to wait as black Gazelles swooped in and soldiers rappelled down to surround the shack. Aboud waited until they were at the door. "OK, do it."

Isn leaped out the back of the shack and set off the charges, darkening the facility and with it, the entire compound.

"I've got a mover!" announced fourteen-year-old dsn, a Life Scout from Troop 40 and the team's tracker. Dsn monitored the in-road detector coils embedded in the streets and intersections around Duluth. A telltale spike in a magnetic sensor at Pétain Airbase aroused his curiosity. "It just left the TOC and is heading north."

Aboud picked up a nurf cube from his desktop. He tapped it on dsn's portrait then inspected the coil's magnetic signature from all sides as he twirled the shape. "That is a big waveform. Lots of hashing on the trace. Probably radios."

"It's gotta be leadership!" said dsn. "One of the general's armored Sherpas. Let's give it to Blackwater. They're in place in the north treeline."

"Blackwater's too expensive," said Archie, dsn's scoutmaster. "They're charging one million sovros a kill. Woody said to use them on HVAs only."

Tanner fanned through his pads until he found a vehicle manufacturer's database and the tranche's Motor Vehicle Registration list. He tapped them with his cube and kept stabbing the foam block with his pencil until he connected the two sides containing his cross-references.

With the pencil now intersecting the databases, he stirred the stick, sending hundreds of makes and models streaking across his visor with each twist. When he found a match between the magnetic profile and the vehicle's VIN number, he stabbed the cube through another side and twirled it to find the owner. "Where is he now?"

Having already tagged the waveform, dsn watched as it drove over another coil three traffic lights away. "He's going east now. He just past Bradley and Lincoln."

"I've got him," said fOrest, in charge of infrastructure controls. "There's a railroad crossing up ahead. I can lower the gate and fix him there."

"Good," replied Aboud. He tapped moto with the cube. "Take this to the Blackwater mortar team. The vehicle belongs to General Faisson. He's HVA."

~ ~

Laval kept checking his mirror for the StanEval agent as he waited for the crossing gates to lift. "They drive blue H3s. Do you see him yet?" asked Faisson, hunched down in the foot well.

"No," replied his lieutenant.

Traffic was stalled twenty-cars deep. They were all waiting for a train that had yet to appear. Faisson began massaging out a leg cramp when he recognized a distant *thup*! from the treeline to the north.

The men looked at each other. "Mortar!" Up above, the shell streaked across the sky and hit a Cooper Electric Mini a half-block behind them. Bystanders left their cars to watch the hybrid burn as another round rocketed to their front and hit a Renault six cars ahead. "They're bracketing us!" Faisson yelled. "*Go! Go! Go!*"

Laval punched the gas and pulled out of line. He smashed through the crossing gates as the car eagerly filling their vacant space was promptly hit and flattened like roadkill. "They know where I am. *How do they know where I am?*"

"StanEval?" asked Laval.

Faisson stuck his head out his window, searching for a drone as a four-ship of supersonic F-105s streaked down Pétain's runway on a bombing pass. "No, it's the Sovereigns. The base is under attack!"

The morning sky lit up with AAA fire as Laval fishtailed to a stop at the next intersection. Out on the flightline, dozens of cigar-looking canisters burst on the ground, shrouding the ramp in black gas. "They're gassing the base!" He looked over to his general but Faisson had already leaped out the door. A shell whistled overhead as the top of his jeep caved in on him. The incendiary splattered the vehicle's insides with spall and sent burning waves of diesel and rubber washing over the lieutenant.

From the safety of his ditch, Faisson raised his head in time to see his aide, black and mummy-like, fumbling in the flames to unlatch his seatbelt. Down the road, a blue H3 approached, sirens screaming. It stopped at each burning hulk to check the remains. Faisson crawled out of the dip and rolled down a hill onto the recreation fields paralleling the ramp. There, thousands of refugees, recaptured after the overnight escape, were being marched back to the barracks. He gave a quick check over his shoulder and ran to join their ranks.

Faisson ducked and weaved through the prisoners trying to stay hidden when his phone rang. It was Laval's number. He answered it. "Phillipe? Is that you? Are you still alive?"

"Not so much," a crackly, distorted voice answered.

Puzzled, Faisson whipped his head around, searching for Laval. He found the agent instead, watching from the embankment above, smiling and waving and holding up his lieutenant's charred, melted Blackberry.

CHAPTER 39
MARCH OF THE
WHITE FLAGS

"Just how stupid is this?" Ahrmenta wondered as she twisted the kinks from her neck. Outside, pedestrians and shoppers gawked as her parade of NSA vehicles cruised through the busy downtown. "Hello, people! Do not be afraid! These big black armored Suburbans are not government vehicles. Please turn around and go about your business." She shook her head and returned her attention to her sniffer. "Jeesh!"

"Where to now, Doctor Brown?" the driver asked over his shoulder.

Brown was in Duluth to find the source of a new wireless sideweb that had just started broadcasting. "I don't know. This whole place is hot. I can't find a point-source."

"Maybe it's not a single node. Maybe the signal's distributed."

"The signals we are picking up are low-power burst-mode," explained the Indian. "The antennas needed for that are big and expensive. We'd see them on the rooftops."

"Not if they're directional," replied her driver.

"Hey, beef-brain. Thanks for the insight, but you asked me to run the op so let me run the op, huh?"

The agent did as he was told and turned the caravan west.

"Whoa!" said the doctor, watching her readouts. "Where were we just pointed?"

"Skyline Drive. Why?"

"I'm picking up spikes. How high is it up there?"

"About fourteen hundred feet."

"That would mean it could broadcast almost forty miles. Maybe higher with a mast."

"I thought our hackers were in the city?"

"Maybe I was wrong," answered Ahrmenta. She tuned her antenna to the hillside and marked one of the spikes. She gave the GPS coordinates to the agent who turned onto the interstate and sped for the bluffs.

The convoy accelerated up the drive and into Swan Lake Terraces with lights flashing and sirens singing. Brown got out first and waited for her agents to secure the neighborhood before inspecting the split-level's insides.

"Not your typical Freemartin stronghold," she said, rummaging through piles of Papa Johns boxes and XBox controllers.

"Sometimes it's just a bunch of slackers looking for a little excitement," replied the driver, tearing up walls looking for weapons. There were none. There was also no sign of the occupants save for the wide-open sliding-glass door in the back. A voice called for Brown from an upstairs bedroom where an agent led her to a homebrew computer. A jury-rigged can of Gourmet Tiger Prawn and Garlic Pringles sat in a nearby window, hooked to the network port.

"What's this?" her chauffeur asked, trying to make sense of the screws and electrodes and bits of PVC pipe hot-glued to its surface.

"A shotgun yagi antenna," she said, looking down the inside.

"In a potato chip can?"

"Yeah, pretty slick, huh? The aluminized interior serves as the collector. Probably can push forty to fifty miles. Sixty in overcast."

"Why use a Pringles can?"

"Because all the parts necessary to build the grown-up version of this array are on the restricted control list. Our little slackers would've been arrested before they left the Radio Shack."

"There's got to be dozens of these around, A. Can't we just generate a pulse and fry 'em all?"

"They're directional and pointed out to the lake" she said, taking in the gray blue expanse of Lake Superior. "Somewhere out there is our point source, a pirate ship, tapping into our backbone. He's using these jury-rigged antennas to hook in so we're going to have to find each one."

"You keep saying *he*."

"So."

"Couldn't it be a woman?"

"Yes, I suppose so."

"But you're hoping it isn't."

Ahrmenta shook off her reveries and turned her attention to the man. "What are you driving at, agent?"

"Nothing." The driver wiped the can with his finger, licked it, then shivered. "I just hope the next place we stop, the guy has a little better taste."

~ ~ ~ ~ ~ ~ ~ ~ ~ ~ ~ ~ ~ ~ ~ ~ ~ ~ ~

Windancer passed Bark Point, just forty miles north of the Twin Ports. Aboud and Team Vger had been in the pit for ten hours and had yet to see the sun. None of them thought they'd be out in time to see it set.

"Don't hide your countenance from me, Oh, Lord," prayed Willowcreek's pastor of Videogame Ministries. He wore baggy pants, spiked-highlighting and had a thick black mono-brow. His name was Cary Templeton, but his creds called him Method. His team ran the network but were having a hard time keeping a line open to Duluth. The born-again found a backup link across the lake at Split Rock. He hooked in, beat his chest and pointed to the sky. "Thank you, Jesus!"

"That pipe is not going to be big enough," said Aboud. "We need to get Duluth back on line. Do we need to boost our signal?"

"No, it's the land links themselves," replied Method. "We're losing them one-by-one."

"Bird's up!" yelled Tentpole, in charge of webcams. The gamer had just hacked into a French drone circling over the Bemidji dropzone and was waiting for its orbit to stabilize. Aboud watched as its thermal imagers came on line and the drone began taking video of friendly ATV Dragoon positions. Tanner grabbed the files and dropped them on zet, who airbrushed in dozens of new Photoshop tanks. Aboud gave the doctored images to moto who drove them to HeatoN who served them up to the horrified French intelligence officers of Task Force 82.

"Disappointed!"

Moto was stuck. The video files were too heavy and made him too slow. As he tried to cross the frontier with the last load, the trees and sky became scratchy and warped before his monitor went totally black.

"You're blocking the road, moto! Back up," said cArn.

"This is my crossing!" moto yelled. "Use your own."

"I've got the radio vger. You've gotta let me through."

Aboud called out to his network team. "Rambo?"

"Signal's good here!"

"ShauGuar? Any reroute?"

"Yes, but my options are dwindling fast."

"Volcano?" Volcano was zoning; sweating into his controller and hammering mercilessly on its buttons. "Volcano?"

"It's NSA. They've found us. They're swarming all around me. I'm getting inbound packets on almost every port. Can I get some help here?"

Aboud sent f0rest and walle to help defend the handful of ports they still had open while the rest of the team unloaded moto and moved him aside.

"Praise the Lord!" whooped Method.

"Not so fast, Jesus Freak. I'm still here," cried cArn. "The crossing closed again."

"Signal's gone!" bellowed Rambo as the screens went dark.

"Our side or theirs?" asked Aboud.

"I don't know. It just blanked out."

Rambo got up to reset his hardware as a huge gray obelisk passed over Windancer, eclipsing the sun and sending a ten-foot wave crashing over her bow. Men and equipment crashed to the floor as Aboud cursed and fumbled in the dark. When the boat righted, Tanner and his team crawled out to the deck and found themselves in the middle of La Royale, the French National Fleet.

~~~~~~~~~~~~~~~~~~~

Spider pulled Snoopy up a few feet to miss Knife Island, hugging the shore as tight as he dare on his approach to Duluth. He put back down and flew among the wave-tops for a few minutes more before the harbor basin came into sight. He struck for the heart of the tranche, laying low and almost touching the green lake bluffs with his wingtip. Passing over Shoremans Stadium, the local semipro team was still practicing, despite its cratered field. Trent rocked his wings for them as they waved. "Watch this, guys," he said as he stroked his after-burners and pointed his nose to the sun.

On the airbase, everyone turned to watch as Trent launched out of the trees like an ICBM. Spider could see the airmen below freaking out as he floated over the runways. *God, I love flying upside-down*, he thought.

He hung in the sky like a giant clay pigeon as the base's four AAA batteries took the bait. The turrets followed Spider and put him in their crosshairs as Beak came in from behind and blew one of them away. Spouts of flame and black smoke poured from the crippled vehicle as tracers from the other guns followed them north. Hoop and Shank unmasked from the south firing on the two western batteries in tandem. Their rounds touched off magazine fires inside and sent sparks out their hatches like roman candles. The lone remaining artillerymen started their engine and headed for the woods where they remained cowering until it was night.

With the air defenses silenced, Spider cleared in the Hercs. The C-130s lumbered in from the harbor and dropped three sticks of Nazi paratroopers along the far side of the field. The 3rd Kompanie, Fallschirmjäger Pionier Batallion 1 hailed from Iowa. They were professional WWII war re-enactors and had volunteered their services to the Sovereigns for their psyop effect. As they drifted down in brown shirts and Waffen SS helmets, the impact they had on the French was visceral and immediate. Other than on celluloid, twenty-first century Europeans had never seen Storm Troopers before, let alone Storm Troopers shooting real Mausers and throwing live stick grenades. As waves of the paratroopers stormed the runway in their Zundapp motorcycles and machine-gun sidecars, the defender's will evaporated. A few ran, some hesitated and ran, most just hesitated and surrendered.

The FUN guards dropped their weapons and fled as the camp prisoners broke rank and joined the fighting. Faisson lost himself in the confusion and sprinted for his alert hanger. As a squad of Fallschirmjägers made an assault on the control tower, the general hid under a fuel truck until he was sure they were gone.

"Komm heraus, Kröte." *Come out now, Frog*. Four massive arms reached underneath the truck, grabbed him by the collar and stood him up in the sun. For a second, Faisson didn't know if he was in America still or Hitler's Germany. These men were not actors to him. They were fit and solid and dour and evil. Their leather faces had scars and their tunics, dried blood. There was no smile to them. If these were not SS, then they were the grandsons of SS.

One of the men dusted off Faisson's stars then gave him a sharp rap in the chest. "Schauen Sie mal, hier ist ein echter General!" We've got ourselves a real general! The re-enactors laughed and mocked him as the StanEval agent rounded the truck and shot the two dead through the back of their helmets.

"Now give me *your* gun," the agent ordered, in a thick Ukrainian accent.

Faisson slumped and handed the man his FAMAS.

"And your little yo-yo."

The Frenchman retrieved his ballistrae and surrendered it, too. The agent smiled then jabbed him in the ribs with his SIG. "Time to pay the piper." Faisson didn't move. The black-suit jabbed him harder. "Come on, I say. Move, you unemployed boy-fucker!"

Over the agent's shoulder, an A-10 appeared, its nose twinkling and its shells impacting the flightline. The man dove for the truck while Faisson stood and glared, pieces of depleted uranium and concrete peppering him. This aircraft had a different look to it, a different sound, but when the jet roared by and dipped its wing, the nose was all too familiar. "*Trent.*"

Faisson looked all about him as his base lay in ruins; his headquarters, burning; his planes, crippled. Prisoners marched by again, only this time they were French.

The American had planned this all from the beginning; feeding him false information, planting Cody inside his inner circle, pimping Laura as a double-agent. He had even turned his Mother France against him and stole his seventh star. What sort of man would risk his own family, his own loved ones, for the selfish pleasure of humiliating others? "John Trent. You won may have won but you haven't paid." The general fixed on a plan and took a step toward the hanger.

"We're not through, Frenchman," said StanEval, drenched to the skin in diesel and standing in a pool of leaking fuel.

Faisson pulled out his cell. "You look wet. Let me dry you off."

"What are you doing?"

"I am calling my lieutenant."

"You mean that crispy mummy I left back there? The one I took the phone fro—"

"That's him!" Faisson hit redial as the agent gaped.

"Stop—*don't!*" said the agent, clawing through his pockets. Faisson hit SEND just as the agent found the phone. As the man wound up to throw it across the ramp, the ringtone started playing the opening bar of Toby Keith's *Red, White and Blue*. The melody never got to the second one as the call turned the phone into a match and StanEval into a torch.

CHAPTER 40
CONVOY

The events of the night had been a fog. A terror. Too many transfers. Too many shoves and herding. Too many fire attacks and rattling machine guns. Now Laura just sat, bleary-eyed, and watched in a passive, unmoving peace that made her wonder if her eyes were closed and she were still sleeping.

Everywhere around her, everywhere she looked—Freemartins, UNCONs, men from her camp—people were dying to keep others from dying. Their courage, bravery and audacity hung in the air like a virus infecting all who witnessed it. It was a strange urge. An urge to preserve. An urge that overwhelmed reason. A dying to save.

She remembered vague vignettes. The barges in the open channel being torn apart by the mortars. Scratching to swim back to the safety of Clough while others swam for the emplacement and charged it with nothing but their fists. She remembered her personnel carrier being rushed by refugees from other camps. How she hit and stomped at them while others gave up their places before running into the maelstrom to fetch more. She remembered the beach, where the big man had laid on her and lie there still.

It was daytime now, the breakout hours in the past. To frustrate pursuit, the escapees had dispersed. Some made for rendezvous points in the backcountry, probing for weak spots in the swamps and forests.

Others made a break for the open waters of Superior, fanning out in dinner cruisers and oil-rig pontoons called whale tugs.

Laura's group headed north to the Iron Range in hopes of meeting up with a Sovereign SAR squadron. They rode in boxy high-wheeled utility vehicles called Unimogs; all the rage with NFL football stars and millionaire hiphop artists. The Unis had been stolen off DaimlerChrysler lots throughout the summer and fitted with kevlar panels and modified with rail bogies. The Freemartins had hoped to use them during the breakout as high-speed trains to avoid the highways and a prying public. Two Harbors was the only big town on their route. If they didn't make it through the city while it was still dark, they would be sitting ducks.

Assembling the convoy had been chaotic and unorganized. Nobody wanted to be last so the convoy departed in clusters. The drivers, unschooled as train engineers, went too fast along the undulating Lake Superior shoreline and slid off the tracks often. Laura's carrier had slid off twice and had almost rolled, a few men being thrown out to their deaths on the lake rocks below.

By dawn, the drivers had gotten their rail legs. They formed into a single column for mutual support and rode through the villages with little trouble. As they marched their way up to the Mesabi Plateau, word of the escape finally preceded them. Now they faced fierce fighting at every crossing, usually French blue-helmets but sometimes technicals. Thankfully, technicals were unambitious and preferred shooting only when the convoy passed by their backyards.

When bullets hit their vehicle, everyone hugged the floor except Laura. A stranger to conflict, Laura now stuck her head out the back to be a witness to it. She gazed admiringly at the victories, plaintively at the losses but was always silently spellbound by the striving and the unwavering clash of wills.

As her rescue neared, she thought of John often. Would John be fighting like these men? Would he be brave and unwavering for others?

Laura didn't know. John had kept his military life to himself and his men. But in their twenty-five years together, John had always been unwavering with her. Neither had he ever caved to the boys or equivocated with others. Whether his acts were big or small, he always had a reason for doing what he did. He shared those reasons with her to show he wasn't arbitrary. So she knew why he thought he was right. This unchangeableness made him steely and unapologetic but also sure and faithful.

Why did I always contend with him? Because he was strong enough to make me submit. Why did I admire him? Because he never did.

Between firefights, Laura put Cody in her lap and stroked his hair. John had been right about him. She knew he needed confrontation, not pampering, but she could never make herself do it. She was missing something his father had. Something that made him cleave to character over compromise. Something that preferred right over conciliation. Was that the reason he hated being wrong? Was that why he condescended to those who didn't share his virtues? Was that why he never asked directions?

The convoy rounded a gentle bend where Laura could see the long line of the Unis. At a road crossing, two squads of Foreign Legionnaires had waited to spring a trap. When the last carrier rolled by, they advanced out of the treeline, attacking the stragglers with rifles and grenades. The truck exploded and came to a stop. As the soldiers approached the burning vehicle, a man jumped out of the flames with a weapon. He could have been a husband, a father or a single man. She didn't know. For a moment, he stood there, one man against twenty. Then, in a blur of action, he shouldered his rifle and a hail of gunfire cut him down.

On any other day, Laura would have called this man stupid since he died for nothing. But today, on this day of so much heroism and sacrifice, she saw the reason: righteousness. Righteousness of cause, of country, of beliefs. And who was more right, more convicted? The men with twenty rifles or the man with one?

Was that what John had been doing all this time? Twenty years ago, standing alone against the Air Force? Ten years later, in his ruined corn field, standing alone against nature? In the doorway, silhouetted against the sun, standing alone against her?

Laura was past shock, was past remorse. She just *was*. She watched the standing-alone-man die and knew he wasn't stupid. He was defending righteousness, *his* righteousness. The righteousness every man needed to give his life meaning and his sons purpose. And for righteousness to be true, you had to let go of everything to defend it. Even your family. Even your life.

~~~~~~~~~~~~~~~~~~~~~~

"We never went anywhere. All's we ever did was farm," Fredrick lamented from underneath his fresh-out-of-the-box-never-used-fire-engine-red Polaris skimmer. "The first thing I'm going to do is kiss her until her eyes pop out then I'm taking her to Las Vegas. I'm going to pamper her. Breakfast in bed, Wayne Newton. Then we're going to find a place to settle down—without cows." He took a pull from a tooth-whitening smoke and held out a hand. "Three-eights-inch socket, please." Patterson rummaged through the wrenches and handed him one. "We really like North Dakota. Good fishing. Friendly people. We could do well there."

"Doing what?" asked Woody.

The big man reappeared, tightened the fuel line coupling, tested the pressurization, then slammed the hood shut. "Sell insurance, real estate. Anything but farm. It's been a hard twenty years and I've put Abby through enough." He opened up his wallet and handed the general a tattered Amway ad. "I've been considering joining. Unlimited pay. Solid future. What do you think?"

Patterson arched his eyebrows.

Fredrick pocketed the paper and looked out over the bare gray brown hills of the Thunderbird Mine. The pit was a giant eight-mile-long feat of engineering in north-central Minnesota. At one time, the mine produced taconite for the steel and auto industries up and down the Great Lakes. Today, it served as a secluded base for the Chinooks and Ospreys of 121SAR to stage its largest extraction operation yet. Wade stood by the railroad tracks waiting for Abby's convoy.

"Thanks for bringing me along, sir."

"Did I have a choice?"

"Nope. I couldn't wait to see her. Why aren't they here yet?"

"Military tactics ain't science. Especially in the SF."

"I'm getting nervous. And I've run out of things to tinker with."

Woody grimaced as he stood and threw his half-burned jag to the ground, swearing at it. "Fat lot of good you fuckers are doing."

"You OK, sir?"

"I've got to get back in the air. I should've started flying months ago. It's the only time I'm not in any pain." Woody paced back and forth a few times before heading to his Bronco.

"You going to look for them?" asked Fredrick.

"Yes, *look*. You stay here and—"

"No. I'm going with."

"There's no seat. And no one's here to help put the skimmer back in."

Wade walked over to the five-hundred-pound snowmobile, lifted the front skis over transom, heaved up the back end and wiggled it into the cargo hold by himself.

"How did you do that?"

Wade held up his newly-lit lucky. "Vitamins."

After a short bumpy takeoff, the pair followed the railhead south through the conifers and hardwoods of the Superior World Forest. Fifteen miles from the mine, they found the Uni convoy racing full-speed for the rendezvous point, FUN infantry vehicles closing in fast. Up ahead, an ancient French VAB joined the chase and began firing its cannon. Smoke billowed from cars behind and the column started falling apart.

"Let me down! Let me down!" Fredrick hollered from the back.

Woody pushed over and accelerated for a head-on pass. He switched to rockets and pressed-in, aiming for the enemy vehicles in front. He fingered his pickle button as the aircraft bucked its way through the morning thermals then pulled off without firing a shot.

"What are you doing? I thought you were a Vietnam ace or something?"

"They're too close to the convoy."

"Then let me down, general!"

"No. Give me your cellphone."

~ ~

Windancer was foundering and taking on water. The yacht's keel was cracked and its mast broken in two. Three Stingrays had gone overboard in the *Richelieu*'s boiling wake as the carrier group left them for dead and sped on for Duluth.

"Do you have a signal yet?" Aboud yelled into the pit.

"Nothing. Some reflections, that's all."

The captain handed a life preserver to Aboud. Aboud slapped it away. "Doctor, I'm afraid I must insist."

"This is not right. We still have people who are counting on us."

"I want to finish, too, but there is nothing to be done. We are going under."

Aboud's phone rang. It was Woody. "General Woody. How can it be you are calling?"

"Aboud, I'm at Tango-Whiskey 900560. A place called Pine Lake. It's got a dam. I need to know if you can open it?"

"Tango-Whiskey what? A dam where?"

"Look, son. I don't have much time. Can your vgers help us?"

"I don't think so. The French ships ran us over. We are sinking and they are blocking our signal."

"I need your magic, son. Those goddamn French pissants are after our rail convoy. If we can open up the sluice gates to that dam, we can cut them off. Wade's wife is in that convoy. So is John's."

"How much time?"

"They'll be there in three minutes."

A commotion erupted on the deck. Tanner turned to watch Nedeau and the men point northward to lake bluffs. There, in the skies above the shoreline, a single B-52 appeared, steaming for the French Fleet.

"Whoa!"

"Whoa what?" asked Patterson.

"A big plane is coming."

"Good. That'll be Mica flight. They're on time. You should have your signal in less than a minute."

Ten Harpoon missiles dropped out of the bomber's belly causing Windancer's crew to forsake their life rafts and watch from the gunwales. As the missiles free-fell to the water, their engines ignited just above the waves, sending them streaking for different parts of the carrier group. As the seas became sketched with brilliant white contrails, the fleet countered by turning into the attack and filling the air with chaff and decoys. Two missiles exploded in midair, taken out by SAMs and self-protection guns. Four of the refurbished sea-skimmers malfunctioned and tumbled into the water harmlessly. The remaining four accelerated on to their targets. Two frigates were hit below the water line, the Harpoons crippling them and sending majestic geysers high into the blue. The remaining two whispered past the picket ships and slithered into the middle of the fleet, looking for the carrier. When they found the big ship, the sea-skimmers locked-on and juked high into the air to escape its guns. At the apex of their maneuver, the missiles changed direction and came straight down into the flight deck, penetrating into the hangars below and exploding in the ammunition magazine. The Windancers cheered as the launch deck flopped over the bow and sent two dozen Rafale fighters into the drink. In forty-five seconds, La Royale's first American engagement was over and they reversed course and limped back home.

"Signal!"

Aboud and his gamers ran downstairs and took up their stations. They had one server and one node. It would be enough. He sent zet off to find the dam site. "Be careful," Tanner warned. "Our private side-web is gone. This is Googlenet, the biggest pipe out there so everyone and his muezzin will be on it."

Zet did not know what a muezzin was. He put on his CGI glasses, picked up his controller and was soon skateboarding down a shadowy virtual path looking for the Pine Lake dam. He found a wooded stream where yellow eyes blinked at him from the dark. Picking up a power charm, zet's skateboard turned into a propellerboard allowing him to quickly motor his way through hundreds of lakes and rivers. When he finally had reached his destination, he radioed a description of the dam to walle who found a match in a software catalog.

The dam's controller code was written in COBOL, a dead language not even Aboud knew how to decipher. Tanner needed to fake out the program instead if he was ever going to get those gates open. "We're going to have to raise the water level," he announced. "If we can trick the code into thinking the lake is overflowing, the logic will open the gates on its own. Anyone have any ideas?"

"MobyNemo," Potti replied. "It's a magic kotaku in a Japanese anime game. You take him out of his fishbowl, throw him in the ocean and he grows into a gigantic whale. Maybe big enough to swamp Pine Lake."

"Find it."

Potti knew exactly where to go for the doll. He broke into the Toys R Us website and ran through the aisles until he saw the animal in a visitor's shopping cart. He grabbed it and ran the doll to Aboud who made copies. One he gave to the Boy Scouts the other, to the Baptists. He gave the original to moto.

"OK, everybody. This is our last mission." The team quieted as Tanner continued. "The whole phreaker nation will be watching so we have to split up. Method and Fnatic, you are the decoys. Head out in opposite directions. Moto and I will head in last and rendezvous with zet. The lives of the camp prisoners are riding on us."

Method and Fnatic went in with he decoys as Aboud waited. When the berserkers of the Internet descended on the two, he snuck into the back woods with moto.

"We're into some weird shit," cried Fnatic. "Pokemon commandos, a platoon of Elvis vampires, even John Madden is shooting at us."

Method was also in trouble. "We're under attack by a bunch of drunk presidents with blood-shot eyes."

"Those are NSA," yelled Aboud. "Keep fighting. Keep them busy everyone. This is a suicide mission."

Tanner was fully immersed in the game-world with moto. He led the way to Pine Lake, firing plasma-throwers and laser cannon into waves of cyber-zombies. When he ran out of those, he cleared a path with a ghetto sweeper and a katana. As the pair neared the dam, Zet sent up a flare for them as a cabal of matrix-cannibals tore into his flesh and stripped him to the bone. Moto ran for the lake and threw in the little fish as more monsters followed. When they were on moto, Aboud gave an Indian yell, jumped into their midst and set off his suicide vest.

CHAPTER 41
ANTIDOTE

Faisson gave the Americans no notice. Even when they commanded him to stop, he continued striding to his hangar. The sense of purpose that exuded from him was so out of place for a Frenchman, the Sovereigns let him go, figuring he was either under someone else's control or he was a part of someone else's psyops operation.

Off to his right, two undamaged Rafale fighters picked their way through the smoldering debris of the flightline. Faisson watched them from the apron as the pilots lit their afterburners in pursuit of the A-10s. A hundred feet into their takeoff roll, the lead aircraft started sinking deeper and deeper into the runway, its wheels crunching heavily into the loose gravel as the pilot throttled-up for more power. Under the intense stress, the jet's delicate landing gear buckled as its struts sheared off and its fuselage plowed nose-first into the screed. Too close to stop, the leader's wingman rammed him from behind, igniting both fuel tanks and touching off a thunderous explosion that sent Faisson sprawling to the ground.

Raising himself up, Faisson found that he was covered in a fine gray powder. Digging his fingers into the pavement, he pulled out a handful of gravel and black dust. The dust tickled his hand and buzzed in his ear like a dentist's drill; the Sovereign's gas was eating his runway. He got up, brushed himself off and stumbled to the shelter where he kept his jet.

The commander's jet came lavishly appointed; leather-upholstered ejection seat, mahogany-inlaid instrument panel, anti-g cup holders. The bubble-canopy was smoked and flecked with gold flakes to shield him from the sun's glare while an iPod-enabled surround-sound stereo system kept out the wind and jet noise. Even though Faisson had little time to fly, his pilots and crew chiefs steered clear of the jet for fear of scratching something. With a hundred French fighters now burning at their bases, such concerns went out the window as the base pilots ran to the hangar and readied the jets for new missions.

"Mon dieu, général!" screamed a young captain as Faisson yanked him out of his seat and threw him to the floor. The pilot's squadron-mates gathered around to help him up. "Where are you going?"

"I am going after the escapees."

"But we don't know where they went."

"I do." Faisson tossed the officers his mobe "The lat-longs are in there. Load them into your nav computers." The general motioned behind them to the other two Rafales in the shelter.

"You want us to be your wingmen?"

Faisson donned his g-suit and helmet, then climbed his ladder. "After you load me with two aGal tanks. And then, only if you can keep up."

Faisson strapped in and started his engine. As soon as the nerve agent was loaded, he jammed his throttle forward, blowing out the back wall of the hangar in the process. He launched across the apron to keep from getting stuck in the pavement and aimed for the grass median between the two runways. When he had reached the far end of the strip, he mounted the run-up pad. The enemy nano-devices had not drifted this far and the concrete held as he had hoped. He stroked his burner, rumbled down the runway and pole-vaulted into the blue Duluth morning just as the pavement below him turned to powder.

~ ~ ~ ~ ~ ~ ~ ~ ~ ~ ~ ~ ~ ~ ~ ~ ~ ~ ~

The computers at the Pine Lake hydrology station sensed Aboud's rising water levels and commanded its dam gates to *full-open*. In moments, the small discharge creek below flooded and washed out the railroad tracks. Two-thirds of the escapees made it across. The rest of the convoy was either swept downstream or stranded on the other side with the FUN in close pursuit.

"Aren't you going to shoot?" hollered Fredrick as the French swarmed the stranded Unis below.

"They're still too close."

"Then let me down," said the farmer.

Woody bellowed back. "Just sit down and behave while I try to figure something out."

Fredrick swore and punched the side of the cargo hold, his fist dislodging a nearby fuel valve labeled CROSSFEED. He turned the handle, and shut off the fuel to both engines as the Bronc's propellers feathered and the cockpit turned silent. Patterson swore.

"You goddamn *ass*! Turn that back on before we crash."

"Are you going to let me—"

"Yes, yes, yes, you smelly piece of cow-shit. Now turn it back on!"

Fuel started flowing as Woody restarted the engines. He turned back toward the lake and descended to its surface. When Wade had fired up his skimmer, Patterson gave the signal and cut away his cargo strap. "You're going to get yourself killed," he said to himself as his chief sailed out the tail.

Fredrick smashed into the water like a jackhammer as he thumbed his gas to keep from flipping. When the Bronco had climbed back into the sky, Wade saw the dam looming for him ahead. With barely enough time to close his eyes, Wade tensed as the snowmobile's skis hit the dike's cement lip and sent him airborne.

At seventy miles per hour, the craft blew apart into an engine, cowling and rider. Wade spun through the air like a discus, landing in the flooded streambed below. When he came back up, he swam for the tracks, gulping water as he went. He hoisted himself up on the rails to get his bearings. To the north lay the convoy, safe and dry. To the south sat its caboose, fighting for its life.

Wade pulled himself the rest of the way out of the water, his head snapping left then right. He agonized over which direction to head when a pistol shot roused him from his starting blocks and spurred him southward after it.

Abby felt her belly kick. "Why have we stopped? Are they letting people out? We've got to pee!"

"Me, too," said Laura, standing. As she made her way to the back of her carrier, she thought she heard shooting.

"Ma'am, it's not safe to come out," said a young levi-clad resistance fighter. "We'll be on our way shortly. Please stay inside."

On the horizon, a lone jet descended out of the blue and rolled out a mile down the tracks. From the distance, it looked like a tiny black triangle as Laura watched it catch the sun and fly straight for her. The fighter dropped a bomb as a nerve-shattering sonic boom rolled over them. The canister hit in the middle of their convoy where it burst open and began leaking a thick green gas.

The canister won't explode, Robillard had told Laura. *It will just pop! Watch the wind*, he added. *The gas will be green.*

The smoke stood still as it billowed out of the tank. When the plume reached the treetops, it caught the breeze and galloped for Laura. "Everyone, get up. Come on. We've got to get out now!"

The young Freemartin held up his rifle. "I said stay inside ma'am. It's not—"

"That's gas!" she said, pointing behind him. "We're being gassed!"

The Freemartin looked nervously at the cloud, its shape swelling like a thunderstorm. "I don't care what it is," he stuttered. "I still have my orders."

Laura stepped over the gate and kicked the boy in the teeth. The prisoners gasped as Laura and Cody jumped down and helped Abby to the ground.

When you see the gas, get inside. If you can't get to a building then find a low-point. A hole. A gully. A lake.

"What are you doing, mom? What is that?"

Laura grabbed both their hands and ran to the front of the convoy. The vapor rolled after them, gulping Unis whole as it went. The blob was heavy and gloomy and had gravity. It blotted out the sun as it approached and muffled her steps while she could hear its. She yanked Cody and Abby sideways and they tumbled down a ditch. "Put this over you, quick!" She handed them a sheet of crumpled white plastic that was laying in a wad among the weeds. "Pull in the edges and sit on it," she said. "Don't let anything get in."

The fog encircled them as a light drizzle fell against the sheet. Laura moved about the tarp to make sure they had a tight seal. All sound stopped; not a voice, or scream or a rustling leaf could be heard. Only the soft hiss of the mist falling softly all about.

The darkness had a green cast while the rain running down their vinyl shelter fell in crimson-red streams. Inside, their breath started condensing, steaming up the tarp. "It's getting stuffy in here," said Cody, after a few minute's vigil. "You sure we're not going to asphyxiate?" He rubbed his finger across the plastic to wipe away a bead of sweat before it dropped on his head.

The agent works by skin contact. A single drop is fatal. Watch for the first symptoms: mucus, tears, blood from the eyes, nose, ears.

"No, Code. Don't touch that. That's not condensation. That's a hole!"

A stream of drool ran down Cody's chin as his cheek began to quiver. The quivering ran down his body to his arms then became great tremors as his eyes rolled back into its sockets and his body began chattering on the ground. "Mom? Mom? *MOM!*"

Abby tried to grab him but couldn't hold on. "Oh my, Lord, Laura, he's—"

"DON'T MOVE!" screamed Laura. "Stay there. You're lifting up the plastic!"

"But we have to do something. What are we going to do?"

These pen-sized tubes are called pyro-injectors. They contain the antidote for the nerve agent.

Laura undid her pants and pulled out the injector kit she had concealed inside a band against her leg. She removed a tube from the case and held it in her teeth as she rolled her convulsing son over onto his stomach.

The antidote is a thick gel. It is delivered into the body by a small charge of gunpowder. Only the rear and thigh can absorb this charge. It will tear the layers of muscle apart, but in a few seconds the lacerated flesh will completely absorb the compound.

Laura held the ampule with both hands and brought it down into Cody's rear. She mashed the red trigger at the end with her thumb as his body jumped from the blast. She cast the empty vial aside, hugging and rocking him. He wasn't breathing.

The antidote will kill if used too soon. The agent will kill if you wait too long. Use your buddy injector only when you see tremors. Don't waste it if you don't see breathing.

Laura cried and rocked her baby some more. He wasn't responding. His quaking stopped and his body went limp in her arms. She examined the injector to see what she had done wrong.

The toxin is precisely metered. Don't give more than one dose. A second charge will be fatal.

Laura dropped her son's limp body to the ground and began pounding on his chest. She didn't see him as a six-foot 185-pound teen anymore. She saw him as a five-pound premie under bilirubin lights barely able to hold on to her finger. She rolled him back onto his stomach, pulled down his pants and hit him again with her last injector.

"Oww! Oww! Oww! Mom! What are you doing? That hurts!" Cody looked over to Abby self-consciously and pulled up his pants. "If you need to take my temperature, just stick it in my mouth!"

"Oh, Cody. You're back!" Laura wrapped her arms around him and kissed his warm neck.

Cody hugged her back, not quite certain why, as he took the strange device from his mother's hand. "What's this?"

Outside, the gas had run its course, thinning and dispersing as it rolled down the tracks. The sky lightened as the sun shone through the haze.

"It looks like it's gone," said Abby, sniffling. "Can we go out now?" Laura and Cody looked behind her where sunlight streamed in from a gap under the plastic. "You don't have a Kleenex, do you?"

Abby's head shivered as her body hopped in place. In seconds, her spine bent backwards and her eyeballs went white. "No, not you, too," she said to her baby, cradling her stomach. Then her limbs went rigid and her body bucked in the dust.

Cody inched away. "Mom?"

Abby was dying. Laura looked at Cody, then back to Abby and her baby.

The injector is optimized for self-administration. Take care of yourself first. Only then can you help another.

With their plastic shelter opening further with Abby's spastic throes, Laura had just seconds to spare before taking the injector from Cody and kissing him on the lips. "I love you."

"I love you, too, mom."

Check your face. The facial muscles are the first to exhibit symptoms. An uncontrollable quivering of the eyelids, cheeks or chin means you've been exposed.

Laura wiped her nose as she flipped up the injector's trigger-guard.

She gripped the pen tightly and pounded it into the meat of her leg.

Hit your thigh as hard as you can as you push the red button. The shock of the charge will cause unconsciousness. Plan for this so your injector doesn't slip.

Laura triggered the charge. As the syringe bucked in her hand, she held it there until she was sure all the antidote had been absorbed. When Abby was done shaking, Laura put a hand on her friend's stomach and gave it a kiss as her own body began chugging like a train and fell over in the dirt.

Thick strings of mucus flung from Laura's mouth as her head spun from stop-to-stop. Her body convulsed in unsyncopated quakes while her spine arched like a gymnast's. As Cody and Abby searched for a third syringe, Laura's eyes fluttered and spun back into her brain.

Inside, John was there, waiting in the sunlit door. This time there were no harsh words, just a smile and his ever present crinkling eyes. He put down his flightbag, came to her side and held her in his arms for the last time.

"*MOM!*"

CHAPTER 42
DOGFIGHT

When the collision of the two Rafales on Pétain's runway evoked whoops and cheers from Beak, Shank and Hooper, Spider keyed his mike to reminded them all to maintain radio discipline. When the two jets burst in a roiling fireball, he decided to let them blow off a little steam.

"Looks like Kermie's having a bad day," said Hooper. "Anybody want to say a few words?"

"Not so much," replied Beak.

"Hogsbreath, we're going back to rejoin the operation," radioed Trent. "How's everyone's state?"

"I'm bingo plus twelve hundred," replied Shank.

"Bingo plus fifteen," reported Beak.

"I'm fat," called Hoop.

Shank and Beak laughed. "We know that, Double Stuf Oreo-ass. He meant your fuel."

The pilots—gritty, hungry and tired—checked their instruments and refolded their maps, readying themselves for their second mission. On the radio, a French air controller broke in, speaking animatedly. Spider turned up the volume.

"Faisson . . . évadés . . . nuerotoxique."

"Are those the turtlenecks?" asked Hoop. "Why are they on our freq?"

"Leper was supposed to put a virus in their radios, disabling their frequency-hopping," said Spider. "It must have worked because they don't know they're broadcasting single-channel. What did they say?"

"Something about General Faisson and escapees?" replied Shank, reliving high school French.

"What is *nuerotoxique*?"

"I think it's *nerve agent*."

Spider pivoted in his seat to see the black triangular wingform of Faisson's Rafale rise from the base and bank sharply northbound. Trent broke out of formation after barely missing Beak. "What the fuck, over?"

"Hoop, you've got the lead. Take the flight to DZ Bordeaux as briefed and waste some Leclercs. I'll join you at the FARP."

"Where you going, Spider?" asked Shank. "You're not going after *that* guy, are you?"

"Spider, leave him alone," added Hoop. "He's not bothering anybody. He's going north probably to seek asylum in Quebec."

"North is also where the escapees went," replied Spider.

"It's a trap," cried Shank. "They broadcast on our channel to spoof us."

"I told you, Aboud hacked their radios. That was the real thing."

"How can you be sure?"

"Because I know this loser. He's got nerve gas and he's looking for revenge."

"Then fuck the mission," said Hooper. "We're going with you."

"No, Woody'll string you up by your nose hairs. This is personal. Spider's got a score to settle." Trent leveled out and lit his afterburners. "See you later. I'm a dot."

Trent's wingmen watched him as he pulled away and got small on the horizon. After a few moments, he disappeared all together. "Dammit, Spider. Quit doing that!"

Snoopy's ancient airframe creaked and groaned under the stress of its powerful new engines, the A-10 sounding like a submarine that had ventured too far below crushing depth. Spider checked his fuel. The afterburners were taking a toll on his reserves but they were also enabling him to keep Faisson in sight.

The two aircraft picked their way north through the rolling forests and sky-blue waters of the Mesabi Iron Range. Just ahead lay the abandoned North Shore Mining mainline. It ran along the plateau's crest, where the convoy had stalled just east of Virginia. Faisson must have found it because his jet turned abruptly and dove to the ground as if on a bombing run.

Trent did not yet see the convoy but knew Faisson could. He estimated the target's position and flew for it as fast as he could. From the left side of his windshield, Trent made out the twin-boom high-wing planform of an OV-10. Some turkey had his fangs out and was flying it straight for Faisson's Rafale, trying to break up the attack. It fired rockets, which missed. As Faisson flew by, the Bronco hit his sonic wave and flipped end-over-end into the forest.

Green gas rose up from the wood-line, thick and bulbous, as Faisson released his munitions and set up for another pass. He took a wide swing north, reversing course and as he rolled back out for another attack, Spider was there with his gatling gun belching fire.

Tracers reached out for Faisson and he winced, waiting for one to hit him. When he opened his eyes, he was staring at an A-10 flying head-on at him.

Spiderman.

The two jets rolled on their sides and passed each other on knife-edge as if they were stunt pilots at an airshow. Faisson tried to get back on course to release his ordinance but could only watch as his last canister tumbled harmlessly into Pine Lake.

Spider turned into Faisson hard as the Frenchman struggled to get into shooting position at his six. Trent lit his first-stage burners, tightening his turn and taking away what little room his adversary had to fire.

Faisson banged the dash with his fist. He had not seen an A-10 perform so well before. He broke off his pursuit, barrel-rolled his fighter to get some much needed spacing and fired off two heat-seeking Micas in frustration.

The missiles slid off their rails without a target. They scanned the sky blindly before locking onto Snoopy's red-hot engines. Trent pulled his throttles to idle and watched the missiles approach from the camera in his ass-backwards Maverick. When he could make out their fins, he released millions of shards of IR-decoys from his chaff dispensers, filling the air behind him with a kaleidoscopic cloud of glass. The micro-prisms confused the seekers and caused them to home on reflections from their own plumes. The missiles reversed direction and chased each other like two rabid dogs until they ran out of propellant and corkscrewed lifelessly to the ground.

Faisson watched Spider trying to gain altitude. He lined up for another attack before the American could get away. As he placed his crosshairs on Trent's helmet, Hoop swooped up from below, filling the general's windscreen with Warthog. Faisson rolled right to keep from colliding with the A-10 while, behind him, two more Hogs had snuck up on his tail. He dove for the dirt.

"Looks like testosterone is still illegal in France," radioed Hooper, in close pursuit.

Cannon-fire followed Faisson on either side as all three wingmen strafed him. Faisson went vertical to see if anyone would take the bait.

"Beak, don't!" yelled Hooper. "You don't have the airspeed."

Beak Brucato pulled and followed Faisson until he was at four thousand feet. Once there, his heavy, ponderous jet floated to a stop and fell earthward on its back. He kicked rudder and flailed his ailerons to get control but not before the Rafale closed to gun range and shot the lieutenant's cockpit full of holes.

The A-10 fell to the ground billowing black smoke as Faisson searched the sky for Hoop and Shank. He saw them below, flying a mile abeam each other. He came down on them head-on, not aiming for either, but splitting the gap. Both pilots padlocked on the general and reversed direction hard into each other hoping to be the first to line him up for a shot.

"Four's in hot!"

"Three's in hot!"

"Four, where are you?"

"I'm over the lake."

"*I'm* over the lake," yelled Hooper. "ABORT-ABORT-ABORT!" It was too late. They ran into each other belly-to-belly and detonated in an inferno that fluttered to the ground in large fiery pieces.

Spider looked down on the fireball from five thousand feet up, a wave of sadness washing over him. He pointed his nose north searching for chutes just as Faisson's wingmen checked-in on the radio, giving away their position. Trent stayed in the sun and watched them come in low. They found him on their radars and fired their heat-seekers. He dove for their formation, sending a burst from his gatling gun as the sun-blinded missiles sailed past.

Trent felt every one of his fifty years as he panted and grunted through the g's of his dive. He pulled out in the treetops, winded, as the Rafales turned and brashly followed. Spider ducked between two ridges and turned right to follow their contours as a long tangle of power lines loomed ahead, drooping across the ravine. He dropped underneath to miss the span only to find more on the other side.

Trent swore. He was sweating and sleep-deprived and making bad decisions. He dropped again and eyed the terrain nervously. Ahead, the two ridges converged and were funneling him into a shallow box canyon. He snapped his head back as the Rafales, not afraid to follow him low, began shooting. Spider saw blue sky above and jinked for the opening only to find it spiderwebbed with still more wires, only smaller.

A large red hay barn appeared on the ridgeline ahead. He couldn't see them but knew a set of electric lines would be running to it from the road. Not wanting to guess how high they would be, Trent ducked into a swath of field corn until the cables came into sight. With tassels slapping at his wings, Spider fortuitously passed underneath.

Wingman Number One never saw the wires. The cables sheared off his canopy, severing his head at the Adam's Apple. Wingman Number Two saw the crash and pulled up in time just as Spider disappeared into a low-hanging cumulus.

WN2 climbed after him. When the Rafale emerged from the cloud on the other side, Spider was waiting. He lined up his camera and fired his Maverick, its rocket engine miraculously restored to working order by Beak and his armorers. WN2 had never seen a missile launch backward before. He froze as it went down his intake and sent hot fan blades into his fuel tank, touching off a small supernova.

"Welcome to America, Kermit. That's how we hug here!"

Faisson shadowed Trent from five miles behind as the American limped back to the convoy in search of his wife and wingmen. When sure Spider was engrossed in his personal matters, the Frenchman pushed his Rafale supersonic and shot out the Hog's tail before Trent saw him coming.

"That might not have been as fun as the first time I had sex," Faisson taunted. "But it certainly was better than the second." The general came around and fired again, taking out the Hog's right engine.

Faisson. Spider recognized the Fran Drescher whine. He leveled off and tried to pick up speed, his burners going in and out as his fuel tanks ran dry. The Rafale rolled out behind him again. Spider waited. "Come on, Tic-Tac. Just a little closer." When Faisson's cannons flashed, Trent horsed his warship into a hard left turn.

Faisson turned with him, turning tighter, trying to stay inside. "You know, major, it is too bad I cannot count your dead wife in my totals today. With all my kills combined, she would have made me an ace."

How could Faisson know Laura had been killed? He couldn't, Trent decided, but he exploded in grief just the same. Spider cut his throttles to force his enemy to overshoot. Faisson cut his. Spider dropped his flaps. Faisson dropped his. Spider lowered his gear. Faisson lowered his.

No matter how hard he tried, the A-10's image kept snowballing as Faisson struggled on the edge of a stall to keep his crosshairs on the American. When he was close enough he couldn't miss, he opened fire. "This is for Gizzelle."

As the shells shimmered for him, Trent popped the speedbrake at the end of his right wingtip. It caught the airstream by surprise and like a giant skyhook, swung his jet up and out of the way as Faisson overshot him below. Out of fuel and out of bullets, Trent had only one weapon left; his ejection seat. As the Rafale passed underneath, he pulled his handles and prepared to die.

Spider's canopy blew off first, hitting Faisson's tail and ripping it off at the root. His ejection seat followed, shooting straight into the general's windshield, pulverizing the cockpit in an explosion of plastic and glass. Both aircraft twisted around each other for a mile like two flaming meteors before finally arcing to the ground and cratering into a swamp.

After an eternity of tumbling, Spider's chute finally opened, snapping him awake. He grabbed his risers and began steering for the train tracks below as a body fell against the canopy above him, tearing it open.

A shape dropped through the hole and grabbed Spider on its way down. It was Faisson. Burned and bleeding, his helmet caved into his skull, the Frenchman mouthed gibberish into the air with nothing but toothless gums. The man drew his dagger as Trent kneed him in the testicles. The general slipped and grappled for a new purchase as Spider raced to unsheathe his own knife. Faisson, younger and quicker, regained his hold, stabbing again into Trent's chest.

Trent grabbed Faisson's arm with both hands to block the blade but was unable to stop its tip from passing through his flightsuit and piercing his skin. He strained against Faisson's weight as the steel dug deeper into his muscle. No longer able to stop its progress, Spider used the last of his strength to guide the blade to a rib where it stopped just long enough for him to retrieve his KA-BAR and gore Faisson in the side.

Faisson screamed and hit Spider in the face. Spider saw white. When his world returned, the Frenchman had both weapons. "Aren't you a little old for this?" Faisson lisped. "Shouldn't you be in a home?" He spit blood in Trent's face and lunged again but not before Spider reached up and pulled his cut-aways, jettisoning his main chute.

Spider fell away from the general as the two tumbled to earth. When his reserve chute opened, he could not raise his right arm to steer. As air whistled through his muscle, Trent saw that he had been slashed from shoulder to forearm. As the pain reached his brain, he sensed he was falling too fast. He checked the canopy above then his boot below, where a knife poked through his foot, the Frenchman hanging on by the handle.

Hanging on by just four fingers, Faisson strained as he used Spider's foot to pull himself up. When he was eye-level with Trent's bloody boot, he swung up with his free hand and plunged his other knife into Spider's thigh, feeling it hit home in his femur. Spider kicked and thrashed as Faisson kept climbing, the Frenchman jerking the knife out of his boot before nailing it solidly into Trent's other thigh. The general kept hefting himself up, climbing Trent as he would a ladder, the blades twisting and ripping the meat of John's legs but holding firm in the bone's soft marrow.

Spider howled until he felt his vocal chords tear away from his throat. With no more energy to fight or block pain, he flickered and blacked-out. When the half-dead Frenchman had ascended to belt-level, he yanked a blade from Trent's thigh and made one last thrust for his bowels.

A violent shudder went through the shrouds causing Faisson to lunge for Trent's waist and drop his dagger. Looking up through his shattered visor, he didn't like what he saw.

Trent was hanging from a single riser now. He had pulled one of his reserve cut-aways with his good arm but with Faisson still hanging on him, was unable to reach the other. Flailing in vain to snatch the remaining release, Trent watched as the Frenchman grinned up to him.

"Give up, cowboy. Life is not always an American happy-ending," he said, reaching for the remaining knife still sticking out of Spider's hamstrings. "It is dim and dreary and full of pointlessness. Better to just give up, my friend, and taste defeat like everyone else in the world."

"Man, you're depressing. The girls must've loved you."

Trent was swimming in pain, his body close to bleeding out. He was reaching for his riser less frantically now, his arm quickly tiring.

Faisson wrenched the last knife free and made ready for his last strike. When he looked up to witness Spider's expression, he found Trent smiling, the last remaining cut-off ring clenched in his teeth.

"No. Do not do that!" Faisson commanded. "You will not win. I will not permit it!"

"This is for America," Spider said through his teeth and gave the ring a solid jerk.

John's pain vanished as he felt the pull of earth. The breeze refreshed his face as he imagined what was coming. He wondered if Woody would be disappointed in him again and if his wingmen and parents would, too. He thought of his second-grade teacher and prom. His first motorcycle and hotdogs. His sons. His grandson. Then he rested his eyes on Laura, the last time he had seen her in the doorway. Would they be going to the same place? Would they meet again? For all his fifty years of searching and wondering, he now knew there was a God. He also knew it was too late to do anything about it.

Trent watched the ground accelerate and come for him. Freed from his pain, a kick of endorphins flooded through him. With one final effort, he reached down and seized the body tumbling below him. As he turned his nemesis to face the ground, he whispered his final command right before they hit.

"My eyes aren't what they used to be, Tic-Tac. Let me know what I'm missing."

CHAPTER 43
AMBULANCE

Woody Patterson's after action report declared Operation Downpour a success. Though both the Sovereign Forces and the UN experienced heavy losses, it was the UN who fell back and gave up ground.

France led the Coax collapse, abandoning twenty thousand square miles of territory in just twelve hours—a modern-day record. With their withdrawal from the line-of-contact, a domino effect was created forcing the retreat of the entire Coax lest they be encircled, too.

The FUN's inordinate fear of Sovereign anti-tank aircraft was the prime factor in the rout. For two years, the French contingent had experienced heavy losses at the hands of the durable A-10s due to their lack of organic AAA assets. These engrams created a panic among the French generals who, when the Warthogs were first sighted on their back step, over-reacted by ignoring the M1s to their front and redeploying their tanks to the rear. With their armor now on forced road marches, FUN command had needlessly exposed their Leclercs to the airborne tank-busters, allowing the SAArm jets to enjoy an ten-to-one kill ratio. If the French had held their ground and kept their tanks massed in their fortified battle formations, the outnumbered Sovereign Forces could not have prevailed.

Stripped of their tanks, French APCs became vulnerable to the Skimmer and Dragoon crews laying in wait along miles of unprotected roadway. The commando's amphibious vehicles were quick and their Predators deadly and when pursued by French infantry, used rivers, lakes and swamps to scamper away and reposition for more kills. Nineteen hundred VABs, VBCIs and AMX-10s were lost during the French retreat along with their attendant crews.

The SF employed many new battle innovations to compensate for their old equipment and low-tech hardware. Some met with wild success, others not. The modified Ski-Doos and ATVs performed reliably under combat conditions but ran out of fuel before noon when the French Air Force reestablished air superiority and prevented resupply from the air. By the end of the day, with no gasoline and captured diesel fuel unusable, the Drop and Shock troops lost their ability to maneuver and became easy targets for dismounted infantry.

The government of Canada were no help to the French. When the FUN demanded Ottawa shoot down Patterson's airborne armada and cut off the FARP, Prime Minister Morgan refused saying his government had the situation under control. The French didn't think so and decided to do it for them. When the French-UN sent their Foreign Legion streaming out of Warroad and into Canada, only then did the Canadians fight—against the French to defend their sovereignty.

Eight thousand Sovereigns lost their lives during the assault. Mostly fuel-starved commando teams that had been stranded deep behind enemy lines. These regulars, volunteers, militia, mercenaries and security contractors came individually and came in groups, be they law offices, bowling teams, karate classes or churches. Their ages ranged from fifteen to eighty, but whatever their origin and whatever their heritage, they were Americans and when they died each one of them took seven-and-a-half Frenchmen with them.

Tactically, there wasn't much to admire about the Gauls. Institutionally, they were arrogant and in their unconventional tactics, slow-witted. They had no moral will and scared easily when their safety was threatened. That was why they had lost the seas to the British in the 1800s. That was why they had lost every war since Napoleon.

Complexity scientists working for the SF factored these traits into contingency equations that told them to locate their dropzones twenty-five miles behind the LOC. The French Task Forces considered these infiltrators to be too far away to be a threat, allowing them to link-up unhindered. Once the Quarterstaff unleashed their A-10s however, the Skimmer and Dragoon teams had a turkey-shoot as the French stampeded for their supply bases in total disarray. By the end of the day, the front had moved fifty miles east and 61,000 French invaders lay in the forests and cornfields of Minnesota, dead.

Such casualty numbers are unheard of in modern warfare, eclipsed only by what the German's had done to the Russians during World War II. But the SF was remorseless and took no prisoners refusing to give their enemies a chance to raise a single white flag. Across the entire Middle States, the Sovereign Forces gave no quarter and shot everything that moved. This was not an edict issued in the rules-of-engagement but an instinct executed by every soldier on the battlefield who wanted the war to be over and the world to think twice before ever invading their country again.

Augmenting Operation Downpour was Operation Testimony, an aerial and electronic campaign designed to kill the FUN leadership in Duluth, liberate their internment camps and destroy UN morale. SF Information Warfare teams proved critical in this effort by crawling the enemy's milnet with the help of the local populace. NSA sniffers took down the network, killing as many sympathizers as they could but not before the hackers penetrated the French Battle Management System, causing confusion, intelligence snafus and friendly-fire incidents. Jump-jets took out most of the administrative tranche, including the UNIFUS Tax Agency, the Hague Annex and the CNNUN studios. Civilian collateral damage was extensive however, due to the lack of precision guided munitions in Duluth and a French gas attack that left three thousand internment escapees dead at Pine Lake.

~~~~~~~~~~~~~~~~~~~~

Aboud held onto the rescue helicopter tightly as it departed Windancer and headed for shore. He must finally look like a commando now because the pilot let him ride the outriggers with the rest of the Stingrays. The wind puffed his cheeks and the pine boughs licked at his feet as the Kiowa climbed the plateau and headed for the convoy.

"Wade!" he called, waving. "Up here!" The chopper banked abruptly and the scientist lost his grip. A rock-chested UNCON snatched him before he fell and tucked him under his arm until they landed. "Wade, it is me. Have you found Abby?"

"I'm still looking. Is the agent still active?"

"No, the persistence should have timed out thirty-five minutes ago," replied the scientist. "But we still shouldn't take any chances."

"I don't have time to put on a suit. Help me. I don't know where to look."

"No," Aboud said, grabbing ampules out of his bag and stuffing them in Wade's hands. "You help me. If you find her, she'll need one, too."

In the mounting heat, flies had already found the bodies as Wade and Aboud dashed from truck to truck and pile to pile. Without exposure suits, medics yelled at them from outside the hotzone. Neither cared. Down the railhead, in the ditch, a piece of plastic fluttered in the breeze. Aboud raced for it. "Wade! Down here!"

Aboud tripped and stumbled down the embankment as Wade ran past him. "Abby! Honey! It's me!"

"Chewie? Is that my Chewie?"

Wade got to the bottom and tore off the covering. The big man lifted his wife as she squealed. Aboud tapped his shoulder and gave him a syringe. Wade put his wife back down and, rolling her on the ground, patted her behind. "Ow! Easy, Wade! We've already had one!"

"We?"

Abby laid on her back and stuck out her belly. "We!"

Aboud frowned at her. "Where did you get the antidote?"

Abby unfolded the tarp. "From her." Laura's glassy eyes looked to the sky. Her hair was a tangle and her mouth in a grimace. Abby bent down and closed her lids then massaged her face until it softened. "From this stupid, idiotic, stubborn, lovely, sweet, lovely, sweet ... " Her voice trailed off and stopped cold. "I got it from my friend, Laura Trent."

Up and down the railroad right-of-way, UNCONs, parajumpers and Freemartins all sat together and ate their lunches while cheering the dogfights above. Cody craned his neck gazing at the white contrails circling there, seeding the sky. He had always thought they were airliners orbiting for landing. Now he knew. A Tigre Eurocopter dashed by overhead, stinging his eyes with sand. It disappeared to the south with two A-7 Corsairs in hot pursuit, their mini-guns hammering the air. He wondered who was winning. He wondered why he cared.

Cody toyed with his eye patch as a medic taped his shoulder. When his sling had been cinched tight, the corpsman opened up the ambulance and Cody climbed in back. Alone in his tunnel, the day lazily ebbed by as the activity and bustle outside hurried it along. Some men brought a litter and placed it gently inside. A slender white hand slid from under the cover and hung in the air. It was mom.

"She had two antidotes," Abby whispered to Wade, following close behind. "She had hidden them the whole time under her clothes. They were supposed to be for her. Her and her son." Seeing Cody inside, she stopped her narrative and hid her head in her husband's shoulder.

"I can't image," Wade said. "I can't imagine what that would take."

"I've got so much to tell you. So many stories. Every time I was ready to come apart, she was there."

A Gator pulled into the clearing as three men in flightsuits hobbled off. They carried their helmets in one hand and helped carry a stretcher in the other. All around them, soldiers cheered and clapped. "Thank you for your applause. Thank you. We appreciate it!" Hooper hailed to the crowd. "We'll try to get shot down more often."

The two put Woody down as Wade came over to shake the general's hand. "I don't believe it, you old goat. I saw your plane crash. I thought you were dead."

"That's why God created ejection seats, Chewie." Woody motioned for a cigarette. Wade lit a Rogaine and stuck it in his mouth. "It's funny. I've got a broken hip, a broken pelvis, three busted ribs and a torn spleen and I've never felt better." He looked at Abby and smiled. "And who is this little flower?"

"General, this is my wife, Abby."

Patterson stuck out his hand as Abby started crying.

"Oh, no. Oh, shit no," mumbled Hoop. "Shit, shit, shit no!"

All activity at the site stopped as another litter approached. It did not veer left nor did it veer right. The body came straight for them as onlookers stood at attention and saluted. The medics drew up to the back of the HMMWV, nudging the pilots aside as they silently glided Spider's body inside. All levity left the group. All conversation ceased.

They were witness to a moment for which all brothers-in-arms know will come but never adequately prepare.

Woody saw Cody huddled in the shadows, shivering. "I'm sorry about your dad, son. Your father was a true hero. A pain in the ass, but the one man I always wanted on my wing."

"He was a legend," added Hoop. "A man of renown. I turned down commands of my own just to stay in his flight."

"We were the biggest group of losers," said Shank. "He kicked the snot out of us and whipped us into shape. He never gave up. I can only imagine how great it must have been to be his son."

Hoop and Shank took Spider's gloves and helmet and laid them across his chest. Woody grunted to them then said goodbye to Wade and Abby. "Let's go, men. Let's let them be together."

Cody didn't look at the sheet-draped forms. He looked straight ahead. He didn't think about them but only about himself. His whining, his rebellion, his trivialities. They were what had defined him for years now and without his parents, they didn't exist. Where would these unhappinesses go now? Where would they find rest?

His eyes flicked to the two stretchers as short snorts flared his nostrils. His eyes burned and he felt as if he were melting and running out the back of the truck. *I was special. I had fierceness*, he said to himself. *When I pushed you were there to push against. But now who's going to notice? Who's going to care?*

He looked at his father and his chest heaved. *I couldn't be you. You were you. I had to be the opposite. Now who am I, what am I, without you?* He looked to his mother and fought for breath, spit now flying from his lips with each rasp. *I couldn't let you love him. I couldn't stand aside. I was always scared you'd pick him over me.*

He heard himself talking as if they were there. *I'm so sorry. Because of my anger, I've thrown away a life. A life you created and wanted to see happy and fruitful. Can I ever put it back? Can I ever start over? Show you what could be?*

He looked at John once more and in three great gulps of air, took off his sheet and kissed his forehead. *I'm sorry, dad. I love you. I love your strength. I love your bad jokes. I love your guiding hand. You gave me something none of my friends ever had: a dad.* He took away his mother's cover and kissed her next. *I love you, mom. I'm sorry* for making you worry. You loved me the most and that made you my baddest habit. Forgive me. Don't cry for me anymore. Whatever evil I did in your presence, it stops now. Today, I'm letting out the life you created.

He covered his parents and took their hands. "You deserved more," he moaned. "You deserved to enjoy a few good years together without a loser son sucking out all of your air." He put his mother's hand in his father's then dropped to his knees and wailed like a lost child.

He never saw his father's squeeze.

CHAPTER 44
PRESS CONFERENCE

Burin Zzgn cleared his scuba mask as he drifted with the current along the Palm Beach seabed. He shook his head as he floated through an artificial reef built of Rolls-Royces, Jaguars and Lamborghinis. Auto Row was part of Sea Turtle World Reserve, the UN's newest wildlife refuge. He chose Palm Beach as the park's site because of the island's prime sea turtle nesting grounds. When he closed the town to protect the species, the Secretary-General doled out the city's vacant mansions and lavish resorts to privileged UN officers and allies as favors. Whatever exotic properties his friends had deigned unworthy came to rest here, no matter how new or expensive. He reached out to pet a Goliath Grouper when his dive watch flashed red at him.

"What is it, Wildfire?" the SecGen said, kicking back to the surface and gasping into his phone. "This had better be good."

"It is President Earle. Should I put him through?" replied his silky-voiced digital assistant.

"I told you to send everyone to voice mail."

"He is requesting your presence at the press conference."

"I brought him to my compound because he said he needed moral support. Now he wants *me* to break the news?"

"There has been a swing in the opinion cloud; twenty-two news channels are broadcasting impeachment segments and blog chatter is spiking around the keywords *senate* and *detentions*."

"For or against?"

"Against, fifty-four to forty-three. Dissenting cellphone traffic is rising even higher."

"For Pope's sake, can't he handle his own people?" Zzgn complained, doffing his tank and rolling into the boat.

"I am event-processing now and consensus is beginning to look like a Vista Curve, the same double-hitch that presaged the Microsoft crash."

"What's the press emo now?"

"Hostile."

Zzgn changed into suit-and-tie on his yacht. When he beached his skiff on the beach, he strode into Rush House with saltwater squishing from his Berlutis. From down the hall, he heard raised voices echoing from the salon.

"Can you give us word on the whereabouts of your brothers, Mr. President?"

"Ron, are you going to settle down or am I going to have to get you a Lamaze partner?" Earle quipped. The pool reporters laughed.

Ron Blair wasn't laughing. "Their campaigns have told us they were taken from their homes in the middle of the night and flown overseas to answer charges in The Hague."

The chief-of-staff launched to the podium, brushing aside his exasperated boss. "That's a bald-faced lie, Ron! Show me your proof."

"There is none," replied the ABC reporter. "UN flights aren't required to file with the FAA."

"We are not here to respond to rumors and innuendo," declared Laird. "We are here to—"

"Is it because they're spearheading the impeachment, Mr. President? Is this how you treat your opponents in Congress? When are you going to tell the American people what is going on?"

"That's why we're here," Laird smiled. "To brief you on our recent setbacks against the SF and—"

"We've seen what's happened in Canada and Mexico, Peter. We've got eyes!"

"—and what went on here during our emergency summit with the Secretary-General."

"Tell us what's going on in the capital. Are we about to come under martial law?" Blair kept prodding.

The president took the microphone and thundered as he shook a finger. "You don't have the brains God gave Paris Hilton! You broadcast that filth and I'll have ABC's license. Now sit your fat white Michelin-man ass down and behave like everyone else!"

"You can't talk to me like that. I'm a—"

From a side entrance, Zzgn appeared. He buttoned his coat and bullied his hair before entering the room. "Burin, you're here!" whispered Earle. "I'm so happy I could pee over a ten-rail fence." He reached out and grabbed the Ukrainian's hand. "These ticks are so bloodthirsty they'd sip on their own mother."

Zzgn smiled, wrestled back his hand and walked to the podium. "Good morning, everyone," he greeted, adjusting his microphone.

Ron Blair stood again and began blurting out questions. "Mr. Secretary-General, not since the Lincoln administration have lawmakers been banned from voting." Zzgn flashed a beguiling grin and motioned him to sit down. "On what authority do you presume to detain U.S. Congressmen," Blair continued, shouting now. "And why only those voting for the president's impeachment? Is this despicable act your doing or is it—"

Zzgn told the man to sit down.

"With all due respect, Mr. Secretary-General, I will not. Not until you answer my questions."

Zzgn motioned to his guard captain. A nose-tackle from StanEval came along side the podium and with his 13-millimeter SIG, shot the reporter through his tie with a loud flame-throwing bark. The ABC-man's heart exploded in mid-beat and he fell over backwards, his lips still mouthing questions.

All stares averted as the journalists inched away from their dead colleague and Zzgn began speaking.

"The enemies of the president have launched a desperate attack against this dependency. I need not tell you, an attack against a dependency is an attack against the world.

"The world cries out for peace, ladies and gentlemen. But before there can be peace there must be justice and to secure justice, there must be continuity of power, continuity of will and purpose. If this single-mindedness is interrupted or any change of course or strategy pursued, the independents will smell our softness and the Coax will fall like a house of cards.

"To that end, the General Assembly has issued Resolution 72/3414 temporarily suspending all U.S. elections for the duration of the conflict." He turned to Earle and Laird. "I have the utmost confidence in President Earle and his administration to defeat this menace—the first to threaten the Alignment—as I have in you to convince the American people to back him." Zzgn stared into the silent pack and dared anyone to raise a hand.

"Don't disappoint him. Don't disappoint me."

EPILOGUE

The two physicians shivered in the dim chill of the Minot Military Hospital's autopsy room. They waited as the orderlies brought in the next bag, complaining how the offensive had doubled their workload.

"You've got this one, guys," one of them told the techs.

"What? You want *us* to? But—"

"You know what to do. You've seen us do it enough times," the stubbly-faced officer explained. "We're getting out of this dungeon to get some fresh air. We'll be at the mini-donut wagon if you need us. See you in a bit."

"Bradley!" replied the orderly's fellow corpsman, unzipping the bag and going to work. "Can we cut him up, too?"

"Sure, you can dissect if you want," answered the doctor. "Just make sure you chart the wounds and inventory the personal effects."

"Yes, sir! We'll be done by the time you're back."

"Why did you have to go and say that for?" asked the orderly, charting the man's external wounds. "What if we do something wrong?"

"I volunteered us because this is a French guy. If we hack off an arm or a leg, who's going to care? He's a toady."

"I guess," said the orderly, poking through pieces of broken skull. "Gnarly. Massive stuff going on in there. Who is he?"

"Nametag reads *Faisson*," replied the corpsman, cutting away the man's clothes. "And lookie here, he's got five stars!"

"A general? Nice, but he's got no teeth," said the other. "I think I'd rather have my teeth."

"Oh, my God, Hal. Look at this!" The corpsman ripped off the general's pants and boots, revealing Faisson's control-top pantyhose and red lacquered toes. "No wonder he doesn't have any visible panty lines."

"Sick," said the orderly. "They've got Chester-the-Molester for a general." He snapped at the hosiery as his friend took out a camera phone. "Hey, what are you doing? You can't do that."

"The guys back at the battalion aren't going to believe this," the corpsman relished. "Prop him up and stick a cigarette in his mouth."

"All right, but cut my face out," said the orderly. "These things always wind up on YouTube."

"I know," replied the corpsman, peer-phoning the video across the Middle States. "Nasty break."

THE END

AFTERWORD

The fall of communism and 9/11 has created an empty void in the literary world; specifically in the arena of war-thrillers. Popularized by the early works of Tom Clancy (*Red Storm Rising*) and Harold Coyle (*Team Yankee*) and General Sir John Hackett (*The Third World War*), these sweeping sagas and epic battles have been replaced by the political thriller, a literary genre that concerns itself with a rouge CIA agent here, a dirty bomb there or terrorist splinter cells everywhere else.

I wrote *Foreign and Domestic* because I was bored with this formula. In this era of Al-Qaeda mall shooters, Taliban beheaders and Iranian yellow cake, the last thing I want to see is a movie or TV show about jihads, terrorists or uranium enrichment (words, by the way, you will not find anywhere in this book but here). I want to be entertained. I want to escape my world. I want to be mesmerized again by cataclysmic clashes and superpower showdowns as army meets army and country devastates country. Where have all these blockbuster global smackdowns gone?

So you see, I have been forced against my will to write this book. However, rather than be a suicidal existentialist about it, I decided to use the occasion to explore some themes that have always intrigued me as a history buff. Specifically, can Americans ever rise up again and sacrifice all—home, family, livelihood—for a dream, an ideal, a piece of parchment? Are there still visionaries out there like Adams, Paine and Washington who can discern the future and are willing to lead with their chins? And if we do have the fortitude to stand strong for our country, what will be the final straw that tips us over the edge?

FND is near-fiction. Near-fiction is a futuristic story that ping-pongs somewhere between non-fiction and science-fiction. It contains technology that may take decades to mature, while at the same time, is driven by events so current Drudge could be posting it right now. Contrary to the definition of fiction, I have not made many things up in this novel. Almost every weapon or bit of tech can be found by surfing the Internet. So it is with this book's events, plots and characters; no matter how over-the-top some storylines seem to be, most are based on historic precedent, be it the Civil War, Vichy France or other well-known White House occupants. While I love breathing new life into forgotten stories, I have no interest in predicting the future. That is why *FND* is chronologically agnostic (no references to years or dates). For a guy who forgets his own wedding anniversary, timelessness is a great invention.

A tale as far reaching as the US-UN War is more than one book can hold. That is why I am writing *FND* as a trilogy. It may seem odd that I am starting with the second book, *Battle for the Middle States*, but that is where most of the action takes place and that is where I was hoping to hook the reader (you can thank George Lucas and *Star Wars* for that). It is my hope the *FND* franchise will resurrect the war-thriller genre. If I can convince a new legion of story-tellers to discard the myopic and start filming in Technicolor, I'll be a happy camper because I'll need another book to read after I'm done with this one.

M. Mannske

ACKNOWLEDGEMENTS

People are more funnel than megaphone. They are made up of so many millions of soundbites, anecdotes, jokes, facts and ideas gathered up during their journey through life that even when they actually do come up with something poignant on their own, they still can't be sure it wasn't something they might have overheard Miss Pageant saying to another teacher during 1st grade recess. That's me.

We are so much the product of those greater than us—our leaders, teachers, authors, parents—who can rightfully claim that what they say is 100% original? I can't. I don't have an original bone in my body (and, yes, not even that phrase is mine). Likewise, who can possibly remember and attribute where every little snippet of stimulus has come from, from conception on? Nobody. All the inputs we collect just become a part of who we are.

That being said, there are some people *I do* remember and want to take the time now to acknowledge.

First off, I wish to recognize Robert McKee for his literary contributions to *Foreign and Domestic*. His book, *Story*, was pivotal to my understanding of the basic principles necessary to take a novel concept and turn it into a good tale. It was his basic building blocks of story spines, fortune reversals and dialog gaps that I have tried to incorporate into *FND*. I recommend it for any of you engineers and pilots out there that may have a good idea but are too scared to write because you have zero artistic talent and have never seen the inside of a blue essay book.

There are many sources I relied on when researching the subject matter, settings and history for *FND*. Beside the Big 4 (OneLook Reverse Dictionary, Wikipedia, Google Earth and BookTV), I wish to thank Thomas Kilgannon, whose book, *Diplomatic Divorce,* supplied me with many insights into the inner workings of the United Nations. Thank you to Harvard Professor Harvey Mansfield and his book, *Manliness,* for so eloquently putting to words what so many of us men have felt and observed throughout the years about our roles in families and society but didn't know how to voice them. Larry Schweikart's unapologetic celebration of the U.S. military in *American Victories* was seminal. And to Joe Soucheray, I say thanks. For all you Gumption County residents who follow the mayor's radio show, the GLisms sprinkled throughout the book are here for a reason; Garage Logic is the official language of U.S. fighter pilots.

A hand goes out to my editors, Dave Sawtelle and Ken Hall, who encouraged and shepherded me through the writing process and whose lives were also sucked dry by "The Beast." I also wish to thank my proofers, Andy Gilman, Fritz Morgan, Sam Sawtelle and my mom, Diane.

Finally, I wish to thank my wife, Leigh, from the bottom of my heart for her sharp eye, constant support and ruthless determination in keeping this book both literarily correct and stylistically engaging. If it wasn't for her strength and sacrifice during these last long 18 months, this book would have never been printed and we would still be living on saltines and water.

ABOUT THE AUTHOR

Michael 'Vice' Mannske graduated from the University of Wisconsin with a Bachelors of Science in Electrical Engineering. He worked on classified military projects in Silicon Valley before flying A-10 Thunderbolt IIs and OV-10 Broncos for the Air Force. He served with the 101st and 82nd Airborne Divisions during the Gulf War as an Air Liaison officer, and currently lives in the Middle States with his wife.

FUTURE WORKS
BY
MICHAEL MANNSKE

Battle for the Middle States Special Editions

Authors Cut Edition (Christmas 2007)
Christian Edition (Christmas 2007)

The Foreign and Domestic Trilogy

The Rise of the Ex-Nihilos (Election Day 2008)
Second Nation (Christmas 2009)

Prequels and Sequels

Captains and Lieutenants
Overwar